who may be powerless individually can band together into a triumphant sororal circle of unstoppable strength."

—*The Star-Ledger* (Newark, New Jersey)

"'Regret' is the given name of the protagonist of Alan Brennert's beautiful, sprawling novel *Honolulu*. . . . Brennert's realization of a character of so different a time, place, and gender than his own is an amazing accomplishment in itself. *Honolulu* is a delight." —*BookPage*

And Acclaim for *Moloka'i*

"*Moloka'i* is a big, generous, compassionate, beautifully rendered epic novel about a largely forgotten, largely ignored chapter in Hawaiian and American history. Alan Brennert has written an exquisitely textured tale of darkness and light, tragedy and the triumph of the human spirit, filled with original, fully realized characters who walk right off the page and into our hearts."

—Jim Fergus, author of *One Thousand White Women*

"Brennert evokes the evolution of—and hardships on—Moloka'i in engaging prose that conveys a strong sense of place."

—*National Geographic Traveler*

"*Moloka'i* is a haunting story of tragedy in a Pacific paradise. The book opens a window on a world of dazzling beauty, ugly disease and fear, and the courage of a young woman in the Hawai'i of a hundred years ago. It is a story of romance and humanity, and struggles with the pain of isolation, in a place far away in time, yet very close in intimacy, vividness, and exact detail, giving us a sense of community and true kinship across time. It is a story of victory." —Robert Morgan, author of *Gap Creek*

"A moving story . . . a vivid picture of Hawai'i before it became the Touristland it is today." —Larry McMurtry, author of *Lonesome Dove*

"A generous portrait of a brave, full life—Rachel Kalama's disease draws her into healing friendships with troubled Sister Catherine,

with roommate Leilani, who was born in the wrong body, with her true love, Kenji, and more, all in a beautiful land that's both prison and refuge. Alan Brennert has brought eighty years of little-known history to engrossing specific life—as inspiring as it is heartbreaking."

—Jonathan Strong, author of *A Circle Around Her*

"A dazzling historical saga." —*The Washington Post*

"Exhaustively researched, *Moloka'i* transported me to a place I never thought I'd want to go—a nineteenth-century Hawaiian leper colony. But Alan Brennert meticulously paints this world, making it resonate with our own, in which disease is still politicized and made a moral issue. Out of the tragedy of the ostracized and the afflicted, he tells a story of triumph and transcendence."

—Karen Essex, author of *Kleopatra* and *Pharaoh*

"A poignant story." —*Los Angeles Times*

"Alan Brennert draws on historical accounts of Kalaupapa and weaves in traditional Hawaiian stories and customs. . . . *Moloka'i* is the story of people who had much taken from them but also gained an unexpected new family and community in the process." —*Chicago Tribune*

"Compellingly original . . . Brennert's compassion makes Rachel a memorable character, and his smooth storytelling vividly brings early-twentieth-century Hawai'i to life."

—*Publishers Weekly* (starred review)

"A superb novel." —Los Angeles *Daily News*

"By drawing on original documents and journals in the Hawaiian archives, Alan Brennert significantly enhances his affecting novel."

—*The Dallas Morning News*

"Moving and elegiac." —*Honolulu Star-Bulletin*

"Brennert's novel combines a historical account of the leprosy settlement with memorable storytelling." —*The Oregonian*

Honolulu

Also by Alan Brennert

Moloka'i

Praise for *Honolulu*

Winner of *Elle*'s Lettres 2009 Grand Prix for Fiction

"A sweeping, meticulously researched saga that sees its plucky hero-ine, a mistreated but independent-minded Korean mail-order bride, through the highs and lows of life in twentieth-century Hawai'i, this book extends our readers' tradition of favoring lush, flavorful histori-cal novels." —*Elle*

"A well-researched and deftly written tale . . . For sheer readability, it's a hit. . . . Brennert has a good eye for places we can't see any-more: plantation life before the unions gained power; Chinatown when it was all tenements; Waikiki before the high-rises started going up. And it's clear he has real affection for the little people and places he so vividly brings to life. He's not just using historic Honolulu as a place to set a novel; he's bringing it to life for people who haven't had the chance to imagine it before." —*Honolulu Star-Bulletin*

"To its core, *Honolulu* is meticulously researched. . . . Brennert por-trays the Aloha State's history as complicated and dynamic—not simply a melting pot, but a Hawaiian-style 'mixed plate' in which, as Jin sagely notes, 'many different tastes share the plate, but none of them loses its individual flavor, and together they make up a uniquely "local" cuisine.'" —*The Washington Post*

"Successful historical fiction doesn't just take a story and doll it up with period detail. It plunges readers into a different world and defines the historical and cultural pressures the characters face in that particular time and place. That's what Los Angeles writer Alan Brennert did in his previous novel, *Moloka'i*, the story of diseased Hawaiians exiled in their own land. He has done it again in *Hono-lulu*, which focuses on the Asian immigrant experience in Hawai'i, specifically that of Korean picture brides. . . . This is a moving, mul-tilayered epic by a master of historical fiction, in which one immi-grant's journey helps us understand our nation's 'becoming.'" —*San Francisco Chronicle*

"[A] sweeping, epic novel. . . . Brennert weaves the true stories of early Hawai'i into his fictional tale, and many of the captivating people Jin encounters are real. His depiction of the effects of the Depression is startling. Let's hope Brennert follows up this second novel with a third and continues to capture this intriguing and little-explored segment of American history in beautifully told stories." —*Library Journal* (starred review)

"[A] poignant, colorful story." —*Kirkus Reviews*

"Brennert's lush tale of ambition, sacrifice, and survival is immense in its dramatic scope yet intimate in its emotive detail." —*Booklist*

"Intriguing . . . *Honolulu* offers endless insights into a culture many readers may never have encountered, and Brennert further enlivens his tale by dropping in historical figures, some fictional, such as Charlie Chan, and some real, such as Clarence Darrow. But it is Korea that's the real focus of this story, and readers get a sympathetic feel for the daily humiliations the native population suffered from the Japanese who conquered the country. . . . [Brennert's] smooth narrative style makes the book a pleasure to read."
—*The Roanoke Times*

"With skill, historic accuracy, and sensitivity and a clear passion for the people and places in Hawai'i, Brennert weaves a story that will move and inspire readers." —*The Oklahoman*

"In this dazzling, rich, historical story, a young 'picture bride' travels to Hawai'i in 1914 in search of a better life. . . . This intriguing novel is a fascinating literary snapshot of Hawai'i during the early years of the last century. The story is compelling, poignant, and powerful."
—*Tucson Citizen*

"This delightful, suspense-filled feminist novel and social history movingly portrays the ambivalence, confusion, and longing suffered by immigrants making their way in a new world, but reveals how women

Honolulu

ALAN
BRENNERT

St. Martin's Griffin ♞ New York

This is a work of fiction. All of the characters, organizations, and events portrayed in this novel are either products of the author's imagination or are used fictitiously.

www.stmartins.com

THE LIBRARY OF CONGRESS HAS CATALOGUED THE HARDCOVER EDITION AS FOLLOWS:

Brennert, Alan.
    Honolulu : a novel / by Alan Brennert.—1st ed.
        p. cm.
    Includes bibliographical references.
    ISBN 978-0-312-36040-5
    1. Korean American women—Fiction.   2. Korean women—Fiction.   3. Women immigrants—United States—Fiction.   4. Mail order brides—United States—Fiction.   5. Honolulu (Hawaii)—Fiction.   6. Korea—Fiction.   7. Psychological fiction.   8. Domestic fiction.   I. Title.
    PS3552.R3865H66 2009
    813'.54—dc22

                                                                        2008034061

ISBN 978-0-312-60634-3 (trade paperback)

20 19 18 17 16 15 14 13 12 11

FOR PAULETTE

my beautiful wahine *from the*
tropical island of
"Milwauke'e"

Me ke aloha nui

Honolulu

One

When I was a young child growing up in Korea, it was said that the image of the fading moon at daybreak, reflected in a pond or stream or even a well, resembled the speckled shell of a dragon's egg. A dragon embodied the *yang,* the masculine principle of life, and it was thought that if a couple expecting a child prayed to the dragon's egg, their offspring would be male. Of course, every family in those days desired a son over a daughter. Only men could carry on the family line; women were merely vessels by which to provide society with an uninterrupted supply of men. So every day for months before I was born, my parents would rise before dawn, carrying offerings of fresh-steamed rice cakes to the stone well behind our home, as the sky brightened and snuffed out the stars. And they would pray to the pale freckled face of the moon floating on the water's surface, pray that the child growing inside my mother's womb would be a boy.

In this they were to be disappointed. On the third day of the First Moon in the Year of the Rooster, their first and only daughter was born to them. In those waning days of the Yi Dynasty, newborn girls were not deemed important enough to be graced with formal names, but were instead given nicknames. Often these represented some personal characteristic: Cheerful, Pretty, Little One, Big One. Sometimes they presumed to be commandments: Chastity, or Virtue. A few—Golden Calf, Little Flower—verged on the poetic. But too many names reflected the parents' feelings about the birth of a daughter. I knew a girl named Anger, and another called Pity. More than a few were known as Sorrow or Sadness. And everyone had heard the story of the father who named his firstborn daughter "One is Okay," his next, "Perhaps After the Second," the third, "Three Laughs," and the last, "Four Shames."

As for me, my parents named me "Regrettable"—eventually shortened to simply Regret.

Koreans seldom address one another by their given names; we believe a person's name is a thing of intimacy and power, not to be used casually by anyone but a family member or close friend. When I was very young, Regret was merely a name to me, signifying nothing more than that. But as I grew older and learned it held another meaning, it became a stone weight in my heart. A call to supper became a reminder of my unfortunate presence at the dinner table. A stern rebuke by my father—"Regret, what are we to do with you?"—seemed to hint that my place in the family was impermanent. Too young to understand the real reasons, I wondered what was wrong with me to make me so unwanted. Was I too short? I wasn't as tall as my friend Sunny, but not nearly so short as her sister Lotus. Was I too plain? I spent hours squinting into the mirror, judging my every feature, and found them wanting. My eyes were set too close together, my nose was too small, or maybe it was too big; my lips were thin, my ears flat. It was clear to see, I was plain and unlovely—no wonder my parents regretted my birth.

In truth, my father was merely old-fashioned and conservative, a strict adherent to Confucian ideals, one of which was the inherent precedence of man over woman: "The wife must regard her husband as heavenly; what he does is a heavenly act and she can only follow him." I was a girl, I would eventually marry and become part of someone else's family; as such my existence was simply not of the same consequence as that of my three brothers, who would carry on the family line and provide for our parents when they became old.

But I knew none of this when I was young, and instead decided it was due to the shape of my nose or the color of my eyes; and for years to come I would fret over and find fault with the girl who looked back at me from the mirror.

I have traveled far from the land of my birth, and even farther from who I was then. More than forty years and four thousand miles separate us: the girl of sixteen who took that first unwitting step forward, and the woman in her sixtieth year who now, in sight of the vast Pacific, presumes to memorialize this journey in mere words. It is a journey measured not in time or distance, but in the breadth of one's soul and the struggle of becoming.

Westerners count their age by the number of years completed on their birthdays, but in Korea one's personal age is determined differently. A newborn child is said to be already in its first year of life, and thus is deemed to be one year old at birth. I was born in the Year of the Rooster—roughly corresponding to the Western year 1897—and upon the next lunar New Year in 1898, I turned two; in 1899, I was three; and so forth. This sounds confusing, I know, so hereafter, when speaking of ages, I shall do so according to Western reckoning.

My early life was typically Korean, at least for Koreans of a certain rank. Our family was *yangban*—we belonged to the country gentry and lived in a fine house with a tiled roof in a little village called Pojogae, not far from the city of Taegu, in Kyŏngsang Province. Pojogae means "dimple," and the village—mostly houses of mud and stone, their roofs thatched with rice grass—rested in a dimple of land surrounded by rolling hills. In winter these hills were draped in snow, but when I was very small my eldest brother, Joyful Day, revealed to me that their white shawls were actually made of rice, the most delicious in all the land: "They're called the Rice Mountains," he explained solemnly, "and people come from all over the kingdom to gather grains to plant their own rice paddies. Why, wars have even been fought over that rice."

I used to beg him to take me there, but he would just smile and shake his head. "The best-tasting rice in the world shouldn't be eaten so early in a person's life," he would say, "but saved for later."

"What kind of rice grows in winter?" I asked once, upon reaching the worldly age of five.

His reply: "Winter rice, of course!"

This sounded eminently logical, and I continued to believe in the legend of the Rice Mountains for longer than I care to admit.

Mine were good brothers—two older, one younger—and for the first six years of my life we played together, up and down the twisting banks of Dragontail Stream, along the entire length and breadth of our little valley. Father would not have approved had he known, as girls were not supposed to have fun with their brothers. But this all came to an end in my seventh year, when Confucian tradition decreed that boys and girls were to be strictly separated, like wheat from chaff. As in most Korean homes, my father and brothers lived in the outermost of two L-shaped wings, each with its own rooms and courtyard, which nestled close together but stood worlds apart. Since only men were permitted to have dealings with the outside world, they occupied the Outer Room. And as the women's realm was that of sewing and cooking and raising children, we inhabited the Inner Room.

Now, the most contact I had with my brothers was at mealtimes, when Mother and I would carry in the dining tables, set them on the floor, and serve bowls of steaming rice and *mandu* dumplings to the men of the house, who always ate first. We hovered nearby, out of sight but never out of earshot, in case they needed more *kimchi*—a spicy side dish made from fermented cabbage, garlic, and red peppers—or a cup of ginseng tea. Only after they had eaten their fill were we women permitted to return to the kitchen and there consume what food remained. In the course of serving them, I might get a wink or a smile now and then from Joyful Day or my second brother, Glad Son . . . but the days of games and companionship between us were over, and I missed them sorely. I missed my brothers' teasing. For the first time I began to feel acutely the lack of a sister.

There were only three females in our household: my mother, my grandmother, and me. Grandmother, never seen without her long bamboo pipe, was Father's mother, and a more rancorous old crone never lived. She treated my mother as a beast of burden, addressing her by a Korean term roughly translatable as "that thing" or "what-you-may-call-her," as in:

"You there, what-you-may-call-her, fetch me some more tobacco!"

"Yes, *halmoni*," Mother said, obeying without complaint.

In this Grandmother was merely following long-standing precedent. New brides moving into their husbands' ancestral home were expected to kowtow to the every whim of their mothers-in-law, who did not hesitate to take full advantage of the situation.

They, after all, had once been daughters-in-law kowtowing to *their* mothers-in-law, and now felt entitled to receive in kind.

"What's that look you're giving me, girl?" Grandmother snapped, having glimpsed a shadow of disapproval on my face.

"Nothing, *halmoni*," I told her.

"You think you know everything, don't you? But you don't. Someday," she said smugly, "you will be me, and then you'll understand."

I gave her a cold look, thinking, *I will never be you, Grandmother,* and retreated into the kitchen to help Mother wash the breakfast dishes.

It was a breezy autumn morning, and through our rice-paper windows I could hear the chatter of fallen leaves scuttling across the ground outside. I was anxious to finish my chores and go out to play. My brothers were leaving for school, and though I had some mild curiosity about what they did there—my parents, like most Confucians, revered learning and stressed its importance to their sons—those chattering leaves spoke more eloquently to me than the vague benefits of an "education," which in any event was only for boys.

When the last dish was dry I hurried outside and joined Sunny, who lived next door; her family, too, was *yangban*, though they owned less farmland than mine and lived in a smaller house. We began a game of shuttlecock in the road, but as often as we succeeded in batting the feathered ball between us, the wind would step in like a third player, scoop the ball up in a gusty hand, and send it spiraling away from us. We found this less frustrating than amusing, and there was much laughing and giggling as we chased the ball down. I raised my paddle and found myself fielding a whirlwind of leaves that swept in between us, swatting not the ball but a windblown scrap of paper that flew up and into my path.

I tore it off my paddle and was about to toss it aside, when I noticed that this wasn't just a scrap of old newspaper, but what looked like a page out of a book. I say looked because at this time I had absolutely no acquaintance with the printed word. I could read neither Chinese characters nor *hangul,* the native Korean alphabet; words were an enigma to me, each letter a puzzle I could not hope to solve. All I could tell from the browned, brittle page was that it was obviously from a very *old* book—perhaps one that had fallen apart and been discarded by its owner, only to have its pages plucked from the garbage heap by a stray puff of wind.

I examined it more closely, noting the elegant black strokes stacked up in neat columns, and though I couldn't fathom their meaning, I was impressed by the graceful and delicate calligraphy.

"Isn't this pretty?" I said, showing the page to Sunny.

Some of the marks were little more than vertical or horizontal lines with crimped ends. Some resembled upside-down wishbones, while others were a combination of circles, squares, slashes, squiggles, and dots. All seemed beautiful and mysterious to me.

"It's *hangul,*" Sunny said, "I think." More than that she couldn't say because she was not able to read, either. Another bellow of wind sent the shuttle ball airborne again and Sunny raced after it.

On a whim, I slipped the scrap of paper into the waistband of my skirt—traditional Korean clothes, or *hanbok,* have no pockets—and resumed our game.

Later, alone in my room, the page presented its mysteries to me anew. I had never had any real curiosity before about these things called words, but the frustration I now felt at my inability to decipher these marks drove me to an uncharacteristically bold move: After supper I sneaked out of the Inner Room and into the men's quarters, where I hesitantly approached Joyful Day as he studied, alone, from a schoolbook.

"Elder brother?" I said in a low tone.

He glanced up, surprised. "Little sister, you shouldn't be in here." But the admonishment was softened by a smile.

"I know," I said, "but may I ask a great favor of you?"

I showed him what I had found and asked if he knew the meaning of the writing on the page.

His eyes tracked across the markings, right to left, then he turned the page over and examined the other side as well. "It seems to be some kind of . . . travel narrative," he said.

"What is that?"

"An account of someone's journey to a faraway place. It appears to have been written by a *yangban* woman, judging by some talk of her maidservants, while visiting a place called Kwanbuk."

I was thunderstruck by this. "Women can write words? Onto paper?"

He smiled at that. "Some do. Some even publish what they write, though for heaven's sake don't tell Father I said so."

"But what does it *say*?"

"Nothing very exciting, I'm afraid. It simply relates how the woman went to view a sunrise."

"Would you read it to me?"

Bemused by my interest, he asked, "If I do, will you then go back to the Inner Room?"

"Yes, yes," I agreed.

He began to read aloud: " 'All was bathed in the serene light of the moon. The sea was whiter than the night before, and a gale chilled my bones . . .' "

I listened, rapt and silent, as he conjured from the cold black type the image of a woman of many years past, shivering in the chill predawn light as she waited for the sun to rise. There was nothing as thrilling or dramatic about the narrative as in the folktales my mother and grandmother sometimes told me—but the woman's vivid descriptions of the lake, the sky, and the rising sun were nonetheless enthralling. The light from below the horizon appeared as "rolls of red silk spread on the sea," and then slowly there arose "a strange object the size of my palm, glowing like a charcoal on the last night of the month."

The words, *her* words, entranced me. For the first time I understood that these lines and slashes contained entire worlds within them. The rising sun was *like a charcoal on the last night of the month*. How could that be? I asked myself. How could something be two different things at once? How could these little chicken scratches contain so much?

Suddenly my brother stopped in mid-sentence, coming up short where the page itself came to an end. "That's all there is, alas. Now, before Father sees you and scolds us both . . ."

I thanked him, took the page, and crept back to my room.

There I used a piece of charcoal to copy some of the markings onto a scrap of butcher's paper. But without my brother's mediation, they were once again an unfathomable collection of lines and squiggles. I knew they held meaning, I remembered the words Joyful Day had spoken, but like a bad magician I could not summon them on my own.

Now each morning I found myself studying my father as he read his morning paper, wondering what those columns of black type might be saying to him. I felt a pang of envy for the first time as my brothers set off for school, and in the evenings I sneaked in and stole glances as they read by candlelight from their school primers. But of course I knew better than to expect I could ever do the same. Girls, at least girls in rural villages like Pojogae, did not go to school; I might envy a bird the power of flight, but I knew perfectly well that I could not be a bird.

And yet—I kept that page. I kept it against the faint, perhaps impossible hope that someday I might learn how to coax the meaning from those enigmatic marks. Until then, it remained silent in my presence—a silence I would be forced to abide for another eight years.

y the time I turned fifteen, in the Year of the Rat—by the Western calendar, 1912—Confucian tradition forbade me from leaving the house without an escort. I was no longer free to play in the street with Sunny, or to go into the foothills to pick wildflowers, and I chafed at having to spend my every waking hour in the Inner Room or Inner Court. On the rare occasions when I was permitted to leave, I was required to wear a long green veil that covered all of my increasingly womanly body but for a slit through which my eyes could peek. From this I drew the conclusion that the physical changes I was experiencing were unsightly to society, thus making me even more insecure about my appearance.

There were only two respites from the tedium of the Inner Room. The first came each afternoon before we began cooking supper, when Mother and I would retire to her room and sew together. This was my favorite hour of the day—what Mother and I called our "thimble time." I had learned how to thread a needle before I was barely out of diapers, or so it seemed. I was proud that after years of practice I was able to sew as many as ten stitches in a single inch—but Mother could stitch twelve! A gifted seamstress, she made all of the household's clothes: the men's waist-length white jackets and baggy white trousers, as well as the short yellow jackets and pleated red skirts I wore as an unmarried girl. But her talents shone most brightly in the wrapping cloths she loved to make.

In the West, people carry bags or briefcases; in Korea, they carry important papers, gifts, indeed objects of all sorts, wrapped in cloths woven of brilliant colors and rich textures. The most elaborate, called *su po*, had once been used in the Royal Palace— back in the days before the Japanese came and deposed our king— and were embroidered with a single design, geometric or pictorial. Favorite images were trees, fruit, flowers, butterflies, or birds. Mother made several such designs for local gentry and each was exquisite:

I remember one that vividly depicted a funnel of windblown snow-flakes against a sky-blue field, and another portraying a flock of cranes dipping their beaks in a river, as gold-flecked fish swam just below the waterline.

But Mother also made another kind of wrapping cloth, one that was usually the province of commoners: the *chogak po*, or patch-work cloths. These were cobbled together from leftover scraps of varying shapes—wedges, squares, rectangles, triangles—and fabrics such as linen, cotton, ramie, silk, whatever was at hand. The different materials, weaves, and patterns were stitched together into a mosaic of crossed lines and no apparent design. There was an abstract beauty to them, to be sure, but one day I asked Mother why she bothered to make these patchworks when she was capable of much more elegant and harmonic creations.

She thought for a moment, then said, "When we are young, we think life will be like a *su po*: one fabric, one weave, one grand de-sign. But in truth, life turns out to be more like the patchwork cloths—bits and pieces, odds and ends—people, places, things we never expected, never wanted, perhaps. There is harmony in this, too, and beauty. I suppose that is why I like the *chogak po*."

I was old enough to know that she meant this as a positive state-ment, and I nodded to let her know that I understood the wisdom of what she had said. But I was also young enough to find the idea that my life was to be made up of odds and ends I didn't want—frayed, ragged remnants like these, together forming a rather mot-ley whole—a little terrifying.

My only other release from the monotony of the Inner Room came on those days when Mother and I would don our veils and carry our laundry in big wicker baskets to the stream, where we would join other village women washing clothes. We were always careful to walk only on the left side of the road; men walked on the right, and whenever we encountered one we averted our gazes, never making the slightest eye contact as we maintained a virtuous silence. But today the only men we saw were a squad of Japanese military police in their glossy brown uniforms, like a swarm of bronze-backed dung beetles, marching somewhere with great urgency. We kept our eyes downcast, less out of decorum than fear.

It had been only three years since our nation, our Land of Morning Calm, had been annexed—swallowed whole by the voracious Japanese Empire, which had long coveted it. Fear had since become as much a part of our daily diet as rice or water. We had accustomed ourselves to the sight of Japanese police—often accompanied by Korean "assistants" dressed in black—descending upon us like vipers to root out insurgents or search for caches of hidden arms. They might come at any hour, breaking down house gates, pulling men and even women from their homes in the hush of the night—a hush broken by the sound of imperious shouting in Japanese and terrified wails in Korean.

But this morning the police merely hurried by, taking no notice of us, and Mother and I let out a shared breath as they passed.

At the stream we rinsed our clothes in cool running water, then pounded and ironed them with laundry bats (an implement resembling a cross between a rolling pin and an American baseball bat). There was something soothing about the rhythmic *thop thop thop* of a dozen-odd laundry bats wielded against stone, like the comforting beat of one's own heart. As we washed, Mother could gossip with neighbors and I would pass the time with Sunny.

"Have you heard?" my friend asked, as she wrung water from a pair of white cotton trousers. "Three girls attending Ewha School in Seoul will be graduating *college*—the first in the whole country!" She added hopefully, "Perhaps *I* might attend it someday."

I sighed. A week did not pass without some flight of fancy on Sunny's part. Without looking up I said, "There's a palace there, too, quite nice by all accounts. Perhaps I might live in it someday."

She looked stung. "It's possible. I *could* go."

"Seoul is as far from Pojogae as the earth is from the sun," I said. "How would you even get there?"

"I don't know. Isn't there a train that goes there?"

I found this conversation more irritating than most of Sunny's fancies, and I let my frustrations out on the skirt I was pounding with my laundry bat.

"When you are attending school in Seoul," I said brusquely, "let me know when the palace becomes vacant." Sunny frowned and said no more on the subject—that day or ever again.

But far more disquieting was the sight that greeted us upon returning to town. The squad of Japanese police we had encountered earlier in the day had arrested a man, beaten him bloody, and was now preparing to demonstrate to our village the brutal folly of harboring rebels. They stripped the man's shirt from his back and tied his manacled hands to a chain hanging from the rear of a horse-drawn wagon. Only then did I recognize their prisoner.

"Mother," I whispered, "isn't that Mr. Hong?"

He was our greengrocer, and the father of a friend of mine.

"Hush!" Mother hissed, and I quickly fell silent.

The wagon driver snapped the horse's reins and it took off at a trot. We watched in horror and disgust but did not dare turn away, lest this be noted by the police. Mr. Hong, manacled and shirtless, was dragged on his back through the streets, the gravel raking and grinding his flesh like pepper in a mill. His left eye was swollen shut, his face purpled with bruises, but he remained defiantly silent, refusing to give up even a single cry of pain.

Then the wagon turned a corner, and none of us ever saw him again.

*I*n fact, the conflict with Japan had begun years before. In 1895, our Queen Min, who was fiercely opposed to Japanese interference in Korea, was stabbed to death by agents of Japan.

Ten years later, Korea was declared a Japanese "protectorate," and five years after that we were annexed. Not everyone in our country would give it up without a fight, and I'm proud to say that our provincial militia in Kyŏngsang-do fought most bravely and bitterly against the Japanese army. But in the end, a dragonfly is no challenge to a dragon, and our province fell like all the others—though there would be scattered guerrilla warfare against our colonial occupiers for years to come.

The Imperial Government insisted that Korean children learn the Japanese language in school. They also banned the teaching of Korean history and language, and burned hundreds of thousands of books that dared to suggest Korea had ever been an independent nation. They were determined to turn the next generation of Koreans into Japanese.

You might think that little Pojogae, far from the corridors of politics, would have been relatively untouched by all this. Yet rural villages like ours were much more central to the conflict than you might imagine. Japan needed food for its people and intended Korea to be its breadbasket. Farmers—and the landed gentry like my father, who leased them their land—were forced to abandon almost all other crops but rice, then saw their harvests confiscated for the exclusive use of the Japanese. We who grew the rice were not allowed to consume it, and had to subsist instead on the small plots of barley, millet, and beans we planted.

My eldest brother's fanciful whimsy of the Rice Mountains had come, in a way, into grim existence.

Meat became a scarcer sight on our table, and we could no longer afford the services of a servant girl from the village who had helped us keep house. Mother—who managed the household finances—was now scrimping and saving scraps of cloth for more than just aesthetic reasons, or turning our clothes inside out and restitching them to get some further wear out of them.

And yet, I must be grateful to the Japanese for one thing, if only one thing: were it not for them, Blossom would never have entered my life.

She simply appeared in our home one morning, a five-year-old moppet with a long braid of black hair down her back and a sweet oval of a face that was everything mine was not: delicate, fine-featured, lovely. She was in the kitchen helping Mother peel a clove of garlic when I entered, still blinking sleep from my eyes. I stopped short upon seeing her, wondering perhaps if she were a new servant girl. Mother didn't even look up from preparing breakfast: "Daughter, this is your new sister-in-law, Blossom, of the Shin clan of Songso."

I stared uncomprehendingly at the little girl, who offered me a small smile. But this was apparently not sufficient response for Mother, who poked her in the arm and said, in a tone I had never heard in her voice before, "Where are your manners, girl? What do you say?"

"Good morning, honorable *shinui*," Blossom greeted me. The word meant "husband's sister," but how could this slip of a child have a husband?

Mother said, "She is betrothed to marry Goodness of the East"—my younger brother—"when he comes of age. In the meantime, she'll live with us and learn how to attend her wifely duties." To Blossom she added reproachfully, "Your husband will waste away and die waiting for you to finish that garlic."

"I'm sorry, honorable mother-in-law," the girl apologized, and quickly finished peeling the clove.

I was still confused, though not, of course, at the idea of the betrothal. In those days all marriages were arranged by one's parents, either directly or indirectly through the services of a marriage broker. As a young girl the notion of marrying for romantic love never entered my mind. Nor was it unheard of for families to take in a *minmyonuri*—a daughter-in-law in training, as it were—though I had always heard it spoken of disparagingly.

No, what baffled me was that my parents had arranged a marriage for Goodness of the East, who was but eight years old, while my two elder brothers and I were still unbetrothed!

I was peeved enough that for the next few days I made no attempt to befriend my new sister-in-law, too busy fretting that I saw no sign of my parents finding a husband for *me*. Blossom and I worked side by side at household tasks, but exchanged few words. We slept in the same room, but at night the only sound was the sigh of warm air flowing through the heating flues beneath the floor.

Then one afternoon—during which, I couldn't help but notice, Blossom braved the wintry cold to carry at least ten buckets of water back and forth from our well—I finished my own chores and entered the Inner Court to take what little sun I could find. There I found Blossom, standing silently at the base of the high wall enclosing the courtyard, gazing up wistfully. Her cheeks were chafed red from the chill; her nose was runny. And there was such longing in her eyes as she looked up—at what, I wondered?—that I asked her if anything was wrong.

"Honorable sister-in-law," she said, "could you help me up to the top of the wall? Just for a minute?"

I was puzzled, but couldn't bring myself to say no. I overturned a large clay flowerpot, stepped onto it, then reached down and scooped Blossom up in my arms. I gave her the boost she needed to clamber atop the wall, where she settled herself on the ledge and peered intently into a distance I could not see. Curious, I pulled myself up and sat beside her, our legs dangling over the edge of the Inner Wall. I followed her gaze across the blue tiled rooftops of the Outer Rooms, but all I saw was the road leading out of Pojogae and into the hills, where dark clouds pressed down on snowy summits.

"Do you see something out there?" I asked.

After a moment she just shook her head. "No," she said quietly. "I just wondered if maybe my papa was coming back for me."

I had built a wall around her in my mind, but with these few plaintive words it was breached as easily as this wall of stone.

Her father, she told me, had been a well-to-do *yangban* farmer, until the Japanese took his farm and cast Blossom's family from their ancestral home. Now penniless, her father went to work as a field laborer, but his pitiful wages were insufficient to feed eight children. Somehow my own father heard of his plight and offered to raise their youngest child as a bride for Goodness of the East. Normally, families of the upper classes would never have resorted to *minmyonuri* marriage, but circumstances were difficult for both clans. Blossom's parents had one less mouth to feed and received four yen in payment—about two American dollars. In return my family received the services of a bride-in-waiting to replace the servant girl we could no longer afford, a virtual slave to the household.

I felt shame for my clan, and guilt when I looked at Blossom.

She spoke of her own family—her parents, five sisters, two brothers—with tenderness, longing, and the fear that she might never see any of them again. I could hardly tell her otherwise; even daughters-in-law wed in the traditional manner seldom saw their birth families again, especially if their new homes were far distant. She began to weep, and without a conscious thought, I took her into my arms, the only comfort I could offer. I held her against me, let her head rest against my breast as she wept, and resolved to myself that from now on I would try to be more than just a sister-in-law to her: I would try to be a sister.

*M*other worked Blossom harder than she had ever worked our servant girl, but I helped her with her chores whenever Mother wasn't looking. When we had free time, we enjoyed board games like *go* and *yut*, or played seesaw in the Inner Court. (Legend holds that seesaws became popular with girls because on the upswing they were able to catch a glimpse of the world beyond their cloistered walls.) Since Blossom was so young, there were no rigid restrictions yet on her movements, and this worked to my advantage as well. I would tell Father that Blossom wished to play down by the stream or pick wildflowers on the slopes of the near hills. Father, of course, wouldn't permit her to go alone and appointed me her escort. I always protested a little for the sake of plausibility, and soon the two of us were free of the stifling sameness of the Inner Room for an hour or two.

On New Year's Day, Blossom and I rose early to help Mother cook the food to be offered to our ancestors on this first day of the Year of the Ox. It was Mother's responsibility to prepare for these ancestral feasts, up to ten a year, though as females we were not permitted to take part in them. We merely carried in the dining tables and set out the food in the appropriate attitudes—fish on the east side of the table, meat on the west. Joyful Day, as eldest son, poured wine into the ancestors' wine bowls, laid chopsticks across the plates, and placed spoons for the soup; then, kneeling, he led the ceremony honoring the past four generations of our forebears, as Mother, Blossom, and I listened from the kitchen.

Afterward we ate, each in our own turn. Mother's New Year's Soup was always delicious, though there was more rice and dough in it this year than chicken, and no pheasant at all. I drank a bowl of rice wine too quickly and got a little tipsy. Grandmother had several bowls and became quite the cheerful drunk: She was much nicer to be around when half-pickled than sober, calling my mother "dear, dear daughter-in-law" as if she had been possessed by spirits—as I suppose she had! Would that we could have gotten her to drink more during the other moons of the year.

As Blossom and I played inside, the boys took the kites they had been building all winter and cast them to the winds. The traditional Korean kite was an oblong or rectangle—a mulberry-paper skin stretched across a framework of bamboo sticks—with a circular hole in the middle, the diameter of which was exactly half the kite's width, for greater stability and control. It was always colorfully painted: A kite with a red half-circle on its face was called a red half-moon kite; one with stripes of green, red, and blue was a tricolor skirt kite; and so on. Some kites were not rectangular but resembled an octopus with eight flapping arms. None had tails. The boys would use a horned wooden reel to let out the lengthening string, and the kites would ascend gloriously into the skies.

During these first two weeks of the First Moon the boys would also engage in kite fighting. They dipped their kite strings in a mixture of glue and glass powder, then dried them to a coarse edge, so when the kites were aloft the strings became razors. Each boy would try to steer his string so that the serrated glass edge would slice like a knife through another boy's string, neatly severing it, and watch his opponent's kite go spinning away on the wind.

Blossom and I observed this pageantry from atop the wall of the Inner Court. From a distance the white, green, red, yellow, and black kites diving and slashing at one another looked like a flock of brightly feathered parrots quarreling amongst themselves, with an occasional bird taking off in a snit for parts unknown.

Then on the fifteenth day of the moon, all the kite flyers wrote the words "Away Evils, Come Blessings" on their kites and took to the skies one last time. It was said that thirteen hundred years before, during a trying time in our nation's history, a famous general had tried to calm civil unrest by sending a kite bearing a burning cotton ball into the night skies. The people saw it as a falling star returning to heaven—a sign that the nation's current misfortunes would be ending. Ever since, on the fifteenth day of the New Year, boys all across the land would unreel their kites, long threads having been attached beforehand to the kite strings. Once the kites were airborne the boys would strike a match and light a fuse to the threads; as the kites flew higher, the sparks would race up the threads and finally reach the strings, which would then burst into flame, setting loose the kites.

From our house Blossom and I could see dozens of flames igniting in midair, and watched the brilliantly colored kites fly free, borne away on updrafts, drifting toward the distant hills.

"How far will they go?" Blossom asked excitedly.

"Very far," I predicted. "At least as far as Taegu."

"Will they reach the ocean?"

"Some of them, I'm sure."

"Will they go all the way to America, do you think?"

"I have no doubt of it," I said with a smile.

From our high perch atop the wall we watched the kites bobbing and spinning on the wind, like caged birds set wildly free. Would either of us have ever dreamed that soon I would be following in those kites' imaginary wake?

Two

*I*f Blossom was one piece of my *chogak po*, another patch would be added later in that Year of the Ox when Mother's elder sister, Obedience, fell ill. Widowed and living alone in Taegu, she was guilty of the worst crime a Korean woman could commit: a failure to produce heirs. "Not even a daughter," my father would say with pity and contempt. Producing sons was the highest duty of every woman, and those who failed to live up to that duty were often ridiculed and shunned. But Mother would not forsake Aunt Obedience and petitioned Father to allow her to go to Taegu to care for her. Father grumbled a bit about it—it was customary to bring lavish gifts to one's in-laws, which we could ill afford—but he did not gainsay Mother the trip. Besides, it was a good excuse to sell some of our eggs at the market in Taegu. I quickly volunteered to help Mother carry the eggs and was delighted when Father agreed that I could accompany her. A trip outside the Inner Room was thrilling enough, but a trip to the city—I was beside myself with glee, though of course it was indecorous to show it.

"I don't know how you can stand that festering sore of a city," Father told Mother. He disliked Taegu and avoided going there, I suspected, because as a member of the country gentry he had no social standing in the city and was not accorded the kind of deference and respect he received in Pojogae. I think that may have been why he took such pains to be a strict Confucian—so none could dispute his aristocratic lineage, even if we weren't rich like other *yangban*.

Mother and I would be gone an entire week, during which one of the village women, with help from Blossom, would cook and clean for Father. We planned to leave before dawn in order to arrive at the marketplace by early morning. The day before we left I went to the henhouse and set about filling up egg cribs. These were long open cradles made of woven straw, each holding about ten eggs—they looked rather like elongated bird's nests, with little loops of straw to secure each egg in place. After I had filled seven cribs Father adjudged that the amount was sufficient and secured them onto a *jige*—two pieces of pine bound together with straw at an angle that makes them look like the English letter A. It also held our clothes, as well as presents of rice wine and sweet cakes for Aunt Obedience. The next day, in the early morning darkness, Mother and I donned our veils, I hoisted the *jige* onto my back, and we began the eight-mile walk to the city. (Other *yangban* women were often transported from place to place in palanquins—an enclosed sedan chair borne on the shoulders of servants—but alas, the days of palanquins were long over for us.)

The day dawned clear and cool and the walk was pleasant, if

long. At one time, I knew, even this much travel would have been impossible for us except at night. It used to be that a town bell would toll in the evening and all the village men had to remove themselves from the streets so that women could leave their homes—to do shopping or errands, or just to take a breath of air, often in the company of servants bearing lanterns to light their way. Only under cover of night could women traffic in the outside world, without risk of being glimpsed by men.

We stopped occasionally to rest or to drink water from a stream, and after three and a half hours we finally reached Taegu. Merchants were just opening their doors to customers but the streets were already busy with pedestrians, palanquins, horse-drawn carts, even the occasional automobile, still an exotic sight. I also noticed that few women here in the city were veiled—perhaps the veils, like the nights of women shopping by lantern light, were going out of fashion.

The closer we came to the town marketplace, the more the streets took on a festive air, bustling with color and commerce. We passed a grain market where customers haggled over the price of wheat and barley; nearby, vendors sold handmade pottery and fine leather sandals. I savored the smells of cooking food from booths selling pungent *kimchi* or sweet rice cakes made with fresh pumpkin. When we arrived at the poultry market I took the *jige* off my back and Mother presented our eggs for inspection to a vendor. She did so while still managing to avoid looking directly at the man to whom she was trying to sell her wares. They bargained over the price in one of the more ridiculous speech forms required by Confucianism, in which a woman interacting with a male stranger addressed an imaginary third party to the conversation: "Please inform the honorable gentleman that these eggs were laid by fine young hens raised in the village of Pojogae, which is renowned for its poultry." "Please tell the honorable lady we might look more favorably upon these eggs at a lower price," and so on. Eventually this tortured negotiation came to a satisfactory conclusion, and we left the market slightly wealthier than we had entered it.

Aunt Obedience lived in a narrow sliver of a house next door to a butcher's shop. The butcher is one of the lowliest and most reviled professions in Korea, and when Auntie's windows were open one could hear the incessant clucking of doomed fowl and the constant chop of the butcher's blade cleaving through meat and bone. I tried not to think about what animal parts were being amputated each time I heard the thump of a blade striking the butcher's block.

Obedience was a kind-hearted if somewhat self-pitying woman with a consumptive cough and a grudge against the world. This was not unusual among Korean women who, after all, had much to feel aggrieved about. "My life has been nothing but suffering," she would say, warming to her subject. "Better I should never have been born!"

Mother would then object, "Sister, you know this is not so."

"Well, at least, I should not have been born a woman. Had I been a man, I might have made something of my life."

"But had you been born a man," Mother said, "I would never have been blessed with such a loving sister." The words punctured Auntie's self-pity and brought tears to her eyes. "Do you remember that old song we used to sing at picnics?" Mother asked with a smile.

"Of course! 'The evening sky holds many stars—'"

"'By the sea there are many sands . . .'"

And so Mother drew her sister into a series of loving recollections of people and places of their youth, which made Obedience smile and even laugh.

Mother quickly took charge of the household and set about cooking a chicken dish known as a health rejuvenator. As this unfortunately required a chicken, I was given the onerous task of purchasing one at the butcher's shop. Auntie insisted on paying for it and pressed a handful of *won* into my hand. Boldly, I decided not to wear my veil. No one on the street seemed to take notice.

My pleasure at being out bare-faced and unescorted was mitigated by my revulsion at the shop, its floor streaked with the blood of fowl, swine, and cattle, whose short lives had all reached the same unhappy end. No one who grows up in the country, of course, is a stranger to such matters, but the concentrated stench of so much dead meat turned my stomach. The butcher offered to let me select a chicken from the coop outside but I merely picked out one of the plucked carcasses already on ice, which he hastily wrapped in slick brown paper.

I paid for the poultry and returned to Auntie's. Mother took possession of the carcass and set about sprinkling it with ginseng while Obedience examined the bill to make certain I had not been shortchanged. When I saw her taking in not just the numbers but the few words of *hangul* on the bill, I blurted out, "Auntie—can you read?"

"I can certainly read a butcher's bill," she said with a sniff.

"Could you teach me?"

"What silliness is this? Why does a young girl of marriageable age need to learn to read?"

My response, I admit, was not without a measure of calculation.

"Because I wish to make something of my life," I said.

I saw the desired flash of sympathy in her eyes, but then, surprisingly, she glanced away in embarrassment.

"Your uncle taught me to recognize certain words and numbers, in order that I might not be cheated by an unscrupulous grocer," she admitted, "but that is all. Forgive me, niece. I cannot help you to better yourself. I wish I could."

There was such shame in her tone that I felt immediate remorse for having raised the subject. Auntie retreated into the kitchen with Mother and I spoke not another word about the matter. . . .

Until that night, when I was awakened near midnight by the

touch of a hand on my arm. I was sleeping on a straw mat in the front of the house—Mother shared a room with her sister—and I opened my eyes to see, in the hovering glow of a candle, Aunt Obedience squatting at my side.

"Niece," she said softly, "do you truly wish to learn to read?"

"Oh, Auntie, please don't trouble yourself over my foolish whims. I understand that you can't—"

"Oh, *hush*." The word came out with surprising gentleness, but it was followed hard by a scraping cough. When she recovered her breath she went on: "I . . . *might* know someone who could teach you. But it would have to be our secret, just the two of us; you understand?"

I didn't, but said that I did.

"Dried-up old women like myself rarely have a chance to better anyone's life," she said with familiar self-deprecation, but an unfamiliar hint of a smile. "At least I shall try."

She stood, and the wobbly pool of candlelight floated out of the room with her. I had no idea what to make of this, but even the faintest hope of learning to read made it difficult for me to fall back asleep any time soon.

*T*he next morning I awoke to find Mother puzzled and concerned because Aunt Obedience had insisted on going out to the market alone, despite her cough. But when Auntie returned an hour later, she seemed fine: "At the market I happened to see my friend Mrs. Li, who has a daughter the same age as Regret," she announced casually to my mother. "I thought it might be pleasant if the two of them met." Mother agreed, and was as startled as I when her sister promptly took me by the hand and whisked me out of the house to meet this new friend.

Out in the street, Obedience smiled again. "She has agreed to meet you," she told me excitedly.

"Mrs. Li's daughter?"

"What! Don't be silly, that was all blather, for your mother's benefit."

"Why can't Mother know what I'm doing?"

"I would prefer that she did not," was all Auntie would say. "And if she asks what you and Mrs. Li's daughter did together, say you spent the afternoon sewing, or cooking, or whatever enters your head."

"Yes, Auntie," I said. "Thank you."

Within minutes we were at the marketplace, where we paused in front of the fish market as Obedience surveyed the crowd in search of someone. As five, then ten minutes crept past, she seemed to worry; until at last she sighed in relief, declaring, "There she is," and once more took me by the hand.

As we hurried forward I followed her gaze, and caught my first glimpse of this person who would be so pivotal to the course of my life.

She was standing at a flower stall, a strikingly beautiful woman no more than thirty years old, with fair skin and piercing eyes. She was colorfully attired in red petticoats and a brilliant blue blouse made of lustrous silk and ramie. Her face was impeccably made up with powder and kohl, as in the pictures of royal women I had seen. But her beauty was not the most remarkable thing I noticed about her.

The woman, you see, was chatting with the flower vendor, and I was flabbergasted to see that she did not deferentially avert her gaze but instead looked *directly at the man* as she spoke to him. Even more astonishing, she *smiled* at him! Her face was not the diffident, expressionless mask that other women decorously presented to men, but warm, open, and even a little flirtatious.

I can scarcely begin to describe the nearly electric shock that crackled through my body at the sight of this. The woman nodded a goodbye to the florist and moved on. I watched in amazement as she brazenly made eye contact with at least half a dozen other men—smiling, speaking a word or two of greeting, even exchanging laughter with one prosperous-looking gentleman. And the men, far from being shocked or offended by her boldness, actually smiled back at her! I had never seen anything like it, and I must confess, my first reaction was one of dismay and disapproval.

As she drew closer, the woman looked up, recognizing Auntie. The warmth in her face cooled a bit, her expression becoming, it seemed to me, merely polite. I expected my aunt to bow first in greeting, as one of lower rank does upon meeting someone of higher rank; but to my surprise the woman bowed first and said, cordially enough, "Good morning to you."

Even more surprising, she used the "high" speech form that a person of lower stature used when speaking to one of higher rank.

"Good morning," Aunt Obedience replied with a small bow. "May I have the honor of presenting my niece to you?" And she gave me a little jab in the side.

I bowed and introduced myself with what I hoped was proper form: "I am Regret, of the Pak clan of Pojogae, and I am meeting you for the first time."

When I told her my name I thought I saw her wince a little, quickly covered by a small smile.

"I am called Evening Rose," she said, "and I have no clan. At least none that matters."

I was startled by this and did not know how to reply.

"Your honored aunt tells me that you wish to learn to read. Is this so?"

"Yes, teacher," I said, using a common honorific. "I do."

"And why is it so important to you to learn?"

I started to tell her what I had told Auntie, that I wished to better myself, but this time it came out a bit differently: "I wish to become a person of value," I found myself saying, "so that my parents might not be ashamed of giving birth to me."

I had only ever articulated this thought to myself, and I felt suddenly embarrassed at voicing it, fearing it might be too emotional and, therefore, in poor taste. Had I said too much?

The woman called Evening Rose looked at me, her expression unreadable, then turned to my aunt and said, "You may come for her at my house in one hour. That is all the time I have to spare today." To me she merely said, "Come along, then," and like a straggling puppy I followed her out of the marketplace.

She walked so gracefully that I felt like a stumblebum trailing in her wake. As we passed men in the streets I avoided their gazes, even as Evening Rose met those gazes openly, warmly. Who on earth, I asked myself, was this beautiful, regal lady who walked so boldly among men?

We arrived at a little two-story white house with a blue tile roof not far from the marketplace, tucked into a quiet corner and half-obscured beneath the billowing green leaves of a paulownia tree. The grounds surrounding it were bright with hyacinth, azaleas, forsythia. Lilies floated on the blue-black surface of a small pond beside the house; a stone lantern guarded the walkway. We ascended three short steps onto a tiny porch and then entered.

The interior was simply yet artfully furnished. Low tables squatted on rush mats that smelled sweetly of sedge. Folding screens—some adorned with mountain scenes, some with calligraphy—broke the main living area into smaller, more intimate spaces. All at once I found myself amid a flock of women as beautiful as Evening Rose, though most were a good deal younger; I'd say between the ages of seventeen and twenty. Like her they were impeccably made up and colorfully attired, some wearing sleeping robes even though it was the middle of the day. I felt acutely inadequate amidst all this loveliness. My hostess rattled off introductions to girls with names like Fragrant Iris, Plum Flower, Moonbeam, and Snapdragon, who each bowed and smiled cordially in greeting.

The sole exception was an older woman with a face as blunt as a mallet, who took one quick look at me, snorted contemptuously, and advised Evening Rose, "Don't waste your time on this one. She's not pretty enough."

My companion frowned. "Curb your tongue, old woman. This girl is my guest, and I shall entertain whomever I please in my room. Oh, and arrange to have some refreshments sent up, will you?" she added sweetly.

She took me by the elbow and guided me past the grimacing old woman, up a staircase to the second floor, passing more beautiful women along the way. I was just beginning to wonder what they were all doing in this one house when we entered my hostess's private room, and all thoughts paled next to what I saw there.

Like the rest of the house, it was simply but tastefully furnished: a sleeping mat separated from the living area by an ornate folding screen, a wardrobe chest made of dark burnished oak, and a vanity table on which was assembled a veritable armada of combs, brushes, powders, oils, and other cosmetics.

Yet none of this is what commanded my attention when I stepped across the threshold. All I had eyes for were the lacquered shelves that covered an entire wall of the room—shelves that were filled to bursting with books. Leatherbound books, clothbound books; short books, tall books, fat books and thin. Their spines, in a variety of colors and textures, stood out like a peacock's plumage, and their sheer numbers dwarfed even my father's quite respectable library.

"Are these books . . . all *yours?*" I asked in amazement.

"Yes, of course."

"You are a . . . scholar, then?"

She laughed for the first time, a pleasant, musical laugh. "Of a sort, perhaps. I am a *kisaeng.*"

"Pardon my ignorance, teacher," I said blankly, "but what is a *kisaeng?*"

A servant girl entered the room carrying a dining table on which were balanced a kettle and two china cups, then placed it beside a pair of cushions on the floor. We sat, and as my hostess poured me a cup of hot rice water she explained, "A *kisaeng* is a kind of entertainer. We are trained from childhood in arts like dance, poetry, song, calligraphy . . . the highest grade of *kisaeng* once performed in the royal palace."

Impressed, I asked her whether she had ever performed for the king.

"I'm proud to say that I did . . . when we still had a king. Before the Wai barbarians came." This was a common pejorative for the Japanese. "Now I live here, and perform at . . . private functions." These latter words contained, I thought, a hint of melancholy.

"And what sort of books are these?"

"Oh, all sorts. Some are novels. Some are *p'ansori*, a kind of song-story. Some are history—Korean history, the kind our oppressors would have us deny."

I asked her where she had learned to read.

"The court schooled me in both Chinese characters and Korean. We had to know these things, you see, if we were to socialize with *yangban* men at royal banquets and other festivities."

"My father says that book reading is the province of men, and great harm will be done if women enter that province."

She laughed a short, less musical laugh.

"Your father is both misinformed and unoriginal. He was quoting the great scholar Yi Ik, who had many enlightened ideas about the underprivileged, but none, alas, for the female of the species. Would it surprise you to know that one of our nation's greatest poets was a mere woman?"

She rose as gracefully as a doe, went to her bookshelf, and almost without looking took down a volume from an upper shelf.

She sat down again and opened the book. "Several remarkable *sijo* poems are handed down to us from a *kisaeng* who went by the name of Bright Moon." She read aloud:

> *You, blue stream, flowing around mountains,*
> *Do not be proud of moving so swiftly.*
> *Once you get to the open sea,*
> *You will never be able to return.*
> *Why not stop for a moment while the bright moon*
> *Gleams down on the world?*

Evening Rose turned the book around so that its pages faced me, but they might as well have been upside down or sideways for all that I could make sense of them. "Someday, perhaps, you will read these for yourself. I am not a teacher by trade or by temperament, but I will do my best."

Now she produced a long black pen and a paper scroll. With the pen gripped between exquisitely manicured fingers, she drew a single character that looked like this: ㄴ

"This is the letter we call *nieun*," she told me. "Say it aloud."

"*Nieun.*"

"Now start to say it again, but not quite. Vocalize only the very first part of the word."

I thought this odd, but did as she instructed: a guttural "Nnnhh" was all the sound that came from my throat.

"Again. And note the position of your tongue as you make the sound."

"Nnnhh," I repeated.

"What position was your tongue in? Was it straight?"

"No, it was bent upwards. Touching the roof of my mouth."

"Like this, you mean?" And she wrote down ㄴ once again.

"Yes!" I said excitedly, the connection now obvious to me.

"Good. You see, *hangul* is what's called a phonetic language—

the characters were designed to mirror the shape of the mouth, tongue, teeth, lips, and throat when speaking them. So when you see this letter, you will think of that bent tongue and know that its name is . . . ?"

"*Nieun,*" I said confidently.

"Exactly right!"

She went on to draw for me the twenty-four basic characters of the Korean alphabet. I was delighted to find how quickly I was able to associate the letter *giyeok* with the "g"/"k" sound made at the back of my throat, or *bieup* with the "b"/"p" sound made with my lips pursed together. In less than an hour these mysterious symbols, whose meaning had once been so utterly opaque to me, were beginning to take on a form I could recognize.

When I marveled at how this could be, my teacher explained, "*Hangul* is an invented language, created to be easily grasped. Chinese characters are ideograms—they represent concepts, not sounds—and there are thousands of them. These letters are fewer, simpler, and more logical in design."

By the time the hour had closed on my first lesson I found that I had learned to recognize a good two-thirds of the Korean alphabet.

Evening Rose said approvingly, "We've made good progress today, but we've only just started. Your aunt should be downstairs waiting. Come back tomorrow at this same time—no sooner, no later—and we shall continue."

She went to her vanity table and I hurried out of the room and down the stairs to where Aunt Obedience was waiting in the foyer. Moments after we left the pretty little house she asked, "Well? Can you read?".

"Not yet," I told her, "but—"

I saw a notice posted in the window of a grocer's shop, and though I could not read the words, I was thrilled to realize that I recognized over half the individual letters. I went up to the store window and pointed to a character I had once thought resembled an upside-down wishbone. "This is the letter *siot*," I declared proudly. I pointed to another character, a nearly perfect circle with a small bump atop it: "This is called *leung*. And this one is *bieup* . . ."

Auntie, suitably impressed, smiled with genuine pride.

"Perhaps when your lessons are over," she said, "you can teach *me* to read!"

For the next twenty-four hours I could barely contain my anticipation. I longed to share my excitement with my mother, with whom I had shared so much, but Auntie insisted on keeping my lessons secret. The following day I again left her house, this time on my own, under the pretense of visiting with Mrs. Li's nonexistent daughter. I was so thrilled that I forgot the route we had taken the day before and had to ask directions from a woman heading to market. But when I described the little white house under the paulownia tree, she gave me a reproachful frown: "What's a girl like you doing going to a pleasure house? You hardly look like you belong there," she said with disdain. I was a bit taken aback, but told her I was meeting a friend there. With a little grunt of disapproval she pointed and told me the house was two blocks north.

I arrived five minutes late and my teacher was not happy about it. "If you cannot be on time," she told me sharply, "you might as well not come at all. I have a schedule to keep."

"I am sorry, teacher. I lost my way. Please forgive me."

My sincere contrition seemed to mollify her. "Very well," she said, motioning me to sit again at the table, "we'll continue where we left off yesterday."

That day we studied the remainder of the Korean alphabet until I was able to recognize all ten vowels and fourteen consonants. Then my teacher handed me a pen and had me copy the letters onto the paper until I could make a passing imitation of her elegantly flowing calligraphy.

"You have a graceful enough hand," she allowed, "but let's try again."

"Yes, teacher."

I copied the letters over and over until my fingers cramped, but I had never been happier in my life.

The next day I made certain not to be late; in fact I was ten minutes early. But this time when I walked into my teacher's room I suddenly found myself face-to-face with a middle-aged man pulling on a pair of baggy white trousers.

"Oh!" I gasped. "I'm so sorry!" Blushing and stammering, I backed out of the room and hid, unsuccessfully, behind a brass Maitreya statue in the hallway. After the man left—throwing me a chagrined smile as he passed—Evening Rose told me to come in, and we proceeded without a word spoken about the incident.

I had never seen a man's private parts before and was barely acquainted with what my own could do, but I was becoming as fascinated with what went on in this "pleasure house" as I was by my teacher's lessons. After a few more glimpses of men slipping in and out of women's rooms, I began to realize that being an "entertainer" apparently meant more than merely serving tea or playing the lute. I admit, I was a bit chagrined by this: The importance of chastity was drummed into every Korean girl from an early age, and such flagrant lack of virtue was at first shocking and dismaying to me. I was confused: Evening Rose was so elegant and refined—how could she be capable of such disgraceful behavior? What would my mother say if she knew this woman was teaching me? Did Aunt Obedience know what went on in this place?

That set me to wondering something else, and one morning when I was alone with Obedience I asked her, "Auntie? How did you and Evening Rose happen to become acquainted?"

An innocent enough question, but it brought out the fire in Obedience's eyes. She said tartly, "It is enough for you to know that we *are* acquainted," and I wisely never broached the subject with her again.

Which is not to say I didn't broach it to Evening Rose, but when I asked her the same question she merely replied, "I am not free to discuss that with you," and I decided that further pursuit of this question was futile.

My teacher went on to demonstrate to me how letters were stacked and combined in syllable blocks, and the syllables then joined to create words. When I correctly deciphered the first word she presented to me, I was so happy and proud that I actually burst into tears, which seemed to both startle and move her.

She then gave me a grade-school primer, not unlike the ones I had seen my brothers reading from, and tasked me with reading the simple words—*cat, dog, house, sky, mother, father*—therein. Over the next several sessions, as my reading skills gradually increased, so did my writing ability. Soon I was stacking vowel upon consonant, consonant upon vowel . . . and as the syllables combined into words flowing out of my pen, I exulted in a joy and a confidence I had never felt before.

"Well," Evening Rose said, pleased, "you seem to have a gift for language."

"The gift is yours, teacher."

"My teaching skills are minimal. I have a talented student."

I beamed with pleasure at this rare compliment. My initial shock and dismay at my teacher's profession had receded to a faint reproof in my mind. It seemed, after all, a small thing compared to what I was receiving from her.

That wonderful, thrilling week in Taegu passed all too quickly. At the end of it I had grasped the rudiments of something I had only dreamed of: the power to take meaning from words. It was a gift I knew I could never truly repay, but I wished to give my teacher something, so I filched one of the bottles of rice wine we had brought for Aunt Obedience and presented it to Evening Rose on our last day of lessons. She accepted it graciously and bowed. "Know that you are welcome to return again anytime," she said, then turned away.

I started to leave the room, when behind me I heard my teacher say, "Your parents were wrong, you know."

I looked back at her. "What?"

"When they named you. They were wrong." She gave me a soft smile. "To these eyes, you are a rare and beautiful gem."

I smiled and left, my heart soaring like a kite.

Later, when I went into Aunt Obedience's room to deliver her some ginseng tea Mother had made, I demonstrated to her how I could now write simple words. "You are a smart girl," she said, looking pleased and proud. "You will make something of your life."

"I can't thank you enough, Auntie, for all you've done for me," and I kissed her on the cheek. Flustered, she changed the subject.

Back in Pojogae, I found a moment alone and surreptitiously took out the browned old page I had kept all these years. Evening Rose had identified it, sight unseen, as from a travel book by a woman writing as Lady Ŭiyudang; and now I let my eyes drift across the columns of printed symbols. To my delight the word *moon* jumped off the page at me. Then *sea*, and *night*, and *sun*, the words blazing like stars in a paper sky. I did not, of course, recognize all the words—but I identified enough to transform the page from a mysterious and unfathomable riddle into something nearly comprehensible, and thrillingly attainable.

Blossom wanted to know everything about our trip, but I worried that a child as young as she might let slip something to my parents, so I withheld the full truth from her. I fell back into my old routine—cooking, sewing, housekeeping, washing.

But having walked the streets of Taegu unescorted—and glimpsed an even broader world beyond that, through words—I found myself chafing even more within the limited confines of the Inner Room.

Doing laundry at the stream, I found that Sunny had a new enthusiasm, and as usual she shared it with me as we pounded our clothes with our bats: "Have you ever heard"—*thop thop thop*—"of a place called"—*thop thop*—"Hawai'i?"

"No," I answered truthfully.

"They say it's a paradise"—*thop!*—"where no one needs money to live, and where the streets themselves are paved in gold."

I regarded her skeptically. "Who are 'they'?"

"Pink Lily told me in church. She said the American missionaries told her about it. And they said that there are"—her voice lowered to a whisper—"*Korean* men there, who need wives!"

I looked at her with unalloyed pity.

"That is without a doubt the silliest tale you have yet told," I declared, and punctuated the statement with a *thop* that ended the conversation.

Looking back, I'm not sure why Sunny continued talking to me. But really, roads paved in gold?

By autumn Aunt Obedience's health was again in decline . . . or perhaps she was just lonely for her sister. This time Mother could only go to Taegu for a day or two, but once again I was able to accompany her, carrying several cribs full of eggs. Our trips to the city now became shorter but more frequent—once every month or so—and on that first visit, while Mother and Obedience gossiped, I slipped out to see Evening Rose.

I was worried that she might be, shall we say, otherwise engaged . . . but when I arrived at her house she came to the door promptly and smiled upon seeing me. "Come in, my little gem," she said, and from that day forward she would never again use my birth name; to her I was always Gem, *Jin* in Korean.

She offered to continue our lessons, and over the course of the next year she helped me further hone my reading skills and exposed me to a breadth of literature I would never have encountered without her: poetry like that of the *kisaeng* Bright Moon, *p'ansori* like "The Song of a Faithful Wife," and romances such as "A Dream of Nine Clouds."

In addition to reading and discussing literature, she taught me a few songs that had found favor at the royal palace and showed me some steps of a *kisaeng* dance, though I felt clumsy and clubfooted. In odd moments I would find myself gazing at her, still musing about her connection to my aunt. Could it be a blood relation, I wondered? Might they be cousins, or half-sisters? I enjoyed the possibility that Evening Rose and I could be distantly related, enjoyed it enough that I did not want it dispelled by whatever the mundane reality might be.

Once I stayed till late in the day when my teacher had to prepare herself for an engagement that evening. I watched with fascination as she made up her face—powdering it with snow-white makeup, applying kohl to her eyes and brilliant red pigment to her lips. I thought her the most beautiful woman I had ever seen, and the wisest, and I said as much.

"To be beautiful *and* clever, that is what men expect of a *kisaeng*." She used a brush to smooth out the white powder that made her shine like a China doll. "*Yangban* men marry obedient Confucian wives, but who is it they seek out for wit and companionship?"

"Teacher, how did you become an entertainer?"

"I was born to it. My mother was *kisaeng*, so I inherited her status; I had no say in the matter. She was owned by the government, even as I am. I can never have the same status as a so-called honorable woman . . . even a commoner's wife." She must have seen sorrow in my eyes at this, because she said sharply, "You needn't pity me, my little Gem. I've learned more in my life than a hundred wives are allowed to know. It's been, all said, a fair trade."

I quickly changed the subject and asked her again of her days at the royal court. When she spoke of the people she had known there, the dances she performed, it was clear that the Japanese had ended what she thought of as the brightest, happiest days of her life. "No wonder you hate them," I said.

Her face in the mirror was dramatically beautiful, her crimson lips accentuated by the white sheen of the powder.

"I hate them for that," she said, "and not least for what they have forced me to become."

She put down her makeup brush and stood, ready for what must have been a humbling step down from entertaining kings and queens. I started to leave, when I remembered another question I had meant to ask.

"Teacher, have you ever heard of a place called Hawai'i?"

She turned her painted face to me. "Why, yes—a former *kisaeng* I knew went there, to work in a place called Iwilei. Why do you ask?"

So it *did* exist, after all! "Is it beautiful? A paradise?"

"It's been called that, but I wouldn't know."

"Are—" I hesitated to even ask it. "Are the streets paved with gold?"

She laughed good-naturedly. "I sincerely doubt it. Now, if you'll excuse me—"

"Of course. Thank you, teacher."

Well! Perhaps I owed Sunny an apology, after all.

$\mathcal{W}$e were home for only two weeks when a message came from a doctor in Taegu that Aunt Obedience had been stricken with pneumonia. Mother and I hastened to reach the city, but by the time we arrived at the sliver of house chockablock to the butcher's shop, my aunt had let go of her shaky grip on life.

Mother was devastated. Sick with shock and grief, she made

the necessary funeral arrangements and we cried together. I could only console myself with the knowledge that I had thanked my aunt for all she had done for me, and that she had been happy and proud of my accomplishments.

This would certainly be my last trip to Taegu, so the day before Auntie's funeral I left the house on some pretext for one last visit to Evening Rose. She greeted me at the door with condolences—somehow she had heard of my aunt's passing—then sat me down at the same table where I had learned to read and said, "There is something I think you should know. About your aunt and myself."

Finally, I was going to know the truth. Was my teacher Obedience's step-sister, perhaps? Would I be able to call her auntie? I waited expectantly.

With uncharacteristic hesitation, Evening Rose began, "Your uncle, of course, was quite a successful businessman."

"Yes. He owned a pastry shop." I smiled at the remembered smells of honey rice cakes and chestnut bread. "He used to give me little red bean pastries to eat when I came to visit."

This only seemed to make her more uncomfortable. "Yes. I met him at some function or other. I found him likable, and kind."

She glanced away from me, something she had never done before.

"Like all men, your uncle desired an heir. But your aunt seemed unable to give him one, and so . . ."

She sighed, as if she was regretting having brought the matter up.

"He . . . took me as a concubine," she said finally. "A 'second wife.' It is not an uncommon practice."

I felt as if someone had pushed me from a moving wagon, and in the middle of a mudslide to boot—the ground shifting beneath me.

This was the last thing in the world I had expected, and I immediately thought, *I've heard enough*—but my teacher went on:

"I was his concubine for the remainder of his life—almost ten years—though I did not produce an heir for him, either. He may have been unable to produce one with any woman—but it was your aunt, of course, who bore the stigma.

"Last year—and this could not have been easy for her—your aunt came to me and told me of your desire to read. She said, 'You owe me this much, at least,' and I could not argue the point. So I agreed to become your teacher."

She looked at me nervously and I now understood the anxiety I had seen in her eyes. "Does my Gem think less of me for this?" she asked.

"No. Of course not." I was shocked, I admitted, but . . . "You were kind to my aunt," I said, "and to me. I can only think well of you for that."

She seemed relieved and happy to hear this.

We both knew that my lessons had come to an end. "I have no diploma to bestow on you," she said, "but perhaps this will serve just as well." She smiled and presented me with a well-worn, but complete copy of Lady Ŭiyudang's Diary of a Sightseeing Tour of Kwanbuk.

Blinking back tears, I thanked her for the book and for all she had given me; we bowed to one another; and I left, feeling dizzy with revelation. I now knew at what cost to her dignity my aunt had purchased my reading lessons, and I appreciated her generosity all the more.

Few mourners attended Obedience's funeral, shunning her even in death, and I prayed that heaven might receive her more warmly than this life had.

ow, as Mother was denied the company of her sister, I was denied that of both my aunt and my teacher. I was surprised at the depth of the void it left behind in my life. Before

I had learned to read, I felt small and incapable. But now I would lie awake nights pondering the meaning of a line in Lady Ŭiyudang's narrative, amazed that I could even pose such questions to myself.

I read the entirety of the book in close to a month, then read it again.

I tried to content myself with my household tasks and the time I enjoyed with Blossom, but . . . it was no longer enough. Evening Rose had awakened in me a thirst for knowledge, a thirst I was hard-pressed to quench in provincial Pojogae. Father's library consisted entirely of books written in Chinese, which was beyond me, and I was desperate for something new to read. So in the mornings, after Father had finished and discarded his morning paper, I would rescue it from the trash and secretly, eagerly, pore over it. I couldn't decipher the front page, which was largely printed in Chinese characters, but page three was written entirely in *hangul* and I consumed it greedily. Published in Seoul, the paper was always a week late by the time it reached us, but I still thrilled to read its mix of politics, world news, society gossip, even the advertisements.

In these pages I also encountered occasional mentions of institutions like Ewha Girls' School and the Hansŏng School for Education. The first schools for Korean girls were founded by American missionaries, but Hansŏng was a public school and was discussed in the paper in a very matter-of-fact manner. I began to see that things were changing in our country, and that it was not impossible for a girl to receive an education in Korea today. I told myself that my father must have seen these same stories and realized much the same thing. He was an intelligent man, a cultured man, who revered learning as all Koreans did. Perhaps if I impressed upon him my sincere desire for education—if I demonstrated my ability—he might consider allowing me to attend school.

It took me weeks to work up sufficient courage, but one evening after supper I approached him after I had removed his dining table. He was starting to get to his feet when I addressed him—in the appropriate "high" speech form one used to address a male elder—"Honorable Father, may I ask something of you?"

He looked at me in mild surprise. He was used to retiring to his study directly after dinner, but he sat back down. "Very well, then. What is it?"

"Father, I . . ." I took a breath and then let the words escape in a rush: "I would like to attend school."

He looked at me in bafflement.

"Is this a joke?" He laughed. The notion was obviously hilarious.

"No. I wish to learn."

"But you are learning," he said. "You're learning how to become a good wife and daughter-in-law. These are the most important things a girl can know."

"But Honorable Father, girls *are* going to school in Korea. You've seen the articles in the *Dong-A Daily*, I'm sure. You must realize—"

"How do you know," he interrupted, "what is in the *Dong-A Daily?*"

"Because I can *read*." There: I'd said it. It remained only to demonstrate it. I picked up that morning's paper. I turned to the third page and began reciting first the headlines, then the lead story, the words tumbling from my mouth.

Father was looking at me like a man whose dog had suddenly started speaking Mandarin.

I was about to finish reading the news story when Father erupted to his feet and snatched the paper from my hands.

"How dare you!" he cried, so loudly it made me flinch.

Koreans place a high value on never revealing their emotional state through their facial expressions. Korean men believe that to display emotion is to be seen as frivolous or feminine. So the anger I now saw openly displayed on Father's face was both extraordinary and terrifying.

"How *dare* you disobey your father's wishes!" he shouted. "What you have done is shameful!"

"No, it's not!" I shot back, bravely but foolishly. "If my brothers can go to school, why can't—"

I never finished. In a fury, Father gave me the back of his hand across my face. I staggered backwards. He lunged forward and struck me again, this time in my left eye, dropping me to the floor.

"A woman without ability is virtuous!" Father shouted down at me. "You are not virtuous! You dishonor your clan!"

My mother rushed in from the kitchen and saw me cowering on the floor. The color drained from her face.

Father yelled, "There is an old proverb: 'Women who read become foxes.' And by your deceit you are the proof of it!"

He stepped forward as if to strike me again, but Mother—in the only time I had ever seen her react with such emotion—stepped between us.

"This is not right!" she told Father, voice trembling between anger and fear. "Look at how you've bruised her eye! Is this what a father should do to his daughter? No matter what the girl has done, surely this is punishment enough!"

For a moment I thought he might strike Mother as well, but instead he merely vented his frustrations on the paper he still clenched in his other hand. He balled it up and threw it at me, and I received it gratefully in lieu of another blow. His face regained some of its normal color and composure, and finally, satisfied that he had put me in my place, he stormed out of the room.

Mother knelt by my side. "Daughter, are you all right?" Gently she touched the swelling on my right cheek. "Come, we'll tend to that bruise."

The next morning Father's eyes were cold and cloudy as milk glass as I served him breakfast. I tried not to flinch as I set down his rice gruel and *kimchi,* as one might leave scraps of food before a crouching tiger. He ate hurriedly and left to deal with some matter of business in town. I told Mother that my eye hurt and I wished to lie down. "Yes, of course, no chores today," she said. But instead I sneaked out of the house and began a long, chilly walk to Taegu.

I had no set plan in mind. Vaguely I thought to somehow get from Taegu to Seoul, where I might be able to apply to a school like Hansŏng, though I knew this would be difficult without my father's permission. I hoped that Evening Rose might be able to help me . . . perhaps loan me enough money to get to Seoul. She would understand, surely, why I left home. Three hours later I was on the steps of the white and blue house beneath the spreading leaves of the paulownia tree.

The door was answered by the blunt-faced older woman I had encountered once before—the housemother, I had learned—and when I asked to see Evening Rose, she looked positively stricken. "Evening Rose is not here," she said stiffly.

"May I wait for her?"

"Evening Rose," she said, "does not live here anymore."

"What do you mean?"

"Stupid girl," the woman snapped, "I mean what I say!" Fearfully she looked up and down the street, then leaned in to me and hissed, "The constables took her! Two weeks ago. They came in the night and they took her! Do you understand now?"

"The police?" I gasped. "But why?"

"Why is the moon white! Stupid girl! She's gone, forget about her!" And like someone chasing a fly from her house, she shut the door in my face.

Three

I simply could not accept what I had just heard. Standing there on the porch like a cow stunned for slaughter, I convinced myself that I must have somehow offended my teacher; that for some reason she did not wish to see me, and had sent this old woman to greet me with a lie. As terrible as that would have been, it was infinitely preferable to the alternative. I had to know the truth—had to know that my friend was all right. I ran to the back of the house. I found a window with no moving shadows behind it, tore a hole in the rice paper covering it, and clambered through. I knew the house well enough by now and stole up the stairs without the housemother noticing me. I bid what I hoped was a casual greeting to the girls I passed, then slowed as I came to my teacher's room. I overcame a momentary rush of apprehension and entered.

A woman sat with her back to me at the little vanity table and in a surge of joy I called out to her. But when she turned in her seat I saw that it was not my teacher, but the young woman known as Fragrant Iris.

"Ah," she said softly, recognizing me. "Her student. I wondered if you would come back."

It was a subtly different room I had entered. It held similar furniture—sleeping mat, folding screen, vanity table—but the lacquered wall shelves were shorn of books. Now they held only a few knickknacks: an assortment of folding fans, one or two ceramic figures, a white porcelain vase. "What's happened?" I asked. "Where is Evening Rose?"

Fragrant Iris approached me, staring at my bruises. "Child, what happened to *you*? Are you all right?"

"That doesn't matter. Where is my teacher?"

"I'm sorry to tell you, the police took her," she said sadly.

The words struck me harder than any of my father's blows. "But *why*?"

"They claimed she was giving money to the Independence Army. Who knows if it was true? They came in the middle of the night and they arrested her. It was true enough for them."

Despite my best efforts to rein in my emotion, tears welled in my eyes. "We—we have to help her, somehow."

Iris noted ruefully, "Once, the idea of constables invading the privacy of a woman's room—even a *kisaeng*'s—would have been unthinkable. We have no influence with the Japanese military police as we did with the royal court. But one of Evening Rose's patrons is a government official. We have hopes that he may be able to use his influence to free her . . . or at least keep her alive."

These grim last words proved too much for me and I wept. Iris kindly took me in her arms and held me as I sobbed. But my shame at expressing my emotions so freely won out over my grief and I forced myself to stop—though not before attracting the notice of the housemother, who now glared at me from the doorway: "What! You again?"

"Go away, grandmother," Iris said coldly. "This is none of your concern." The old woman muttered darkly under her breath but did move on.

I again took in all the empty shelves. "What happened to her books?"

Iris sighed. "I'm afraid those didn't help her case. When the police saw them—the histories, in particular—they stripped the shelves bare, piled the books in the street, and burned them all."

I could almost smell the smoke, and it made me sick.

"We were fortunate," she said, "they didn't shut the whole house down."

"I want to *do* something. What can I do?" I asked helplessly.

Fragrant Iris just shook her head.

"There is nothing to be done," she said gently. "Go home. Go back to your village. Pray if you are of a mind to. We have no further recourse."

The walk back to Pojogae took a hundred years. I had ample time to reproach myself for not remaining in Taegu and doing something to help my friend, though I was hard-pressed to think of what a seventeen-year-old country girl could have done to help. But at least my troubles with Father now seemed inconsequential. My absence had not gone undetected by Mother, who had feared, correctly, that I had run away; when she saw me safely home again she was so relieved that she did not think to punish me. More important, she did not tell Father. She had even lied for me: when I missed supper she told him I wasn't feeling well, and he accepted this at face value. When I saw him the next morning I caught him glancing at my swollen, discolored eye and I finally saw a twitch of guilt disturb his stony face. We never spoke again of my ability to read, though he now made a point of carefully disposing of his daily paper after he had finished it. He was thankfully unaware of the copy of Lady Ŭiyudang's book I kept hidden beneath the bottom drawer of the wardrobe chest I shared with Blossom.

I took what comfort I could in the rote exercise of my daily chores—in the chorus of laundry bats at the stream, in sewing with my mother—and in Blossom's sweet presence. After a few weeks of good behavior I asked for and received permission to take her on a "flower picnic" in the hills, where we snacked on jellied soybean slices as we tried to name all the various flowers that were blooming that summer. Blossom correctly identified the Yellow Day Lily, also known as Forget-Your-Troubles; the Mountain Iris, or Servant-of-the-Rainbow; and a purple-flowered peppermint whose leaves we both tasted approvingly.

But among those she did not know was a long-stemmed flower with a white-and-violet bloom that looked something like an open mouth—on the "tongue" of which were two small white bumps resembling grains of rice. She asked, "What is this? It's so pretty," and I started to tell her, then caught myself.

It was called a Daughter-in-Law Flower, and I knew well the story from which it took its name: Once a long time ago there lived a woman and her daughter-in-law, so poor that the only food they could find were a few cups of unshelled rice. The mother-in-law instructed the girl to hull the rice, then left to search for more food. She returned to find the daughter-in-law chewing something, and when she demanded to know what she was eating, the girl admitted it was two small grains of rice which had fallen to the ground—and she stuck out her tongue to show her. Furious, the mother-in-law choked the girl to death. Later, a green shoot sprouted from the daughter-in-law's grave, becoming this flower which bloomed in her memory.

"I don't know this one," I lied, and quickly moved on to another.

I saw in the Daughter-in-Law Flower more than just Blossom's future, of course; I also saw my own. In its open mouth I divined endless days and nights trapped in the Inner Room, a lifetime of servitude to a husband and mother-in-law. I told myself that this was no less than what I had been facing a year ago, and back then I had even fretted about whether I *would* find a husband or end up like poor Aunt Obedience, childless and reviled. I told myself to forget about school: I would never know more than I knew now, and that was the end of it.

There is a uniquely Korean emotion known as *han*—one of the fundamental aspects, it is said, of our psychology. It is a kind of fatalistic acceptance of defeat and suffering, a despairing resignation to one's lot in life. Korean women particularly understand *han*, but it is also rooted in the Korean people's history and our nation's endurance of many trials and misfortunes over the centuries. Yet we *do* endure, have endured, will endure—and from that we derive the fortitude to go on, to continue the struggle even if our efforts be doomed.

So even as I told myself, *I will never know more than I know now*, my sense of *han* gave me the strength to endure what lay ahead of me—and that strength gave me the courage to challenge it.

A week later, after telling Mother I was going to spend the afternoon sewing with Sunny in her family's Inner Room, my friend and I instead found ourselves sitting on a straw mat in the home of a *ke-man*, a matchmaker, named Mrs. Kim—a smiling, grandmotherly woman in her sixties, who came recommended by the American missionaries at the Methodist church. Her manner was at once maternal and businesslike: "You know how hard life can be in Korea," she told us, "so it should come as no surprise when I tell you that some fifteen hundred Korean gentlemen are today living in a place called Hawai'i—a lush and fertile group of islands in the middle of the Pacific Ocean—which is a part of America.

"Many of these men journeyed there as bachelors and have since become wealthy and prosperous, but they have a problem. There are not enough Korean women there for everyone to marry, and most will not consider marrying non-Koreans. So, what to do?" She gazed earnestly at us, as though this dilemma had kept her awake nights. "Well, it's my business to help these lonely men find wives. I consider it a patriotic duty, aiding Koreans who are far from home and in a bad way. I'm proud to say that I've signed up nearly two dozen young women from Kyŏngsang-do, and they are all now happily married women in Hawai'i."

"What sort of a place is this Hawai'i?" I asked.

"Oh, a beautiful land," Mrs. Kim said with enthusiasm. "A tropical paradise, where food grows so abundantly that if one is hungry, all one needs to do is reach up and pick something off a tree to eat! Money is scarcely needed to live, so it can be sent back to one's family in Korea. The Chun clan has recently been receiving lavish gifts of food and clothing sent by their eldest daughter, now married to a wealthy businessman in Honolulu."

"But how would we get there?" Sunny said. "It sounds very far."

"It is, but it's only nine days' travel by steamship. Your fare will be paid by your fiancé. He will also send you two hundred yen—one hundred American dollars—which you may use for spending money or give to your family."

Two hundred yen! Sunny's eyes popped. What Mrs. Kim was proposing, of course, was not so very different from what went on in Korea every day. If one's parents could not find their son or daughter a suitable spouse, they might easily engage the services of a marriage broker; few Korean women married men they actually knew before the wedding. "So we would see these men for the first time when we arrive in Hawai'i?" I asked.

"Not at all," Mrs. Kim replied. "In fact, you may see them right now." She reached into an envelope and took out a handful of photographs of solemn-faced young Korean men. She laid them down on the table one by one, like cards in a Tarot deck presaging our futures.

"This is Mr. Kwon," she said of a good-looking young man in a Western-style business suit. "He lives on the island of Kaua'i. This is Mr. Kam," and she laid down a photo of a handsome man in his twenties. "He resides on the island of O'ahu. This is Mr. Li, of Honolulu," and here we saw a picture of a man in a dark suit and bow tie standing in front of an expensive house shaded by exotic trees.

As I studied the photographs I felt a shiver of excitement I could not at first name. Then I realized that for the first time in my life I was looking directly into the eyes of a strange man! It was a startling, scary, thrilling sensation.

"And we are to pick one of these men to marry?" Sunny said wonderingly.

"Or they can pick you, when they see your pictures."

"I'm so plain, I don't know that any man would choose me for a wife," I muttered, feeling a stab of my old insecurity.

"Nonsense," Mrs. Kim said, "you're a pretty enough girl as you are. But we have ways of making you even prettier."

Even this much choice into one's own spouse was simply unheard of. Despite my apprehension, I found the idea subversive and appealing.

But there was one thing I needed to know.

"Do they permit girls to attend school in Hawai'i?" I asked.

"Yes, of course," Mrs. Kim said cheerfully, as if I had asked, "Does night follow day in Hawai'i?"

In that instant I made up my mind.

A few days later Sunny and I again sneaked out of our homes, this time to accompany Mrs. Kim to a photographer's studio. There the matchmaker skillfully combed and braided my hair, then applied judicious strokes of lipstick, rouge, and kohl to my face. I balked at first, but Mrs. Kim claimed it was "just to provide some contrast to your features" in the black-and-white photograph. When she had finished I looked into the mirror and saw a strange girl staring back at me, like a daisy pretending to be a rose. I was still not sure I would have called her pretty, but Sunny and Mrs. Kim seemed to think so.

The photographer took the film into a closet that served as his darkroom. Once our photographs were developed, Mrs. Kim said, she would write our names and ages on the backs, then mail them to Hawai'i—though she warned us that it would probably take several months to receive a response. Now there was nothing to do but wait. I was excited by my newfound prospects, but felt spasms of guilt at the thought of leaving my mother and, even more difficult, Blossom. I told myself that if I married a wealthy man, I would send Blossom a steamship ticket and bring her to Hawai'i as well. After all, she was only seven years old; her wedding day was still many years in the future. Surely I could save her, too, from becoming a Daughter-in-Law Flower.

Sunny, ever the optimist, suggested we start taking English lessons. We arranged to do so with the American missionaries, an elderly couple from someplace called Minnesota (it sounded Japanese to me), who were only too happy to tutor us. Once a week we stole away to their home for our instruction in speaking and reading the English language. I found English, a phonetic language like *hangul*, relatively easy to grasp—my lessons with Evening Rose most certainly helped in this—but Sunny had more trouble and we spent many hours in her Inner Court, secretly studying together when we were supposed to be sewing.

But perhaps the most interesting part of these lessons was the missionary couple themselves. I was startled to see them sharing household chores, asking each other's opinion, occasionally even arguing, all of which would have been unthinkable behavior for a husband and wife in Korea. And they were affectionate as well, in a way I had certainly never seen my parents act toward one another. I found it both strange and charming, like a shell you might find on the beach in a shape or color you've never seen before.

At last, after nearly three months, Mrs. Kim sent word that two men in Hawai'i had chosen us to be their wives. We skipped our English lesson the next day and went straight to the matchmaker's home. We learned that Sunny had been selected by a Mr. Lim— young, fair-skinned, a bit thin but with very intelligent eyes—and I had been chosen by a good-looking, broad-shouldered man named Mr. Noh. I found him so handsome that I could not at first believe he had chosen me for his "picture bride" and I asked if perhaps there had been some mistake. But Mrs. Kim turned over the photograph and on its back I could plainly see where he had written, "My name is Mr. Noh and I choose the girl named Regret."

I was ecstatic. To be marrying a handsome and prosperous man was thrilling enough, but to be going to a place where I could further my education—it all seemed like a waking dream.

Now Mrs. Kim informed us we had to apply for a passport to leave Korea, and to do that we would need copies of our birth certificates: "Your parents can apply for these at the police station, and then you can have your name transferred to Mr. Noh's family register." I despaired to think that not only would I have to tell my father about my picture marriage, I would actually need his cooperation in obtaining a passport.

After much deliberation I decided to tell Mother first. At first she couldn't believe I was serious. When she came to realize that I was, she began to weep. I felt like a horrible, traitorous daughter and even reconsidered whether I ought to go through with this if it were to cause my mother such terrible pain. But when I showed her the picture of my intended groom, and read aloud what he had written on the back, she began to understand how much this meant to me. And the truth was, even if I were marrying a man only two leagues away, Mother might never see me again either. At last she made her peace with what I was doing.

The next morning I worked up my courage and informed my father that a great opportunity had been afforded me—that a marriage had been arranged for me to a man in Hawai'i. His response was more muted than I expected. He just stared for a moment, then said to Mother, "You see? A girl with a little education will always behave recklessly." He turned back to me. "Put this nonsense out of your head. You will marry whomever your parents say you will marry."

"Respectfully, Father, I wish to go to Hawai'i and pursue an education."

"Don't be ridiculous. No respectable girl chooses her own husband! You will not bring dishonor to this clan. This discussion is over."

He retreated to the Outer Room, where we could not follow, and brushed aside any further attempts to raise the matter. I enlisted Eldest Brother in my cause, hoping his support might help sway Father, or at least blunt his wrath. But though he tried, Joyful Day reported that Father was immovable on the subject: "We may talk until we choke, but he will never agree to this." And without Father's permission, there could be no passport, no visa to America.

Dispirited, I could see no solution to my problem. For a few days I moped as I did my chores, wondering whether I should simply go back to Mrs. Kim and tell her to call off the engagement.

Then one morning I awoke early, Father's recriminations still ringing in my head, and I knew all at once what I had to do.

After breakfast, when Father retired to his library to study the Chinese classics, I slipped quietly out of the house. When I returned a few hours later, I served Father his midday meal and again declared that I wished to obtain a copy of my birth certificate in order to apply for a passport.

His expression was impassive, but his gaze was flinty. "Didn't I say that this discussion was ended?"

"It cannot be ended because we still have much to discuss."

He jumped to his feet, knocking his lunch from the table.

"Insolent whore! Must I beat you again before you understand? I will not have you bring disgrace to this family!"

"I already have," I told him.

This caught him unawares. "What?"

"I have already brought disgrace to the family. Today I went to everyone we know in Pojogae and told them that I was betrothed to be the picture bride of a man in Hawai'i."

He stared at me in disbelief. "You did not."

But I had, and I rattled off the names of every family whose household I had visited that day as I had eagerly spread the news.

"So you see," I said, "you might as well help me get my passport, as I have already dishonored our clan and as such you would be well rid of me."

By this time Mother and Joyful Day had heard the commotion and joined us, and they were treated to the uncommon sight of Father at a complete loss for words. His face was flushed, his eyes bulged, and for a moment I thought he would indeed strike me again. But he seemed paralyzed—not merely with rage, I knew, but horror at the idea that this village, which showed him such deference and respect, would now be whispering about him behind his back, gossiping about the disgrace his brazen daughter had brought to the Pak clan.

To Koreans, deliberately causing shame and embarrassment to others, even complete strangers, is anathema. Yet I had willfully brought such shame onto my own parents. What I had done was far, far more than just an insult to them; it was an insult to society.

Finally my father's paralysis ended. But instead of a blow, he gave me only a cold smile.

"You have lived up to your name," Father said.

As I had hurt him, now he hurt me, and his aim was never truer.

"Go, then," he said contemptuously. "Marry whomever you like. But should things not work out as you hope, your ship might as well sink into the Pacific Ocean, because you shall never set foot in this house again."

These were the last words he would ever speak to me.

*T*hat night I tried to console a weeping Blossom by telling her what I'd told myself these past months: that as soon as I had enough money I would bring her to Hawai'i, where she could live with me and my husband. I held her in my arms, rocking her asleep with this lullaby of paradise and promises. I wish I could say I rested as easily, but the truth is I cried myself to sleep, uncertain if I truly was doing the right thing. Yet there was no turning back after what I had done, and in my heart I did not want to. I wanted to go to America. I wanted to learn.

Sunny's parents took her news far better than mine had—they were touched that their daughter so desired to help her struggling family that she was willing to "sell herself" to a man three thousand miles away. After we both received our birth certificates, I joined Sunny in applying for my passport, which when it came bore the despised words IMPERIAL JAPANESE GOVERNMENT. We then applied for visas from the American Embassy in Seoul.

Within six weeks, the hundred *yen* for my steamship ticket arrived, along with two hundred more for incidental expenses. I gave half of this to my mother to use for the household, and promised to send more once I was settled in Hawai'i. I was also required by law to deposit a portion of this money in a bank as a kind of insurance that I would go through with the picture marriage (some women, flush with spending money, had reneged on their engagements but kept the cash).

Now that our plans were out in the open, Sunny and I boldly came and went as we pleased, increasing the frequency of our English lessons to an hour each day. By the end of these lessons we were conversing, simply but effectively, in English with our American teachers.

Mother made two new dresses for me, in colors more befitting a married woman. As the day of departure neared, I packed these and my other clothes in a bag along with a sewing kit and the book my teacher had given me. The morning I left I bid goodbye to my family—all but Father, who had left for town before dawn. My clan surprised me with lovely and touching farewell gifts. Blossom, bravely trying not to cry, gave me some pressed flowers she had picked in the hills. My mother bestowed upon me a silver hairpin—traditionally worn only by married women—to place in my hair on my wedding day. And finally, Joyful Day and my other brothers presented me with a package of writing paper and a fountain pen—"so that you might write us and tell us of your life and education in America, and keep us all as close as your pen." This meant more to me than I can say: it was both an acknowledgment of my literacy and an approval of my aspirations. I embraced each member of my family in turn and wept without shame.

Sunny's parents took us on ponies to Taegu Station, where we boarded a train for the port city of Pusan. There, in the towering shadows of Mount Hwangnyeonsan and Mount Geumjeongsan, we transferred to a ferry bound for Yokohama, Japan. Though Sunny and I were sad to leave our families, being together made us feel less lonely; and the excitement of being aboard a ship for the first time, so far from everything we had ever known, was as bracing as the salty air. In Yokohama we were given physical examinations for smallpox and trachoma, and more embarrassingly were required to provide stool samples, which were to be tested for parasites. We knew it would take a day or two for the results, so we had made reservations at a local Korean-style inn, where we were made welcome and fed a fine dinner of *kimchi*, seafood soup, red bean paste, and, of course, rice.

At the inn we met other Korean women who were traveling to America as picture brides. One, aptly named Beauty, was an exquisitely lovely sixteen-year-old with a melodious Kyŏngsang accent. In fact, all of us turned out to be from the same province. Within thirty seconds of introducing herself Beauty had pulled out a picture of her fiancé in Hawai'i. "Isn't he handsome?" she asked, showing us a small portrait of a serious-looking young man with penetrating eyes. "Such a fair complexion, so scholarly!" She was clearly smitten with her intended, or perhaps just smitten with the idea of being smitten.

Another woman, a well-dressed city *yangban* with features sharp as a paper crane's, glanced at the photograph and announced airily, "Fair . . . but common."

Beauty wilted like a flower in a dry wind.

The *yangban*, whose name was Jade Moon, quickly produced her own fiancé's photo. He cut a dashing figure in a Western business suit, holding a Panama hat in one hand as he posed jauntily with one foot on the running board of a Whippet automobile.

"*This* is an uncommon man," she declared.

A tiny young woman named Wise Pearl, no more than five feet tall, spoke up, quoting an old proverb: "An empty cart rattles loudly," she said, meaning, One who lacks substance boasts loudest. Sunny and I laughed, which seemed to annoy Jade Moon more than the jibe itself.

I asked Wise Pearl why she chose to become a picture bride. She admitted that her parents were poor, that there wasn't always enough to eat, and the promise of abundant food as well as money to send home was what first attracted her. "But it also promises to be a great adventure," she added enthusiastically.

With no prompting from me, Jade Moon volunteered the information that while there had been much interest from many *yangban* families in having their sons marry her, she found them all too "common" and was much more taken with the idea of marrying a successful and socially prominent man in America.

"You'd best hope," Wise Pearl said impishly, "that such a man does not find *you* too common."

With a look of great forbearance, Jade Moon excused herself and retired for the evening.

Two days later, Sunny and I tested negative for parasites and were cleared to leave on the next ship bound for Honolulu: the *Nippon Maru*, a 6,000-ton steamship that at 440 feet was longer than Pojogae's entire main street. The first of Japan's great ocean liners, it had two big smokestacks like a steamer, but also three tall masts and an elaborately carved bowsprit like a sailing ship. As we walked up the gangway I was pleased to spy Wise Pearl among the crowd, as well as Beauty, who looked excited enough to levitate to Hawai'i.

The *Nippon Maru* was well past its glory days—its once-glamorous luster dulled by years of service as a military troop ship in the Russo-Japanese War—but it was still a queenly and impressive sight to a pair of young girls from the provinces. Our quarters, however, were considerably less impressive. We were situated belowdecks in third-class steerage, so called due to its proximity to the ship's steering system. It was a huge, cavernous compartment—I had never seen an enclosed space so large—broken up into tiers of wooden bunks covered with straw mats, or "silkworm shelves" as they were sometimes called. Passengers were segregated by sex, except for families traveling together, and by race—Chinese, Japanese, and "Other." Koreans fell into the latter category, along with a smattering of Okinawans, Filipinos, Indians, and Siamese—lumped together in what often was referred to as "Asiatic steerage."

When the *Nippon Maru* finally set sail, we did not do so alone. This was February of 1915, the earliest days of the First World War, and just weeks earlier two Japanese passenger liners—*Tokomaru* and *Ikaria*—had been torpedoed and sunk by German U-boats. So the *Nippon Maru* was to be escorted across the now-perilous waters of the Pacific by two Japanese warships that were always visible off our bow. At night we also had to observe a blackout, which made for plenty of stubbed toes and short tempers in the overcrowded steerage compartment.

Thankfully, we never encountered any U-boats in our journey across the ocean, but that is not to say the voyage was a pleasant one. The first few hours we enjoyed calm seas, and then for nearly the remainder of the trip the ship rocked up and down like a seesaw. It was bad enough on deck, but down in steamy, poorly ventilated steerage the motion seemed even more violent, and it moved many a traveler, myself included, to nausea. Soon the hold smelled not merely of sweat and urine (from the too-few lavatories) but of vomit as well. If that wasn't sufficient to kill one's appetite, the dinner menu was: stewards brought in big pots of rice, vegetables, and overcooked meat, shoveling the food willy-nilly into bowls. We ate on our bunks, and afterward had to rinse our dishes under the lukewarm tap water in the lavatories.

The atmosphere in the hold became suffocating and drove most of us above decks (not strictly allowed for us bottom-dwellers) in search of fresh air. One chilly night, Sunny and I hid inside a lifeboat, huddling together against the cold but unwilling to exchange it for the stifling humidity below. Nothing could be done, though, about the pitch and roll of the ship itself, which often sent us sliding from one side of the lifeboat to the other like marbles in a game of *yut*. The next morning, after we had crawled out from under the lifeboat's canvas top, we passed the first-class dining room—out of which emerged a happy and well-fed Jade Moon. "You're traveling steerage?" she said, wide-eyed. "*My* fiancé arranged for a *first*-class cabin." Were we not so exhausted and seasick, we might well have thrown her over the side.

Another time, as I settled in for the night on a spot of open deck in the lee of a smokestack, I heard someone say something in Japanese. I didn't realize I was being addressed until I heard, in English: "Excuse me, is this taken?"

I looked up. Standing above me was a young Japanese woman in a patterned kimono, her hair done up in a high pompadour, holding one of the cheap cotton blankets we had been issued in steerage. "May I sleep here?" she asked.

I shrugged, and gratefully she settled in beside me.

"Thank you," she said. She smiled in a friendly, open way I had never associated with the Japanese. "Are you traveling to Honolulu or San Francisco?"

I hesitated a moment, then said, "Honolulu."

"I, too. I'm to meet my new husband there." She drew the thin blanket up to her chin and shivered in the chill damp air. "They say it is paradise," she said, smiling, "but this trip is the opposite, is it not?"

She was a mere girl, barely older than I, but in her face I saw only the face of those who had abducted my teacher and taken Blossom's home away from her.

"Excuse me," I said, and abruptly got to my feet.

Carrying my blanket, I moved to the other side of the deck. The woman looked after me with what might have been hurt—but I did not wish to consider, at that point, the notion that Japanese could feel hurt.

After nine days we finally sailed into Honolulu, past the headless sphinx of an old volcano crater unlike anything I had ever seen before, and into the crowded boat harbor. We were all surprised at the size of the city—indeed it was hardly even a city by Korean standards, just a collection of low buildings gathered between green mountains and blue sea. We had imagined that we were moving to a great metropolis, but on first sight it looked more like some tropic backwater. This was to be our first disappointment.

The *Nippon Maru* slipped into its berth and its passengers began to disembark. The many hundreds of us who were emigrating were taken to an imposing stone immigration building that stood on some mud flats offshore; we crossed over to it on a long wooden causeway known as "the China walk." I was dismayed to note that there were steel bars in the building's windows, hardly a welcoming sign. Inside, we queued up and prepared for a long wait, but the immigration staff moved at a fairly brisk clip, clearing almost a hundred applicants in the first hour. Finally Sunny and I were "processed." This consisted of a literacy test in Korean—we had been warned of this by Mrs. Kim and so I had coached Sunny in the rudiments of *hangul*—and then once again we were subjected to physical examinations for diseases like "pink eye," trachoma, and asked for the inevitable stool samples.

This latter alarmed me, as I recalled how long it had taken for our results to come back in Yokohama, and indeed we were informed that we would have to remain here on Quarantine Island until we were cleared to leave. We spent the next two days in cramped quarters, eating mostly Japanese foods, until finally our tests returned negative, our passports were stamped, and we were told by the officials that our husbands-to-be were waiting for us outside.

Sunny, Beauty, Wise Pearl, Jade Moon, and I crowded at the window to catch a glimpse of them—but none of us was prepared for what we saw. Standing in the yard of the immigration station was a ragtag group of men in worn, threadbare suits and straw hats. All were deeply tanned, nearly as dark as the Hawaiians we had seen strolling along the docks. In Korea, the fairer a man's complexion, the more refined and desirable he was perceived to be. These men had the dark weathered skin of manual laborers—like fruit left out in the sun too long to shrivel and discolor.

But the tropic sun alone could not account for the wrinkled faces now turning hopefully in our direction. They were all at least twenty years older than we, much older than their pictures had represented them. Wise Pearl's fiancé looked to be about forty years old, his eyes obscured behind thick glasses, with thinning hair visible beneath his straw "boater." Sunny's intended appeared even older, perhaps fifty, with graying hair and deep smallpox scars on his face that hadn't shown up on his photograph. Even Jade Moon's husband-to-be, who had looked so rakish posed against his shiny automobile, was considerably darker and older than his portrait.

"Aigo," Wise Pearl said softly.

Jade Moon expressed a somewhat stronger, and more colorful, sentiment than *oh my,* which caused me to blush.

But the cruelest joke had been played on the loveliest of us all. Beauty's fiancé—barely but sadly identifiable from his photograph—was a wizened old man who appeared to be at least seventy years old. He grinned happily when he saw her at the window, a smile that did not, alas, hold a full complement of teeth. Beauty gasped when she recognized him, then clapped her hands to her mouth. "No!" she cried. "There must be some mistake!"

"Oh Heaven, what have we done?" Sunny moaned.

Only I was not completely dismayed at the sight of my future husband. True, he was older than the photograph he had sent, but he still appeared no more than thirty-five years old—and though as tanned as the others, he was still a handsome, strapping man. I was relieved, but embarrassed that I alone should have escaped this awful trick that had been played on my friends.

"What shall we *do?*" Beauty asked, pale with shock.

"We all need to stay calm," I suggested.

"*You* can stay calm," Sunny said, "your husband isn't a hundred years old!"

"Mine is *two* hundred," Beauty said miserably.

We turned away from the window so that these men, over whose portraits we had once swooned, could not see the unseemly panic in our faces.

"I can't marry that ugly old man." Sunny's vehemence was startling in someone so usually the optimist.

"What other choice do we have?" Wise Pearl asked. "The authorities here won't let us into the country unless we marry them. We cannot go back to Korea without return steamer fare, and I gave all my spending money to my family."

Jade Moon's tone was one of dread. "I could not return to my parents' house after failing as a picture bride. The loss of face would be too great. I think I would rather die."

Of her fiancé Wise Pearl said thoughtfully, "He may not be young or handsome, but I didn't come here just for that. If he can help my family, all well and good. But I'm in America. That is enough. I will marry him."

Jade Moon stole another look at her intended, then nodded slowly. "Yes," she agreed, "much is forgivable if they are truly as wealthy as we were told."

Sunny was unconvinced. "Mine looks like he's wearing the same suit he wore when he arrived here, who knows how many years ago," she said with agitation. "Do these look like prosperous men to you?"

Beauty began to weep. I took her hand in mine consolingly.

"Consider this," Jade Moon said soberly, in what seemed a sincere attempt to comfort Beauty. "Your groom has one foot in the grave; maybe two. It will, at least, be a *short* marriage."

Beauty stared at her, aghast.

Sunny looked again at her betrothed—at his leathery, pock-marked face so clearly seen in the bright Hawaiian sun—then snapped open her change purse and rummaged around inside it. "How much is steamer fare?"

"A hundred *yen*," Wise Pearl told her.

Sunny quickly counted up her cash. Her eyes brightened.

"I almost have enough!" she said joyously. "I need only twenty more *yen*." She turned to me, imploringly. "Regret . . . do you have the money? Oh please, I promise, I'll repay it somehow, can you lend it to me?"

The thought of entering this strange country without my old friend at my side frightened me, but there was even greater fear in Sunny's eyes.

"I can't go through with it," she said softly. "Forgive me. I just *can't.*"

I opened my purse. I had already converted my *yen* to dollars; I handed ten of them to Sunny, the equivalent of twenty *yen*. She took it and clasped my hand gratefully. "Thank you, dear friend. I will miss you. I wish you only happiness." She embraced me, then turned and hurried back to the immigration authorities who had just cleared us for entry into Hawai'i, and was soon lost from my sight.

Beauty eventually resigned herself to her fate and we all went out to meet our new husbands. I felt sorry for Sunny's fiancé, Mr. Lim, who only slowly came to realize that his bride would not be forthcoming and eventually drifted away like a breeze. But I admit, I only gave him a passing thought; I was too nervous about meeting my own fiancé, Mr. Noh. I could not keep my eyes off him as we left the immigration building and entered the yard where the men were waiting. I waited expectantly for him to recognize me, but his gaze just swept past me as he searched the crowd emerging from the station. Finally I approached him, bowed, and identified myself in the proper "high" speech a wife uses to address her husband: "Good day. I am Regret, of the Pak clan of Pojogae."

He turned and looked at me.

Because Koreans try not to openly display our feelings, we have developed ways of seeing past the inexpressive facades we present to the world. Using something called *nunch'i* we interpret nonverbal clues to read a person's inner state. A Westerner studying my fiancé's expression would have seen only a look of vague dispassion. But I could detect subtle yet unmistakable signs of surprise and disappointment—the same kind of disappointment my fellow brides felt when they first laid eyes on their men.

If he knew that I saw this, he did not betray it. He bowed in greeting, and in Korean introduced himself: "I am Righteous Son, of the Noh clan of Pyŏngyang. Welcome to Hawai'i." Around us I could hear similar introductions being made between Wise Pearl, Jade Moon, and Beauty and their fiancés.

"Are you hungry?" Mr. Noh asked me.

Even though I was, I said no, to spare him the trouble. This social ritual obliged him to ask me again, to make sure I wasn't declining out of humility, but before he could we were interrupted by one of two immigration officials who politely inquired whether we brides still wished to marry our husbands-to-be. When we each responded yes—Beauty's voice catching like that of a little girl who could not yet convincingly lie—he announced that the man beside him was a "justice of the peace." He called out the name of Wise Pearl's fiancé, Mr. Kam.

On the spot they were married in a brief civil ceremony. Wise Pearl and her new husband looked traditionally solemn (even when bride and groom were genuinely happy, there were no smiles at Korean weddings). Now the official called out the name of Jade Moon's betrothed, Mr. Ha, and they, too, were joined in marriage. Beauty was next, and if I could see the pain in her face, surely her elderly fiancé Mr. Yi could, but he showed no indication of it. Finally Mr. Noh's name was called. We stepped forward and were told to join hands. The calloused flesh of my fiancé's hand closed around mine, my skin crawling at the hardness of his touch. Then like those before us, he and I were quickly and efficiently wed.

It all happened so fast that I had forgotten to put my silver pin in my hair. I would do it later when I combed out my hair, exchanging the braids of my maidenhood for the smooth rolled hairstyle of a married woman.

After the ceremonies we brides walked the customary three feet behind our husbands as we all crossed over the wooden causeway to the harbor's esplanade, the men chatting among themselves in English. They no doubt assumed that none of us knew enough of the language to understand their conversation, or they would never have spoken as they did. Mr. Kam was congratulating Beauty's husband, Mr. Yi, on getting "the pick of the litter." Mr. Ha remarked, "Mine's not bad for seconds, eh?" And then my husband shrugged and said, in a disgruntled tone, "Beggars can't be choosers, I guess," an American expression I did not know but the meaning of which seemed self-evident.

Everything else was now self-evident, too: Mr. Yi, clearly the wealthiest of the men, obviously had had first choice from among our batch of picture brides. I would later learn, in fact, that he had bribed the marriage broker, who then allowed him to pick the prettiest girl—Beauty—for himself.

My husband, on the other hand, appeared to be the least affluent, and had to settle for what was left. Me.

Somewhere I could hear my father laughing.

All of us save for Wise Pearl—whose husband took her away in a battered old wagon—walked to a nearby Korean inn, the Hai Dong Hotel, located a few blocks north of the harbor on the appropriately named Hotel Street. Mr. Noh and I were given a pleasant room with a bed, table, lamp, and window. We ate a well-prepared dinner of *kimchi*, noodles in black bean sauce, and fresh vegetables. Throughout this my new husband and I barely exchanged more than half a dozen sentences. Silence during meals was the norm in Korea—the better to appreciate the food—but I suspected my husband's coolness toward me was more than mere custom, and I thought I knew why.

I had been last choice, yes, but even at that he must have looked at my picture—at this young woman wearing lipstick and kohl, all the artifice with which the matchmaker had prepared me to be photographed—and he must have thought, Well, she's not too bad. And then he saw me in person for the first time at the immigration station and he realized that he'd been fooled—even as he and the other men had fooled us—by a doctored photograph. I did not need *nunch'i* to tell me that he was probably feeling humiliated and angry. Could I blame him?

I never expected love or even passion that night, but I was to be denied even a trace of tenderness. In our room my husband simply told me to undress, which I did, quite self-consciously. He told me to get into bed, and I obeyed. Then he lay atop me and entered me without so much as a kiss or a soft word. I barely remember the rest of it; certainly I felt no pleasure. Soon afterward he fell asleep. I lay there beside this stranger, trying not to awaken him as tears slipped silently down my cheeks. But even as I tried so hard not to make a sound, I became aware of a muted sobbing not my own— though it could have been mine, imbued as it was with pain and loneliness. The sobs seemed to be coming from the other side of the wall behind our bed, and I remembered now that Beauty and her husband had taken the room next to ours. Through the thin clapboard wall I could hear the sound of Beauty's weeping, in chorus with my own unvoiced grief. And though it would be some time before I learned what the locals called this little inn, I already knew all too well the singular character of a wedding night spent at the Hotel of Sorrows.

Four

The next morning Mr. Yi—by all accounts a successful Honolulu dry-goods merchant—spirited Beauty away in a new Model T Ford. She looked unmistakably like someone who had spent half the night crying, her eyes still red and swollen with remembered sorrow, but otherwise she maintained the stoic dignity of a woman who understood the meaning of *han*. I wished her well, wondering whether I would ever see her again. Jade Moon's husband, Mr. Ha—despite the photograph of him posing impressively beside the Whippet automobile—did not seem to own a vehicle of his own, and they accompanied Mr. Noh and me to the nearby railway station. There the four of us were to board the *Leahi*, a steam locomotive bound for the northern shore of O'ahu. My husband was in a more cheerful mood today, in seeming good spirits as he and Mr. Ha chatted three steps ahead of us on the train platform. As we walked past, but not into, a luxurious mahogany-paneled passenger car, I realized that once again we were traveling steerage. In this case that meant second-class seats in a "combination car"—one that carried a mix of passengers, baggage, and mail. It also served as a smoking car, as I discovered not long into our trip when various prosperous-looking white men wandered in from first class and lit up a form of tobacco I had never encountered before. I was inured to the smell of Grandmother's bamboo pipe, but nothing could have prepared me for the foul gases given off by these fat brown sticks called "cigars."

I sat by the open window, taking in deep breaths of the fresh sea air as we passed the harbor. Seeing the world-famous flag of stars and stripes flying from the masts of the many battleships at anchor brought home for the first time that I was actually, finally, in America. As we steamed up the leeward coast of O'ahu we saw swaying fields of tall green sugar cane, the occasional water buffalo working a taro patch, and gangs of Chinese *kulis* plowing rice fields. We skirted groves of algaroba trees and tall coconut palms bending in the wind as if bowing to us as we passed. I found myself unexpectedly captivated by it all. The train slowed and stopped at a succession of sleepy little stations with exotic names like 'Aiea, Waipi'o, Leilehua, 'Ewa, Nānākuli. Then the lush green hills and rolling farm fields gave way to black rocky promontories that I first took to be coal, but which, my husband told me, were forged from long-cooled volcanic lava. Such unique natural beauty! Hawai'i was more than living up to Mrs. Kim's description of it as a paradise. I was heartened by what I saw, as I think Jade Moon was too, though we seldom spoke during the trip and remained quiet, like good Korean wives.

After two and a half hours the *Leahi* finally pulled into a tiny station announcing itself as WAIALUA. Jade Moon and I obediently followed our husbands off the train and out of the station, where a horse-drawn wagon was waiting for us. This was a far cry from Mr. Yi's Model T; its driver was a laborer of some sort, wearing a kind of checkered cotton shirt I would come to know as a *palaka*. He exchanged greetings with our husbands, who responded warmly, lifted our baggage into the rear of the wagon, then helped us up onto a wooden bench in front. In minutes we were on our way and I worked up the nerve to ask, "Honorable husband, where is it we are going?"

"Mokuleia Camp," he replied. This meant nothing to me until we crested a small hill. Now we found ourselves looking down at a vast expanse of green—thousands of acres of sugar cane, an army of man-high green stalks marching toward a shoreline of pristine white sand. Irrigation water gushed like rivers down gullies cut in the rich red soil, and in the fields were stooped hundreds of laborers hoeing, cutting, watering, and hauling cane. And as if standing watch above all this, like a lighthouse somehow stranded far from shore, was the tall smokestack of a sugar mill, from which rose a constant plume of sweet brown smoke.

Jade Moon glanced at me with mounting anxiety as our wagon bounced along a dirt road bordering the cane fields, the wheels kicking up a great cloud of red dust. We passed through the first of many laborers' camps: in one we saw nothing but Japanese faces gazing at us as we rode by; in the next, Portuguese; in the third, a mix of Chinese and Filipino; until we entered a camp that seemed to be shared by both Korean and Spanish workers. The driver reined in the horse and brought us to a stop. As in the other camps, there was one long barracks-like building as well as row upon row of small bungalows, all of which had tidy little front yards and not-so-tidy chicken coops in back. My husband helped me out of the wagon, and again I flinched as his calloused fingers clasped mine.

Mr. Ha looked up at a dun-brown bungalow with white trim and cheerfully announced, "Here we are."

I was dismayed, but Jade Moon's expression was one of undisguised horror. "What do you mean?" she asked her husband. "Why have we come to this place?"

"Why, this is our new home," Mr. Ha replied proudly. "You can smell the paint, it is so new! I lived in that horrible old barracks for years, but you and I have our very own house."

Jade Moon stared at her husband in disbelief. "But you . . . sent me a first-class ticket—"

"Yes, nothing but the best for my new wife! Like this house. Come, come inside." Head held high, Mr. Ha entered the bungalow, expecting Jade Moon to follow. I alone saw the terrible disappointment and betrayal in her eyes: her "uncommon" man was, in fact, a common laborer.

Shamefaced, she followed him inside. What other choice did she have? What did I?

My husband now led me to our own house, a few hundred feet farther on. It was nearly identical to Jade Moon's, a wood frame cottage painted brown with white trim, its small front yard enclosed by a brown picket fence. It stood on a raised and slatted foundation a few feet off the ground; to enter it we had to ascend half a dozen porch steps.

In Korea, living spaces did not necessarily have inherent functions: a room became a bedroom when you unrolled a sleeping mat, and it turned into a dining room when you brought in a low floor table on which to eat. Here, I learned, things were different. Our home consisted of three small rooms: a bedroom, defined by a mattress surrounded by mosquito netting; a so-called living room furnished only by a straw mat and kerosene lamp; and a kitchen that looked out pleasantly on a leafy banana tree in the backyard. Nowhere was the difference between the two cultures more apparent than in the kitchen, in which stood a wooden table at least three feet high—more than twice the height of a Korean floor table. "Husband, what is this for?" I asked, puzzled.

"It's a dining table. It's where we will eat."

"But we're not eating now. Shall I take it away?" In Korea, dining tables were set out before meals, then taken away afterward.

"No, it is the custom here to have the table out at all times."

"But it's so high. What do you sit on, these things?" Tentatively I lowered myself into one of the straight-backed chairs. "Why does one need such an uncomfortable perch when there's a perfectly good mat to sit on?"

He shrugged. "I never claimed it made sense."

He showed me the backyard with its still-unpopulated, tin-roofed chicken coop. Between our home and our neighbors there was a communal toilet with two stalls reserved for our household by a stenciled sign reading NOH. All told, the house was barely a step above the kind of dwelling a peasant family in Korea might occupy, but with none of the warmth or charm of a typical Korean home.

Mr. Noh wasted no time in putting me to work. It was nearly midday and he had to go to work, belatedly, in the fields. He said, "Wife, pack me a *bentō*," then went into the bedroom to change out of his frayed business suit and into a pair of dungarees and a shirt. I stood there in a panic. What on earth was a *bentō*? The word sounded Japanese but I had never heard it spoken by any Japanese in Korea. Since it was something to be "packed," I thought it might be some article of clothing, so I began rooting about in the bedroom closet, hoping something would present itself as being particularly *bentō*-like. But my husband just looked at me quizzically and said, "What are you doing over there? I told you to pack me a *bentō*." I swallowed, apologized for my ignorance, and told him I did not know what that was. He blinked at me, then conceded, "No, I suppose you don't. Back home we call it a *do-sirak*"—a box lunch. "There's a denim bag in the kitchen. Pack me a water bottle and something to eat."

Relieved, I thanked him for his explanation and went into the kitchen, which was another problem altogether. The pantry was poorly stocked—some uncooked rice, tinned salmon, another tin of sardines, a jar of fermenting *kimchi*, a bottle of rice wine. I found a loaf of bread that had not yet gone stale and sliced off a few pieces. The *kimchi* seemed ripe enough and I poured some into a smaller jar. I filled the water bottle, threw in the tinned salmon and a pair of chopsticks, and hoped it would suffice. Mr. Noh took his lunch, said offhandedly, "You can wash my work clothes while I'm gone," and left for work.

The minute he was gone, my legs buckled under me and I sank into a sitting position in the middle of the kitchen floor. Where was I? What world was this? What had I *done*? I cursed myself for a fool and wept, trying desperately to think of a way out. But the reality was, I was now married to this man—and even if there were some escape from that, how would I get back to Korea? And what would I do once I got there? There was no returning to my father's house. Surely this one could be no worse—could it?

After long and careful consideration, I decided that the only thing to be done was the laundry. And so I got up off the floor.

I found Mr. Noh's clothes easily enough—they were piled high as a burial mound in the bedroom—and could just as easily see that they were encrusted with the blood-red dirt that seemed to permeate everything on the plantation, even the air itself. Korean soil did not stick to the shoe even when dry, like this did. Each pair of trousers was so stiff with dried mud that I was tempted to see if it could stand up on its own legs. I took the clothes behind the house, where I washed a pair of pants in a cement sink, then wrung them out. But no matter how many times I rinsed and wrung, the pants continued to bleed into the sink.

After half an hour of this, my plight was noticed by a woman in the adjoining yard, a young Spanish housewife with flowing black hair named Marisol, who hurried over to set me straight. "No good, no good," she told me in a kind of English that was not quite

English, "too *duro*—hard. Mo' bettah this way." From under the sink she produced something I'd never seen before: a steel scrub board. She draped the dungarees over the board, then pounded them with a wooden paddle not unlike our laundry bats back home. She alternated the pounding with a hard brush, and now when she rinsed out the pants I could make out the blue of the denim for the first time.

"You see difference?" she asked.

"I see," I told her. "Thank you."

"No mention," she said with a smile. "You like *flan*?"

"What is that?"

"It's *ono*, you like. I bring." Minutes later she carried over a bowl of delicious custard unlike any I had tasted in Korea. I thanked her again, then spent the next several hours scrubbing, pounding, and wringing my husband's work clothes until the last drops of red were squeezed from them and I was able to string them out on the clothesline to dry.

In the midst of this I heard the piercing blast of a steam whistle, but thought nothing of it; I merely assumed a train was passing by and continued with my washing. Not long afterward, my husband returned from the fields. I quickly learned that the workday ended at four-thirty in the afternoon and, rather than complimenting me on the fine job I'd done on his clothes, Mr. Noh glared at me and demanded to know why dinner wasn't ready. I scrambled to throw something together from what little I found in the kitchen, cooking a pot of rice on the kerosene stove and throwing in some wine to flavor it. When the rice was ready, I served it along with some of the *kimchi* and the sardines. Mr. Noh looked at his plate as if at some abomination of nature, but he did eat it, in much the same way I once ate a bug on a dare from my brothers.

At eight o'clock the steam whistle sounded again, this time signaling it was time for "lights out" in half an hour. In bed I lay beside my husband, only to have him grope me tiredly, then doze off.

I turned over on my side and closed my eyes. I did not cry myself to sleep this night; I was too numb with exhaustion.

*T*he whistle blew again at four-thirty the next morning, waking me from a deep sleep into a recurring nightmare. Mr. Noh was furious that I was not already up and preparing his breakfast: "How is a man supposed to work in the fields all day without a proper meal to begin it!" he raged. He snapped up the hand-wound alarm clock beside our bed—again, something I had never seen before, much less known what to do with—and threw it in my direction. I jumped as the clock flew past me and into a wall, where it expired with a jangled ring. I rushed to fix a hurried breakfast of leftover rice and *kimchi*. My husband ate it silently, then on his way out barked, "For God's sake get some decent grub in here!"

I watched him leave camp with the other men, marching to the fields like a ragtag army uniformed in denim pants, checkered shirts, and boots. Most wore a variety of straw hats; a few were bareheaded. To my surprise, I saw several women—bundled up in long-sleeved blouses and gathered skirts, heads covered by bonnets or wide-brimmed hats—heading into the fields as well.

Even a foolish girl from a far land could intuit the meaning of "grub," so I wasted no time in getting to the plantation store. I was disappointed to find that they didn't carry much in the way of fresh produce, but I used a large portion of my remaining money to purchase more rice, soy sauce, some tinned beef, honey and sesame oil to make rice cakes, and a fresh loin of pork that I decided to make for dinner that night. The store owner, Mr. Fujioka, asked me if I wanted to "charge" them on my *"bango,"* but since I hadn't the faintest idea what either word meant I just shook my head and handed him the cash.

On my way back I was heartened to see children running and

playing through the camps, which made them seem more like a place where people lived and not merely labored. Passing through the Japanese camp, I encountered a peddler selling fresh vegetables and I eagerly bought a head of cabbage, green onion, garlic, ginger, and red peppers to make fresh *kimchi*. This left me with less than a dollar in cash, but at least we would have food on the table.

After I stocked our pantry, I was feeling lonely and sought out Jade Moon—as inappropriate as she may have been as a potential source of comfort. But when I knocked on the door of her bungalow there was no answer, and I saw no sign of her in her yard. Had she run away, as I wished I could?

I went home, pressed Mr. Noh's clothes, and washed my own laundry after nine days at sea. After that I began preparing dinner, determined to make up for the pathetic meal I had served last night. I made *bulgogi*—"fire beef," though pork worked just as well. I cut the pork loin into thin slices and steeped them in soy sauce, sesame oil, garlic, chili pepper, and red pepper paste. As the meat marinated I cooked a pot of rice, another pot of bean-curd soup, and prepared *kimchi* for fermenting. The minute the four-thirty whistle blew I began grilling the marinated pork slices.

When my husband came home to a house filled with the smells of cooking pork and rice, his after-work sullenness evaporated like water on a skillet. He sat down to dinner and, as was customary, I humbly belittled the meal I had spent so much time preparing: "Please forgive me, as I am not a very good cook. I hope you will not be too disappointed." I doubted he would be, but just to be safe, I poured him a bowl of rice wine, which he quickly drained.

After a few bites of meat he looked up and declared, "This is excellent." He took another bite and actually smiled. "I have not had *bulgogi* this good since I left Pyŏngyang." I stood basking in his praise, then he noticed that I had not set a place for myself. "Come. Sit. Eat."

I must have betrayed my surprise at the invitation. My husband sighed and said, a bit reprovingly, "We are not in Korea any longer. In America, men and women sit at the same table and eat together. I don't know if this is a good thing or a bad thing—it just is. Please. Sit down."

I got myself a plate, spoon, and chopsticks, and sat down at the same table as my husband. Tentatively I helped myself to some rice and a slice of pork—but this all felt so strange. What were men and women supposed to do under these circumstances? Nervously I broke the customary silence by asking, "You are from Pyŏngyang?" This was in the north, a world away from Pojogae.

He poured himself another bowl of rice wine and nodded. "I left there in the Year of the Snake—1905. I was a soldier, but those were bad times for the army. We never had enough to eat and were reduced to foraging off the land. One day I saw a notice that said workers were needed at sugar plantations in a place called Hawai'i. I deserted the army as it had deserted me, made my way to the nearest port, and shipped out on the next boat to Honolulu."

I didn't know whether it was the food or wine or both that was making him so suddenly voluble, but I found that the more he talked the more I liked him. "So you have been at Waialua for ten years?"

"No, no. I started at 'Ewa Plantation, near Honolulu. It was a terrible place. The head *luna* was a despot of a Frenchman. He would curse at us, and if we weren't working fast enough for him, he would sit smugly on his horse and snap a whip at us. As if we were slaves, or bridled horses."

"*Aigo,*" I said.

"When my contract at 'Ewa expired, I went to the island of Kaua'i and worked at Makaweli Plantation. It was even worse. At least at 'Ewa if you worked, you got paid. At Makaweli they had the *poho* system."

"The what?"

"If the *luna* didn't like the way you were cutting the cane, or if you left a small piece on the ground, he'd say, 'You *poho'*—Hawaiian for 'out of luck.' He'd take money out of your wages. Fifty cents, five dollars, as much as he liked. And that money went straight into his back pocket. Here we were, making eighteen dollars a month, and he had to steal from us?" He shook his head in disgust.

"After that I worked for a while at Pu'unene Plantation on Maui. At Pu'unene I heard that Waialua was a good place to work, so I came back to O'ahu. They do treat you well here, and the housing is better than most. But the pay is still a joke. Ten years later and I still only make twenty dollars a month, including bonuses. Nobody gets rich here except the bosses." He downed the rest of the wine, then smiled unhappily. "Guess I'm just *poho,* eh?"

Twenty dollars a month sounded like a lot to me, but clearly he didn't agree. Still, after ten years, I assumed he must have saved up a fair amount . . . perhaps even enough for me to go to school, though I was not about to broach that subject yet.

He yawned and pushed away from the table. "A fine meal," he said, "but I'm very tired." He went straight to bed and was dead asleep in minutes. With two hours until lights out, I opened my luggage and took out my copy of *Diary of a Sightseeing Tour of Kwanbuk.* As Mr. Noh snored away in the bedroom, I sat in the living room and, by the sallow light of the kerosene lamp, reread portions of Lady Ŭiyudang's travels. It cheered me; in a way I felt as though I were following in her adventurous footsteps. I thought of Evening Rose, wondering where my friend was this night, praying she was safe. I wondered what Blossom and Mother were doing. I took out my writing paper and pen and began composing a letter to Joyful Day, careful to paint as rosy a picture of my circumstances as possible:

Honorable Elder Brother,

*It is with great pleasure that I can inform you I am arrived
safely in Hawai'i. The journey here was a pleasant one. My
husband and I were married in a ceremony beside the ocean and
have moved into our lovely new home, which is situated amid
much natural splendor. Hawai'i is truly as beautiful a place as I
had been told, and my life here is* [here I paused in thought,
at last continuing:] *like nothing I could have imagined in
Korea . . .*

As I wrote I saw my family's faces so clearly, and missed them
all the more keenly. I felt somewhat guilty for the flagrant exaggerations, if not outright lies, I was telling them; but at the end I
was able to append at least one honest line:

*Tell little sister-in-law that there is no tropical bud here
more beautiful than my Blossom.*

Smiling, I folded the letter and slipped it into an envelope, which
I then addressed. For the first time since coming to Hawai'i, I began
to hope that perhaps things were going to work out after all.

*L*ife on the plantation was hard, but once I settled into a
routine it became tolerable. I accustomed myself to rising
at three in the morning, ironing my husband's clothes, then preparing his breakfast in time for the 4:30 A.M. whistle, as well as his
lunch to take with him into the fields. I would then clean the
house, attack the laundry (a pair of trousers could be worn no
more than twice before it mummified), or tend the vegetable garden I started in our yard—I planted seeds for red peppers, carrots,
lettuce, cabbage, and garlic.

But there were things I could get only at the plantation store, and all I had left was fifty cents. I told my husband I needed to buy more groceries, but instead of giving me cash he said, "Just charge it to my *bango*." Again this mystifying phrase. "I am woefully ignorant of this word," I admitted. He reached inside his shirt and pulled out a small brass medallion that hung like a necklace around his neck. "My worker number," he said, showing me where the medallion was stamped with the numerals 2989. "You can buy food and the cost will be deducted from my wages." I thanked him and committed the number to memory.

That day I went to the store and gathered an armful of canned goods and raw beef, but when I gave Mr. Fujioka my husband's number, he frowned: "Is that Noh's *bango*?"

"Yes."

"You are Mrs. Noh?"

This brought me up short for a moment. Korean women retain their family names even after marriage, though one cannot call them "maiden" names as they are called in America: in Korea I would be known as "Mrs. Pak," wife of Mr. Noh.

So I simply replied, "I am Mr. Noh's wife."

"He owes me ten dollars he hasn't made good on. When he pays up, then you can buy more. Not until then." He snapped up the items I had set aside and began reshelving them.

Embarrassed, I didn't know what to say, so I just left.

When my husband came home from work and I told him what happened, he grimaced and said, "That damned Jap! He likes to give Koreans a bad time, that's all. Just make do until payday," he directed, and sat down for supper.

I scrimped as best I could, stretching out our dwindling supply of rice, and with my few remaining coins I bought the cheapest items I could find at the plantation store: sardines were only five cents a tin, bread a penny a loaf, and *aku*, a tasty local fish, was available at three to five cents per pound. Marisol also kindly gave me some eggs from their chicken coop and cabbage from her garden.

But the larder was looking bare indeed when one Saturday morning before work Mr. Noh announced, "Payday today. I'll be home a little later—six, maybe seven o'clock." I assumed it took that long to disburse wages to the thousands of the plantation's laborers. Relieved, I scraped together a meager dinner of bean paste, *kimchi,* and rice that could simmer in its pot until Mr. Noh came home.

The four-thirty whistle blew and soon the other men in our camp came home with smiles on their faces and gold coins jingling in their pockets. My husband was not among them, but I didn't worry since he had told me he would be late.

I waited for him on the porch, watching the dusty parade of workers straggling home, and took note of one of the women among them. Her face shaded by the wide brim of a straw hat, her eyes downcast, she plodded along with the same bone-weary posture as the men. She had almost shuffled past me when I recognized the long face and sharp features, nearly masked by a veil of red dust. It was Jade Moon.

So startled was I that I called out her name, a terrible breach of etiquette. She looked up, dismayed and embarrassed that I had seen her.

She stopped, the other laborers continuing on around her like the waters of a river flowing around a mired tree branch. With a mirthless smile on her face, she held up a *bentō* bag in a hand covered with a kind of work mitten. "An amusing sight, eh?" she called to me. "How elegant is the city girl from Seoul! How fashionably she dresses." She lifted a leg to show the calf-high boots hiding under her skirt. "The latest in ladies' footwear! Are you not envious?"

I hurried down the porch steps and to her side. "I looked for you at your house, but it never occurred to me you were working in the fields!"

"It would not have occurred to me, either," she said with a sigh, "three days ago."

"Come inside, let me get you something to drink, we can talk—"

"Some other time. I must make Mr. Ha's dinner."

"Would you like some help? Mr. Noh won't be home for—"

She suddenly exploded at me, "I need nothing from you! What could you possibly give me? How could you possibly help me? *Leave me alone!*"

I was startled but not really offended by the outburst. She turned away and continued on down the road, and in her slow, weary shuffle I saw a proud woman brought low. Perhaps she was right: What words of comfort could I offer her?

Six o'clock passed with still no sign of my husband, then seven. At the blast of the eight o'clock whistle I threw manners and custom aside and ate my dinner alone. Finally, just ten minutes before the eight-thirty lights-out, I heard a noise from outside, followed by a loud curse in Korean.

I opened the front door to find Mr. Noh sprawled facedown on the porch steps. I rushed to his aid as he struggled to stand. "Husband, are you all right?"

He raised his face to mine. I recoiled at the sour reek of alcohol on his breath.

"Goddamned steps," he muttered, and got unsteadily to his feet.

I guided him through the doorway and into the house. Once inside he stubbornly pushed away from me and staggered to one of the dining chairs, into which he awkwardly deposited himself.

I had no idea what to do next; I had no experience with inebriated men. Then Mr. Noh declared, "I'm hungry," and grateful for something to do, I hurried to get him his supper of *kimchi* and rice.

But when I put it in front of him he looked disgusted: "No meat again?"

"There will be plenty of meat," I assured him, "now that you've been paid."

His mouth twitched. He shoveled a spoonful of rice into it, chewed, then mumbled around the food, "No money this week."

"What?" I prayed I hadn't heard that right. "You didn't get paid?"

He picked up some *kimchi* with his chopsticks, swallowing it almost without chewing. "I was *winning*," he said heatedly.

"Winning what?"

"You should have seen my hand!"

I looked at his hand. "What's wrong with it?"

"I had an *inside straight*," he said, spouting more nonsense.

"Husband," I asked anxiously, "what happened to your pay?"

"Four queens happened to it!"

Despite the unfamiliar nomenclature, I began to see the general outline of our misfortune. "Were you—gambling?"

He suddenly spit out a gob of half-chewed rice onto his plate. "This is slop!" he shouted. "I thought you could cook!"

"And what will we eat," I asked helplessly, voice raised in panic, "if you've gambled away your earnings?"

This was a mistake, one I would never make again. As my father had done, my husband jumped to his feet and struck me. But where Father had given me the back of his hand, my husband delivered a fist across the mouth. I staggered backwards. I felt as though a spike had been driven into my lip, splitting it open, and I tasted my own blood.

"You have no right to question what I do with my money!" he yelled at me. "A wife is to offer her husband respect, not reproof! You are a poor excuse for a wife, and if you don't improve, I will have you sent back to Korea!"

He stood there, nearly vibrating with rage, glaring at me with such fierce rebuke that I feared he might strike me again and again until I "improved." My heart pounded in my chest almost as a clapper sounded inside a bell, its terrified peal drowning out even the words I now forced myself to speak: "I . . . I am sorry, honorable husband. Please forgive my callowness and stupidity. I promise, I will try and be a better wife."

This seemed to mollify him somewhat, and when his hand next lashed out it was merely to snap up his dinner plate and hurl it against the wall. I flinched as the plate shattered, smearing the wall with rice and *kimchi*.

He staggered into the bedroom and collapsed just short of the bed. I did not dare try to move him for fear he might awaken.

I could not bear to be in the house another second, and despite the eight o'clock curfew I ran outside and up the red clay road bordering the cane fields. When I had run half a mile or so, far enough away that I thought no human could hear, I unburdened myself of my tears. I sat there amid the cane stalks and cried in the dark for the better part of an hour, my emotions swinging from pain to anger, anger to fear, and thence to panic. In that panic I convinced myself that this was all my fault; had I not come here under false pretenses, the lie that was my photograph? Did my husband not have the right to be disappointed in me? And I *had* been callow and stupid to criticize him. I thought of the night a week before when he praised the meal I had cooked and had allowed me to sit and eat with him. He was not a bad man; I was a bad wife. I would have to become a better one, that was all. It was the only way I could walk back into that little bungalow: to embrace the illusion that I could somehow change the situation, that I had some say over it. To admit that I had no say—that was too terrifying to contemplate. And so I sat there on the ground, weaving an illusion from strands of desperation, until at last I got up and started the long walk back to my husband's house.

$\mathcal{T}$he next morning Mr. Noh awoke with a violent hangover and no apparent recollection of what transpired the night before. He eschewed breakfast but seemed grateful for the hot coffee I served him, even thanking me for it, and was out the door without a mention made of anything that had passed between us. I was grateful for this second chance, and resolved to make the most of it.

Once more I surveyed our pathetic larder and realized that if it was ever to be filled again, I was going to have to do something to earn some money of my own. My encounter with Jade Moon fresh in my mind, I saw only one option.

I went to the plantation offices and requested to be assigned field work. The clerk took my name, my bungalow address, and had me fill out some forms. In short order I was assigned a *bango* of my own and given a medallion like my husband's, but bearing its own number. I who began life as a girl called Regret, who was addressed here in America as "Mrs. Noh," would now also be known—by the *lunas* in the fields, and by the paymaster on payday—as Number 3327.

Five

The next morning Mr. Noh woke to discover that the wife who was preparing his breakfast was doing so not in traditional Korean attire, but in plantation work clothes—a denim blouse, long gathered skirt, and a pair of most unwomanly boots, all of which I had charged against my future wages at the plantation store. My husband looked at me in utter bewilderment: "What are you doing dressed like that?" I replied casually, "Just a little *hanahana*"—a plantation term for work—"to make some extra money." He seemed flustered, uncertain what to make of this, so he sat down to eat his rice gruel and *kimchi*, both of which were reassuringly normal. After he had finished he reached for his *bentō* bag, saw another one sitting beside it that I had packed for myself, gave it an unsettled look, and hurriedly left for the fields.

I strapped on a straw sunbonnet and a neckerchief, and followed him into the world of work. It took me twenty minutes on foot to reach my assigned cane field, and I was already perspiring mightily by the time I got there. But I'd been told that these heavy clothes, as hot and uncomfortable as they might be, were absolutely essential to protect me from the sharp spines of the cane leaves.

I had been assigned to a work gang made up of about twenty *wahines,* or women—Japanese, Filipinos, Chinese, Portuguese, Okinawans, but only two Koreans, myself and Jade Moon. When my erstwhile shipmate saw me walk into the cane field, she made a beeline toward me. She is probably as happy to see a country-woman here as I am, I thought.

"Are you a fool?" she greeted me. "What are you doing here?"

So much for the camaraderie of countrywomen.

"I want to make money," I replied. "Why else would I be here?"

"Unless your husband is forcing you to work in the fields," she said, scowling, "I suggest you earn your pin money by selling vegetables from your garden. This is no place for women."

"These are all women," I pointed out. "*You're* a woman."

"Yes, and this is no place for me either!"

"Does your husband make you work in the fields?"

"No! I'm just offering you advice, thankless as it may be."

"I need to make money," I told her, "and I intend to work for it."

She was, I could tell, on the verge of another withering remark when the head *luna,* a white man—or *haole,* as Caucasians were called here in Hawai'i—swaggered up to us and declared gruffly, "No jabbering! Get to work, both of you!" He thrust a hoe into my hand; Jade Moon shook her head at my abject stupidity and headed back into the fields.

I was put to work doing *hoe hana*—weeding row after row of

cane that stood a foot taller than me and seemed to stretch almost infinitely into the distance. Wielding my hoe I broke up the hard soil, then yanked out the obstinate weeds by hand. A line of cane comprised about thirty feet; we were expected to weed on the order of a hundred lines a day. When you tried to stand up straight to ease the pain of bending over, the *lunas* would shout, "3327! Stop lazing around and get back to work!" Quite often we worked from six to eleven in the morning without once standing up, and by then my back and shoulders ached like a rotten tooth. It was also blazingly hot in the open fields, mitigated only somewhat by the cool trade winds. Our wide-brimmed hats—made of what the Hawaiians called *lauhala*, pandanus leaves—more than adequately shaded our faces, but did nothing to discourage the wasps and mosquitoes that unfailingly found our few inches of exposed flesh, or the caterpillars that wriggled up our legs and into our boots.

Nor did my gloves offer complete protection when, later, we were assigned to strip away dried leaves from the cane stalks—this was called *hole hole*. By evening my hands were scraped and bleeding from dozens of cane cuts, so blistered and raw that I had to soak them in a solution of Epsom salts.

The *lunas* warned us not to talk among ourselves, but the women got around this by singing as they worked. One tune sung by the Japanese women came to be understood by all the races at work in the fields:

> *Wonderful Hawai'i, or so I hear*
> *One look and it seems like hell*
> *The manager's the devil and*
> *His* lunas *are demons.*

I was reluctantly impressed by these women, who often worked with infant children strapped to their backs, or would make a kind of playpen out of the towering cane stalks and suckle their babes between lines of weeding.

At 11:00 A.M. the whistle blew and we were given thirty minutes for *kaukau*—mealtime—gathering in groups to eat and talk. I ate my rice in the Korean manner, with a spoon, and my *kimchi* with chopsticks, and I was startled to see that the Japanese women used only chopsticks for all foods but soup, which struck me as somewhat vulgar. But I was frankly appalled as I watched the Portuguese women scoop fish or beef out of tins with their fingers, as Hawaiians did with fish or this taro paste called *poi*—in Korea it was strictly forbidden to eat food with one's hands, and I did my best to conceal my horror.

I must have been staring too long at one of the Portuguese women, who misinterpreted it and asked me cheerfully, "You like try?" She broke off a piece of some sort of pastry and held it out to me. I couldn't gracefully decline, so I smiled a little nervously and used my chopsticks to pluck the offering from her hand (which seemed to amuse her). But my dismay at her table manners quickly paled next to the sweetness of the pastry. "This is delicious," I told her.

"*Ono*," she said.

"It's called *ono?*"

She laughed. "No no, this *malassada*—what the *haoles* call a 'doughnut.' '*Ono*' means delicious."

"It is very *ono*, then," I said. "Thank you."

As short as it was, mealtime was the high point of a day in the fields. In those that followed I would discover such delights as Portuguese bread, Okinawan potato *manju*, Hawaiian *haupia* pudding, and a sweet Japanese confection called *mochi*. In return I would share the *mandu* dumplings, honey rice, and *kimchi* I prepared for my own lunch. We also exchanged recipes, and now for supper I would occasionally make Chinese eggplant in hot garlic sauce or Spanish *paella* as a complement to traditional Korean fare. My husband had tasted many of these dishes before and made no objection when I served them.

At first, it was a bit difficult communicating with these women. I thought I had learned adequate English from the American missionaries, but people on the plantation seemed to speak something entirely different. When a worker wasn't done with a task, she would tell the *luna,* "No *pau* yet, wait bumbye!" (It took me forever to realize that "bumbye" was a contraction of "by and by" and meant "soon enough!") If something was the best or the worst it was *ichiban,* "number one." To *kompang* was to work together or to share, and when I looked blankly at any or all of this, someone would invariably ask, "You no *sabe?*" or "You no savvy?"

What I finally came to "savvy" was that when the plantations brought laborers to Hawai'i from various countries, there needed to be a common language in which the bosses could communicate with the workers and the workers could communicate among themselves. What evolved was Hawaiian "pidgin," a kind of shorthand dialect whose foundations were English and Hawaiian but whose grammar and sentence structure owed much to Portuguese, Spanish, and Cantonese. Hawaiian words like *keiki* (child) when added to "sugar cane" became "*keiki* cane," meaning young seedling cane stalks; *sabe* came from the Spanish *saber,* to understand, but also sounded like the English word savvy; *ichiban* and *bango* were Japanese; *kompang* was Filipino. *Kaukau* sounded Hawaiian, but was actually derived from Chinese pidgin: *chow-chow.* The more pidgin I heard, with its distinctive lilt and blunt poetry, the more I understood, and the more I came to appreciate it.

But for all the good fellowship in the fields, the work itself was long, tedious, and brutal. We were bent over, under an unforgiving sun, for ten and a half hours each day. When we were doing *hoe hana* our backs ached as if broken; when doing *hole hole,* despite the heavy clothing we wore, the razor-sharp spines of the cane leaves made pincushions of us. And the *lunas* treated us as beasts of burden, certainly as nothing human.

Then one day into my second week of work, the cane fields truly became the hell that the Japanese women sang of in their lament. The trade winds that normally cooled the fields had vanished in the night. The sea offered up not so much as a breath of relief, and the light rain showers that often refreshed us in the afternoon also failed to appear. With neither air nor water mitigating the heat of the day, the tropic sun became a blazing furnace. The air we breathed parched our throats and the *lunas* had to bring in barrels of extra drinking water, which itself was hot as soup. I perspired so much inside my protective clothes that they became soaked, but I dared not take anything off for fear of wasp stings and cane cuts. None of us had the strength to sing, or even to talk over lunch. The scorching sun climbed higher into the heavens but seemed as if it were floating only a few hundred feet above us. Waves of heat shimmered the air, making me wonder if perhaps I was dreaming all of this.

The other women called this "Kona weather," and by 1:00 P.M. at least one of them was overcome by the heat and had to stop working. But when a *luna* ridiculed the poor woman for her weakness, I resolved to go on as long as I could, though I swung my hoe at the weeds with slowly diminishing force.

Around three o'clock I heard a commotion and looked up to see a knot of women gathered at the end of a nearby cane row. From their midst came the disturbing sound of a woman's sobs—not the soft weeping I had heard in the Hotel of Sorrows, but something that was both a gasp and a moan.

I hurried over and caught a glimpse, through the thicket of *wahines* surrounding her, of a woman sitting cross-legged on the ground, wildly tearing off her hat, her kerchief, her heavy denim jacket. Between sobs she cried out, "Damn it! Damn it! Too *hot*."—in Korean.

It was Jade Moon.

A Chinese woman tried to calm her, but was rebuffed with an angry shove. "Eh, you *pupule!*" the woman snapped at her. The other women now backed away, but I pushed through them, even as Jade Moon started to unbutton her denim blouse. I squatted down and put a hand on hers.

"It's all right," I told her, "we'll get you some water—"

She was looking directly at me, yet despite this I believe she didn't recognize me. Her face, like all of ours, was dusted red from the soil, and her tears had traced dark red rivulets down her cheeks, as if she were weeping blood.

"I *can't*," she cried. "I can't *do* it anymore—"

She wrenched her hand free from mine and tore at her shirt buttons, snapping the threads with a pop. She sighed as the air touched the exposed skin of her neck.

"What in hell's going on here?"

I looked behind me. One of the *lunas* was glowering down at us.

"This woman suffers," I told him in English. "She must get out of the sun."

"She's just lazy," he said with a sneer, "like all of—"

Jade Moon's fingers fumbled at her buttons, exposing the upper crescents of her breasts for all to see. The *luna's* eyes widened: "What the hell is she . . ."

I grabbed her hands in mine, looked her in the eye and, seeking to shock, hissed at her: "Stop this! *Are you a fool?*"

She stopped, brought up short by her own words of a week ago. I believe she dimly began to recognize me.

"Go on, get her out of here," the *luna* said, finally realizing that Jade Moon wasn't faking. "I'll only dock you each half a day." I helped my friend up onto wobbly feet and supported her as we trod out of the cane field. It took twenty minutes to get back to our camp, with frequent drinks from my water bottle, but at last we reached my bungalow, where I had her lie down on our bed. I dabbed her face with water, both to cool her and to wipe away the crust of red dirt, and gave her as much to drink as she could swallow.

All this time she had not spoken a word. Now, as she drained a glass of water, she looked at me with embarrassment and said quietly, *"Mianhamnida."* There is no precise English equivalent of this word—it can express both gratitude and apology, as in "Thank you, I am sorry for the trouble I have caused you."

"You have nothing to apologize for. It's a hot day, it might have happened to any of us."

"You probably think me a silly city girl unacquainted with hard work," she said with a frown, "and you would be right. I know nothing of manual labor. My first day in the fields, I thought I was going to die. At the end of the day, I *wanted* to die. My body had never hurt so much in my life." She added with chagrin, "That is what I tried to tell you, badly, when you came to work in the fields."

I now recognized her characteristic frown for what it was: not a scowl of disdain for me, but a reflection of her own self-loathing.

"Then why do it?" I asked. "Does your husband make you?"

She shook her head. "My father is *yangban,*" she said, "and spends his days in scholarly pursuits. His family inheritance was exhausted years ago. He applied for the civil service, but was turned down; and to take another kind of job would be beneath his dignity. So while he sits in his den and studies the Chinese classics, my mother works herself to the bone—raising vegetables to sell at market, taking in laundry, anything she can think of to support a family of five. I thought that if I married a rich man in Hawai'i . . ." Here her voice faltered. ". . . I could send back enough money that my mother would not have to work herself to death. She's so small, so frail . . . and she works so very hard. I thought I could help, but—" She laughed ruefully. "The joke is on me. I came all the way to Hawai'i just to marry a pauper who spent every cent he had to bring me here! Hilarious, isn't it?"

"So you work in the fields," I said, "to send money to your family?"

"Yes, but I'm not strong enough, God help me. I am weak and spoiled, a terrible daughter! I wish I were dead!" She broke down again into sobs; I took her in my arms and held her as she let loose her shame and exhaustion. When she had cried herself out, I spoke up:

"Listen to me," I told her. "You are no weaker than I am. You hate yourself no less than I have hated myself. You are not alone.

"You have endured much. You have suffered much. You will suffer more, and you will endure that as well. Is this not what it means to be Korean?"

I saw a shadow of her dignity return to her. She nodded slowly.

"Yes," she said. "This is so."

Then a small smile even tugged at her mouth. She reached up and playfully straightened my neckerchief.

"And are we not," she added dryly, "so very fashionable?"

We both laughed, and I went to the kitchen to prepare her something to eat.

Saturday, twice a month, was payday, and no one was awaiting their wages more excitedly than I was. I stood in line at the manager's office, and when it was my turn I proudly showed the paymaster my *bango*. "Number 3327," he read from his ledger. "Worked eleven and one-half days at forty-six cents a day, for a total of five dollars and twenty-seven—"

"Wait—that cannot be right. I was told field workers were paid seventy cents a day."

"*Men* make seventy. Women make forty-six."

"But we do the same work!"

"Do you want your money or not?" he barked. Grudgingly I nodded. He counted up the appropriate number of coins, placed them in my hand. "Next!"

My annoyance at making only two-thirds of a man's wages was outweighed by the pride I felt as I hefted the money in my hand, money that I had earned from my own effort. I put the coins in my skirt pocket and happily listened to them jingle all the way to the plantation store, where I purchased enough food to last us at least two weeks. And I even had a dollar left over, one I could perhaps send to my mother or save for schooling. I felt great joy and satisfaction—almost as much as I had felt upon learning to read—as I carried the groceries home and proceeded to restock our bare pantry.

I was surprised and pleased when only a few minutes later my husband came home. I had prepared myself for the possibility that he might again stay out late gambling and drinking, but here he was, sober and on time.

I went into the living room and greeted him, utterly unprepared for the fist that struck me in the nose like a hammer. My face seemed to explode, I saw flashing lights as my head jerked backwards, and I fell to the floor.

I lay there, blood gushing from my nose, gazing up with a total lack of comprehension at my husband, who towered above me, quivering with rage.

"You shame me!" he shouted, and I heard again my father's voice. "My wife, working in the fields like a man—as if I am not man enough to provide for you! They were all laughing at me behind my back, did you hear them?"

Oh Heaven, I thought. I put a hand to my nose, trying to staunch the flow of blood, but even the slightest pressure on it hurt beyond imagining.

"I . . . I am sorry, honored husband," I said, trying to find the words that might dampen his rage. "I was only trying to help."

He took a step toward me, and for a moment I thought it was to give me a hand up. Instead he kicked me in the side, the tip of his boot stabbing like a dagger in my ribs, and I screamed in pain.

"Where is the money?" he asked. I couldn't even catch my breath. He reached down, grabbed me by my shirt, and shook me hard. *"Where is it?"*

Through a red fog of pain I reached into my pocket and brought out the few coins left over from my wages.

"Where's the rest of it?" he demanded.

"I—bought food." I braced myself for another blow of the hammer, but he just took a step backward and dropped the coins into his pocket.

"You are not to work the fields anymore," he ordered.

"I . . . won't," I said between gasps. "I promise."

"I'll be home late. I will spare you the trouble of preparing dinner."

He turned and stalked out of the house, the slam of the door behind him making me flinch.

I lay there unable to move for at least ten minutes, finally gathering the strength to stand. My ribs burned when I took a breath. I quickly found a rag and pressed it against the bridge of my nose. I felt lancing pain, but I kept up the pressure and eventually the bleeding stopped. I looked into a mirror and saw a face ruddy with dust and blood—but beneath the rust was a shocked and terrified pallor.

From somewhere I found the fortitude to walk to the plantation dispensary, where I told the doctor that I had fallen coming home from the fields. I couldn't tell him the truth; I was too ashamed. Whether he believed me or not he adjudged my nose fractured and gave me an icepack to reduce the swelling, which was by now prodigious. Then he examined my ribs, which were luckily only bruised, not broken. The swelling on my face gradually decreased and the pain subsided, but it left me with a black-and-blue swath across my nose. I went home with instructions not to touch it or sleep on it, as well as a bottle of aspirin for the pain and the doctor's insistence that should the bleeding start again, or should pus appear, I was to return to the infirmary.

As I walked home I wondered—in an oddly detached manner I would recognize only in hindsight as shock—what to do next. My husband had forbidden me from working in the fields, but I knew he would come home tonight having once more gambled away his wages. Fortunately I had purchased enough food to last several weeks—but what then?

Worrying about food when I should have been worrying for my life, I arrived home and fell exhausted into bed. My nose still throbbed and I took two aspirin as instructed. Tomorrow was Sunday and I did not, blessedly, have to rise at four in the morning to prepare breakfast. I slept in till nearly six. When I woke my husband was in bed beside me and he made no mention of my bruised and swollen face. He even seemed rather chipper. I did my best to stay out of his way for the rest of the day, preparing his favorite meals and saying not a whisper to antagonize him. When he left in the afternoon to play something called "softball" with his friends, I went to the management office and turned in my *bango*.

By Monday the shock had worn off and I was again gripped by fear. The first time Mr. Noh struck me he had been drinking, but this time he had been cold sober. That meant that an attack could happen at any time, for any reason. The thought paralyzed me: What did I do, what did I say around him? How did I live with this explosive presence? I was anxious to talk with Jade Moon but she was in the fields, as I should have been. In desperation I sought the counsel of other Korean housewives in the camp, but found that they held a very Confucian view of marriage. "It is a husband's right to treat his wife as he sees fit," one told me, while another quoted the old Korean adage, "Women and dried pollack should be beaten every three days," and admitted that her own husband occasionally had to "discipline" her.

Only one of the women I spoke with thought that what my husband had done was wrong: "This is America, not Korea. Women are not chattel. Take the train and speak to the pastor at the Korean

Methodist Church; perhaps he can help you." When I protested that I had no money for train fare, she thrust some coins into my hand and said, *"Go."*

My family was Confucian, not Christian, and Namsanhyun Methodist Church was fifteen miles away in Kahuku—the last stop on the O'ahu Railway main line. But with no better alternative, after my husband left for work the next morning, I stole away to the railway station and purchased a ticket for the 11:45 train. It took half an hour to reach Kahuku Station and from there I was able to walk to the church, where I asked to speak to the pastor.

But though the reverend was sympathetic to my plight, and made clear he did not countenance violence, he advised me, "We are far from the lands we knew, and Koreans are a small minority here in Hawai'i. If we are to preserve Korean culture and tradition, we must preserve family unity. Look into your heart, child, and forgive your husband his transgressions."

"As he forgives me?" I asked. "With his closed fist?"

"What other choice do you have?" he asked, adding gently, "This is the life you chose, child. You must learn to make the best of it."

I took the 2:20 P.M. train back to Waialua. As the station neared I was sorely tempted to remain sitting—to let the train take me as far from Waialua and Mokuleia Camp as I could travel. For a few moments I thought I might actually do it. But after the locomotive shrieked to a stop in Waialua Station, I lost my nerve, got up, and got off the train.

Perhaps everyone was right. Perhaps I had needlessly provoked my husband into violence by taking a job in the fields without his permission. But even if I accepted the blame for that, the problem still remained: how to survive on the few coins remaining after my husband's gambling?

Marisol generously introduced me to her friend Luisa, who ran a thriving business washing, ironing, and mending clothes for the single men living in the barracks. She charged them five cents a shirt, and needed another hand to help her: for every shirt I washed, pressed, or stitched, I would receive two cents. But I was not brave enough to accept her offer then and there; I could not risk my husband's wrath again by going behind his back. Instead I brought the matter up one evening after dinner, choosing my words carefully:

"Honorable husband," I said, "you were right to be angry that I took the field work without asking your permission. You are the Outside Master"—a Korean term for head of the household—"and I should have come to you first."

He looked at me impassively.

"But I see how hard you work," I went on meekly, "and how the *lunas* cheat you, and I wish to help in some way. A woman here in the camp takes in laundry for the men in the barracks. She has asked me to assist her, for which I would receive a few pennies in payment. I respectfully ask the Outside Master to consider allowing me to go to work for her, and thereby contribute some small sum to the household."

I steeled myself for a possible eruption, but he didn't look angry, merely contemplative.

"Laundry," he said after a moment.

"Yes. Washing shirts, ironing, mending."

"Would anyone else know you are doing this?"

"No. We would do all the work at Luisa's home, and she would deliver the laundry to the barracks."

Whether it was the deference I displayed or the fact that laundry was more traditionally women's work, I don't know; but at last he nodded and said, "You have my permission."

I bowed my head in gratitude. "Thank you, my husband."

I went to work for Luisa the next day. There I would spend eight hours beating the mud out of trousers and shirts, soaking them in a steel wash drum, and stirring the mixture like some kind of foul, bloody stew. I was so proficient at stitching and patching that Luisa eventually entrusted me with all the sewing that needed doing. I found that I was able to work on perhaps twenty shirts a day, earning a daily wage of forty cents—nearly as much as I would have been paid for working in the fields. Then, before the four-thirty whistle blew, I would hurry home and begin preparing Mr. Noh's dinner.

I was soon earning almost ten dollars a month, though I decided not to share that exact figure with the "Outside Master." I would use most of the money for groceries, then give my husband some (but not all) of what was left, which he could gamble away with his own wages if he was so inclined. But I was always careful to set aside a dollar or two each month for unforeseen emergencies, hiding the coins in a jar that I buried in our vegetable garden.

The tensions between Mr. Noh and myself lessened; the household was at peace again. I would never feel completely safe around him, but neither did I live every day in constant terror. His better nature surfaced now and then—he would make a joke or do something thoughtful for me—and it was during one of these harmonious interludes that we had marital relations again. I found myself completely disconnected from the act, almost as though I were sitting in the corner of the room, watching my husband straddle me and thrust himself into my body. I was not afraid, I was not pleasured, I simply *was*. I did not dare be anything else.

A few weeks later I woke feeling nauseous, but forced myself to go to work. The queasiness lessened as the day wore on, but then I began to feel more and more fatigued as well. I had to relieve myself every hour or so, then would suddenly find myself crying about it, as though it were the most terrible thing in the world—and forget about it just as quickly. That month I missed my menstrual period. In those days there were no blood tests to determine pregnancy, but the plantation doctor knew the signs and congratulated me.

I sat in the infirmary and said wonderingly, "I'm going to have a child?"

He smiled and allowed as how that was the usual sequence of events.

I walked home, elated, though part of me worried how my husband would react. But when I told him that evening, to my relief he broke into a wide grin; he seemed delighted by the news. And for the first time since the night he had spoken so kindly to me over dinner, I too was happy.

*T*he months that followed were good ones. With a child on the way, Mr. Noh exhibited a newfound sense of responsibility: he stopped drinking, no longer went out on payday, and abstained from gambling. I asked him to do none of these things; he embraced them on his own, and seemed genuinely eager to save money to raise a family. We talked about baby names, though he never considered the thought that it might be anything but a boy. "We won't stay on the plantation forever," he promised. "I'll get a job in town. As a carpenter, or a yard man to a rich *haole*. Our son won't grow up with red dirt between his teeth."

When I told Jade Moon, she admitted that she, too, had missed a period and feared she might be pregnant; she didn't relish the prospect of doing field work with a baby strapped on her back. The possibility of having to give up work altogether had not occurred to me, but in my third month my fatigue became so chronic and acute that I was unable to continue working for Luisa—it was all I could manage to do our own laundry, cooking, and housekeeping. Mr. Noh was understanding and supportive.

But whereas in the past it was my salary that went to pay for food and other necessities, now it was Mr. Noh's. I had paid off his debt with the plantation store and once again we could charge our purchases, but when next he received his wages—less the cost of groceries I had already purchased—he was shocked to walk away with fewer than two dollars. The next payday he netted even less, as we had purchased baby blankets, diapers, and other nursery items.

When he had been single, my husband had not had to worry about purchasing food: he lived in the men's barracks and ate the meals they served there, the cost automatically deducted from his salary. But now he was feeding two people—soon to be three—and he watched his money evaporate like the afternoon rains here in Hawai'i. This began to weigh heavily on him. He withdrew into himself, becoming quieter, more irritable. The happy dream I had been living turned tense and anxious once more. He complained about the cost of food, about my cooking, about any and everything. Each payday, with its meager handful of coins, only seemed to worsen his mood.

I tried to tell him that things would be better after the baby was born, when I was able to go back to laundry work, but he snapped at me, "What kind of man would I be, to be supported by my wife?" I wisely refrained from pointing out that I had been doing exactly that until just recently.

More and more he referred to our unborn infant not as "our baby" but "this child," as in, *This child will need a crib. This child will need clothes. This child changes everything.*

The tension grew along with the life inside me. Then one Friday night late in my fourth month, Mr. Noh came home from the fields two hours late—and very drunk. It was not payday; I knew he had no money to be gambled away. Perhaps he had just needed a drink or two to relieve his stress. Don't do anything to provoke him, I told myself. Act as if nothing is wrong.

I said, "I've kept your dinner warm on the stove. Are you hungry?"

He looked at me in disgust.

"No, I'm drunk," he said combatively. "You goddamn blind?"

"Then I'll make you some coffee," I said, and went to put on water.

His hand shot out and grabbed me by the arm. "Did I say I wanted any damn coffee?"

His fingers gripped my arm like an ever-tightening coil. I felt a wave of sickening fear and tried desperately to think of what to say next.

"All right," I said finally, blandly. "No coffee."

In the face of my refusal to confront him, his grip on me only hardened. I tried not to cry out, to say anything at all that might trigger his rage. But I should have realized, the trigger had already been pulled.

He squeezed harder, and before I could stop myself, I cried out in pain.

He smiled like a wolf that had scented its prey, and with a jerk of his arm he sent me spinning into space. I crashed into the pantry, the collision knocking the wind from me. I collapsed onto the floor and he was suddenly there, kicking me. The first kick was to my ribs, but as I yelled and reflexively rolled over, his next kick found my stomach. I screamed, begged him to stop, but of course that only encouraged him. I covered my belly with my hands to protect the baby, but he kicked me in my arm and the jolt of pain forced me to let go, exposing my stomach again. He kicked my belly again and again, sending lightning flashes of pain and grief through my body. I heard my child scream in the lightning, felt its helpless agony, until it was too much for me to bear and blackness swallowed both the lightning and the thunder of my husband's rage, and I lost consciousness.

In the safe quiet darkness I wept, as my child—my *daughter*, I somehow knew—enfolded me in arms that were not arms and gazed at me with eyes that were not eyes, and told me sadly that it was not meant to be. And she left to go somewhere else, somewhere I could not reach.

Then even the darkness went away.

When I woke, not long after, I was still lying on the kitchen floor. I looked down at myself and saw my skirt sodden with blood—felt it trickling out of me along with my broken water—and at this I blacked out again, mercifully so.

*M*y husband passed out not long after he assaulted me and killed our child. When he awoke, he had no memory of what he had done, a gift that was to be denied me. He saw me lying bloodied on the floor and ran in a panic to the infirmary. I'm told I was taken there in an automobile, and one of the first things I recall was the plantation doctor, Dr. Jaarsma, telling me that I was lucky that the blows had not damaged any of my internal organs.

I did not feel lucky.

He also assured me I had not been hurt so severely that I would not be able to bear another child. The prospect terrified me.

Then the doctor, sitting beside my bed, soberly asked me if I wished to file a charge of assault against my husband. I was lost in grief, and strangely empty of rage. "Would men in your country," I asked him, "really put another man behind bars merely for beating his wife?"

"Well," the doctor allowed, "he might serve a few months, at least."

"And what then?"

He had no answer for that.

I told him I would not file charges. He started to rise. I asked whether my baby had been male or female.

"It was a girl," he said. I just nodded.

Soon Mr. Noh came to my bedside, wallowing in guilt and repentance. He wept and promised that he would never strike me again, that he would never take another drink, so help him God. He begged my forgiveness, but if I could not bring myself to have him jailed, neither could I forgive him—or believe that his promises would stand the test of time and temptation. I said nothing and closed my eyes as if drifting to sleep, denying him the absolution he so ardently craved.

Other wives in the Korean camp—including some of the very ones who had advised me to take my husband's beatings without complaint—brought me bowls of seaweed soup, a common Korean restorative for women who have just given birth. They also urged me to spend the traditional thirty days afterward in bed, a tradition I was happy to observe: for at least the first week I could not have gotten out of bed had I tried.

While in the infirmary I received an envelope postmarked in Korea. Because it took so long for mail to cross the Pacific in those days, I was only just receiving my elder brother's response to my letter home:

> *Honorable Little Sister,*
>
> *We are all happy to hear from you and to know that you have safely reached your destination. I read your letter aloud to Mother and Blossom; little sister-in-law had me read it to her twice, and says to tell you that she misses you, as do we all.*
>
> *Congratulations to you on your wedding. From your descriptions, Hawai'i truly seems like a paradise. How wonderful it must be to live there. It pleases us all to know that you are happy and fulfilled in your new life . . .*

I cried myself to sleep that night.

After three weeks I had recovered sufficiently to be discharged from the hospital. I could still barely walk, and Mr. Noh had to make his own breakfast and pack his own lunch. Marisol helped me do laundry and prepare dinners. I forced myself to walk from one end of the tiny house to the other, slowly gathering stamina. Gradually, I came back to myself, and found the strength to do what I knew I must.

It went against all I had been taught a good Korean wife should be: loyal, sacrificing, obedient. But I could not remain in this house and possibly deliver up another child for the slaughter. I told only Jade Moon of my plans, and she did not discourage me; she even offered to give me money, but I thanked her and declined. I had money, at least a little.

And so it was that one morning after my husband had left for work, I dug up the jar of gold coins I had buried in the garden, packed my suitcase, and walked the mile to the train station at Waialua, where I purchased a ticket for the end of the line, the farthest point from Mokuleia Camp and Mr. Noh—removing my silver wedding pin from my hair as I boarded the next train bound for Honolulu.

Six

This time the lush green landscape rolling by held no charms for me, and the exotically named stations we passed seemed merely signposts in a country of despair. The shriek of the brakes as we pulled into each station unnerved me, and the drumbeat of the train along the tracks took on a pounding, reproving tone. No escape on my part, it seemed to say, could bring back my daughter—and nothing else seemed important. I sat there wondering what her voice might have sounded like . . . tried to imagine the shape of her smile, or how her eyes might have caught the morning light. I tortured myself with all the infinite lost possibilities until at last I felt the train slow and heard the conductor call out, "Next stop,

Honolulu!"—the end of the line, nowhere else to run. I got up and disembarked the train.

Outside, clutching my suitcase, I stood blinking for a moment in the shade of the gabled railroad depot. Now that I was here, where *was* here? I found myself facing a commercial street crowded with storefronts, ordinary but for what loomed behind: the spent volcano crater known as Punchbowl. It looked a bit like one of the many hills surrounding Pojogae, but with its summit disturbingly lopped off, as if by some giant's blade. I was only a few steps from this wide avenue called King Street, busy with pedestrians and populated by a wide variety of shops. On this block alone I noted two Japanese apothecaries, a Chinese grocery, a Portuguese tattoo artist, even a Korean shoemaker. From more than one storefront I heard the sounds of commerce being conducted vigorously in pidgin. It felt almost as if I had never left the plantation.

Nearby the depot was a lodging house, the Railroad Hotel, which reminded me of the last time I had been at this railway station: the day after my dockside wedding. Realizing I was not far from the Hai Dong Hotel, I began to retrace the route we had taken that day, instinctively seeking the familiar comfort of the little Korean inn. I walked down King Street to River Street and up River to Hotel Street; but when I finally reached the Hai Dong, I was seized by apprehension. What if the innkeeper, Mr. Chung, recognized me as the bride of Mr. Noh? What did I say if he asked where my husband was? If he realized I was running away, might he not try to contact Mr. Noh and tell him where to find his errant wife? The possibility froze me to the spot. I longed to go inside and be surrounded by at least the trappings of home—but I simply couldn't take the chance. I turned and hurried back the way I came, not daring to risk the fellowship of other Koreans.

By the time I returned to the railway depot I was hungry and spent some of my meager savings on a bowl of rice at a Japanese restaurant on King Street. I daydreamed that it might have come from the Rice Mountains, which only made me all the more home-sick. I yearned to jump aboard the next ship bound for Korea, but even if I could somehow scrape together the steamer fare, where did I go once I got there? Not back home to Pojogae or to Taegu—Aunt Obedience was gone; so was Evening Rose. No, better to be here in Hawai'i, as distant as it was, than to be in my homeland yet unable to truly go home.

Out on the street again I had no more idea where to go next—or even where I was—than before. I went back to the railway station and asked a heavyset porter loading bags into a carriage, "Excuse me? What is this place called?"

"This?" he said. "This is Iwilei."

He pronounced it *EE-vee-lay*—as Evening Rose had when she spoke of the friend of hers who had gone to work there.

I felt a jolt of recognition and excitement. "It is?"

"Yeah, this side of the street, anyways." He grunted as he lifted a heavy bag. "Other side, that's Pālama, but here"—he jerked a thumb toward a nearby road that intersected King Street at an angle—"this is Iwilei."

I thanked him and instinctively headed toward the intersection.

Without knowing her name, of course, I harbored no real hope of finding my teacher's friend. But Iwilei seemed worth a look, if only to be closer, for a moment, to the memory of Evening Rose. And I had, after all, no pressing engagements elsewhere.

I followed a group of pedestrians, most of them male, flocking like pigeons down the intersecting street, along with an increasing number of passing motor cars that bounced along the scored and pitted roadway. The first building we came to was an imposing coral-block structure, surrounded by a high wall, which looked like a medieval fortress and turned out to be a prison. Hardly the most auspicious of sights, it stood silent and forbidding at the fork of two roads; across from it, equally uninviting, squatted a row of ramshackle houses. I followed the crowd down the more traveled of the two roads, and as we passed by the prison I heard a chorus of barks and yelps coming from a dog pound situated behind the jail. The poor animals seemed to be crying out for their freedom, in contrast to the stoic silence emanating from the prison.

The barking of the dogs slowly gave way to the raucous cheers and catcalls of men, many arriving by car to join those traveling on foot. This road was even more heavily trafficked than King Street, and most of the pedestrians were men in some sort of military uniform. I recognized only the livery of the Japanese navy, but from their varied faces and the many languages they spoke, I could see that there were sailors here from all corners of the world, obviously on shore leave.

The street seemed increasingly designed to cater to such men, as evident by the number of saloons out of which floated rude laughter and coarse dance-hall music. Here, too, was a barbershop, a billiards parlor, a tobacconist, and a penny arcade. Even the air seemed to take on a masculine aspect, pungent with the smell of shaving lotion, cigar smoke, and liquor. The mood in the street was festive, as if we had stumbled into the middle of a party—and indeed, the men around me were acting more and more like revelers.

But not all of them were entering the saloons and arcades—not even the majority of them, who continued purposefully down the road. We passed several canneries and a few more boardinghouses, then found ourselves approaching a high wooden fence at least fifteen feet tall, beside which an affable-looking police officer was stationed. He let the men pass through the gate without a word, but when he saw me carrying my bag he asked, "You new to Iwilei, Miss?"

"Yes," I told him, "I am."

"Go on in, then"—he gave me a wink and a smile—"and make yourself at home."

"Why, thank you," I said. Did the police here greet all visitors so warmly? Such a friendly place! I walked inside, feeling welcome.

On the other side of the gate, and on both sides of the street, I now saw row after row of neat little wooden cottages—each painted green with white trim, and each with its own tiny *lānai*, or porch. They looked not unlike the tidy little bungalows we had lived in at Waialua, and for a moment I wondered if I had wandered onto some sort of plantation. In a way I had, but it was a much different kind of crop that was sown here at Iwilei.

The honky-tonk dance music of the saloons had been replaced by an inharmonious medley of songs, each issuing from a gramophone in the individual cottages: one tapped out a sprightly Spanish flamenco; from another blared the German ballad "Auf Wiedersehen"; and more than one played a then-popular tune called "On the Beach at Waikīkī":

> *Honi kāua wikiwiki*
> *Sweet brown maiden said to me*
> *As she gave me language lessons*
> *On the beach at Waikīkī*

The occupants of the bungalows were *haole*, Japanese, Chinese, and Hawaiian, and all appeared to be female—again, not unlike Waialua, where few but women were at home during the day. But though it was only late afternoon, these women were clearly wearing evening clothes: bright, gaudy dresses made of silk or satin, with plunging necklines and slitted skirts that shockingly revealed more flesh than I had ever seen displayed in public. They all wore bright lipstick, heavy makeup, and musky perfumes, and were either sitting on their porches—smoking cigarettes, fanning themselves in the heat—or visible through a window as they sat inside, chewing gum and reading movie magazines. The men around me slowed as they approached a house, eyeing the women inside like shoppers at one of those stores along King Street.

Suddenly a woman standing on her *lānai* leaned forward over the wooden railing to grin at a passing man—and her breasts burst out of the scant restraints of her dress! She made no move to cover herself, nor did she display the slightest trace of embarrassment. But I was blushing enough for the two of us.

> *She was surely teasing me*
> *So I caught that maid and kissed her*
> *On the beach at Waikīkī*

As I finally began to "savvy" where I was, I turned and started to hurry back the way I came, away from these unassuming little "pleasure houses." But in my haste I must have called attention to myself, and now an obscenely obese *haole* in a white suit and Panama hat stepped in front of me. It was as if a wall of pale flesh and linen had descended from the sky, bringing me up short. "You are new," he said in an accent that was unfamiliar to me.

"No, I—I am not a—" I struggled to think of the English word for *kisaeng*, then realized that I didn't know it; this was a term my missionary teachers had somehow failed to acquaint me with.

The man ogled me from beneath his sweaty brow and smiled. "I like new. Are you *very* new? Perhaps *brand*-new?"

I tried to step around him, but again he blocked my path. "I am not what you think I am," I told him. I turned away, but his hand shot out and clammy fingers closed around my wrist.

"Let go!" I cried out, struggling to break free of his grip.

"How much?" he asked me.

"I am *not*—"

"Hey. Russkie," someone called out.

I glanced up to see a pretty, curvaceous, blond-haired woman standing on her *lānai*, fanning herself with a folded newspaper, her expression one of mild boredom as she took in my plight. "Back off. Can't you see she ain't selling?"

"We are negotiating," the obese man insisted.

The blonde nonchalantly stepped down off her porch steps, ambled over to us, then calmly raised the newspaper and gave the fat man a mean swat across the back of his head. His hat flew off; his grip on me loosened.

"Get your fat ass outta here!" the blonde bellowed impressively at him. "You want virgins, go jump in a volcano! G'wan, get lost!"

The obese Russian bent to retrieve his hat, then quickly did as he was told.

My rescuer turned to me. "Sorry about that, hon. We don't get many civilian gals in here. You okay?"

"Yes," I said, but my voice was trembling. It had been too familiar, too much like the treatment I had become accustomed to in my own house. Without meaning to, I suddenly burst into tears.

"Aw, hell," the blond woman muttered. I tried to stop crying, but found that I couldn't. She sighed. "Okay, c'mon, take a load off."

Through tears I said, "Pardon me?"

"*Sit.* Come in and sit down a minute."

I leaped at the opportunity to get away from the sweat and swagger of the men around us. The woman took my bag, and as I followed her up the porch steps I felt a bit calmer, reining in my tears as we entered the bungalow. "So what gives, hon?" she asked. "You F.O.B.—fresh off the boat?"

This much I understood, and thought it wise to say that I was.

"You take a wrong turn at the docks and wind up here?"

"Yes," I said. "A wrong turn."

Her little bungalow, like all of them here, consisted of just three rooms: a parlor or sitting room; an adjoining bedroom; and behind the bedroom, a tiny kitchenette. The only furnishings in the parlor were a lamp, a gramophone playing "On the Beach at Waikīkī," and an artistic rendering of a nude woman hanging above a worn couch. Over the latter was draped a pair of stockings with several long runs in them, a few garish dresses also in various states of disrepair, and a large orange cat dozing with its head on its paw.

"That's Little Bastard, don't mind him." Of course the name meant nothing to me, another failing of missionary education. My rescuer pushed aside the dresses to clear a place for me to sit. "So what's your name, kiddo?"

A casual question, but it threw cold terror into me: Could I trust anyone here with my true name? What did I tell her? Then Evening Rose seemed to gently whisper in my ear and I found myself saying, "My name is Jin."

She laughed. "Yeah? I've got a friend named gin, you want to meet her?"

Confused, I merely smiled, which she took as assent. "I'm May," she said, going through the bedroom and into the kitchenette, "May Thompson." As I heard her pouring something I idly reached over to pet the cat, which now opened its eyes, regarded me skeptically, then flopped over on its back, presenting an ample tummy to be rubbed. I began stroking the soft fur of its belly when the cat's paws suddenly closed around my wrist and its teeth sank into the back of my hand.

I yelped in pain and tried to yank back my hand, but the cat held on with both paws and teeth. I tried to shake him off—once, twice, three times—then on the fourth try he finally let go, perhaps out of boredom, and landed on his feet to resume his lazing position on the couch.

Two bubbles of blood welled up on my hand. May reentered the parlor with two glasses of what appeared to be water, saw me rubbing my hand and the cat licking himself for a job well done. "Ah, Little Bastard makes another friend," she said, handing me a glass. "Here you go. Bottoms up, toots."

I was quite thirsty and had taken a large gulp when I realized the liquid was not water. I choked on it at first, but whatever it was felt comfortingly warm as it worked its way down my throat—a feeling that soon radiated throughout my whole chest. It was not unwelcome. I took another swallow.

"You okay, honey?" May asked. I nodded a response. She downed her drink in two gulps, as if it were lemonade.

There was a knock on the open door. A young American sailor with hair the color of wheat stood impatiently on the porch: "Hey, Maisie, you busy?"

"Gimme a sec, okay, hon?" May turned to me. "Finish your drink, toots, money just walked in the door."

I did as she said, draining the glass. The warmth in my chest spread to my arms and legs as well.

"You feeling better, kiddo?"

"Yes," I said with a smile. "Fine. I should go. Thank you for your help."

I stood up. The world tipped on its side, then started spinning.

I toppled backwards like a felled tree, onto the couch. The last thing I heard before I passed out was May's voice saying, "Oh *shit*."

Whatever that meant.

I woke once, around midnight, from a disturbing dream in which I was being pursued by a herd of squealing mice through our barn in Pojogae. I opened my eyes, but alarmingly, the sound did not go away. I was lying on May's couch, a pillow under my head, a cotton blanket draped across me. The only illumination came from moonlight seeping around the drawn window shade, framing it in a ghostly white light. Slowly I identified the sound as the squeaking of bedsprings from the adjacent room— further punctuated by the occasional grunt, pant, gasp, and moan.

I had heard similar sounds at the pleasure house in Taegu, so I was hardly shocked. As it droned on like some lewd drinking song endlessly repeating its blushing refrain, I was reminded that there is nothing quite so amusing as the sound of other people having sexual relations. At long last a man cried out in pleasure, and less than a minute later a disheveled sailor—though not the one with wheat-colored hair—was spat out of the bedroom like some finished product on a conveyor belt. I shyly retreated under the blanket as he left, peeking out in time to see the next customer, an eager Chinese, sprint into the bedroom and shut the door behind him. In moments the bedsprings began singing tenor again.

I felt almost as if I was back in that little house beneath the paulownia tree, and it was not an unpleasant feeling. I closed my eyes and drifted asleep to the strains of this bawdy lullaby.

When I woke again, bright sunlight was now gilding the edges of the drawn shade. I sat up, my head still a little woozy. A clock announced it was half past nine in the morning, and the house was now silent but for the faint snoring of May in the bedroom, and a kind of wheezing purr from the vicious little cat who still dozed atop the back of the couch. I went to the window and pulled up the shade: the street outside was deserted, the houses all silent, with no sign of their occupants, all presumably resting after a long night's work.

I went back to the couch, wondering where to go from here, when I noticed that some of the clothes that had been draped across the couch the night before had been stuffed into a trash basket in a corner of the room. I picked from the trash a red silk evening dress with a ripped seam and a blue satin slip with torn, brocaded trim. They were damaged, certainly, but it seemed wasteful to simply throw them away. And it now occurred to me I could also repay in some small way this woman's kindness in rescuing me. I took my sewing kit from my travel bag, settled down on the couch again, and carefully started taking the seam of the dress apart. Finding some red cotton thread in my kit that was a close match to the color of the dress, I began to restitch the seam.

As always, sewing had a calming effect on me, and for the next hour or two I felt relaxed and happy, almost as if I were back in Mother's room, sharing our thimble time. Oh, how I wished that I were! I did not look once at the clock, and in what seemed like no time at all I heard:

"Hey. Toots. You still here?"

I looked up. May, wearing only a flimsy pink camisole, stood in the doorway between bedroom and parlor. She appeared surprised to see me. "Figured you'd have been on your way by now," she said, somewhat pointedly.

"Oh. I'm sorry," I said. "I . . . lost track of time."

"Yeah, makes two of us. I kinda went into extra innings last night myself." Indelicately, she rubbed the inside of her thigh. "Geez, is my pussy sore."

I nodded.

"Yes," I agreed. "He *is* ill-tempered."

May stared at me—then roared with laughter. Once again I had apparently misread her meaning. Pidgin was easier to grasp than the strange English this woman spoke!

When she finished laughing she said, "Sit tight. Lemme put some water on." As it turns out she meant this quite literally. She disappeared into the kitchenette, and emerged a few minutes later with two cups out of which steam was rising. "Here, have some," she said, handing me a cup.

I took a sip, expecting perhaps some sort of tea, but blanched at its acrid taste. "What *is* it?"

"Hot water with a teaspoon of limestone phosphate. I read in the paper you ought to drink some every day before breakfast— cleans out the kidneys and bowels, purifies the blood."

I put the cup down unfinished, content with the purity of my blood as it was. May drank the ghastly concoction quickly, then noticed for the first time what I had been working on. She picked up the red silk dress, examining it with surprise, if not outright amazement: "Did you fix this?"

"Yes, but I'm sorry, I did a very poor job," I said with requisite Korean humility.

"Sakumoto the tailor fixed this once, but the seam busted open again. Told me it couldn't be repaired."

"That is because he used silk thread to repair the seam. Silk is too strong, it cuts the fabric. With a dress made of Chinese silk, better to use a weaker, softer thread, like cotton."

May picked up the night slip, examining that as well. "Damned if these don't look good as new."

"You are too kind, but thank you."

May seemed to regard me with new eyes. "C'mon, let's rustle up some grub." I followed her through the bedroom—past a canopied bed in considerable disarray, a chest of drawers, a vanity table—and into the kitchenette, where she heated up a skillet, cracked four eggs into it alongside several strips of bacon, and put on a pot of coffee. In a few minutes we were sitting down at the little kitchen table to eat. Her cat wandered in, quickly sniffed out the food, and let out a small but demanding *Nyep.* He went to May's chair, raised himself up on his hind legs, and reached up with a paw, which fell a few inches short of May's plate. She fed him a strip of bacon, then lifted him into her lap and began massaging his neck. In her hands he purred con- tentedly, though oddly it sounded more like a bird's trill.

"So," May said as she took a swallow of coffee, "I take it you're looking for a place to hang your hat?"

"A what?"

"A place to live."

"Oh. Yes."

"Maybe here in Iwilei?"

This would certainly be the last place my husband would think to look for me. "Yes, perhaps."

Casually she said, "So who you running from?"

My heart skipped a beat. "What do you mean?"

"Honey, nobody jumps at the chance to live in a place like this unless she's on the lam from somebody. And Oriental gals like you can't even enter the country if they don't have somebody lined up to marry 'em. You're here all alone, so you gotta be running from somebody. Who is it? Husband? Pimp?"

I did not know this second word, but I sighed and admitted, "My husband."

"He try to sell you on the street?"

I was shocked. "No! Is that—does that happen?"

"How do you think most of these Japanese gals wound up here? They came as, whatayoucall it, picture brides? Their husbands either put 'em to work, or sold 'em to someone who did."

I felt cold inside, wondering if this fate had befallen any of my friends from the *Nippon Maru,* praying it had not.

"Is that how . . . you got here?" I asked. "Someone sold you?"

"Hell no. Nobody sells me but me. I'm strictly an independent contractor."

"No one sold me, either," I said quietly. "My husband merely beat me."

Soberly she took that in, then nodded.

"Okay. Just so long as we're being square with each other."

" 'Square'?"

"Honest." She broke open the cellophane from a small package labeled LUCKY STRIKES. "So . . . you laying low till you can file for divorce?"

I did not know this "laying low," but I understood, and was shocked by, the latter half of her statement. "Women here may divorce their husbands?"

"Yeah, sure. They can't in your country?"

I shook my head. "In Korea only men can ask for *ki-cho*. It means 'abandoned wife.' "

"Honey, I'm starting to see why you left home." She lit a cigarette, which further astonished me: aside from Grandmother's pipe I had never seen a woman smoke before. "Okay," she said after inhaling and releasing a noxious plume. "So me and the other gals here, we might be able to use somebody like you—somebody good with a needle and thread. This job's hell on your wardrobe, all that groping and pawing . . ."

"Yes, I could help with that," I said eagerly.

"In exchange, I can give you room and board here, with me— not for long, mind you, just till you can get on your feet."

It *was* unlikely Mr. Noh would find me here, and the truth was I had precious little money to spend on lodging. "I would be most grateful for that."

"Just remember: this is a business, like any other. That's my office in there"—she indicated the bedroom—"and I keep regular hours, four P.M. to two A.M. You can sleep on the couch, like you did last night, but if you've got a problem with the acoustics—the noise—then go check into the Y instead."

"I was not bothered by the . . . noise," I replied honestly.

Her laugh was coarse but genial. "Good. Because I like a *lot* of noise."

She did not mislead me on that score. In fact, May Thompson was easily one of the most popular women in Iwilei— "entertainers," the government called them, here as in Korea. Prostitution in Honolulu was tacitly sanctioned by the authorities as a necessary evil, but restricted to this "red light" district. The hundred-odd women who worked here were supposedly examined for venereal disease on a weekly basis—in practice far less often, though Chief of Detectives Arthur McDuffie came each week to collect their "health certificates," along with something May called "kickbacks," cash payments to the police that assured the stockade would not be closed down.

That first day May introduced me to some of our neighbors, told them I was a seamstress, and within the hour I found myself knee-deep in a pile of dresses, skirts, blouses, and lingerie. I immediately went to work mending tears, patching linings, and raising hemlines far above what might be generally considered a respectable length. One woman, Lehua, asked me to repair something called a *sarong*, which I found fascinating in its brevity. From Lehua I also learned that *iwilei* is Hawaiian for a unit of measurement roughly equal to the length of an arm—to which May added cynically, "Yeah, and that's just how the decent, God-fearing folk of Honolulu like to keep us: at arm's length!"

Indeed, the women of Iwilei were even legally constrained from visiting certain sections of the city, and May would often send me out on errands for her into the "respectable" neighborhoods she was prohibited from visiting.

In my first few days at Iwilei I returned from one such shopping trip—to purchase silk underwear, May's one indulgence, at Gump's Department Store downtown—to find that she had installed the oddest-looking device in the corner of the sitting room. It looked vaguely like a mechanical bird with a needlelike beak, perched atop a wooden table standing on metal legs; below the table were a series of gears and levers the function of which I could hardly guess.

"Hey, kiddo, we're in luck," May told me with enthusiasm. "One of the gals is shipping out to San Francisco and she didn't want to lug this back with her, so I picked it up for a ten-spot. It's a few years old, but it's a genuine Singer."

"It sings?" I said. "Is it some kind of phonograph?"

"No, no, no! Christ. It's for you, it's a sewing machine."

"For me? But I have no use for such a thing."

"If you're going to be a seamstress, you need a sewing machine. Go on, give it the once-over, it won't bite."

I had heard of such machinery, of course, but I had never seen one, and as I approached it I noted that it was aesthetically quite pleasing to the eye. The "head" of the machine was painted black and decorated with ornate gold and red adornments, or "decals." The "beak" of the bird was in fact a needle, and instead of tail feathers it sprouted a silver metal wheel of some unfathomable purpose.

"But I have no idea how to operate such a device," I protested.

"It's a snap," May assured me. "I'll teach you."

"You?"

I must have betrayed my shock at this: May looked a bit indignant. "Hell, yes. What kind of lousy mother wouldn't teach her daughter how to sew? You think when I was ten I said to her, 'Sorry, Ma, I don't need to learn to sew, I'm gonna fuck for a living'?"

I blushed. "I'm sorry. I did not mean to suggest—"

"I had a mother, too." With wounded pride, May shouldered me aside, sat down, and proceeded to demonstrate the operation of the Singer, starting with the treadle—a foot pedal which, when pumped, moved a series of gears that made the sewing needle go up and down. "Trick is," May explained, "you've gotta alternate your heel and your toe till you get a steady rhythm going . . . otherwise you can spin the balance wheel in the wrong direction, see?"

She tutored me in the proper use of this treadle until I was proficient, then showed me how to set and thread the needle. I was surprised to discover that where I would hand-stitch two pieces of fabric together by weaving the needle and thread in and out of both pieces, the machine's needle actually created stitches on both sides simultaneously. When May pumped the pedal slowly, the machine made a dozen stitches in a matter of seconds; when she pumped faster, it stitched even more. "And this is an old foot-operated model. The new ones have an electric motor that *really* goes to town."

I could scarcely believe it: This device could sew more stitches in a few minutes than I could in half an hour! My initial aversion was quickly forgotten; the machine won me over with its remarkable speed and consistency. By the end of the day I was comfortably doing these new "lock-stitches," amazed at how much more quickly I could work with this Singer.

This was fortunate, as sewing jobs continued to come at a steady pace. Much of my labor here was spent letting out dresses by another inch or two or three, which I considered an enormous waste of time. Korean clothes, both men's trousers and women's skirts, were of one size, with waistbands that could be tightened or loosened as needed. Koreans know that the human body is always changing—so why try to make one's body fit into some garment of arbitrary size? But Americans seemed quick to bow to the tyranny of a fitted garment—and just as quick to cheat that fit when they could not live up to its restrictions.

Many of the fabrics I worked on were satins, silk, or this new "artificial silk," soon to be called rayon, so they required delicate handling; but I was used to working with such fabrics, as my mother's wrapping cloths often utilized silk and ramie. With some of these I relied on my hand sewing, as I was not yet confident enough that I could make machine stitches without tearing them. But immodestly I must admit that the ladies of Iwilei seemed quite happy with my handiwork and regularly gave me "tips" in the form of sweets and potables—the latter of which I would usually pass along to May.

The women who worked at Iwilei were as colorful as their clothing. The most renowned was a madam, "Society Sal," whose house offered up a constant flow of liquor and pretty girls to serve it. She had some small competition from the remarkably trouble-prone Annie White, who had been arrested by the police on at least seventeen different occasions, always for selling liquor without a license, never for prostitution. Then there was the enterprising Dolly Gordon, who not only owned a telephone but boldly listed her number in the city directory under "businesses." Most infamous, however, was the loud and contentious Dorothy Palmer, who was continually getting into arguments, even fistfights, with other women—earning her the dubious title of "Queen of Iwilei," bestowed by one of the local newspapers.

More sobering to me was the revelation that a good third of the stockade's residents were regular users of what May called "dope"— primarily opium and morphine—perhaps to blunt the numbing toll the nights took on them. May's sanguine attitude about her profession was not a common one, perhaps owing to the fact that she had only been practicing it a few years. When I asked her how she had happened onto this way of life, she shrugged and said, "I like men and I like sex. And getting paid for it, hell, what could be better than that?" Born in a place called Nebraska, restless at an early age and at odds with her divorced parents, she eventually moved to San Francisco, where she took up her trade. There she heard tales of the "harlot's heaven," Honolulu, and of how money earned there in prostitution "couldn't be touched" outside of Hawai'i. She packed her bags, set sail aboard the SS *Ventura*, and never looked back.

The stockade was also home to a dozen or so men—"procurers," as polite society called them. Some supposedly held reputable jobs as chauffeurs, jewelers, or employees at the local billiards parlor, but in fact they lived off the earnings of women. May called them "pimps," and rarely had a good word to say about any of them.

Needless to say, none of this was subject matter to be raised in one of my letters home; and for that matter I was not even sure what to say to my family about my change of circumstances. I could not allow too much time to pass without writing, for fear that Joyful Day might send a letter to Waialua and receive back a missive from Mr. Noh informing him of my betrayal of my marriage vows. I could not bear the shame of that. But I was fearful of giving anyone my current address, lest it accidentally find its way into Mr. Noh's hands.

The solution came in the form of something called a "picture postcard" sent to May from a friend of hers living in some far place called Western Samoa. I had never seen such a card, and when I asked May if there were "postcards" here in Honolulu, she just laughed: "Well, if you look real hard," she told me, "you *might* find a few."

Indeed, at a five-and-dime store downtown I found dozens of such cards featuring hand-tinted photographs of local attractions like Diamond Head, Waikīkī Beach, Kilauea Volcano, as well as assorted waterfalls, tropical flowers, surfboard riders, and beautiful native women in *hula* skirts. Many of these scenes seemed strange even to me; I could only imagine my family's startled reaction to the sight of brown-skinned men on long wooden boards, standing astride ocean waves like gods straddling the seas. I finally settled on an aerial view of the harbor, the city, and the impossibly green valleys and mountains, bearing the legend TERRITORY OF HAWAII— CROSSROADS OF THE PACIFIC, and wrote a short, carefully vague message in the small space on the back of the card allotted for it:

My new home, Honolulu!
Life moves very fast; opportunities abound.
Will write soon with new postal address.

Was that vague enough, yet specific on the point that my old address at Waialua was no longer valid? At least it purchased me some time to consider what I might do next.

wilei was home to more law-abiding residents as well, at least outside the stockade. A peninsula built in part on fishponds that had been filled in with coral dredged from the harbor, it was also the site of two pineapple canneries, the city gas works, a lime company, a kerosene warehouse, a soap works, an asphalt factory, and a fertilizer manufacturer. Indeed, it was hard to forget the presence of these industries since, depending on which way the breeze was blowing, you took in the sweet smell of pineapple laced with tar, soap flavored with pineapple, sulfurous pineapple gas, or old-fashioned manure—with a twist of pineapple, of course. And since much of Iwilei was also girdled by a mile's length of railroad tracks—looping around the railway terminal to the east and Kapālama Basin to the west—there was no escape from the rattle of incoming or outgoing trains whose whistles woke us shrilly at dawn and keened on the hour.

Not long after I arrived here, I was out walking along the shoreline when I crossed paths with a group of small boys who were eagerly gathering the yellow pods—fallen *kiawe* beans from the ubiquitous algaroba trees—that littered the beach. Laughing and running, the children collected the yellow bean pods in big gunny sacks, and seemed to be having fun doing it. One of them—a dark-skinned Hawaiian boy who looked perhaps eight years old—was lagging behind the others, and they were teasing him for it:

"Eh, slowpoke, c'mon, try catch up!"

"'Ey, Joe, you sure one lazy *kua'āina!*"

Flustered, the Hawaiian boy tripped over one of the exposed tree roots and spilled half of his beans back onto the ground. The other children found this hilarious and continued on running up the shore, clutching their burlap sacks.

The Hawaiian boy looked about ready to cry when I came along and offered to help him.

"*Mahalo,*" he thanked me. He was very soft-spoken, and with a shy smile he bent down beside me and we began gathering up the pods.

"What do you do with these?" I asked him.

"Oh, we sell 'em," he said. "Make big money."

"Sell them? To who?"

"Fertilizer company. They use 'em for horse feed. Fifteen cents a bag!"

"That *is* much money. Let's make sure we get them all." We spent the next several minutes recovering all the beans he had spilled and then some, until his bag was brimming. It was now almost as heavy as he was, and I offered to help him carry it home.

"My name is Jin," I said as we walked, increasingly comfortable with the name. "What's yours?"

"Joey."

"How old are you, Joey?"

"Six. I was born Christmas Day."

"You are big for your age."

"Yeah," he said proudly. "Mama tells me, 'Joey, you one fine *keiki*.'"

"What was that your friends called you? The Hawaiian word?"

He frowned a little at that.

"*Kua'āina*. Country boy. They make fun 'cause I come from Maui."

He was trying not to seem bothered by it, but I could tell it mattered to him. "Did you like living on Maui?"

"Yeah, you bet. Had my own train!"

"A toy train?"

"No! Real big." He stretched his arms wide. "Bigger'n the house I live now."

I smiled, attributing this to youthful imagination. "You know, Joey," I told him, "I also am from the country."

"Yeah?" He looked at me. "You from Maui, too?"

"No, I come from a place called Korea. It's very far away, but we have country people there too, and city people also make fun of them sometimes. No matter what your friends say, there is nothing wrong with being a country boy."

He smiled a beautiful smile. "Yeah? No lie?"

I nodded. "No lie."

Joey's home was one among scores of small cottages and shacks clustered between the Honolulu Gas Works and the Hawaiian Fertilizer Company, where many of the residents worked. It resembled a plantation camp, but with a mix of nationalities—Hawaiian, Chinese, Japanese, Portuguese, a few Koreans—all living together. It was nearing supper time, and from the shared outdoor stoves came a host of delicious smells, which almost, though not quite, obscured the odors from the gas works and the fertilizer factory.

Joey took me into his small cottage and introduced me to his family: "This is Jin. She's a *kua'āina,* too! She helped me carry." Proudly he showed them the sack filled to bursting with bean pods, and his mother Esther—a tall, slender, dignified woman who clearly doted on her son—congratulated him and thanked me for my assistance. Joseph Kahahawai Sr. was a large, bespectacled Hawaiian, about thirty years of age, with a soft-spoken manner not unlike his son's. Joey's younger sister Lillian was sweet and pretty.

Esther announced, "I'll put out another place for dinner," and so it appeared I was staying for supper.

"My dad's a fireman," Joey informed me.

I wasn't certain about the nomenclature, but I guessed, "He puts out fires?"

"Other way around, more like it," Joseph Sr. said with a smile. "I stoke the boiler on trains for O'ahu Railway and Land."

"Yeah, but at Lahaina he *drove* the train," Joey said proudly.

"At the sugar mill," Joseph explained with a shrug.

I laughed as I realized, "So you really *did* have a train bigger than a house?"

"Yeah, you bet," Joey said, adding wistfully, "It was one fine ride."

We sat down to dinner and my hosts, devout Catholics, bowed their heads as Joseph Sr. recited, "Bless us, O Lord, and these Thy gifts which we are about to receive from Thy bounty, through Christ our Lord. Amen." We enjoyed delicious *aku*—raw whitefish caught by Joseph that morning, marinated in ginger, onion, soy sauce, and chili peppers—with cooked sweet potato and freshly baked pineapple pie, made from scraps of fruit discarded by the canneries.

"You live in Iwilei?" Esther asked. I said that I did, hesitating a moment before admitting that I worked as a seamstress for the women of the stockade.

Esther seemed mildly scandalized by this, but I explained that I was new to Honolulu and was working there in exchange for room and board.

"That's all?" Esther said. "Room and board?" I nodded. "I sew a little myself. How many stitches do you do in a day?"

"Oh, I mend perhaps . . . eight or nine dresses a day."

"Well, you might be interested in knowing that those *ladies*," she said with disdain, "pay only fifteen dollars a month in rent, and even the ugliest of them earn twenty dollars *a night.*"

I let out a gasp at this extraordinary sum. Joseph looked at his wife and said, "How do *you* know what those ladies make?"

"Everybody in Iwilei knows what they make."

"I don't."

"Good thing, too," she said. Her husband laughed, but Esther fixed me with a sober look: "Either you're being underpaid for your services, or you're overpaying on your rent. Either way, you ought to take it up with your 'employers.'"

"You could get a job with the Gas Company," Joseph Sr. suggested. "They lease out cottages like this to employees for a dollar a month, and they pay two and a half dollars a day." This was a generous wage by plantation standards, and I said as much.

"You worked on the plantation?" he said.

"Oh, no," I said quickly, "but I have heard."

I found myself envying this family: If only someone other than Mr. Noh had chosen me, I might have been sitting in my own little house, looking into my own child's bright eyes.

When I was ready to leave, Esther told me warmly, "*Mahalo* for helping my boy. *He hale kou.*" She explained that this translated roughly as, *You have a house*—or in other words, "You're always welcome here."

Then her expression turned businesslike again. "And if I were you, I'd have a long talk with those *ladies* about your salary."

I promised her that I would, though I could hardly have foreseen under what circumstances this talk would take place.

The winter of 1915–16 was an unusually wet and stormy one for the island of O'ahu, and the afternoon of January 13 was like many others of late, with a light drizzle falling from mottled skies. I was in the sitting room of May's cottage, hand sewing a piece of lace, thinking about what Esther had told me and pondering how I might ask May about getting paid more. While I did not wish to seem ungrateful for her help, I felt dependent upon her for everything: she gave me money to buy food at the grocery store, but I had none of my own. Clearly I could not remain in this situation forever if I wished to earn enough to someday bring Blossom to Hawai'i.

May had just finished entertaining a client and was strumming a tune on her ukulele—she was actually quite good—when we heard the sound of raised voices from outside. We stepped out onto the *lānai* to see a group of perhaps a dozen soldiers standing outside the bungalow of one Lena Stein next door. That would hardly have been unusual, but for the color of the soldiers' skin.

These were black men wearing the dark blue dress uniforms of the United States Army—members of the Ninth Cavalry, as we would discover later, on their way to Manila aboard the transport ship USS *Sheridan*. And they were engaged in pitched argument with Lena, who stood defiantly on her *lānai:*

"I toldja, *no!*" she yelled at the men.

"Why the hell not?" one of the soldiers yelled back.

"'Cause you're colored, why the hell d'you *think?*"

"Color of our money's the same as anybody else's," another man snapped. "Ain't that all whores like you care about?"

I confess, I had never seen a black man before, and I stared at them in mute fascination, which probably only added to their discomfort. But May did not hesitate to stalk over to Lena's porch and take her aside.

"Jesus Christ," she said in a low tone, "what the hell's your beef? You've screwed *kanakas* darker than these guys."

"It ain't the same."

"It's all the same equipment, toots. Standard issue."

"I don't screw niggers!" Lena said heatedly, not bothering to lower her voice, which only further incensed the soldiers.

May threw Lena a disgusted look, then turned to the men with a bright smile: "Hell with her, fellas—my house is wide open for business. Who's first?"

She looped arms at random with one of the men, then led him up the porch steps to our house.

"You always did like the dark meat, Maisie," Lena said with a sneer, but May ignored her and ushered the soldier inside the bungalow. I tried not to gape at him as he passed by. Actually, he seemed rather handsome once I had gotten used to his complexion, so different from any I had ever seen in Korea.

The rest of the soldiers made their way down the street, seeking other willing partners. But with the exception of two or three women who, like May, cared only about the color of money, doors were slammed in the soldiers' faces; normally bawdy women suddenly became shy and reclusive.

In the few weeks I had been here, I had seen these women take into their houses men of sometimes unsurpassed repulsiveness—ugly, unkempt, and malodorous—and yet these neatly groomed men wearing the colors of their country were turned away solely because of the color of their skin. They left Iwilei feeling frustrated, indignant, and angry.

The rain began to fall more heavily. I went back inside and returned to my sewing, as best I could with the usual noisy distractions from May's bedroom.

By seven o'clock that evening, the rain was heavier still and the street outside was now a mud flat, and largely deserted. Even men hungry for sex did not venture into the sodden streets of Iwilei when the weather was this bad. I was inside sewing; May was standing on the porch, smoking a cigarette and watching the gray sheets of falling rain, when I heard her mutter, "Uh-oh."

Something in her tone prodded me to join her. "Is something wrong?"

Silently she nodded down the street.

Through a curtain of rain I could make out a large group of men—dozens of them—passing through the stockade gates. As they grew closer I noted two things they all had in common: they were all wearing the uniform of the United States Army, and they were all black.

May discarded her cigarette, grinding it out with her heel. "This sure as hell ain't good," she said, rushing inside.

I watched transfixed as the men of the Ninth Cavalry emerged like dark specters out of the storm—side by side, as we would learn later, with soldiers of the Twenty-Ninth Cavalry, an all-Negro regiment stationed at Fort Schafter. And there weren't merely dozens but *hundreds* of them, all converging on Iwilei.

I hurried inside, where May gathered up as much of her money and jewelry as she could find, threw it all into a bag, and slung it over her shoulder. She looked around for Little Bastard, but the sound of marching feet must have already alerted him to the coming trouble and he had taken off for parts unknown.

We would read in the paper the following day how the members of the Twenty-Ninth had thrown a *lū'au* for the men of the visiting Ninth Cavalry, consuming much liquor, as word rapidly spread of how badly a number of them had been treated by the women of Iwilei. But at seven-fifteen that evening, we did not need anyone to tell us what was happening—we knew.

The mob paused when it reached Lena Stein's house, but there was no sign of her and the window shade had been drawn down. For a moment the only sound we heard was the tapping of rain on the rooftops around us, like a disembodied drummer's corps accompanying the soldiers.

Then someone threw a brick through Lena's front window, shattering the calm as well as the glass, and more than just rain descended upon us.

One of the soldiers who had been rebuffed by Lena now jumped up on her *lānai* and with his bare hands tore off the top bar of the porch railing, then used it as a club to break down Lena's door. I heard her scream as he rushed in, dragged her out, and pitched her headfirst into the street. She hit the ground like a stone skipped across a filthy pond, her face quickly buried in inch-deep mud.

Then the floodgates opened wide. Soldiers pounded up her porch steps and into her bungalow, breaking windows, overturning furniture, smashing her gramophone, looting the house of all valuables.

Lena attempted to crawl away unnoticed, but a soldier gave her a glancing kick in the neck for good measure.

The mob might well have let May pass by unmolested, but she was not taking any chances. She grabbed me and we jumped out a side window, as behind us the mob literally tore apart Lena's house, then stampeded over the rest of the stockade like a herd of wild stallions.

Iwilei, never the quietest of places, now resounded with the terrified wails of a hundred panicked women fleeing for their lives, overflowing the street as well as the narrow alleys between houses. Their pimps provided no protection—they too were driven out, and offered scant resistance to the rioters.

May and I inched our way from house to house in the crawl spaces beneath the bungalows, as above us the floors shuddered with fury. Covered in mud, we scurried along like half-drowned rats as we caught glimpses of half-naked women pulled from their homes. A few were injured by flying bricks or glass, but by and large the drunken, furious soldiers seemed less intent on doing the women physical harm than in laying waste to their houses and possessions.

The police guards who patrolled Iwilei did their best to stop the rioters, but they were a bare handful of men and soon retreated, calling for reinforcements.

For the next twenty minutes, May and I were trapped underneath a house, unable to move in any direction, while bedlam reigned around us. Finally the mob moved on and we scrambled out from under the house, running in the only direction we could: up toward the workers' camp behind the Hawaiian Fertilizer Company. Some of the little cottages were closed tight as drums; others were guarded over by their tenants, who stood defiantly on their doorsteps with guns or clubs, determined to fight off the rioters if necessary. One of these was Joseph Kahahawai Sr., who saw me—heaven knows how he recognized me, covered as I was from head to toe with mud—and ran up to us. "Get inside! Hurry!"

In the temporary shelter of the Kahahawais' home, Esther helped us wash up and gave us a pair of clean dresses—"Mother Hubbards," May called them—to wear. Neither she nor anyone else in the camp knew what was going on, and when I explained what had happened, Esther just shook her head in disgust. "All these *malihini haoles* coming here," she said, "bringing their hate with them."

I appreciated their help, but it was not they who were the object of the soldiers' wrath. I whispered to May, "We cannot put these people in danger by staying here," and grudgingly she agreed. We thanked the Kahahawais, Esther made the sign of the cross on our behalf, and we ran out and up Iwilei Road. Dozens of other women were also fleeing this way, and barely a hundred feet into our flight we encountered the prostrate form of a neighbor, Jennie Barr, lying in the middle of the road. The back of her dress was torn and blood oozed from a gash between her shoulder blades. We pulled her to her feet, and though dazed she ran with us up toward King Street.

But as we neared it we were scarcely prepared for what we saw: a battalion of U.S. Army troops, most of them white, deployed across Iwilei Road between O'ahu Prison and King Street, with another contingent bordering 'A'ala Park. This was the Second Infantry from Fort Schafter, which had been summoned to quell the riot. They stood in battle formation, with rifles at shoulder arms, facing us.

And not just us. Behind us we now heard voices, and turned to see that large parts of the rioting mob, having finished their near-demolition of the stockade, were now retreating the only way they could—up Iwilei Road—with the three of us caught between them and the *haole* battalion ahead of us.

"Shit!" May cried, and as one we ran toward the soldiers ahead of us.

We ran as fast and as hard as we could, until Jennie slipped and fell. May and I picked her up, then carried her between us as we rushed toward the battle lines drawn ahead. Fortunately, one of the *haole* officers signaled two of his troops to come and assist us, and the men soon ushered us safely behind their lines.

Meanwhile, the rioters were headed straight for these same lines.

A soldier sounded a bugle, and the men of the Second Infantry obediently attached bayonets to their rifles—but the mob did not slow.

Another blow of the bugle, and the Second began to load their rifles.

We braced ourselves for a battle, but the rioters finally seemed to comprehend the gravity of the situation. They recognized the second bugle call as the order to load and, apparently not prepared to meet the barrels of their comrades' rifles, they quickly retreated and dispersed into the back alleys and corners of Iwilei.

The riot, it seemed, was suddenly over.

A soldier took us to the Honolulu police station at the corner of Merchant Street and Bethel Avenue, along with most of the other displaced women of Iwilei. Many were barely clothed, railing about the ransacking of their homes and the theft of all their worldly goods. A handful of refugees had, like May, managed to escape with their money and jewelry and now entrusted thousands of dollars in cash with Chief McDuffie (notably not including May, who preferred to keep a closer eye on her funds).

The Second Infantry quickly clamped down on Iwilei, closing the sole entry road and issuing permits to enter and leave so the last of the rioters could be ferreted out and damage to the stockade assessed. But May insisted to McDuffie that she be allowed back into Iwilei to look for her cat, and a determined May Thompson was not a force to be trifled with. Finally, another detective standing nearby—a short, wiry Chinese-Hawaiian in a neat suit, with an impressive scar bisecting his right eyebrow—volunteered, "I take 'em, Boss."

McDuffie acquiesced with a sigh. "Okay, okay. They're all yours, Apana. Get a pass from the provost marshal and a uniform to drive you." Sternly he told May, "In and out in an hour, Maisie, cat or no cat—you got that?"

May assured him that she did and we obediently followed the Chinese detective. "We go bumbye, one stop," he told us, leading us to his desk where he retrieved not a gun or a billy club but a coiled black bullwhip made of braided rawhide, hanging from a hook on the wall.

I glanced uneasily at May and whispered, "Do all policemen here carry whips?"

"Naw, only this one," she said, apparently recognizing him. "Apana, huh? Ain't you the guy who shut down that *che-fa* lottery in Chinatown last week?"

He nodded matter-of-factly and led us out of the station house.

May told me, "We got us a four-star escort, kiddo. This is Chang Apana, who holds the department record for most arrests." She turned and asked, "You rounded up, how many, seventy guys at one time, single-handed?"

"Oh, no, no," the detective objected modestly. "Only forty."

I looked at this little fellow, even shorter than I—no more than five feet tall, perhaps a hundred and thirty pounds—and could hardly imagine him subduing so many men. "How many guns did you need?" I asked.

"No gun. Just this." He hefted his bullwhip, then smiled slyly and added, "Cool head, main t'ing."

Apana said something in fluent Hawaiian to a uniformed officer, who left to get a patrol car. Then the detective spoke with the Army provost marshal, who reluctantly signed a pass and handed it to him. In minutes we were in the patrol car, on our way to Iwilei. The uniformed officer drove; Detective Apana did not have a license to operate an automobile, apparently liking cars only slightly better than he liked guns.

As we turned a corner, Apana noticed a group of young men loitering under a street lamp. He yelled out the window, "'Ey! You no savvy curfew? Go home!" For emphasis he swung his arm out the window and snapped his whip, which uncoiled like a snake and cracked the air like a gunshot, scattering the young men.

Amid the wreckage of Iwilei we drove to May's cottage, which had fared a little better than its neighbors. May and I got out of the car and I began calling sweetly, "Little Bastard? Poor Little Bastard, where are you, Little Bastard?"

Detective Apana laughed uproariously and kindly shared with me the meaning of the cat's name. I blushed, I think, down to my toes.

It was Apana—who told us he had begun his law enforcement career as an officer for the Hawai'i Humane Society—who finally found the miserable little feline dozing contentedly under a neighboring house. May scooped him up and stuffed him into a canvas bag. I half expected him to claw her to pieces for this indignity, but with May he was remarkably compliant.

She also took the opportunity to rescue her gramophone, which had survived the riot unscathed, as had the sewing machine. She asked me to carry the cat, but I offered instead to transport the gramophone, which was heavier but far less hazardous.

The damage to the stockade was evident all around us: broken windows, smashed porches, shredded wire screens, gutted furniture upended in the street. All told, it would total some five thousand dollars in damage—not counting the money, jewelry, and clothing also lost in the riot.

Back at the station house, May and I took note of a dazed Lena Stein sitting on a bench in the lobby, a blanket wrapped around her, nursing a cup of hot coffee. May tossed her a sarcastic smile as we passed.

"Thank God we preserved your white maidenhood," May said acidly.

Lena muttered an obscenity; we left the station to check into a hotel.

or the next two days we rented a room at the strangely named Silent Hotel in downtown Honolulu—at least until the managers got wind that May was entertaining men in her room and summarily ejected us. We then hastily checked into the Railroad Hotel on King Street, where I persuaded May to behave herself until we were allowed back into Iwilei.

I found the entire experience frankly terrifying, and seriously considered finding other quarters in a less colorful—and less volatile—neighborhood. But the grim reality was that I still barely had enough pocket money to rent a room for a single night, and so I instead brought up the matter of salary with May as we sat at a table in our room, playing a card game called "gin rummy."

I began by telling her that I very much appreciated her hospitality and kindness to me, but that I needed to begin earning money of my own so that I might eventually be able to bring a family member here to Hawai'i. I started to tell her about Blossom, but halfway through my explanation she interrupted: "Wait a minute. This kid's parents . . . *sold* her to your family?"

"There is a Korean word for the custom, but—yes."

"And she was only five years old?"

I nodded.

May stared at me, and for the first time since I had known her, she seemed genuinely at a loss for words. In lieu of them she stood up, went over to her tin of money, and took out a thick wad of currency. She came back to the table and laid out in front of me approximately fifteen dollars in cash.

"What is this?" I asked her.

"It's the money the other gals have been paying me for your sewing."

I looked up at her, and it was my turn to be shocked.

Defensively, she said, "Hey, I've got expenses like everybody else, okay? But go on, take it. From now on, I'll have the gals pay you directly, and only the work you do for me will be charged against my overhead."

Embarrassed, she got up and put a record on the gramophone, which began playing a familiar tune as I stared at the wrinkled bills in my hand and smiled.

> *Honi kāua wikiwiki*
> *You have learned it perfectly*
> *On the beach at Waikīkī.*

Seven

In hindsight it is easy to see the riot as the beginning of the end for Iwilei, but it hardly seemed so at the time. It was true, in the wake of the violence the local newspapers published heated editorials calling for the closure of the red-light district. There were even a few "citizen's committees"—mostly white society women from the "better" neighborhoods—formed to lobby for its closing. But with the sailing of the USS *Sheridan* a few days later—and no apparent action taken against the soldiers who had participated in the riot—the whole incident seemed quickly forgotten by the public at large. Carpenters were already busily repairing the damage to the stockade's houses, and by the following Monday Iwilei was once again open for business.

Also back in business were the saloons, arcades, pool halls, and other seamy establishments that benefited from the sex trade at Iwilei. Among these was a boardinghouse on Iwilei Road in which interested parties could find games of poker, craps, and the illegal lottery known as *che-fa*. Each time I passed this house I was asked by someone loitering outside whether I wished to place a wager on the *che-fa*—but even if Mr. Noh had not gambled away his salary I would hardly have been tempted to part with the few dollars I earned each week from my job, which now included the making of entire dresses or *sarongs* from patterns and fabrics provided by Iwilei women.

I also took time to make some new clothes for myself: Western-style dresses like the ones I saw being worn by *haole* and Hawaiian women on the streets, replacing the traditional bright red, blue, or orange blouses and skirts that immediately (I feared) identified me as Korean. In my first few months in Honolulu, I had been afraid to venture far outside of Iwilei lest someone might recognize me and Mr. Noh—now relegated to the province of nightmares in which I felt again the lash of his hand, and the pain of losing our child— might come and reclaim me as his wife. I even avoided shopping at a conveniently located general store in Iwilei run by a Korean named Kim Yuen Tai.

Eventually those fears abated somewhat, aided by the camouflage of my white shirtwaist dress: I might have been Chinese for all anyone here could tell. So now in my free time I began to explore my new home, while still avoiding areas like adjacent Pālama, where resided a greater concentration of Asian immigrants.

My first impression of Honolulu from aboard the *Nippon Maru* had been of a tropic backwater barely qualifying as a city. This was not, it turned out, a fair assessment. Downtown Honolulu— with its staid bank buildings, impressive government offices, and beautiful churches—could certainly lay claim to being as modern an urban center as anything I had seen in Korea or Japan. But then

I walked only a mile farther down King Street—to where it intersected with Kapi'olani Boulevard—and found myself gazing out upon acre after acre of duck ponds, rice paddies, banana groves, taro patches, and pig farms. It was almost as if I were back in Pojogae. I had never before seen a city give way to country quite so suddenly and unself-consciously, and I found it quite charming.

I would wander from Iwilei to Kapi'olani Park, from Waikīkī to Punchbowl and back again. (A streetcar cost five cents to ride, a waste of a nickel when I could just as easily get there by foot.) On these travels I made a point of stopping at every school I saw— public or private, from McKinley High School to Kawaiaha'o Girls School—to inquire about the possibility of my enrollment. But I was now nineteen years of age: far too old for primary school, lacking the requisite education for middle school, and college was out of the question. Mrs. Kim had told the truth, as far as it went, when she said that girls in Hawai'i had the opportunity to attend school. What she did not tell me—perhaps did not know—was that that opportunity was already long past for girls like myself.

But then, not all education is received in schools. One morning, on one of my walking tours of downtown Honolulu, I noticed a rather long line of people standing outside the wrought-iron gates of a palatial private home on Beretania Street. It was a white coral-block house with rows of tapered white pillars forming colonnades on split-level balconies wrapping around both upper and lower stories. It stood at a modest remove from the street, graced by greenswards and flower gardens. A lush arbor of palm and monkeypod trees shaded it from the tropic sun. I assumed on first glance that it was the home of some wealthy *haole*, to judge by the architectural style (French Colonial, I was told later).

But what were all these people doing queued up outside? The line extended from the street through the wrought-iron gates, down a long driveway, and into the home itself. These were not the sort of guests one would expect to find on the doorstep of some rich *haole*: men, women, and children of largely Hawaiian descent and obviously modest means were proudly dressed in their best Sunday apparel even though it was a weekday. Many held fragrant *leis* strung of plumeria, carnation, or jasmine blossoms; some carried bouquets of ginger, lilies, and anthuriums; others had come bearing fruits, *poi* wrapped in *tī* leaves, sweets, even the occasional live chicken. There was a festive air to the crowd, as if today were some kind of holiday, though I was relatively sure it was not.

I followed the queue halfway down the block until I came to its end, where a Hawaiian man in a dark suit was holding a toddler as his wife quieted a fidgety six-year-old. I asked him politely what he and the others were waiting for. He seemed surprised that anyone would have to ask.

"We're here for the levee," he said.

" 'Levee'? What is that?"

"The reception. To see the Queen."

I was nonplussed by this: "I did not know America had a queen."

The woman responded coolly, "We are not Americans by choice," which only confused me all the more.

Her husband, however, laughed good-naturedly. "*Hawai'i*'s queen. From before the revolution." He looked me over, amused. "You a *malihini*, eh?"

Yes, I admitted, I was a newcomer, and apologized for my ignorance. The man explained to me how Hawai'i had for centuries been a kingdom, ruled by the *ali'i*, the royalty. For most of its history each island was ruled by separate chieftains, until united by Kamehameha I more than a century ago. Then in 1892 a thousand years of autonomous rule came to an end when a cabal of greedy businessmen—aided by the collusion of the American ambassador—seized control of the government, and under the implicit threat of American military might, forced Queen Lili'uokalani to abdicate. Twenty-five years later, this "*haole* elite" of businessmen still ruled

Hawai'i, now a territory of the United States. They were known as the "Big Five" companies—sometimes called "the Invisible Government," owing to their power behind the scenes of the Republican Party that dominated Hawaiian government and politics.

All this was a revelation to me, stirring feelings I had not considered in many months. I thought of our murdered Queen Min, and of King Sunjong, deposed by the Japanese a decade later. Suddenly I saw this place where I was living, this Hawai'i, in an unexpected new light: as a country that had suffered as Korea had suffered, lost face as a people, lost sovereignty to foreign occupiers.

Of course these Hawaiians would not think of themselves as Americans—did I consider myself Japanese?

"The queen lives in this house now?" I said. "And you may come see her?"

"Yeah, sure. Used to be she gave levees all the time; not so much since she been sick. People come, pay respect, bring her *ho'okupu*—tributes. Show her she's still our *mo'i wahine,* our queen. Always will be." The depth of feeling in his voice as he said this was quite the opposite of what a Korean might show on speaking of our royal family—but it was a feeling we shared in common.

"May anyone pay their respect?" I asked. "Even a *malihini?*"

"Yeah, sure thing."

I got in line behind them and they generously shared some of their flowers, so that I might have a tribute to give the queen. I hoped I looked presentable enough to meet royalty. We stood in the hot sun for half an hour as the queue slowly made its way up the street, through the gate, and onto the grounds.

We entered the house through a light and spacious entryway, then into a dining room lushly appointed with flowers and gifts. Seated in a high-backed wooden chair was a woman in her late seventies wearing a black silk dress with a yoke collar. Her face was strong and open in a way I had come to expect from Hawaiians.

Her hair was mostly white, with a few strands of black threading through it like old memories. Flanked by attendants wearing bright yellow feather *leis*, she sat with a proud, queenly bearing, as if she were still on a throne.

Some of her visitors approached on their knees, chanting their genealogies as they entered her presence. They kissed her hand, presented their tribute, then, as I was told court etiquette demanded, backed out of the room again. A few women curtsied before her. I grew nervous as I drew closer—what should I do when I reached her? What would be appropriate for a *malihini* like me?

When the time came, I decided to emulate the deep, formal curtsy I had seen others perform. I kissed her hand, gave her my floral tribute, then stepped back and said to her, "May it please Your Majesty to know I am called Jin, and I come from Korea, the land of morning calm. We too had a queen we loved above all else, and a king who was deposed by agents of a foreign government. They reign in our hearts until the day our land, and yours, are again sovereign nations."

Lili'uokalani was frail and gray, but her warm brown eyes looked at me first with surprise, then with quick interest, and finally a gleam of approval. She smiled, and raised a thin hand in a little motion that seemed to take in everyone in the room.

"These people," she said proudly, "*are* my nation."

I curtsied again, then backed out of the room as I had seen others do.

In minutes I was back on Beretania Street, blinking in the bright morning sun; everything was the same as before I entered, but from that day forward I could never think of this adopted home of mine in the same way. Now, whenever I looked in the faces of the Hawaiian people I would meet, I would see a kinship, a shared burden. Because now I knew that Hawaiians, too, understood *han*.

On my way home, I happened to pass that certain boarding-house on Iwilei Road in which games of chance were known to be played. As I went out of my way to avoid being asked whether I wished to place a bet on the *che-fa*, I carelessly bumped into a man—not very tall, wearing a blue woolen cap and a black sailor's peacoat—who was on his way into the house.

"Oh! I'm sorry—" I began, then noticed that the man's cap was pulled down low over his forehead—but not low enough to obscure a very distinctive scar above his right eye. And peeking out from under his peacoat was what appeared to be a bullwhip coiled around his waist.

He looked up, and I found myself staring into the face of Detective Chang Apana. He recognized me too, and hushed me with a finger to his lips and a wink of his eye. Then he hurried past me and into the boardinghouse.

Well, I thought, this promised to be of no small interest. I crossed the street and lingered for a while in Kai Kee's grocery store. Minutes later a rowdy commotion erupted from the boardinghouse—shouts, curses, a loud popping sound that was not quite a gunshot—followed by a stream of gamblers spilling out the front door like a flock of chickens fleeing a henhouse, one step ahead of a wolf.

Ah, but no wolf ever presented a sight as memorable as that of Chang Apana chasing down a houseful of wrongdoers, cracking his blacksnake whip above his head as if he were herding cattle (which he once had, as a *paniolo* on the big island of Hawai'i). With calloused hands gripping the handle, he snapped the whip at a fleeing felon clad in an undershirt. The air cracked again as the whip literally exceeded the speed of sound, the stinging tip lashing the man's back, toppling him. Apana followed up with a sharp kick to the ribs, which occupied the man's attention for some time. In moments, the braided leather thong had coiled itself like a python around another felon's arm; the detective yanked on the whip, sending the man spinning like a top into the side of the house. When a third criminal tried to get past him, Apana chose a more direct approach, tackling him to the ground amid a cloud of red dust and pummeling him into submission with his bare hands.

He was going after yet a fourth man when I heard the wail of a police siren and saw two patrol cars racing down Iwilei Road. They braked to halt just a few feet from where the detective was holding his prey in what I believe is popularly known as a "half-nelson." Several patrolmen burst out of the cars, guns drawn, as well as Chief McDuffie, who took in the scene with exasperation and bellowed, "God *damn* it, Apana, how many times do I have to tell you: *Wait for the goddamned back-up to get here!*"

Apana grinned as he rounded up the unlucky gamblers and herded them like dazed cattle into the police cars. I no longer harbored any doubts about his arrest record and remembered what he'd told me that night: *Cool head main t'ing.*

After the entire gambling ring had been taken away, Detective Apana came up to me and asked, "So howzat little bastard of yours, eh?"

I laughed and told him the cat was fine. I congratulated him on his arrest.

"One thing I hate, it's gambling," he said vehemently. "My wife, she like to play the *mah-jonng*, you know? Alla time, *mah-jonng, mah-jonng*. Drive me crazy. What am I gonna do, arrest her?" He shook his head, disgusted.

"Yes," I agreed, "every week my husband used to gamble away all his—"

I stopped before I said too much, but not before catching Chang's attention. "You married, eh?"

"Widowed," I said, too quickly.

"He Korean too?"

I nodded. His eyes held me in an odd, gentle way, as if this meant something to him, then he said, "Anybody get rough with you—husband, pimp, anybody—you let me know, I take care, okay?"

"But I'm not a—"

"You just let me know, 'ey?" He gave me a paternal pat on the arm and walked away. I sighed and chose not to argue the point. Chances were that he would not have believed me, no matter how many times I assured him I was not a prostitute—even more so in light of what I would shortly be asked to do.

One afternoon in July, a madam named Mrs. Miyake—who with her husband ran a brothel in a nearby lodging house—came to May with a problem. I was sewing in the parlor when Mrs. Miyake, standing with May on our *lānai*, told her how she had recently been approached by a Korean man perhaps fifty years old who was looking for something called a *"kisaeng."*

This single word of Korean stood out sharply amid a babble of English I had only been half listening to. I put down my sewing.

When Mrs. Miyake admitted to the customer she had never heard the term before, he explained that what he was looking for was similar to a *geisha*. "Ah, yes, we have *geisha*," she affirmed, but the man insisted he did not want a Japanese girl; she had to be Korean, schooled in Korean ways.

"Jin's a civilian," I heard May tell the madam.

"May I speak with her myself?"

I could almost hear May shrug: "It's a free country."

By the time they walked in I was already on my feet and declared, "No!"

The madam said, "Jin-san, hear me out—"

"I am not *Jin-san*, and I am not a prostitute!"

"Mr. Lim does not want a prostitute," she replied. "He wants a *kisaeng*."

I knew the difference, but I was surprised that she did. "No bed work," she explained. "He has had that with a number of my ladies. What he wants is not sexual release, but elegance, sophistication, entertainment."

This was, of course, what a certain level of *kisaeng* had always been: an entertainer, or "skilled woman." Evening Rose had been of this highest grade, but that was back in the days of the royal court, and since annexation most *kisaeng* in Korea were either concubines or prostitutes.

May was wary. "This joker ain't some kind of screwball, is he? He doesn't want to dress up like the emperor while she licks *sake* off his toes?"

"No, no. None of my girls has ever had a problem with him." To me she added, "It is much the same as when Japanese men go to a teahouse to drink and flirt with *geisha,* but do not always take them home. This is all he wants."

"But I am not even pretty enough to be a *kisaeng*," I objected.

"Under all that makeup, who will know? The important thing is, can you serve wine without spilling it?"

"Yes, but—"

"Do you know any Korean songs?"

I knew some taught me by Evening Rose, but I lied and said, "Just folk songs," not wishing to give her more reason to pursue this silly notion.

"Then you are the closest thing there is to a *kisaeng* in Hawai'i," Mrs. Miyake said. "And since this man has been away from Korea for fifteen years, he will scarcely notice the difference."

May noted judiciously, "Talking takes longer than doing. I usually charge double when there's no nookie."

"He is willing to pay a higher rate."

I glared at May. "Please do not help!"

"Honey, trust me, you need an agent." She turned back to Mrs. Miyake. "Two bucks for the first hour, time and a half after that."

"I am sure that can be arranged."

Had I heard this correctly? "Two . . . *dollars?*"

May asked the madam, "What kind of split did you have in mind?"

"Three ways. You and I and Jin."

May shook her head. "Two ways, me and Jin. I take ten percent off the top, the rest goes to her."

Mrs. Miyake said in exasperation, "And how do *I* profit from this?"

"By keeping a good customer happy, so he'll keep coming back to your gals when he *wants* nookie."

The madam sighed heavily. "All right, but I have to charge you for the room. And for incidentals—makeup, clothing, wine . . ."

May nodded. "Fair enough."

Both women now turned to me.

"What do you say, hon?" May asked. "Two bucks for pouring a little tea and singing a song. Not bad for a night's work, and a pretty good start on that steamship ticket for your sister-in-law."

I found this all quite absurd. To be a *kisaeng* was, in my mind, to be Evening Rose: elegant, poised, beautiful. I was none of these things, hence I could not be a *kisaeng*. But still . . . two dollars *was* a great deal of money. And for Blossom, I would do almost anything.

I found myself asking, "Is he . . . he's not from Waialua, is he?"

"No, he's lived here in Honolulu for quite some time."

I considered this a moment, then said firmly, "I will not touch him in any way."

"Absolutely not," Mrs. Miyake agreed.

It was absurd, but it was done.

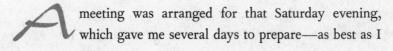 meeting was arranged for that Saturday evening, which gave me several days to prepare—as best as I

was capable of preparing. Using May's battered old teapot I practiced pouring tea in the ritualized but graceful manner I had seen Evening Rose do so. I also practiced pouring wine into wine bowls and then handing them to a (nonexistent) man. As for my musical performance, I knew that while urban *kisaeng* like Evening Rose often recited sophisticated *p'ansori*, those from rural regions merely performed local folk songs, so in the mornings I practiced a few that I remembered from my childhood. I soon learned that Westerners found Korean songs to be somewhat discordant, as my efforts brought May loping out of her bedroom to complain, "Jesus H. Christ! Do you call that yowling *singing* or is Little Bastard getting laid again?"

"Do I complain," I asked sweetly, "of the music made in *your* bed?"

May muttered a vulgarity and withdrew back into her bedroom. I gathered I had won the argument.

I made certain the room Mrs. Miyake was providing in her lodging house was appropriately decorated with folding screens, mats, serving table, a porcelain tea set, and a pair of wine bowls. I attended to my wardrobe myself. Because *kisaeng* wore only the lushest fabrics and most brilliant colors, I selected my brightest Korean dress—of red and blue silk and ramie—to wear that evening.

As the day drew nearer, however, I grew increasingly anxious that this man would laugh me out of the room before I'd even had a chance to open my mouth. How could anyone mistake such a homely country girl for an elegant *kisaeng?*

On Saturday afternoon one of Mrs. Miyake's girls, Shizu—who had some training in hair styling—washed and rolled my hair, pinned it up in a semi-pompadour, then decorated it with lovely porcelain combs. All the while she chattered about men she had known and men she wished to know—"You see this new movie man, Douglas Fairbank? Ooh, he one sexy *haole*"—

punctuating her conversation with a sweet infectious laugh. Shizu was happy with the end result, and I was impressed as well—not just by the elegant upsweep of my hair but by Shizu's amiable presence. For the first time I did not feel wary or hostile toward a Japanese person, and at the end I bowed to her and said, *"Kansha suru"*—Japanese for "thank you," words I certainly had had no occasion to utter in Korea.

I walked carefully back to May's, terrified to do anything that might injure the delicately assembled hair piled high on my head. Once home I sat down at May's vanity as she helped me apply my makeup. I was afraid to look into the mirror, afraid I would see how ridiculous I looked and call off the entire charade. I had already scrubbed my face with astringent and moisturized it with cold cream; now, as I had seen my teacher do so often, I applied a coating of white pancake as a foundation, dabbing it on evenly with a sponge, followed by a layer of white powder, which I brushed smooth so that my skin shone like a china doll's. May then tortured me by plucking my already-sparse eyebrows with tweezers and reshaping them with a black brow pencil, giving them a more graceful arch.

She followed this with what she called "the latest thing from the mainland," something called "mascara," which involved the fiendish application of hot wax to the tips of my eyelashes. "Oh, stop pissing and moaning," May chided. "Didn't your mama ever tell you that beauty *hurts* like a sonofabitch?" Indeed she had not. Thankfully the application of black kohl powder to accentuate my eyes was painless. Then there was the matter of my mouth, and heaven knows there was no shortage of bright red lipstick in May's cosmetic case. She traced what she called a "Cupid's bow" on my lips.

When we were finished, I stared in wonder at the girl who looked back at me from the mirror. With her white porcelain skin, ruby lips, and kohl-rimmed eyes, I would have thought I was looking at one of the women from the little pleasure house in Taegu. But then I blinked, and raised a hand to my mouth, and the woman in the mirror did the same. I smiled in unexpected pleasure; she smiled back. I felt as if I were a puppeteer manipulating a marionette, my thoughts the strings that animated it to do my bidding. But *I* was the marionette, as well as the puppeteer, and it was quite a wonderful feeling! For the first time in my life I truly felt *pretty*. I could have cried tears of delight but for the fear I would destroy my carefully applied kohl and mascara.

I donned my blue and red dress and walked the short distance to Mrs. Miyake's boardinghouse. Along the way my dramatic appearance elicited a number of startled and admiring stares from male visitors to Iwilei, and this time, I must admit, I found the attention flattering. At Mrs. Miyake's I was told my "client" was waiting and I was handed a tray bearing a carafe of rice wine and a small bowl. I carried the tray down the hall to the room, opened the door with one hand while balancing the tray with the other, then entered.

The man was sitting on a mat in front of the low tea table, and as I entered he looked up and smiled at me. It took all my experience as a Korean woman, trained not to betray her emotions to a man, to hide my recognition—and my shock.

It was Mr. Lim, who had been at the immigration station the day I was cleared to enter Hawai'i. The same Mr. Lim who had been engaged to marry Sunny, and who left the docks empty-handed when she balked and fled back to Korea.

Aigo, I thought as I lowered the tray onto the table. My hands trembled a bit as I transferred the wine from the tray to the table. When I was done, I stood up straight and bowed in greeting. "My name is Gem, and I am honored to be meeting you," I said in Korean, struggling to keep the nervousness from my tone.

He bowed in return. "I am Third Son, of the Lim clan of Youngnam." His eyes met mine, intently, and I forced myself to meet his gaze directly, as any good *kisaeng* would. But my skin was cold and clammy beneath my powdered face. Did he remember me? Did he recognize me as the bride of Mr. Noh?

But he just smiled and said quietly, "You are very beautiful."

I smiled in relief. "Thank you. You are very handsome."

This was not quite the case, but neither was he as bad-looking as Sunny had seemed to think. He was in his early fifties, I judged, his complexion far from fair, his skin leathered by years in the sun. Beneath his deep tan he bore the pocked scars of smallpox, like freckles that had deepened and pitted his face. His hair, it was true, was thinning and gray. But his smile seemed to reflect genuine pleasure at being here with me; and as I had never had a man express any pleasure at being in my presence before, I was disposed to think favorably of Mr. Lim.

I spoke the dialogue I had rehearsed many times over the past several days. "Would you care for some wine?"

"Perhaps a little."

I filled his bowl to the rim. "A half-cup of wine brings tears," I said, quoting an old proverb, "a full cup brings laughter." This had nothing to do with getting tipsy, as you might think, but with the generosity extended to a guest.

Mr. Lim seemed delighted by my erudition. "Indeed so. Thank you."

He took a sip of the wine, his eyes never leaving me. I was hardly accustomed to such attention from a man and was a little flustered, though I tried not to show it. "And how long has Third Son of the Lim clan been in Hawai'i?"

"Too long, alas. I came here fourteen years ago, dreaming of riches. I was told Hawai'i was a golden mountain just waiting to be scaled. I found only a mound of red clay to be shaken off my boots." I laughed appreciatively at his wordplay. "And how long have you been a *kisaeng?*"

I replied, not entirely dishonestly, "I began my studies three years ago, with one of the most refined and sought-after *kisaengs* in the city of Taegu."

He nodded, impressed. "Your own refinement does her proud."

Suddenly I was blinking back tears from my kohl-rimmed eyes.

"Did I say something wrong?" he asked quickly.

"No, no, not at all. Pay it no mind."

"But something *is* wrong, I can see it. How have I offended you?"

In order to allay his fears, I admitted that the woman I had studied with in Taegu was arrested by the Japanese last year.

"Oh—I am so sorry," he said.

"I'm sure she is all right," I lied.

He asked me what things were like back in Korea: Had the Japanese truly committed all the depredations he had heard about? I reluctantly confirmed that they had, and told him some of what I had seen. He asked me about Taegu, and I did my best to describe it from my last visit. He drank it all in like a man thirsty for home, parched for the sights and sounds of his native land.

I brought in some sweet rice cakes Mrs. Miyake had gotten from Kim Yuen Tai's store. Mr. Lim could easily have purchased them himself, and in truth they were a little dry and lacking in flavor; but they were apparently made far more delicious being served by a *kisaeng* and he expressed delight with them. Afterward, I sang him a song I remembered from flower picnics when I was a girl:

> *My fresh fragrant lily,*
> *In deep valley blooming alone.*
> *And oh! Lovely girls of sweet sixteen*
> *Are blooming in their rooms unseen.*

Mr. Lim clapped when I was finished, and it was clear to me now why he had requested a *kisaeng*. All he wanted, really, was to look at the painted face of a smiling Korean girl, to listen to her musical laugh, and to be reminded of the places of his youth. When I asked him if he ever considered returning to Korea, even for a visit, his eyes dimmed and he admitted that he could not afford such a trip. "I had saved enough money for a ticket, but I . . . invested it poorly."

Yes—invested in bringing a picture bride to Hawai'i, who then turned around and left, leaving him with no money and no bride. My heart cried for him. When I looked at him I could not see the old pockmarked laborer who sent Sunny running for home: I saw only a sweet man too poor to reclaim his past, and too old and hurt to believe in the dream of a future.

I thought of how I might console him, of how much he needed consolation . . . as, for that matter, did I. And had I been somewhere else—had I not been wearing this makeup—I might well have given him such consolation. But then, had I not been here pretending, would I ever have set eyes on him again? Would he ever have opened himself up to me as he had tonight?

I ached to take him to my bed . . . but as fondly as I felt toward him, I could not. As much as I admired and loved Evening Rose, I could not be her . . . could not become what she had become.

So at the end of the evening I simply stood, bowed, and thanked him for his company. "It is I who must thank you," he said, bowing deeply in return. "I have not enjoyed an evening more in fourteen years."

My heart longed to betray me, but I turned on my heel and left the room.

On my way out Mrs. Miyake gave me the cash I was due: two dollars, less fifty cents for room rent, wine, and rice cakes. I accepted the money, then gave it all to May when I got home, asking none in return. I sat down at May's vanity to remove my makeup, taking one last look at the girl in the mirror—the pretty, powdered face of a woman whom a man had actually desired, and who, much to her own surprise, had perhaps too much self-respect to do anything about it.

The girl in the mirror smiled at me, and I smiled back.

*I*n the days that followed, the more I thought about Mr. Lim, the more annoyed I became at Sunny for having abandoning him. I knew I could not put off writing my clan any longer, so I sat down and wrote another carefully composed letter to my brother, one that provided some details of my life in Honolulu, while withholding others. Fortunately, since it was Korean custom for a woman to retain her family name, I did not have to worry about what to use in my return address: it was, as ever, "Pak." I spoke of my move here in the most general of terms—"There is more money to be made in the city than on the plantation"—with no mention made of my husband, but nothing that would preclude his presence here, either. I told them of my sewing work, but not the profession of most of my customers. And I filled out the rest with descriptions of the islands' great natural beauty, and of how, more truthfully, I missed my family and wished they could be here with me.

But in addition to this letter, I composed a second one, to Sunny. I began by inquiring after her health and conveying my best wishes to her parents, then told her some of the same selectively edited stories of my life here:

> It is too bad that you did not give Hawai'i more of a chance, for it is, in many ways, the beautiful land of which Mrs. Kim first told us. It may not be true that the roads are paved in gold, but women have much freedom in this country . . . even as all Koreans here live free from Japanese persecution.
>
> I recently encountered, quite by accident, your former fiancé, Mr. Lim . . . and with all respect I believe you did not give him enough of a chance, either. He is a good man and a kind one,

and would have made you a fine husband. Might you reconsider
your decision not to marry him? He may not be handsome, but
I have learned that a pleasing face can cloak a most unhand-
some temperament; and by the same token, a homely face can
hide a handsome heart.

This was the closest I dared come to alluding to my own failed marriage. I held no great hope that Sunny would change her mind, but I felt I owed it to Mr. Lim to at least try. Within two months' time, I received a cordial reply from Joyful Day, who if he suspected anything odd about my circumstances had the grace not to inquire. But I never received a reply from Sunny. I knew she could read and write *hangul* because I had taught her to do so, in preparation for the literacy test of which Mrs. Kim had warned us. Perhaps she was embarrassed by her reneging on her marriage to Mr. Lim; perhaps I should not have broached the matter and subjected her to such embarrassment. Whatever the reason, I never heard from her . . . and soon had other worries on my mind.

First, there had been the race riots in January. Then at the end of May, a newly arrived prostitute was shot to death in an Iwilei cottage by an estranged lover who had followed her from San Francisco. She did not live far from us, and I heard the three shots her paramour fired into her, as well as the fourth shot that ended his own life.

If "respectable" Honolulu citizens were questioning how safe a place Iwilei had become, I was beginning to wonder the same thing.

The earliest omens of our dispossession appeared that fall, though few in Iwilei took the signs seriously at first. In recent months there had been increased agitation against the district, including a self-appointed public "vice commission" intent on closing the stockade. At the end of October, this commission began threatening legal action against Iwilei landlords unless they ordered their tenants to vacate by November 1. Many landlords, fearing publicity or jail, reluctantly complied; but one, a Chinese businessman named Y. Ahin, publicly vowed to fight any attempt to evict his tenants.

Within a matter of days, a warrant was issued for Ahin's arrest on charges of keeping a "disorderly house."

May, however, was untroubled. She assured me this was all so much bluster, and would "blow over" in a few weeks, "once the blue-nosed old ladies in the Mānoa Valley are done beating their drums."

Mrs. Miyake told me much the same thing. "Every six or seven years, in a great show of decency, someone in government decides to break up the stockade," she said, citing closures in 1901, 1908, and 1913. "But we always open again. Why? Jin-san, do you *know* how many soldiers are stationed on this island?"

But then Mrs. Miyake's husband, returning from a trip to Japan, was suddenly prevented by immigration authorities from returning to Honolulu. He was held at Quarantine Island as the authorities debated whether or not to deport him—and his wife—back to Japan. This was enough to convince many of the Japanese prostitutes to vacate Iwilei out of fear they, too, might be deported.

When one landlord's representative came and told us we could remain, "providing your cottages are not used for immoral purposes," May laughed out loud and asked, "So what do we do, teach Sunday school? And how do we pay the rent? Or is that on the house?" The landlord, it seemed, was not *that* interested in promoting morality.

More reassuring was Chief McDuffie who, on his regular visit to receive the women's health certificates, told them that Iwilei would not be closed "by any damn reformers." Presumably the police department was not prepared to lose the kickbacks that paid for the blind eye cast toward Iwilei.

A few days later, on November 3, it was announced that a territorial grand jury would be formed to investigate whether Ilwilei should be continued as is, modified in some way, or shut down completely. This occurred even as Mrs. Miyake was arrested on charges of conducting a disorderly house.

Most of the remaining Japanese girls quickly decamped for other quarters. That night all of the houses on the 'ewa, or eastern, side of Iwilei Road were shuttered and dark. But those on the Waikīkī side were as garishly lit and loudly raucous as always, with the popular song of the moment—"I'm Down in Honolulu Looking Them Over"—blaring from a dozen different gramophones:

> *I'm down in Honolulu looking them over*
> *I'm down in Honolulu living in clover*
> *Try and guess the way they dress*
> *No matter what you think it is, it's less . . .*

The following Tuesday, at two-thirty in the afternoon, the fifteen public-spirited men of the grand jury visited the district whose fate they were to decide. They sniffed around like cats, intensely interested in the smell while making it clear they were haughtily above such things.

Soon adding their voice to the debate were twenty-one manufacturing, transportation, and other legitimate businesses based in Iwilei, who requested of the city attorney that the stockade be shut down because their officers, employees, and business guests have to "pass over the same road that is used by prostitutes, pimps, runners, and other hangers-on of the vice industry . . . in close proximity to factories where large numbers of women and girls are employed."

When I read this on the front page of the *Honolulu Star-Bulletin*, I began to wonder whether the closure of Iwilei was less a matter of morality than of commerce.

But I believe Iwilei's fate was truly sealed upon news of the arrest of two local boys, both fourteen years old, who had been running errands for what the papers called "the painted women" of Iwilei. Since prostitutes were legally restricted in the places they could go in Honolulu, they sometimes sent enterprising young boys off to purchase groceries (and perhaps other, not so innocuous items like liquor) for them. Alas, this would not win us any friends on the grand jury.

That night, on my way home from visiting the Kahahawais, a man fell into step with me—a man wearing a wool cap and a sailor's peacoat. Before I had a chance to greet him, Chang Apana asked, "You start looking new place to live?"

"Not yet," I admitted.

"Try find. Iwilei *pau*."

"People say it's been finished before. And Chief McDuffie told us—"

"Ah, McDuffie got head up ass," he said disgustedly. "Not up to him anymore. Federal case now." Before I could inquire what this meant, he added soberly, "Make quick an' get out, or you stay Iwilei, all right—in O'ahu Jail."

Having delivered this stern fatherly warning, he melted into the crowd of soldiers and sailors still thronging Iwilei Road. I didn't know why Chang had taken such a benevolent interest in me, but I took his words seriously. I went home and, after May's last client left at two A.M., related to her what the detective had told me. When I mentioned his saying this was a "Federal case," her eyebrows shot up and the skepticism in her face drained away.

"What does this mean, 'Federal'?" I asked innocently.

"It means we start packing tomorrow," she said, and went to bed.

A little after three A.M. we were awakened by the roar of automobiles into the stockade, followed by the bangs and crashes of doors being kicked in and the sounds of shouting and fighting. May and I ran outside, fully prepared to find police storming our *lānai*, but the officers—including one identifying himself as a United States marshal—seemed to be targeting only a few houses, out of which they soon dragged, ungently, a baker's dozen of men, all of them procurers. The only women being arrested—for now—were those living with the pimps.

"Apana's right," May said soberly as she watched the men being forced into patrol cars. "Iwilei is *pau*."

This all occurred early on Monday morning. Monday night, Iwilei was dark: the few women who remained sat behind locked doors and drawn shades, the muffled sound of phonographs from within a tinny echo of Iwilei's former brass. By Wednesday the grand jury had returned indictments against one hundred and fifteen women at Iwilei on charges of "commercial prostitution." Bench warrants were issued. Miraculously, May's name was not on the long list of women who would have to surrender and face a hearing in Judge Ashford's courtroom at ten o'clock on Friday morning.

By this time, of course, we were long gone, having packed up our belongings—including a rather truculent Little Bastard—and secured rooms at a small, out-of-the-way hotel off Richards Street.

On Friday morning, in Judge Ashford's court, all but seven of the stockade's women pled guilty and received suspended sentences—with the judge warning that should they be arrested again within the next thirteen months, they would not be so fortunate. Virtually as one they all headed for the steamship offices, most of them to purchase tickets to "the Coast"—San Francisco or Los Angeles.

May surprised me by joining the exodus, booking passage aboard the SS *Sonoma,* bound for someplace called Apia, in Western Samoa.

"Ah, I've had it up to here with all this so-called 'civilization,'" she told me as she packed her bags. "Gimme a little grass shack in

Samoa, least till all this blows over. There's a gal in Apia who'll front me for a job as a barmaid. I'll set up shop there for a while. Maybe once things've cooled off here, I'll come back."

"I will be sorry to see you go," I told her.

"Yeah," she said, "it's tough shit, ain't it, kid?"

May was quite the sentimentalist.

"But listen, hon—they won't let me bring Little Bastard into the country. Think you could keep an eye on him till I get back?"

I quailed at the thought, but smiled blandly. "Of course. But how will you find me when you return?"

"You'll stay in touch with Esther and Joe, right? I can always ask them. Don't worry, it's a small island. I'll find you."

She peeled off a handful of bills from a thick wad she kept in her purse. "Here, this'll pay for the little guy's upkeep, and help get you set up in a place of your own. You can keep the sewing machine, too."

"Thank you. That's very kind."

May picked up the cat, bounced him in her arms, and told him, "Okay, pal, I'll be gone awhile, but Jin's gonna take good care of you till I get back. Treat her like you would me, and don't give her any trouble, okay?"

He let out a small *Nyep*, which I took to mean, "I make no guarantees."

May deliberated endlessly about what to take with her, finally deciding on two suitcases of clothes, her gramophone, her ukulele, and several bottles of gin. She fretted even longer over what to wear onto the ship, finally settling on a white dress, white hat, white stockings, and white kid leather boots. We were very late getting to the docks, but May wasn't worried the ship would leave without her: "I know the purser. They'll wait." In fact they did. She hurried up the gangway with her gramophone, its morning-glory horn tucked under her arm like some rare and enormous bloom, and onto the deck of the *Sonoma*. She waved a farewell to me, winked at a ship's officer, and vanished like a pale shadow onto the ship. It lifted anchor at seven P.M., a dockside band sending it off to the tune of "I'm Down in Honolulu Looking Them Over."

I went back to the hotel and found Little Bastard sitting on the bed on his hind legs, howling as if he knew he had lost his best friend. Taking my life in my hands, I sat down beside him and stroked his head, but he did not bite or claw me; he even curled up in my lap and nuzzled his head against my hand, which I considered an outright miracle.

Then, after ten seconds of amity between us, he emitted an irritable little *Nyep*, bit me on the hand, and jumped out of my lap.

Neither of us, it seemed, expected to see May again anytime soon.

Eight

In nearly a year of thrifty living at Iwilei I was proud to have saved about thirty dollars, the bulk of which I was determined to set aside for Blossom's steamer fare. Now I began searching for a furnished room, but soon discovered that the better rooms rented for at least seven to ten dollars a week. At that rate I could see my savings quickly evaporating, especially if I was unable to secure employment right away. Even a room at the YWCA cost a dollar and twenty-five cents a day. More than one landlord suggested, "Try look Pālama or Chinatown, rents more cheap," so I quelled my fears of being found out as a runaway wife and began exploring those neighborhoods that stretched from King Street to School Street, and from Nu'uanu Avenue to Liliha Street.

Here, crowded within less than one-quarter of a square mile, were thousands of Chinese, Japanese, Hawaiians, Portuguese, Koreans, Puerto Ricans, and Filipinos, living in a patchwork of racially mixed neighborhoods. Some of these neighborhoods took their names from the native Hawaiian language: Pālama, 'A'ala, Kamakela, Kauluwela. Some borrowed plantation terms: Tanaka Camp, Nishikiya Camp. Others were more colloquial: Tin Can Alley, Hell's Half Acre, Corkscrew Lane, Mosquito Flats, Blood Alley. I started in Pālama and worked my way *mauka*—toward the mountains—past fish markets, hardware stores, grocers, Chinese herbalists, and more, all reminding me of the marketplace in Taegu.

But I was not prepared for the sight of ramshackle tenements sprawling across entire blocks, their walls often rough and unpainted, as though still awaiting finishing years after they were built. Most looked more like long wooden sheds than apartment buildings— identical rows of them facing each other, like images in the same sad mirror. Some were single-storied, while others teetered on stilts—flimsy matchboxes stacked one atop the other. And these were luxurious accommodations compared to the tar-paper shacks that squatted amongst them, trade winds wailing through cracks in their cardboard walls.

I was frankly horrified at the thought of living here, but I worked up my nerve and entered one of the tenements in search of a manager—who told me there were no vacancies, but directed me down the street to another building, this one no more commodious than the last. It was actually two buildings built side by side, each two stories tall, connected by a sinew of stairways and clotheslines from which were strung freshly laundered shirts, trousers, dresses, and underwear. On the walls outside each room, pots and pans hung from hooks and crude shelving held brown water jugs, iron teapots, and other utensils of daily life. Most of the residents appeared to be either Hawaiian or Chinese. Children played in the muddy midway between buildings; men sat on stools or benches outside their rooms, smoking and playing cards. A dog was curled up nearby and when it saw me it got up, barked once, then, having fulfilled its obligations, returned to its rest.

The manager, Mr. Leung, showed me to a vacant room on the second floor as the *keiki* laughed and chased each other up and down the creaking wooden stairs. "This one nice unit," Mr. Leung told me as he opened the lockless door. I stepped inside and tried not to show my dismay: it was tiny and narrow, like a shoebox with a window. Its only furnishings were a dining table with two chairs, a moldy old throw rug, and a bed draped with what appeared to be a horse blanket. On the far wall there was a single cupboard, but neither sink nor stove. A dry stratum of dust coated all of it.

"And where is the kitchen?" I asked.

"Out here—off verandah." Mr. Leung led me down the long balcony to a communal kitchen, its rusty, coal-burning stove smeared with a thick scum of grease. Even worse were the shared bath and toilet facilities, of which I will not speak further. (Suffice it to say that rather than immerse myself in the scabrous old tub, I would wash my face at the sink and took to using, once or twice a week, the facilities of a local Japanese public bath, which was kept much cleaner than this. A shower cost only ten cents, and once a month, for a quarter, I would treat myself to a hot bath—complete with bar of soap, towel, and a washcloth.)

The room rented for nine dollars a month. It wasn't worth even that, but I signed a lease and moved in. Little Bastard walked the length of the room, surveying it with what seemed a contemptuous sneer. I couldn't say I blamed him. I did my best to make the place livable, washing, dusting, and scrubbing everything twice over, but I could not work miracles, for which the cat never forgave me.

To be sure, these unsightly tenements were a thorn in the eye, and amazingly they stood barely a mile from stately homes on the slopes of Punchbowl Hill. I was told these slums had their beginnings in the wake of a fire that destroyed the greater part of Chinatown in 1900. Shanties and shacks sprang up beside government-built temporary housing for the displaced, but eventually that temporary housing became the very permanent slums of Kauluwela.

Now that I was situated, however grimly, I turned to the matter of employment. Esther Kahahawai suggested I apply at the Hawaiian Pineapple Company in Iwilei. Although the cannery was nearing the end of that year's "ratoon" harvest, they apparently needed a few extra workers and hired me as a "white cap"—after the white headcaps we all had to wear over our hair—and put me to work in the trimming and packing room. "Brown caps" were women who relieved white caps who had to go to the bathroom or couldn't keep up with production, and "blue caps" were the strict forewomen who oversaw the department. As on the plantation, I was issued my own *bango* and identification number, as well as a white gown and a pair of rubber gloves.

At the heart of each production line, in a room separated from us by a dust-proof partition, was an elaborate mechanism called a Ginaca machine—a massive collection of gears, chains, turrets, and rotating knives which, when operating, looked like the machinery of Hell itself. Pineapples were pushed by a "feed chain" into the maw of a rotating "sizing" knife that removed the outer skin of the fruit with surgical precision, leaving behind a cylinder of pineapple. While a mechanism quaintly called an eradicator squeezed the juice from the discarded skin, another guided the fruit cylinders into something resembling the six-barreled chamber of a revolver. A tube then removed the core of the cylinder, which was eventually cut into doughnut-shaped slices to be canned at the rate of fifty pineapples a minute.

My job was to inspect the cylinders for quality as they rolled past me on a conveyor belt, grabbing them with my thumb in the core hole, and trimming away with a knife any rough edges or blemishes. This may sound relatively easy, but I assure you, having fifty pineapples a minute lobbed at you like mortar shells can be more than a little intimidating. I was dismayed and embarrassed when a brown cap had to step in and catch some of the blemishes and pineapple "eyes," which I had failed to trim as they rolled past me. And I was told by fellow workers that I had only three days to master the task or I would be let go.

Have I mentioned that all this took place against a background of the most ungodly noise I had ever heard? The Ginaca machines produced such a hideous clamor—together with the clatter of tin cans as they rattled along the conveyor belt—that workers and forewomen often had to communicate through a series of hand signals: "stop work," "come here," "hurry up," and so forth. The trimming room was also hot and muggy, and I quickly tired of the sickly sweet, ever-present smell of pineapple. By the end of each day my wrists throbbed, and sometimes my arms would even go numb up to the elbows. But the worst part was the acid burns I would get on my fingers from the pineapple juice, which managed to penetrate even the gloves I wore.

I was distracted and nervous at first, but as my reflexes and facility with the knife improved over the next several days, I soon fell into step with production. Most of the women on the line were also Asian and the room was filled with gossip and chatter in English, Japanese, Chinese, even Korean. They asked me where I was from, when I arrived in Hawai'i, and I answered truthfully, up to a point; then, when I reached that point, I claimed to be a widow, forced to move to Honolulu to seek work.

I was cordial with these women but did not encourage friendships outside of work. I was too wary of someone putting the lie to my story. I was far lonelier than when I had been living with May in the stockade.

And I was poorer as well: the job paid only fifty-nine cents a day, or about fifteen dollars a month. After rent, that left me with all of six dollars a month for other living expenses. Fortunately, rice sold for less than ten cents a pound, and I was able to subsist on that and canned salmon (fifteen cents each), sardines (a nickel a tin), and *kimchi* (the ingredients for which cost mere pennies apiece). But this left me with almost nothing left over at the end of the month. Clearly, I was not going to be adding much to Blossom's steamer fare while working at Hawaiian Pineapple.

I wrote my brother with my new address—heaven knows what he thought of all these moves, but if he suspected anything was amiss he did not embarrass me by inquiring about it. In my loneliness I became rather voluble, and found myself telling him:

> *Work is hard, of course, as it is everywhere . . . but at least here a woman can work if she so desires. She can walk the streets without a veil, can go anywhere she wishes to go, without an escort or having to ask permission from a man. She is not condemned to live her life within the same three rooms. She is not a prisoner of tradition. It is a freedom I cannot ever imagine myself giving up.*

I had never articulated this thought before, even to myself, but it was true: Now that I was here, now that I knew what it felt like to be truly free, I realized I could never go back to wearing the shackles of Confucian dictates.

I was grateful for the companionship of the Kahahawais, and often visited them after work. Joey was growing taller by the day, and the boy who had stumbled gathering *kiawe* beans was developing prowess as an athlete. I spent several afternoons on the athletic field at Kauluwela Grammar School, watching him play a game of softball on a team that included his schoolmates Henry Chang, "Mack" Takai, Benny Akahuelo, and Horace "Shorty" Ida—the

"Kauluwela Boys," as they liked to call themselves. The first time I saw a player wielding a bat, I did wonder about this supposed boys' game that appeared to be played with laundry implements, but I was proud of Joey as he swatted the ball over the fence and onto the grounds of the Japanese hospital next door, necessitating someone to chase it down as Joey ran the bases.

I had been working at the cannery perhaps a month when—as I entered the main building one morning along with hundreds of other workers on my shift—I first noticed a man staring at me from across the building's lobby. Like me, he was part of the work force crowding inside: he wore denim overalls over a *palaka* shirt, with a dungaree hat tilted back on his head, and his face beneath the brim of the hat was recognizably Korean.

I felt a stab of panic and quickly looked away, wondering whether he might be someone who had worked at Waialua Plantation and was now trying to place my face. When I dared to glance back in his direction, his figure was lost amid dozens of other men going to work, and I exhaled in relief.

A few days later, as the steam whistle signaled the end of my shift, I was disturbed to notice the same man looking at me from a closer vantage point as we left the cannery. I didn't know how long he had been gazing at me, but I was growing more certain that he recognized me. Could I have stood in line behind him at the paymaster's office at Waialua? Or passed him while shopping at Mr. Fujioka's store? Worse—could he have been one of Mr. Noh's gambling acquaintances, who now wondered what his friend's wife was doing working here?

I hurried out of the building, doing my best to melt into a mass of female white caps making their way up Iwilei Road. I didn't look back until I reached King Street, and when I did, the Korean man was thankfully nowhere to be seen.

I was terrified to go into work the next day. I even considered quitting my job before I was exposed, then chided myself for my timidity—and for what were, as yet, baseless fears—and forced myself to go back to the cannery.

That afternoon, I glanced up to see the man standing only about twenty feet away from me, at the far end of the trimming line.

I let out a startled gasp, which he could scarcely have heard over the din of the Ginaca machines. He seemed to be trying to get my attention with hand signals, as the foreladies did to make themselves "heard" above the clamor, but these were hand signals I had never learned and did not recognize. He pointed first to me, then to himself; made a kind of ladling motion with his hand; and motioned toward the exit. At a complete loss to understand him, I told one of the brown caps I needed to go to the bathroom and, working up my courage, went up to the man and asked in Korean, "I don't know that signal, what does it mean?"

He smiled and said, "It means, 'Will you have lunch with me tomorrow?'"

I was so surprised and relieved that I just laughed and told him, "Yes, certainly."

He smiled again, said he would come by tomorrow at lunch time, then bowed and left the trimming room. Not only had I not been exposed, I now had, as May had sometimes called it, a "date."

I was of two minds about this, of course. I feared getting to know anyone who might uncover my secret, but at the same time I was gladdened that a man, any man, had noticed me in this way. The next day he showed up at the trimming room in his checkered shirt and dungaree hat. It may sound odd, but even though his face had for days been so prominent in my thoughts and fears, it wasn't until today that I really considered what he looked like. He was not unhandsome, with cheerful eyes that brightened his long, typically stoic Korean face, but he was much older than I. It turned out he was thirty-eight, hardly a doddering ancient—but to a girl of twenty, all I could think of just then was that he was nearly twice my age.

He bowed and formally introduced himself as Jae-sun of the Choi clan of Pusan. His given name translates into English as "prosperity and goodness," but as that is somewhat awkward, I shall refer to him hereafter by his Korean name. (The vowel *ae* sounds like the English *a* in "bat," and "sun" is pronounced somewhere between "sun" and "soon.")

I introduced myself as Jin of the Pak clan of Pojogae. "Ah," he said with a small smile, "and a gem you are, amidst all these diamonds!"

This was a reference to the diamond-shaped segment on the pineapple's skin, and it seemed amusing at the time. I laughed. And I had to admit, I was enjoying the opportunity to speak again in my native tongue.

Instead of taking me to the company cafeteria, Jae-sun picked up a large basket and a mat, and led me outside to a grassy spot near where the newly harvested pineapples were warehoused. He laid down the mat on the grass. "I beg your indulgence," he said humbly, "as it is a poor table I set before you."

The table was anything but poor. Out of this magic basket he produced a miraculous array of foods: spicy-hot eggplant *kimchi;* sesame balls filled with sweet red-bean paste and raisins; and *naeng-myeon,* cold noodles with vegetables.

"This is delicious," I said between bites. "Where did you get it?"

"You are too generous. I made it myself, for better or worse."

I had never met a Korean man who could cook, much less admit to having done so. "For better, I think. You are an excellent cook."

"Being a bachelor, I am a cook out of necessity. But I do enjoy it. I used to watch my mother preparing dumplings and fire beef, and asked her to teach me how, but she told me the kitchen was not the proper realm for boys."

"In Korea, perhaps. But here you could be a chef at a restaurant."

"I have dreamed of such a thing," he admitted, "but my English is not sufficient to the task of running such a business. And most of what I know to cook is Korean—there are no such restaurants in Honolulu."

"There are many Japanese restaurants; you might get a job at one of them."

His cheerful eyes suddenly hardened. "No," he said sharply. "I will not work for the Wai barbarians who have stolen our country from us."

Startled but not shocked by his vehemence, I changed the subject and asked how long he had been working at the cannery and what it was he did. He told me he worked in the facility that ground up the pineapple shells into bran for use as cattle feed, loading twenty-pound bags of pineapple bran onto conveyor belts. He had been here for four years, having worked at Waimānalo Plantation for eight years previous to that. He was a widower, he said, though he did not elaborate.

"We are both widowed, but only one of us may marry again," I said. Widows in Korea were prohibited from remarriage; I brought this up to discourage his interest in one who was, unbeknownst to him, still a married woman.

But he just laughed at that. "In Korea it would not be seemly for a man to cook in his home—and yet are you not even now eating my *kimchi* and noodles?"

I had to smile and concede the point. I was impressed. Was he truly so liberal a thinker that he would sanction a woman to marry for a second time? Or was he merely pretending to be enlightened, as my husband had appeared at first?

I enjoyed our lunch, and the next day, when Jae-sun asked me out to dinner that weekend, I found myself accepting. We ate at Hop Hing Lun's restaurant on 'A'ala Street, where I told him about my family in Korea and even about my desire for an education, which did not appear to alarm him. I did not volunteer any details of my marriage and he did not ask for them. By this time the difference in our ages no longer seemed so important, but I wondered whether it was cruel and futile to encourage his attentions when I was still legally married to Mr. Noh.

It was on a Wednesday evening in mid-January, as I pondered this question while sewing, when I heard a knock on my door. I assumed it must be either my landlord, Mr. Leung, or one of my neighbors—but when I opened the door I was staggered to see a familiar figure in white on my doorstep, a pile of luggage at her feet, and a gramophone tucked under her arm.

"Hiya, toots!" May greeted me brightly. "Ain't this a kick in the pants?"

She barreled past me and into the room, depositing the gramophone with a thud on my wobbly table. "Boy, am I sick of lugging *this* goddamn thing halfway around the Pacific!" She took in my cramped, narrow quarters and blanched. "Jesus! Put a couple of handles on this place and you've got yourself a coffin." I laughed: it was true. Suddenly an orange ball of fur propelled itself off my bed and into May's arms. "Hey, there he is!" she cried out happily. "There's my Little Bastard!" She stroked his mane and, transported with bliss, the cat climbed up her chest and wrapped himself around her neck like a stole, purring contentedly.

I asked, "Did you not go to Samoa?"

"Oh yeah, I went, all right."

"And what happened? Why are you back so soon?"

"Oh, baby, that's a long story. Listen, I'm starving. You got a kitchen in this dump?"

"Why, yes," I said airily, "it's off the *verandah*."

In the communal kitchen I stir-fried some vegetables, water chestnuts, and tinned salmon while May used the facilities. She came back and announced, "No offense, kiddo, but this rattrap makes Iwilei look like 'Iolani Palace."

"It is the best I can afford at the moment."

"You find a job?"

"Yes, at the cannery. I cut out pineapple eyes."

"Smart. That way they can't see it when you slice 'em to pieces." She opened the cupboard and rummaged through it. "Any hooch in here?"

Finding the cupboard hoochless, May went out onto the balcony and called down to a small boy playing in the courtyard. "Hey, kid! I'll pay you a quarter to go down to the corner and pick me up a fifth of gin!"

She flipped him a quarter and the cost of the gin, and the boy took off like a bullet, returning in record time. We brought the food back to my room and May finally told me about her trip. "So here's the straight dope," she said around a mouthful of food. "I'd had a bellyful of 'civilization' and all I wanted was that little grass shack in Samoa. Which isn't to say I didn't want to have a good time getting there, so I threw a little party in my cabin. Lasted about ten days." She hooted with glee. "That's the beauty of being aboard ship—there's no shortage of available men! I was pretty tight the whole time, and I couldn't give you their names if you put a gun to my head, but let's just say I worked my way up through the ranks. If we'd been at sea another day, hell, maybe the skipper himself might've signed on for a hitch."

As usual with May, I understood every third word but somehow gleaned her meaning.

"Couple cabins down from mine, there are these two *gentlemen*." Her words dripped with uncharacteristic disdain. "The younger one's American, kinda good-looking . . . I invited him to my cabin, but he gave me the cold shoulder. The older guy's an uppity Brit who looks me over like something he found on the bottom of his shoe. And while they're looking down their noses at me—'*Tsk tsk, bad job, isn't she, Gerald? That she is, Willie*'—these two queers are pretending to all the 'respectable' folk on board like they're not goin' back to their cabin and buggering each other's brains out!"

I had absolutely no idea what this meant, and said so. When May explained, I was shocked: I had never heard of such a thing.

"Honey, it takes all kinds," May said with a shrug. "I got no problem with how anybody gets their jollies, long as they don't judge *me*. So wouldn't you know, not only do I get a snootful from Willie and Gerald, I get another one from some holier-than-thou missionary couple, hauling a shitload of salvation down to the aborigines. They'd give me the evil eye, and just to piss 'em off I'd wiggle my ass in their faces whenever I saw 'em.

"So we sail into Pago Pago Harbor, but there's some bushwah about an outbreak of smallpox on the schooner that's supposed to take us to Apia—and we all have to put up in some fleabag of a rooming house outside Pago Pago till the quarantine's lifted! And it's *raining*. Jesus, I never saw so much goddamn rain in my life. For five whole days, it's pissing down so hard we can't even drive the three lousy miles into Pago Pago for a little entertainment!

"But thank God for the red, white, and blue: Pago Pago is in *American* Samoa, and there's a U.S. naval base nearby. I got the quartermaster of the *Sonoma* to wangle me a tour of the base. My escort was tall, dark, and handsome, and oh boy, pretty soon shore leave's not lookin' so bad after all."

Little Bastard was curled up in May's lap and as she massaged his neck he emitted a wheezy purr of contentment. "But just my luck—I'm in this fleabag rooming house and on one side of me I've got the missionary and his wife, and on the other, Mr. and Mrs. Willie! The preacher raises hell with management about me having a man in my room, the Brit gives me a hard time about my playing music . . . I mean, here we are, stuck in this miserable little dive at the ass-end of nowhere, and these killjoys are bellyaching about a girl getting a little recreation! What the hell did I do to deserve *this?*

"The missionary tried to get me tossed out, but it was the damn Brit who really got under my skin. He'd call downstairs to his lover boy, 'Teatime, Gerald!'—and I couldn't help myself, I'd bang on the wall and yell, 'No, it's *nookie* time, you bloody limey!'" She laughed uproariously. "I'd still be there partying if me and a friend hadn't decided to take a midnight swim in the bay, in the altogether. How the hell was *I* supposed to know that was the *governor's* motorboat pier?"

"I do not understand."

"They kicked me out of the goddamn country! And here I am again!"

May stayed that night with me, the two of us sharing my small bed, precipitating the only instance I can recall of May Thompson appearing demure: "Now, you just stay on your side, honey, okay? I ain't that kind of specialty act." The next day she rented a room for herself in Chinatown, where the city's remaining prostitutes had quietly settled after the closure of Iwilei. The absence of an unofficially sanctioned red-light district seemed to placate the righteous elements of Honolulu society, and women like May promptly went back to plying their trade, albeit a bit more discreetly.

We stayed in touch, occasionally even going to a movie together—always a matinee in advance of her "business hours"—but Jae-sun now occupied most of my social life. We had lunch several times a week at the cannery, and by mid-March I could not deny my growing attraction to him. Then one day he asked me, somewhat to my surprise, if I would accompany him to church that Sunday.

He explained matter-of-factly that he had converted to Christianity after his wife's death, finding it a comfort. When I asked him how his wife had died, he told me it had been an accident on the plantation. "She was coming home from a long day in the fields, carrying our newborn son. In the dark she stumbled and fell into an irrigation ditch. She hit her head on a pipe and fell facedown into the ditch. She and our son both drowned."

To a Westerner his expression would have seemed stoic, but I could clearly see his pain—in his eyes, in the tightness around his mouth, even in the way his hands lay in his lap as he spoke. "My wife had wanted us to leave the plantation and move to Honolulu, but I was afraid I would not be able to make a living here, and so we stayed. I should have listened to her," he finished quietly.

I was unprepared for such a sad and terrible response.

"I am so sorry," I said, feeling guilty for my own ruse of widowhood, which now seemed venal and self-serving. "How many years has it been?"

"There is no point in counting the age of a dead child," he said, invoking an old Korean maxim. "But I go to church, and I pray for them."

I told him I would be honored to join him.

That Sunday we attended services at a Korean Methodist church on Punchbowl Street, where we listened to a sermon by the pastor, Reverend Song. The hymns the congregation sang sounded lovely to my ears, and I could see how Jae-sun derived comfort from this community of believers. However, the presence here of so many of my countrymen and women heightened my fears of being exposed as the wife of Mr. Noh, and I found myself anxious for the service to end.

Finally we began filing out of the large wooden church shaded by tall palm trees, but just when I thought I had escaped detection, I heard a high breathy voice exclaim, in Korean: *"Regret?"*

My heart pounded at hearing my childhood name again, and fearfully I turned in the direction of the voice.

It belonged to my old friend Beauty, whom I had last heard sobbing through the thin clapboard walls of the Hotel of Sorrows.

But now she seemed anything but sorrowful. She ran toward me, a bright smile on her face, and as she came up to me she happily clasped my hands in hers.

"Oh, do forgive me the rudeness of using your name! I was just so stunned to find you here. You look wonderful, dear friend. Is this your husband?"

Jae-sun blushed.

Beauty, of course, had met Mr. Noh at the docks, and now I saw her dawning realization that this was not him.

"My husband is dead," I said quickly. "This is my friend, Mr. Choi."

Beauty's elderly husband, Mr. Yi, slowly hobbled up to join us and introductions were made; I explained to Jae-sun that Mrs. Yi and I had arrived together in Hawai'i as picture brides aboard the *Nippon Maru*. If Mr. Yi was shocked at the idea of Jae-sun courting a widow, he did not show it. We all chatted amiably for a few minutes, then Beauty insisted I must come visit her that week; I promised that I would. But even as we left the church grounds, I worried over how much longer I could keep Jae-sun from learning the truth.

*B*eauty's husband owned a general store on Liliha Street that was enjoying considerable success, to judge by the number of customers when I came to visit. At seventy-two years of age, Mr. Yi no longer worked long hours at the store but left the running of it to his two sons from his first marriage (his previous wife was deceased some five years). Beauty worked as a sales clerk, and they also employed as a stock boy a young Hawai'i-born Korean in his early twenties, Frank Ahn, the son of a couple Mr. Yi knew from his plantation days.

Mr. Yi encouraged his wife to take a few hours to visit with me, so we walked to their large and well-appointed wood-frame house on Morris Lane. Beauty made a pot of hot rice water and we sat in the backyard amid a blaze of orange helliconia blossoms and the soft perfume of Chinese jasmine, or *pikake* as it was called here. When I told Beauty that her husband seemed as considerate as he was prosperous, she nodded. "He is a good man and he treats me kindly. And he is a good father to his sons, though I'm afraid neither cares much for me. It doesn't help matters that I'm pregnant."

"What?" I said. "Congratulations! What could be wrong with that?"

"Mr. Yi's sons would prefer not to share their inheritance with a sibling from their father's second marriage. I would just as soon oblige them in this, but from the start my husband seemed intent on raising another family." Her previously sunny face now looked like a rainy day. "I work long hours at the store; I don't mind that. But—the nights are difficult. Mr. Yi *is* a kind and generous man; I don't wish to seem ungrateful. I think of him as a daughter does a father . . . but not as a woman feels for a man."

I told her I understood, but that her circumstances could be worse. I related Mr. Noh's behavior toward me, her eyes widening as I described my year of married life. *"Aigo,"* she said softly. "No wonder you looked stricken when you saw me at church. But then, what is Mr. Choi to you?"

"He is everything that my husband is not. At the moment he is only a friend, but I suspect he will shortly wish to be more, and ask me to marry him. I will have to tell him the truth then, and that might well change his mind."

"But it is beside the point. You are already married."

"Then I will ask for a . . ."—I had to use the English word, as *ki-cho*, "abandoned wife," hardly applied—"a divorce."

I did not entertain the idea as casually as I let on, but Beauty was horror-struck: "Oh, no, no, dear friend, you mustn't! Bad enough being a Korean widow who dares to remarry, but divorce?"

"This is not Korea. Divorce is not uncommon here."

"But there is such stigma against it in the Korean community—in the church, especially! I knew one woman who dared seek a divorce, and the whole neighborhood shunned her, as if she were a leper from that hospital in Kalihi!"

"What am I to do, then? Hide like a mouse in a hole the rest of my life? Do I not deserve some happiness, with a man who is tender toward me?"

She looked at me miserably.

"I have asked myself that same question many times," she said quietly, "and I cannot pretend to have an answer."

I left feeling sorry for Beauty, but her unhappiness only strengthened my growing resolve to put my marriage to Mr. Noh behind me, regardless of the consequences.

As production slowed on the trimming line, I was assigned other tasks at the cannery, including packing various products for shipment to customers on the mainland. Depending on the size of the package, I might have to pad the boxes for transport, and there was a large stack of old newspapers available for this purpose. It was no less tedious than working the line, but considerably easier. When I grew bored I might sneak a look at one of the news stories, but most of the time I was barely conscious of what was on these sheets I was crumpling into ballast.

Then one morning my attention was caught as I stuffed a newspaper page into a box. Curiously, I withdrew it and, as I had done years ago to that old page from Lady Ŭiyudang's book, I smoothed it out. What I saw was no less memorable, but hardly beautiful. There on the front page of the *Pacific Commercial Advertiser*, dated May 25, 1915, was the headline:

BRIDE MURDERED ON BUSY STREET

Pretty Young Korean Stabbed and Slashed
By Husband While On Way Home

> Walking hand in hand with a girl friend on her return
> home from a pleasant evening spent in a moving pic-
> ture theater, pretty nineteen-year-old Kim Pak Chi
> Ser, a Korean bride, was fiendishly attacked by her
> husband, a Korean man, and stabbed to death on a
> public highway, right in the heart of one of the busiest
> districts of the city, at half past nine o'clock last
> night . . .

I read with understandable interest and increasing alarm the
story of "Kim"—referred to as if this were her given name and
not her family name—who was brought to Honolulu as a picture
bride by a man "of considerably less education than she." The
story went on, "After a time the husband commenced to ill-treat
his wife, and the attention of the authorities being called to the
existing state of affairs between them, the girl was placed in the
Susanna Wesley Home on King Street." She soon found work as
a domestic for a local family, and was walking home from a
movie with some of them when her estranged husband "pounced
upon his wife . . . 'like a big beast would jump on a little one.'
He placed his hands over her mouth until she screamed out in
terror . . . there was the sound of a shot and the girl was seen to
stumble . . . on the ground with her husband kneeling over her
and thrusting at her head with something that gleamed in the
moonlight."

That something was a knife, and the girl died of her wounds on
her way to Queen's Hospital.

All this was chilling enough, but bringing it even closer to my
own life—into the realm of the terribly possible—was the name

of the family for whom Kim worked, and in whose company she died:

> Kim Pak Ser had for the past month or so been in the employ of the family of Apana, the well-known police officer, and last night she and several members of the family attended the moving picture theater near Liliha and King streets.
>
> The show over the party started to walk leisurely home. Mrs. Luhiwa Apana and her daughter Helen were walking some distance ahead of Mary, a fifteen-year-old daughter, and Sam, a little son of Apana . . .

I stared at the wrinkled newspaper in what were now trembling hands. I read and reread the words, feeling for myself the panic and terror this girl must have experienced: the jolt of surprise as her husband sprang at her out of the shadows; the suffocating fear of his hand across her mouth; the sound of the gunshot that missed its mark; and the cutting pain of the knife that did not.

It made sense now: Detective Apana's paternal interest, his friendly protectiveness toward me. I reminded him of someone whom he had not been able to protect. He was not on the scene, according to the story, when the girl was murdered; had he accompanied his family to the movies that night, he might have disarmed the wild-eyed husband in time and poor Kim Chi Ser would still be alive.

But he had not been there, and she was dead.

And if a girl like her could be killed in the way she was—on a brightly lit, well-traveled street, in the company of the family of a prominent police officer—it could happen to me, too. Just as easily, and just as quickly.

I folded the newspaper page into quarters, placed it in the

pocket of my work gown, and promptly put all thoughts of divorce out of my mind.

A gainst my own desires, I began to distance myself from Jae-sun. I had no phone at home and the only way he could reach me was at the cannery, so I asked to be given a different work shift, hoping to simply avoid him. When that did not work, I found reasons not to lunch with him. When he asked me out to dinner the following weekend, I told him I had plans to see a motion picture with a girlfriend. He could clearly sense my new aloofness, and I readily saw the pain and confusion in his eyes. I told myself this was best for both of us, but it made me miserable to contemplate; and by Saturday, consumed with guilt and loneliness, I turned my lie into truth by calling on May to see if she would like to go to a movie. We went downtown to see the new Charlie Chaplin film, *Easy Street*, in which the Little Tramp improbably becomes a police officer, but I could not enjoy it. Afterward, as we walked to a coffee shop, all I could think of was poor Kim Chi Ser, and I fought back the irrational panic that my own estranged husband might appear from around the next corner to attack me.

"So what's eating you?" May asked as we settled into a booth.

"Oh, perhaps just a cup of tea."

May rolled her eyes.

"No, not what are *you* eating, what's eating *you*? As in, you look like somebody ran over your dog and then backed up to finish off your mother."

I told her about my conversation with Beauty, as well as the newspaper story I had stumbled across. I admitted my fear of what might happen to me should I seek a divorce from my husband; or at the least of how Jae-sun might reject me for it. I laid out the impossibility, as I saw it, of a future with him, which was why I had decided to stop seeing him.

May listened patiently as she smoked a Lucky Strike, then when I was finished she asked me one question: "Are you in love with this guy?"

"Whether I love him, or he loves me, does not matter. There are too many reasons we should not marry."

May stubbed out her cigarette in an ashtray and said, "You're an idiot."

For once I understood her perfectly, and I was both taken aback and hurt.

"Why do you say such a thing?" I asked.

She sighed heavily, as if about to reveal something she would rather not.

"Remember how I told you," she said, "about that tour I got of the naval base down in Samoa?"

"Your 'shore leave'?"

"Yeah. My escort was named Iosefo—Joseph. He was Samoan. Big handsome guy, with a smile like a goddamn sunrise. Not a mean bone in his body." She smiled in a way I had never seen her smile before. "We took to each other right off. He called me his 'number one *vahine*.' And all the time I was down there, he was my number one man. I could've had any and all of those sailors at the base, but all I wanted was Joe.

"And baby, what a lover! He was sweet and he was fire. We couldn't get enough of each other. He'd sneak out of his barracks and we'd spend days at a time in that fleabag room, ordering up steaks from the kitchen. I'd play my records, or strum the ukulele . . ."

She lit up another cigarette, breathed in the smoke and let it out again, like a cloud of thought in a newspaper cartoon.

"Well, hell, I went there to get away from civilization, right? To live in a little grass shack in Samoa? So one night I say to him, 'Joe, let's go get married.'"

I must have looked dumbfounded at this. May smiled: "So help me God, it's true. I was crazy about him, and he was crazy about me—so I thought, why the hell not? I had money, we could do whatever we wanted. So I drag Joe's ass over to the courthouse and we apply for a marriage license.

"But turns out the judge is a good old boy from Florida who looks at us like I just asked for a license to marry a kangaroo. Gives us some bullshit about how we'd have to apply to the territorial governor. See, it's okay for all these horny white guys to screw, even marry, the *vahines;* but when a white woman wants to marry a guy whose skin is darker than hers . . . well, you get the picture.

"Then the goddamned missionary gets wind of this, raises hell with Joe's CO—and the next thing I know the chief of police is banging down my door in the middle of the night! I told 'em to go to hell, I know my rights—but Joe's in the Navy, and he figures they'll toss him in the stockade if he resists, so . . ."

The anger and frustration in her face was plain to see. "They haul Joe in front of the hangin' judge from Tallahassee, who says, 'Don't you know it's wrong, Joseph, to be with this white woman every night in her room?' Joe hung his head, but I piped up, 'It's none of your damned business if Joe and me keep company! We'll go back to Honolulu to get married and to hell with alla you!'

"The judge says, 'You're going back to Honolulu, all right, but not with him. He's in the United States Navy.'"

She sighed and took a swallow of coffee. "So the bastard deported me. Bam, just like that, I'm back on board the *Sonoma,* heading for Honolulu."

For the first time since I had known her, May Thompson looked fragile, and broken.

"Did you . . . see Joe again before you left?" I asked.

"Naw, they wouldn't let me near him. I smuggled him a note, promising I'd pay his steamer fare to Honolulu, we could get married here, no one would bat an eye. I've written him two letters already since I got back. But . . ." She hesitated. May never hesitated.

"He has not written back?" I said quietly.

She shook her head. In the silence I clearly heard her disappointment and hurt. She drained her coffee and smiled cheerlessly. "Civilization—what a laugh."

She stood up and dug into her change purse.

"If you want to marry somebody, Jin, for Chrissake—*do* it." She flipped a quarter onto the table as a tip. "That's why you're an idiot. Look, I gotta go."

On her way out a heavyset man at the counter whistled at her, and I saw her throw him a smile. But it was an empty smile, a mere sales tool. I rose to leave. The man preceded me, hurrying out the door to catch up with May as she sashayed up King Street. Within half a block they were walking arm in arm toward the nearest hotel, and I wanted to cry.

I began looking for an attorney the next day.

Nine

The dissolution of a marriage in Korea was no trifling matter, and in most cases was initiated by the husband's parents. A wife could be expelled from marriage for one of "seven evils": adultery, thievery, jealousy, insolence toward her in-laws, failure to produce a son, a mortal disease, or excessive talkativeness. *Ki-cho* was an even greater stigma for a woman to bear than sonlessness. By failing as a wife—due to her inherently "dark and ignorant nature"—a divorced woman became a pariah. No respectable clan would allow their son to marry such a woman; her own parents often banned her dishonorable presence from their household. Women who committed adultery were made slaves of the state, and for those who willfully abandoned their husbands, the legal penalty was death by hanging. Many a disgraced woman died by her own hand before it came to that.

With such fearsome associations, a divorce was not something I considered lightly, but America, I told myself, was not Korea. May was the one who advised me to obtain the services of an attorney, and recommended one she knew who had represented women of Iwilei. His name was Tillman and his offices on King Street were modest at best. A short, dark, rumpled *haole* in his late thirties, he took careful notes as he quizzed me about the date of my wedding, how long my husband and I had lived together, and my reasons for seeking a divorce. When I informed him of my husband's drunken attacks on me and my subsequent miscarriage, he looked up from his notes: "Were you treated by a doctor at that time?" I told him yes. "What was his name?" I provided him with the name of the plantation doctor. When Mr. Tillman had finished his questions and I had finished answering, he told me, "I believe you have more than adequate grounds to seek a divorce. Now, is there anything *you* would like to ask *me?*"

Hesitantly, I worked up the courage to ask, "Do wives who abandon their husbands in Hawai'i risk punishment by hanging?"

He had the jaded air of a man not usually surprised by much in his line of work, but now his eyes widened and he sat a bit straighter in his chair, as if for a moment he embodied the entire American legal system. "No. Certainly not."

"Will I be forced to confront my husband in court?"

"If he doesn't contest the petition, no. If he chooses to fight it—yes, I'm afraid so. But there will be bailiffs—guards—there to protect you."

"Will they protect me once I have gone home, and my husband will now know where I live?"

He admitted they would not.

I asked him how much this would cost. "Normally," he said, "for a divorce, I'd charge between fifty and a hundred dollars."

When he saw my shock at this he amended, "But in this case I'll do it for thirty. If we win, of course, I'll seek to have your legal costs paid by your husband."

Thirty dollars represented almost all of my savings—but what else could I do? I had only the vaguest concept of American law, and could hardly navigate the legal system on my own. I agreed to the terms.

Within two days my attorney had filed with the First Circuit Court of Honolulu a "libel" for divorce—on grounds of "extreme cruelty" and "habitual intemperance"—and a summons was issued to Mr. Noh directing him to appear in thirty days' time before Judge William Heen to answer the libel.

I could only imagine my husband's reaction at receiving such a summons, and tried not to consider what his feelings might be about it, and about me. Were I to dwell too much on that, I did not know how I would find the courage to walk into the courtroom thirty days hence.

A source of equal anxiety to me was Jae-sun, as I knew that I finally had to reveal to him the full sum of my life. He was happy when, after a week of keeping my distance, I approached him at work and said I needed to speak with him. I think he was a bit puzzled that, instead of taking him aside at the cannery, I suggested a walk along the Iwilei shore after work, but his pleasure that I seemed friendly again clearly outweighed any confusion, and he readily agreed.

At the end of the workday, as we walked amid fallen *kiawe* beans on the beach, I gathered my nerve and told him, "I must beg your apologies. There are things about myself that I have kept from you. I have not been honest with you about my past."

He seemed undisturbed by this. "I am sure you could never tell me anything that would require an apology."

"I will let you be the judge of that." My heart fluttered like a leaf in the wind and I began telling him the whole truth of my life. I spoke of my marriage to Mr. Noh—his drinking, his gambling, the violent storms in which I was swept up—and of the child I lost to his temper. I hung my head in shame as I admitted that I was not, in fact, a widow: I recounted how I ran away from Waialua, and the lie I was living, the lie I had told him. This revelation brought him to a sudden stop, and though he tried to hide his shock, I could see it clearly in his eyes and in the way he rolled slightly on his feet, as if he had taken a physical blow.

Finally, I informed him that I had filed for a divorce from my abusive husband . . . and to my distress, that word brought the reaction I had feared.

"Divorce?" His tone was as horrified as if I'd said I was considering murder.

You must understand: In Korea at that time, a divorced woman was by the very fact of her divorce a criminal, a contemptible person—a thief, an adulteress, or at the least a jealous harridan or insolent daughter-in-law. Abandonment of one's marital duty was no less of a black mark. Respectable Korean society made little distinction between a wife who betrayed her marriage bond and one who stole, slandered, or fornicated. I could have been a gossiping, thieving, licentious she-devil and I would have been met with a roughly equal measure of scorn.

However liberal Jae-sun might have become in his years in Hawai'i, he was still Korean enough to be aghast at what I just told him—repulsed not merely at what I had done, but at what I was about to become.

"I am sorry," I said quietly. "I know that does not begin to make amends. I humbly ask your forgiveness."

He looked at me a long moment, at a loss for words.

"You . . . you cannot go through with this," he said at last.

"What should I do, then?" I asked. "Go back to a husband who beat me? Who murdered our child?"

He winced, knowing such pain all too well. "No," he conceded. "But how . . ." There was no mistaking the anger and accusation in his tone. "How could you have *lied* to me as you did?"

I flinched and nodded. "You are right. It was wrong even to have agreed to have lunch with you that first day."

"Don't you know," he said, in growing alarm, "that it is a sin for a man to be with a woman who is already married?"

I felt guilty, but there I had to draw the line: "Don't be silly. We have not committed adultery."

"Silly?" he said, raising his voice. "You think it is silly for a man to think the sort of thoughts about a woman that I have thought of you, and then to learn that she is legally and morally bound to another?"

"But you did not know," I protested. "God knows what is in your heart, doesn't he?"

"That is exactly the source of the trouble!" he yelled, and I flinched again. "God *knows* what is in my heart!"

He was more furious than I had ever seen him. He did not attempt to hide it, or the pain, betrayal, and confusion he was feeling. Then he turned and started back up the beach, away from me.

"I am sorry!" I called after him, in tears now; but neither my words, nor his heart, pulled him back.

That night I cried both for the hurt I had caused Jae-sun and for the loss of the first man I had had any feelings for since poor Mr. Lim. I was despondent, but told myself that this was no less than I deserved for having misled Jae-sun. The fact that I had done so out of fear and worry did not excuse it. And now my worry was multiplied, like a knot in the tangled threads of my life, as I feared what I might expect when I met Mr. Noh in court. But what was done, was done; and I had to admit, alongside my fear and anxiety was a relief that everything was at last out in the open.

The next morning I came to work to discover that a small envelope with my name on it had been left with my forewoman, who made it clear to me that she did not appreciate being used as a postal box. In it was a short note written in *hangul*:

> *Please forgive my unseemly show of emotion yesterday.*
> *Where once I thought I would never lack for things to tell*
> *you, I find now that I do not know what to say to you.*
> *Until I do, I think it best to say nothing.*

I took from this what little encouragement I could—at least he cared enough to tell me he was staying away—but my hopes that he would forgive me receded with the tide of time that passed without any further word. After several weeks, I tried to reconcile myself to life without him. But I missed his cheerful eyes, his laugh, even the tilt of his silly dungaree hat. I consoled myself with the knowledge that even if I was not meant to be Jae-sun's wife—and that thought pained me more than I could express—then at least my days of being Mr. Noh's wife would soon be at an end.

On the appointed morning, my attorney escorted me past the gilded statue of King Kamehameha I standing outside Ali'iolani Hale and into the grand hallways of the Territorial Courts Building in downtown Honolulu. I had never been inside a courtroom before, much less an American court, and though Mr. Tillman had given me a rough idea of what to expect from the hearing, there was still much in the proceedings I would find surprising. Not least was the city magistrate overseeing the case. Judge William Heen was both relatively young—in his mid-thirties—and Chinese-Hawaiian, the first person of such background to be appointed a judge in the territory. The last thing I had expected to see behind this imposing bench was someone with facial features even remotely similar to mine. He had just finished adjudicating a traffic violation and the courtroom was being emptied of the previous litigants. We waited for them to leave, and then my attorney showed me to what he called the "plaintiff's table" in the front row.

Behind his tall bench, Judge Heen was signing some documents for the bailiff. Like most Hawaiians he smiled easily, and laughed at something the bailiff said to him. I was just beginning to feel a bit more relaxed when out of the corner of my eye I noticed someone standing in the aisle to my right, and I turned.

Mr. Noh stood there in the aisle, looking at me.

I jumped, though his was not a threatening look of any kind. He was dressed in the same threadbare dark suit he had worn to the docks the day we were married. His shoes were not polished. He held a battered felt hat in his hand.

He bowed slightly and greeted me in Korean. He took a step toward me and my whole body tensed; I had to fight the blind instinct to run.

My lawyer, seeing my panic, quickly stood and interposed himself between us, though he was at least a head shorter than Mr. Noh. "If you have something to say to my client," he told him, "you may say it through me."

"This is my *wife*," Mr. Noh said, looking aggrieved.

Mr. Tillman said calmly, "Please take a seat at the respondent's table"—he pointed to one on the right-hand side of the room—"and wait for your attorney."

Mr. Noh snorted in derision.

"I do not need an attorney," he replied confidently, but took his place at the table as directed.

My pulse pounded in my head like the roar of the surf, drowning out the bailiff's voice as he announced the case number and the court was called to order.

Learning that my husband was not represented by counsel, Judge Heen asked him whether he understood that he had the right to engage an attorney. This was in the days before courts would appoint free counsel for a defendant, so when Mr. Noh repeated that he did not need a lawyer, no one seemed at all concerned that perhaps he could not afford one (or, more likely, that he had gambled away any legal funds he might have had).

"So you wish to represent yourself in this matter?" the judge said. "Under the Constitution you have the right to argue *pro se*—in your own behalf—but I don't recommend it."

Mr. Noh pointed to me. "By what right does a wife bring such an action against her own husband? In Korea only a man may seek a divorce, never a woman."

"That may be the case in Korea," the judge said, "but you were married in the Territory of Hawai'i and under our laws either husband or wife may sue for separation and divorce."

"But we are Korean," Mr. Noh insisted.

"As long as you are living in Hawai'i you will abide by our laws. Do you understand that?"

Reluctantly, Mr. Noh grunted an acknowledgment.

"Was that a yes?" the judge said. "For the record?"

"Yes," Mr. Noh replied.

"Very well, then. Let the record show that respondent has chosen to serve as his own counsel. Mr. Tillman, you may make your opening statement."

My attorney briefly summarized the facts he promised would come out in testimony: the manner of my engagement to Mr. Noh; what I was told about him in Korea and how this measured up to the facts as I learned them when I came to Hawai'i; my husband's habitual drinking and gambling; and finally the violent acts he committed against me. As he spoke of the latter, I stole a glance at Mr. Noh and saw the anger and humiliation in his face rising like mercury in a thermometer. Mr. Tillman also made clear that I was not seeking alimony and there was no property to be divided or custody of children to be considered.

When my attorney had concluded, the judge asked Mr. Noh if he wished to make his opening statement now or wait until after Mr. Tillman had put on his case. When Mr. Noh seemed uncertain as to what this meant, the judge patiently explained it and added, "If you are unfamiliar with American trial procedure, the court *is* willing to grant a continuance—a delay—so that you might engage the services of a private attorney. Are you sure you don't wish to do so?"

Mr. Noh stubbornly shook his head. "No delay. I will tell my story after she tells hers."

"Let the record show that the respondent has reserved the right to make his opening statement after the completion of plaintiff's case in chief," the judge told the court stenographer. "Mr. Tillman, you may proceed."

My attorney called me to the stand and asked me a series of questions with which he had previously made me familiar. But it was a far different thing, answering in this imposing courtroom in front of complete strangers. As Koreans, we are taught that to make public one's emotional or family problems is a shameful acknowledgment of personal inadequacy, as well as a burden to the community. So I was nearly as embarrassed as my husband as I told of how he would drink and gamble away his wages; how I tried to bring money into the house but was physically attacked for my efforts; how I felt nearly constant fear when I was living with him; and finally, how he assaulted me and murdered our unborn daughter.

"So you left Waialua out of fear for your life?" Mr. Tillman asked me.

"Yes. I was certain he would kill me next time."

"Are you still afraid of your husband?"

"Yes."

"Could you ever see yourself continuing to live with him?"

"No, never."

"Thank you, Mrs. Noh. That is all. Your witness."

Mr. Noh looked puzzled. The judge explained, "You may cross-examine the witness—ask her questions. In light of her stated fear of you, however, I suggest you ask your questions from where you are."

My husband looked at me and said condescendingly, "It is unnecessary for me to question my own wife. She cannot tell me anything I do not already know."

Mr. Tillman and Judge Heen exchanged astonished looks, then the judge turned back to Mr. Noh. "You waive your right to cross-examine this witness?"

"Yes."

"All right, let the record reflect that. Mrs. Noh, you may step down."

Relieved, I returned to my seat beside Mr. Tillman, who now called on the plantation physician at Waialua, Dr. Jaarsma. He confirmed that on the evening of November 5, 1915, I was admitted to the plantation infirmary with multiple injuries including a concussion, lacerations to the head and torso, two broken ribs, a bruised kidney, loss of blood, and the spontaneous abortion of the fetus I had been carrying. Upon this last utterance I lost my composure and began sobbing despite myself. I had been able to recount these horrors myself without breaking down, but hearing it from another was too much to bear. I was by this act doubly shamed. My attorney paused in his questioning to give me his handkerchief. The judge asked if I would like a "recess," but I shook my head and forced my tears to a stop. My attorney then turned back to the witness.

"Did Mrs. Noh tell you at that time how these injuries came about?"

"She told me her husband had assaulted her."

"And were her injuries consistent with such an assault?"

"Yes."

"Had you observed injuries like this in Mrs. Noh before?"

"Yes, she had come in another time with a broken nose and bruised ribs."

My attorney then had my medical records entered into evidence.

This time, when offered the chance to cross-examine the witness, Mr. Noh thought for a moment, stood, and asked the doctor, "Do you believe any man in full possession of his senses would seek to kill his unborn child?"

"I can't answer that," the doctor said. "Some might."

"Can men who have had too much to drink commit acts they later regret, and"—there was, I admit, genuine emotion in his voice—"wish they could undo?"

The doctor glanced at the judge for guidance; Heen nodded an assent.

"I suppose they can," Jaarsma replied.

"That is all I wanted to ask," Mr. Noh said, and sat down.

My attorney was again on his feet. "Redirect, Your Honor."

"Go ahead, Counselor."

"Doctor Jaarsma, in your experience, does such regret on the part of alcoholics stop them from committing further acts of violence?"

"No," the witness testified, "not in my experience."

"Thank you, sir. Nothing further."

It was now my husband's turn to present his case. Eagerly, he took the witness stand. His tone as he started was quiet and earnest.

"I do not deny my bad drinking," he admitted. "It is a shameful vice, and its poisonous effects led me to do something for which I can never make amends. Surely even the death of a daughter is to be regretted."

I knew perfectly what he meant by that, but it seemed to mystify Mr. Tillman. Judge Heen, being part Chinese, may well have understood.

But soon enough, Mr. Noh's calm voice took on a different tone:

"I entered into this marriage with honorable intentions," he told the court. "I chose this girl from the many pictures the matchmaker presented to me. As you can see, she is a plain girl, lacking in most feminine graces, and she is fortunate that anyone chose her at all."

I fought back sudden tears. This casual cruelty stung all the more for being so public, but I was determined not to add to my shame by weeping again.

"I went to great expense to bring her to Hawai'i," Mr. Noh went on. "I sent her fifty dollars for passage from Korea, and another hundred to be used as she saw fit. I am not a rich man, no matter what exaggerations the matchmaker may have told her about me; yet I gave her a roof over her head and food to eat."

I recalled this a bit differently.

"But from the start, she was an inadequate wife. Often she did not have dinner ready for me on time, though in truth she was a good cook when she put her mind to it. She was only a fair housekeeper. And she knew nothing of what went on in the bedroom, but I will not go into that."

My attorney almost interrupted him, then apparently thought better of it.

"All this I could have ignored," my husband continued, "but then my wife sought to become more than a wife—she wished to be a husband! She brought shame to the household by going to work in the fields, and this I could not tolerate.

"There is an old Korean saying: 'If you don't beat your woman for three days, she becomes a fox.' My own mother told me, 'Son, a woman needs reminding of how to be a good wife. Do not spare her the back of your hand, you are doing her no favors.'"

He smiled at this, but no one else did. I began to see why my lawyer had made no objections to this testimony.

Judge Heen asked, "Are you admitting, Mr. Noh, that you inflicted these injuries upon your wife?"

"I admit to disciplining her. Granted, in my drunken state, I did this to excess, and I regret it—but would you fault a father for giving a wayward child one too many straps of his belt? A wayward wife is no different, certainly.

"She then aggravated her misdeeds by forsaking her marital duties and running away, causing me great shame. Now she adds to that shame by seeking this divorce. But despite all this, I am willing to forgive her these transgressions and take her back—if only she makes an effort, this time, to be a good wife."

There was a moment's silence as we all came to realize that he was finished with his testimony. My attorney rose from his seat and asked, "And if she does not live up to your ideal of a 'good wife,' are you prepared to beat her again?"

"I hope it will not come to that," my husband said, sealing his fate.

"No further questions, Your Honor."

"Mr. Noh," Judge Heen said with barely concealed distaste, "do you wish to put on any other witnesses?"

"No."

"Do you wish to make a closing statement?"

"I have just made my statement."

"Mr. Tillman, rebuttal?"

"I don't think that will be necessary, Your Honor."

What happened next was unusual, but not unprecedented, according to my lawyer. Judge Heen announced, "Inasmuch as there are no questions of custody, property, or alimony to consider in this case, its disposition seems straightforward. Plaintiff has amply demonstrated the injury she suffered at the hands of the respondent, who has admitted under oath to having been the cause. As there is abundant evidence that this marriage has been irreparably breached, the court therefore finds for the plaintiff on grounds of extreme cruelty and habitual intemperance, and further directs the respondent to pay the plaintiff's legal fees.

"This divorce decree shall, per statute, go into effect in thirty days' time."

He rapped his gavel, and almost before I understood what had just happened, I was a free woman. Or nearly so.

Mr. Noh looked truly astonished—as if he had never doubted that the court would see the propriety of his actions.

My attorney and I thanked the judge for his ruling and quickly left the courtroom. Outside, on the courthouse portico, Mr. Tillman explained to me how territorial law required a "cooling-down period" of at least a month in order to discourage "hasty" divorces . . . but after that, my marriage would be legally ended.

I was so thrilled at our victory that I did not notice Mr. Noh bearing down on us until he was but a few steps away.

His loss of face in the courtroom now stoked a fury easily matching that which I witnessed on the night he killed our child. He raged at me, "How *dare* you bring such shame upon your own husband!"

"You are no longer my husband," I replied, as calmly as I could, even as I fought to quell the terror rising in my throat.

My attorney again stepped between us, but this time Mr. Noh grabbed him by the collar and threw him aside as easily as I might cast open a window curtain.

"Schemer! Whore!" He spat each word into my face. He raised his right hand and balled it into a fist. I had absolutely no doubt he wished to kill me.

Fortunately, I had taken certain precautions.

Before Mr. Noh knew what was happening, someone had grabbed his left arm and twisted it behind his back like a stick of taffy. Mr. Noh yelped in pain and surprise, dropping the hand that had been raised to strike me.

Chang Apana now seized that arm too, bending it backward

with a snapping sound, and Mr. Noh cried out again. The detective quickly spun my would-be assailant around and propelled him into the side of the courthouse. Its concrete face met Mr. Noh's with what I believe is called a "wallop," and my husband let out a whimper of pain. I saw blood trickle down the wall.

Apana yanked him back from the wall and asked, "*Hana hou?* Do again?"

"No!"

Chang laughed. "You like beef, 'ey? Only not so tough when da beef's not with *wahines*."

"Thank you, Detective," I said. "Mr. Tillman, are you all right?"

My attorney nodded. "Yes. Fine."

Chang asked him, "You want press charges?" To Mr. Noh he said, "We go station, thirty days' jail, eh?"

Mr. Tillman looked at me and said, "We won't press charges—if Mr. Noh agrees to return to Waialua and stay away from his former wife."

But my husband, despite his pain, was unrepentant.

"She is *still* my wife!" Mr. Noh spat out. "I do not recognize—"

Calmly, Detective Apana again bounced him off the brick wall. Mr. Noh's face came away even bloodier than before.

"You one dumb sonuvabitch," Apana said. "Like try again?"

Mr. Noh groaned and capitulated. "All right," he said. "I will go!"

"And you stay go?" Chang asked, not yet loosening his grip.

"Yes! Yes!"

"Good." Apana yanked him back from the wall and pushed him toward the courthouse steps. "Start now."

As we watched my soon to be ex-husband stagger dazedly down the steps and onto King Street, Apana shook his head and said to me, "Some *puka* head you marry." *Puka* is Hawaiian for "hole," as in "hole in the head."

"*Mahalo*, Detective. I'm sure he would have killed me this time."

"No mention," Chang said with a smile. "He give you any more *pilikia*, you let me know, eh?"

As he followed Mr. Noh down King Street, making certain he was headed for the train station, I couldn't help but wonder whether the detective was thinking of poor Kim Pak Chi Ser—and if he was feeling some solace today that there was, at least, one young Korean girl in Honolulu whose life he *had* been able to save.

A week later I was on the "line," trimming pineapples, when I looked up to see a familiar face making an equally familiar hand signal over the din. This time I knew what it meant: "Will you have lunch with me?"

I felt a surge of joy, smiling and nodding my assent to Jae-sun, then counted the minutes until lunch hour.

We did not sit out in public on the lawn, but alone in one of the storage rooms, where we could speak privately. As we ate the delicacies Jae-sun had brought in his lunch basket, I told him about my divorce hearing and how, in less than a month's time, I would no longer be married to Mr. Noh. He merely nodded at this. I told him of my husband's most recent attempt at assaulting me and he seemed both shocked and relieved for Detective Apana's intervention. Finally he said, "I have been thinking a great deal in the time since we last spoke."

Like most Korean men, he was reluctant to speak of things he felt deeply about; but unlike most Korean men, he overcame his inhibitions.

"After my wife and child died at Waimānalo," he said, "I wondered why I was being punished so, why such a terrible thing should have happened. A woman on the plantation who claimed to have been a *mudang*"—one of the female fortune-tellers common in every Korean city—"said I was troubled by ghosts, which seemed self-evident to me. She told me I could free myself from their grip by worshipping and serving my ancestral spirits. So I made an ancestral altar out of a wooden crate, carried out the appropriate rituals and prayers to my ancestors . . . but it still brought me no peace of mind.

"Finally, in desperation, I went to the Christian church, where I was told that I was a sinner and needed to repent. I thought, if I had not been a good enough man in the eyes of God, perhaps that was why I was being punished. So I prayed for the souls of my wife and my son, for their eternal bliss, and I repented my sins in hopes of becoming a better man.

"And once I began to feel that perhaps I had—I found you." He smiled a tender smile. "I thought you were my reward."

Tears welled up in my eyes at this.

"But then," he said, "to find out that I'd sinned again—even unknowingly—I did not know what to think any longer."

"But how can it be a sin," I asked, "if you did not know you were sinning?"

He sighed and shook his head, clearly at a loss for an answer.

"I do not know. I have struggled with the morality of it. I have read my Bible. I've prayed to God for guidance. And at the end of it, all I know is this:

"You may not be my reward . . . but to lose you would be a punishment I could not bear."

For the first time, then, he kissed me.

The truth was: He was *my* reward.

The next weekend, I thanked May for giving me the courage to change my situation. Perhaps my actions emboldened her as well, because a few weeks later, in early June, she again showed up on my doorstep carrying her old gramophone with its metal trumpet flower, announcing that she had booked passage to San Francisco aboard the SS *Maui*—and that she and Little Bastard would be leaving within the week.

"What? Why?" I asked, surprised and dismayed.

She placed the phonograph on my table and shrugged. "I need a change of scenery. Fewer palm trees." She tried to let it go at that, then took one look at my crestfallen expression and sighed. "Aw, hell, what's the use? You might as well know all of it. You got any hooch?"

"I have a little rice wine that Jae-sun and I did not finish." She pulled up a chair and I brought over the half-full bottle. I knew better than to bring a glass. May swigged the rice wine, and then, properly anesthetized, went on:

"So down in Pago Pago, I had kind of a . . . lousy moment at the docks. I was standing there watching everybody else board the schooner for Apia, and me, I'm about to get my ass kicked back to Hawai'i. Feeling sorry for myself, I guess. The schooner leaves, I go back to my room and start to pack . . . and that's when it hit me: My entire life fit inside two crummy suitcases. *Two suitcases.* Jesus Christ!" She shook her head and drained the last of the wine from the bottle. "Gotta be something wrong with that."

"Yes, I see your point. But . . . could you not simply purchase a few more suitcases . . . and stay here in Honolulu?" I asked hopefully.

"I can't stay here, hon," she said, in as weary and honest a tone as I had ever heard from her. "I just gotta get the hell out of paradise."

I heard the pain in her voice and I nodded. "Will you be . . . staying in San Francisco, then?"

She shrugged again. "Maybe. Maybe I'll go back to Nebraska for a while. I'll know when I get there, right? Anyway, I wanted to give you a wedding present before I left, and . . . I thought you might like to have this." She presented me with the trumpet-flower gramophone, which I was honored to accept.

"Thank you," I said. "It will remind me of you, and Iwilei."

She laughed. "That might be one place you'd rather forget."

"I cannot and will not. I went there alone and frightened, but a friend was kind and took me in."

She seemed pleased, perhaps even touched, by this.

"Good luck, kiddo," she said fondly. As she stepped out the door she gave me a small wave and promised, "I'll keep in touch."

But she did not. I neither saw nor heard from May Thompson again.

Yet, in a way—I did.

*S*ome years later, I was reading the morning newspaper when I happened to notice a small advertisement for a motion picture about to open at the Princess Theatre downtown. It pictured a line drawing of a woman in a wide-brimmed hat, flirting with a man in a uniform, and the text surrounding it read:

STARTS TOMORROW—2:45 · 7:45—FOUR DAYS

An Outcast Girl of San Francisco's Underworld

A Marine Sergeant—Pago Pago

Gloria Swanson

in

"SADIE THOMPSON"

THE SCREEN VERSION OF "RAIN"

I found myself staring at the advertisement, the words not so much "ringing a bell" in my mind as jangling in some nagging, disjointed manner. It was not merely the familiar surname in the title that drew my attention, but its juxtaposition with other familiar phrases: "A Marine Sergeant," "Pago Pago," "An Outcast Girl of

San Francisco's Underworld"—the latter surely a euphemism for prostitution.

Even the badly drawn picture showed the character wearing a floppy white hat not unlike the one May—Maisie, as she was sometimes called—had worn the day she had left aboard the SS *Sonoma*.

And then there was that line at the bottom: "The screen version of 'Rain.' "

"I never saw so much goddamn rain in my life."

I tried to dismiss it all as merely an odd coincidence, but despite my best efforts it kept bobbing to the surface of my thoughts. The film was playing here for only four days; if I wanted to satisfy my curiosity about it, I would have to do so soon.

The next day, Thursday afternoon, I went downtown to the Princess Theatre, paying my nickel admission for the 2:45 matinee of *Sadie Thompson*.

Raptly, I watched this story of a "painted woman" from San Francisco, Sadie Thompson—cheery, vulgar, sensual—arriving in Pago Pago, where she and the rest of the ship's passengers, quarantined due to an outbreak of smallpox, are forced to stay in a run-down rooming house. There she loudly plays her gramophone, falls in love with a U.S. Marine stationed at the naval base, and runs afoul of a self-righteous "reformer" who pressures the governor to have her deported.

There the similarities to the story May told me ended: The man "Sadie" falls for isn't Samoan but white—"Sgt. Timothy O'Hara"—and the film goes on to portray her browbeaten conversion by the reformer who himself turns out to be more human, and prey to sin, than he imagined. At the end of the film, Sadie Thompson remains in Pago Pago, eventually to marry her very white Marine.

It seemed almost a cruel parody of what had actually happened to May in Samoa. And there was one dialogue title that stuck in my mind for its eerie resemblance to what May said to me before she left Honolulu for the last time:

"I'm on my way—don't know where but I guess I'll get there."

Again, I tried to dismiss the similarities as merely coincidence. How could something that happened to a Honolulu prostitute, half-way around the world in Samoa, find its way to Hollywood and the silver screen? It was silly even to contemplate.

Yet I could not stop contemplating it.

The film was based on a long-running mainland stage play called *Rain*, which itself was based on a short story by one W. Somerset Maugham. When I went to the public library and inquired if they had a copy of the story, I was given a collection of Mr. Maugham's fiction titled *The Trembling of a Leaf*.

The short story was titled simply, "Miss Thompson."

With a kind of baffled wonderment, I read the story of Sadie, who fled Iwilei after its closure. Maugham described her as blond, pretty in a "coarse" way, curvaceous, and wearing "a white dress and a large white hat," with white cotton stockings and white boots "in glacé kid."

This was, I remembered, precisely what May had been wearing that December day in 1916 when she boarded the SS *Sonoma*.

What's more, Sadie Thompson not only looked like May Thompson, she spoke like her, with the same colorful blend of foul language and hard-boiled slang.

I went back to the library and asked the librarian if she knew what the "W" in Mr. Maugham's name stood for. "William, I believe," she told me.

William. "Willie"?

"It's nookie time, you bloody limey!"

Could it be true? And if so, how could I ever know for sure?

"You might try the 'Passengers Departed' column," the librarian suggested. These were brief notices of passengers leaving, and arriving in, Honolulu—a quaint mainstay of the local papers for as long as I had been in Hawai'i.

I thanked her and, remembering quite vividly when May and I left Iwilei, I asked to see copies of the local papers from December 1916.

It did not take long to find. There on page eleven, column three of the *Pacific Commercial Advertiser* for December 5, was a list of travelers who had left Honolulu the previous day aboard the *Sonoma:*

"Somerset Maugham, Mr. Haxton, W. H. Collins, Miss Thompson."

Aigo—it was true! They had sailed together and, almost certainly, stayed together in that rundown little boardinghouse in Pago Pago.

Little had May dreamed that the "uppity Brit" in the room next door—who "looked down his nose" at her, and whose pomposity she took such delight in puncturing—would one day exact his revenge on her by appropriating her for a character in a short story. He had even used her real family name, though not her given one. Perhaps he never knew it.

The whole world knows "Sadie Thompson" now, but surely I am one of the privileged few who knew the real woman on whom she was based. I knew her cheerful vulgarity—her cunning, her wit, her generosity—and her sorrow, shared with few, perhaps none, but me.

Today, as I sit looking at the tarnished old brass morning-glory horn of May's gramophone—as brassy as May herself—I wonder whether she ever saw any of the three motion pictures inspired by this small but significant part of her life. In a way it is painful to imagine her sitting in a movie theater, watching as a private hurt of hers was laid bare, even in fictionalized, literally "whitewashed" form . . . and with a happy ending that likely never graced her real life. But somehow I doubt she ever saw the movie, or was aware of the revenge Maugham had taken on her. Because if she had seen it, I can't help but envision her sitting in the theater in a righteous lather, as the lights come up and the last frame of film fades from the screen.

"Jesus H. Christ on a bicycle!" I hear her cry out, indignantly. "So where the hell is *my* piece of the take?"

The "Sadie Thompson" *I* knew would have sued—and won.

Ten

Summer in Honolulu brings the sweet smell of mangoes, guava, and passionfruit, ripe for picking; it arbors the streets with the fiery red umbrellas of poinciana trees and decorates the sidewalks with the pink and white puffs of blossoming monkeypods. Cooling trade winds prevail all summer, bringing what the old Hawaiians called *makani 'olu'olu*—"fair wind." On one such radiant Sunday morning in July, I proudly slipped my silver wedding pin back into my hair as Jae-sun and I were married by Reverend Song. The ceremony was Methodist and our wedding attire American: My husband wore a dark suit and tie, and I, a white wedding dress I made myself. In other ways, however, it was a typically Korean wedding. Beauty and her husband appeared properly solemn, though Esther Kahahawai, here with Joey, was distressed by the wedding party's somber demeanor, taking me aside before the ceremony to ask if everything was all right. I tried to explain to her that smiles were regarded as bad form at Korean weddings, and assured her that I was happier than I had ever been before. She looked at me as if this were the saddest thing she had ever heard, then accepted it with a small shrug. I was happy that one of my first friends in Honolulu could be here today, though I was disappointed that Joseph Sr.'s new job as a streetcar conductor kept him from attending.

The ceremony was a sunny antidote to my first, bleak dockside wedding. Afterward, Jae-sun and I toasted with a wedding wine called *jung jong,* and our guests feasted on a banquet that my husband himself had prepared, as well as Esther's delicious pineapple cream pie. Joey gulped a little of the wine and got very light-headed. Gazing at the jolly smile on his face, I thought of my tipsy grandmother back in Pojogae and wished that my mother could have been here today. But of course I could not tell my family in Korea of my second wedding, any more than I could tell them of my divorce: they would have been mortified for me, and deeply shamed. Easier to simply let them believe, when in the future I would mention "my husband" in letters home, that I had had the same one all along. And we were forced to maintain a similar fiction—that of my "widowhood"—with Jae-sun's church, or else we would not have been allowed to marry here at all.

Since our wedding coincided with the height of the summer pineapple harvest, and thus the busiest time of year for the cannery, our honeymoon was limited to a single day and night—most of it spent moving my belongings out of my tenement room in Kauluwela and into a slightly larger tenement room Jae-sun was renting on Kukui Street. I could not bear the thought of another wedding night at the Hai Dong Hotel, so we simply retired to our new shared home and suppered on leftovers from the wedding banquet. What this may have lacked in finery it made up for in feeling. I had longed for some trace of tenderness that night, three years before, at the Hotel of Sorrows; tonight I felt it in my husband's every touch. For the first time I felt as though a man were actually making love to me, rather than merely drawing some selfish pleasure from my body. To finally know such joy and intimacy—such gladness of heart—was a bounty I had never expected, and afterward I wept for my good fortune, for the gift I had been given in Jae-sun.

Then the next morning we arose, packed our lunches, and reported to work at the cannery.

Strange as it may seem, I liked this. I liked the fact that the happiest night of my life was followed by a day like any other. It seemed to say that such happiness, so long denied, was now a part of my everyday life.

"I will see you at lunch, *yobo*," my new husband told me before heading to his job on the loading dock. I smiled. I liked the way he called me *yobo*—"dear." I had never felt as though I were truly dear to anyone before.

In summer the cannery was in operation twenty-four hours a day, with three rotating shifts of workers to accommodate the tons of pineapple being processed. Jae-sun and I were soon assigned different shifts, and often the only time we saw each other was in passing on our way to and from work. But the end of the summer harvest also marked the end of my employment at Hawaiian Pineapple. By October I was pregnant; Jae-sun fretted over my being engaged in manual labor, and in truth we were both tired of seeing so little of one another.

I applied for work as a seamstress at tailor shops, dry-goods stores, dressmakers, laundries—all enjoying robust business in the wake of America's entry into what was then being called the Great War. Honolulu was the base of operations for America's Pacific fleet, and a major port for American allies like Japan—the presence of whose warships, slipping into the harbor like fat gray sharks, infuriated Jae-sun and other Korean nationalists. But it meant boom times for Honolulu's tailors, who were kept busy fitting, repairing, and replacing uniforms for the men of the American, Australian, and Japanese military.

I was hired by a tailor named John Ku'uana, an affable Hawaiian with a small shop on King Street, directly across from the O'ahu Railway terminal. Since it was a short walk to the cannery, Jae-sun and I were able to continue our occasional custom of sharing a *bentō* at lunchtime. At my new job I soon found myself doing everything from hemming ladies' skirts to patching bullet holes in a seaman's cap. The work was no less demanding than my job at the cannery, but it was far more satisfying and even paid somewhat better, close to a dollar a day.

I also learned much from Mr. Ku'uana about the history of clothing here in Hawai'i. For the many centuries Hawaiians had lived in serene isolation from the outside world, they had woven fabrics from the inner bark of the paper-mulberry tree—*kapa*, or "bark cloth." Women and men alike had worn only a kind of loose wrap around their waists, but the missionaries quickly put an end to that. After trade with the rest of the world was established, Hawaiians enthusiastically began to import foreign fabrics—calico, cotton, gingham, satin, velvet, muslin—and adopted more Western-style dress. Women took to wearing long gowns called *holokūs* outside the home and yoke-necked *mu'umu'us* inside it. Affluent men favored Western-style business suits, while laborers wore the rugged, checked *palaka* work shirts and "sailor *mokus*," blue denim pants. Also popular was a Filipino shirt called the *barong tagalog*, which was of lighter weight and usually worn loose over one's trousers. At Mr. Ku'uana's shop I often found myself assembling *palakas* from bolts of checkered cotton, but I was as likely to be asked to mend the collar on a Mandarin jacket, or to fashion a kimono from colorful *yukata* cloth that a customer had purchased from a dry-goods store like Musa-Shiya Shoten.

One morning in November, however, Mr. Ku'uana came to work with an unusually somber cast to his face. When I asked him what was wrong he grimly informed me that the waters of the harbor were filled with schools of 'āweoweo—a bright red fish whose appearance inevitably tolled a death knell for Hawaiian royalty.

Tears came to his eyes. "It's her time," he said softly, and I did not have to ask who he meant; she had been in ill health for quite some time. On the following Sunday, November 11, as the red fish had augured, Queen Lili'uokalani passed away at the age of seventy-nine. The islands were draped in mourning for a week as the queen's body was borne by hearse from Washington Place to Kawaiaha'o Church, to be viewed by thousands of grieving visitors who came to pay their final respects.

I was privileged to have met Lili'uokalani in life and felt obliged to bid her farewell now. I joined a long procession of mourners who filed through the coral-block church for one last glimpse of this woman who might have lost a kingdom but never the hearts of her subjects. They paid homage to her with ceremonial wails and chants, visceral expressions of grief unlike any I had ever heard. Finally, I neared the casket on its funeral bier, surrounded by attendants bearing the distinctive royal staffs. I gazed down at the queen in her ivory silk *holokū*—at her white nimbus of hair resting on a yellow pall—and I bid goodbye to this woman who had, by the grace of her dignity and courage, become my queen as well.

On Saturday, her body was taken to 'Iolani Palace and to a place she was able to return to only in death: her former throne room. It was here that her state funeral took place the following day. Government officials who had conspired to depose Lili'uokalani now eulogized her amid the enshrined beauty of a monarchy that safely existed only in memory. Later, *kukui* torches lit her way to the Royal Mausoleum in Nu'uanu Valley, where she was laid to rest, the last of the reigning *ali'i*, near her brother David in the Kalākaua Tomb.

Seven months later, when the time came to name my newborn daughter, I had occasion to think of Lili'uokalani. Jae-sun and I agreed that since our daughter was to be born an American, she should have an American name. But I wanted her to have a Korean name as well, and one in particular: "Eun," which means "blessing." And as I lay abed with this tiny, precious newborn at my breast, I promised her that she would never, ever feel that she was anything but a blessing to her parents.

But "Eun" can also mean "grace," which reminded me of Lili'uokalani; and so it pleased me in many ways to christen our daughter Grace Eun Choi.

*N*ow, in accordance with Korean custom, I, too, became known by a different name. As strange as it may sound to Western ears, from this point on my husband would usually address me as "Grace Eun's mother." Even in identifying myself to others I would most often tell them, "I am Grace Eun's mother." Admittedly, this was an antiquated holdover from Confucian tradition, in which a woman was defined by the children she had borne. But as someone who had had many different names already in a relatively young life, one more did not particularly bother me . . . especially when it held within it the name of my daughter.

Like the Japanese women on the plantation who carried their babies into the cane fields, I now brought Grace Eun with me each day to the tailor's shop. Mr. Ku'uana enjoyed having a little *keiki* around, and at first Grace merely dozed amid swaddling in a cardboard box as I stitched away beside her. When she started to crawl, I constructed a playpen for her out of wardrobe racks on rollers.

The tailor shop was not far from Mr. Yi's general store; I would sometimes go there to meet Beauty and we would eat at an excellent

Chinese restaurant next door. On one such day she was shelving some yard goods when I arrived, and upon seeing me enter the store holding Grace, she waved to me, picked up her purse, and started for the door.

How I wish I had looked away just then! Had I glanced out the window, or down at my feet, or anywhere else, I would not have seen the young stock clerk, Frank Ahn, as he caught Beauty's eye from behind the counter and smiled fondly at her. Nor would I have seen her smile back—so tender a glance that I blushed to witness it. Flustered, I turned away and earnestly began considering some tableware stacked in a display near the door.

When Beauty joined me moments later, I said nothing about what I'd seen. Nor did she say anything to me, which was a source of great relief. The matter was none of my business, after all, and thereafter I did my best to ignore, if not quite forget, the whole embarrassing moment.

Now that I was no longer living in dread of revealing my whereabouts to Mr. Noh, I wrote to Jade Moon at Waialua Plantation, telling her of my new life in Honolulu, my husband and daughter, and my job at the tailor shop. In her return letter she expressed an interest in knowing how much I received in salary. This discussion of money made me somewhat uncomfortable, but I dutifully responded that I made between fifteen and twenty dollars a month depending on the hours I worked. "But of course, these are poor wages in this wealthy city," I added, trying not to seem as though I were bragging.

There followed a lag in our correspondence, and the longer I did not hear from Jade Moon the more I worried that I had offended or embarrassed her.

Then one afternoon I was in the midst of mending an Australian naval uniform—I'd had some trouble matching its coarse, canvaslike fabric until I hit upon the idea of using sail-cloth from a sail maker's shop down the street—when Mr. Ku'uana came into the back of the store and told me, "'Ey, you got visitors. Look like *'ohana*." I had no family here, of course, other than Grace and Jae-sun. Thinking perhaps it was Beauty and her daughter, Mary, I went out to the front of the shop to greet them.

But it was a different picture bride who was waiting: I was startled to find Jade Moon standing there in the shop, a baby in one arm and a suitcase in the other. Her husband, Mr. Ha, was carrying in three more pieces of luggage, including a large steamer trunk.

"We have come to live in Honolulu," Jade Moon announced with no preamble. "Can you recommend a place to stay?"

I was dumbstruck. Mr. Ha turned to his wife. "*Yobo*, we've disturbed her during working hours. Perhaps we should come back later."

"Don't be ridiculous," Jade Moon chided him. "Let me handle this."

Her husband acquiesced quickly, meekly: "Yes, *yobo*."

I finally found my voice. "It . . . it's wonderful to see you, dear friend, but—what made you decide to come to Honolulu?"

"*You* did," she declared. "You make as much money here in a month as my old man and I do combined! So why in heaven should we stay on the plantation?"

The phrase Jade Moon used to denote her husband—"my old man"—was common idiom in Korean for one's husband and not a deliberate slight concerning his age. Or so I hoped.

"I liked Waialua," Mr. Ha said wistfully. "I liked our little house."

"Don't talk nonsense. For thirty dollars a month you do not have to like where you live."

The smile that came to Mr. Ha's face was a very Korean smile of embarrassment. He had the look, it seemed to me, of a man who had awakened one day to find himself clinging to the cattle catcher of an express train: under the circumstances, all one could do was to hang on.

Mr. Ku'uana generously gave me the afternoon off to help settle my old friend and her family in Honolulu. As we all struck up Nu'uanu Avenue in search of rooms, with Jade Moon and I both hoisting our children aloft, I inquired of the toddler in her arms, "And what might your name be, little one?"

"His name is Woodrow," Mr. Ha said proudly, "after President Wilson."

His wife said, "I wanted to call him Screaming Voice in the Night, or perhaps Endlessly Hungry and Teething, but I deferred to the boy's father."

"He's very sweet."

"Yes, I suppose he is," Jade Moon allowed. "And another is on the way."

"That's wonderful," I said.

"Yes, I suppose it is," she said with a sigh. "We'll need at least two rooms."

They had sufficient funds for a two-room flat in one of the less ramshackle tenements in Kauluwela, but even so Mr. Ha appeared appalled at the living conditions. When he started to object, Jade Moon threw him a look that cowed him into silence. She negotiated the price with the landlord and paid the first month's rent in advance. After the landlord had left, she told her husband, more gently, "We won't be here long, *yobo*. We have to start somewhere."

He nodded, clearly hoping she was right.

Though the tourist trade had slowed to a trickle due to the war, the military presence, as I've noted, created many new jobs. Mr. Ha found work in a rice mill and Jade Moon was soon employed as a laundress in a hotel (one that also housed one of the city's ubiquitous billiards parlors). Like me she brought her young *keiki* with her to work, finding ways of keeping him occupied as she soaked and wrung dirty laundry. On one of my visits to her workplace I was struck by how different she seemed from the woman I had met at the inn in Yokohama—her fair complexion darkened by a piti-less sun, her hands rough and chapped from field labor. Yet she still held herself like a proud *yangban,* even when stringing sop-ping wet shirts on a clothesline. "Have you been able to send any money home to your mother?" I asked her.

"A little. But my father, the worthless layabout, opened the let-ter first and used the money to buy more of the Chinese classics. After that I began mailing the cash to a neighbor, who gives it to my mother."

Little Woodrow, his head barely poking out of a large card-board box, began crying, perhaps out of boredom. Casting about for something to occupy him, Jade Moon left the laundry room, only to come back a minute later carrying a red billiard ball with the number 3 on it, which she deposited in Woodrow's playpen. When I appeared dubious, she told me, "It will help him learn arithmetic," and indeed he took to it immediately, happily rolling, dropping, and sucking on it.

"Look at the clothes these rich *haoles* wear," Jade Moon said, admiring a woman's floral cotton dress. "Someday I will wear clothes like this and pay other people to wash them! We'll start a business, set aside enough money to send to my family in Korea, and buy a little house here. My husband may be old, but he has a strong back and is a hard worker. We will do it."

"And are you happier now with Mr. Ha?" I asked.

She looked at me as if I were the most pitifully credulous crea-ture that ever walked the earth. "What does happiness have to do with anything? There are diapers to be changed and suppers to be cooked, and one leads inevitably to the other. Are *you* happy?"

"Yes," I said, "I think so."

She stared at me, then fairly snorted in disbelief. I changed the subject.

The more time I spent with Beauty and Jade Moon, the more I realized how fortunate I was—and how unusual among Asian women—to have a husband of my own choosing. We were bound together not by parental fiat or a matchmaker's deceit, but by common feeling for one another. I had a beautiful daughter, a roof over our heads, and I had even been able to put away some thirty-nine dollars toward Blossom's eventual steamer fare.

When my eldest brother wrote and told me that he was betrothed to marry a young *yangban* girl from a neighboring village, I sensed an opportunity. With a full-grown daughter-in-law shortly to enter the household, perhaps this was the time to broach the subject of Blossom. So I took up my pen and revealed to Joyful Day for the first time my interest in bringing her to Hawai'i. I hoped to receive some words of encouragement, perhaps even an offer to broker terms with my father (I knew I would have to compensate my clan for the loss of a daughter-in-law and was prepared to pay them considerably more than they had paid Blossom's clan). But within a month I received this reply:

Little Sister,

You must banish from your thoughts any foolish notions about bringing sister-in-law to live with you. I can tell you without equivocation that Father would not hear of it. Grandmother is in failing health and Mother cannot do all the work of the Inner Room by herself, even with the help of my new bride. And what of your youngest brother? Does he not deserve a wife of his own?

Little sister, I am happy for your freedom and your new family in America. I understand, truly, that the life of a Korean woman is often, as in the old adage, like that of the frog living at the bottom of a well, who believes the whole world is wet and cold and made of stone. You know better now—but Blossom, I am afraid, is fated to live her life at the bottom of that well. Only one frog in each family may leap to freedom.

These last words were stinging enough to bring tears to my eyes. Was it true? Had I selfishly pursued my own happiness and so condemned Blossom to life as a Daughter-in-Law Flower? I was still weeping when my husband came home from work. "Grace Eun's mother," he said, "what is it? What's wrong?" I showed him the letter and took some solace in his arms, as he reassured me, "She is still but eleven years old. We have time to think of ways to soften your father's resolve. Don't cry, *yobo*."

I chose to accept his consolation and told myself it was true: There *was* still time, wasn't there? Perhaps if we saved even more money, we could offer Father a sum so large—a hundred dollars?—that he could not refuse it. I would just have to work that much harder to bring it about.

Another rude shock came the following Sunday, when Jae-sun and our family attended one of Joey's softball games on the grounds of Kauluwela Grammar School. Though Joey continued to grow by leaps and bounds and to improve athletically, today he seemed off his game—"striking out" at bat, missing an easy catch in left field. He seemed almost disinterested in playing, quite uncharacteristic for him, and his team lost 12–3, also atypical.

Afterward, along with Joey's teammates and their parents, my family and I enjoyed a picnic supper at 'A'ala Park. Notably absent again was Joseph Sr., and Esther seemed as listless as Joey. I asked her whether there was anything wrong and she finally confided that she and Joseph had separated and were filing for divorce. She did not go into the reasons and I discreetly did not inquire, though she did say that Joseph was now living in Kailua, on the windward coast, and today notwithstanding, was still very much a presence in his children's life.

I did my best to console her, pointing out that divorce, after all,

230

was not just an ending but a beginning as well. "I am certainly proof of that," I pointed out. "You will find someone, as I found Jae-sun."

"I don't worry about that," she said, "as much as I do about Joey, growing up here in the city. I can't help wishing we'd never left Maui."

It was true, Hell's Half Acre was hardly the best place for boys to grow up: the crowded tenement houses rubbed shoulders with pool halls, gambling houses, speakeasies, and brothels. Neighborhood clubs—like Joey's "Kauluwela Boys"—evolved all too easily into gangs that drifted into fighting and petty theft.

"He will be fine," I told Esther. "He's a good boy."

Joey's detachment during the game now made sense, and when shortly afterward I saw him sitting alone, picking at his *poi* and *haupia* pudding, I went and joined him.

"Mack and Shorty say I played like a dumb old *kua'āina*," he said glumly.

"The last time I saw you play, you hit a home run and won the game. They weren't complaining then."

"Last time I didn't play like a dumb old *kua'āina*," he muttered.

"No one can win every game they play, Joey."

"Why not?" he said angrily.

"It's not the game that's bothering you, is it?"

He got up suddenly, kicked a fallen coconut with his bare foot, and sent it hurtling across the park in an impressive if pointless display.

When he sat back down, I saw there were tears in his eyes. "Aunt Jin . . . why are Mama and Papa so mad at each other? Is it something I did?"

"Oh, Joey, no, no—it's not your fault." I lay my arm across his shoulders and told him, "It's just that . . . mothers and fathers get married because they fall in love, and sometimes . . . they fall *out* of love, and have to stop being married."

"Why?"

"Because they do, that's all. But I promise you this, Joey: the one thing they never stop loving is their *keiki*."

He looked at me hopefully. "No lie?"

I squeezed him to me and smiled. "No lie," I said.

*T*he Great War soon ended, but in my homeland another sort of battle was now engaged. Not long after the New Year, Honolulu's Korean community received the stirring news that a group of thirty-three brave Korean patriots—inspired by President Wilson's postwar utterances about the rights of smaller countries to be free—had conspired to compose a document they called "The Proclamation of Korean Independence," which asserted Korea's sovereign right to be free of Japanese domination. On the morning of March 1, 1919, the conspirators gathered at the Pagoda Restaurant in Seoul, signed the highly illegal and seditious document, then politely telephoned the nearest police station to turn themselves in.

At two o'clock that afternoon, three million courageous citizens all across Korea participated in a series of carefully synchronized demonstrations. Shopkeepers closed their stores; *yangban* and peasants alike took to the streets, where the proclamation of independence was read aloud to cheering crowds. Protesters proudly waved the banned Korean flag and cried, *"Mansei! Mansei!"*—"May Korea live ten thousand years!" It was by all accounts one of the most inspiring moments in our nation's history: men, women, and children joined in solidarity and love of country, love of freedom, proclaiming—demanding—their liberty. Even a few Korean policemen were moved to discard their black uniforms and join the protesters. There was no violence at first: The architects of the demonstration had laid down strict instructions not to provoke the Japanese military police and to submit peacefully to them.

But as the demonstrations continued over the next several days, with stores remaining closed and students refusing to attend schools, the Japanese authorities engaged in bitter reprisal. Unarmed, unresisting protesters were pounded with clubs or silenced with sabers. In one notably gruesome instance, a man's ears were chopped off and his body hacked to ribbons by swords. Women who were not killed were often gang-raped by Japanese soldiers. There were massacres at places like Sungohun and Suheung, whose names went from obscurity to infamy in a matter of days.

In the span of just seven weeks, some two thousand Korean men, women, and children would die in the name of the bloodred sun of Imperial Japan.

In Hawai'i, we first learned of all this in Sunday church services and the community's response was predictably one of horror and outrage—inciting a militant nationalism in even those who had not previously been politically minded.

"The Japanese have finally shown their true face to the world," our pastor declared. "Now it is time *we* show solidarity with our fellow Koreans!"

The founder of the Korean Christian Church, Dr. Syngman Rhee, was named head of a "provisional government" in exile, and his Korean National Association solicited donations on behalf of this government. Every family was exhorted to contribute five dollars for each adult member of the household. At a time when the average Korean family earned barely thirty dollars a month, this was a not inconsiderable sum; but we gave willingly, enthusiastically, in the common cause of our native country's freedom.

I joined the newly formed Women's Relief Society, whose members would often forego one bowl of rice each day in order to make rice cakes to be sold for fund-raising. Like many in the community, we boycotted Japanese goods such as soy sauce and bought our rice from Chinese merchants. Jae-sun, never kindly disposed toward the Japanese, seemed to harden his heart against them even more.

But by the start of the Year of the Monkey, in February of 1920, these distant horrors were eclipsed by one right here in our midst.

Eleven

$\mathcal{I}$n December an epidemic of Spanish influenza broke out in Honolulu as it already had worldwide, going on to claim eighty-one lives in the islands in January alone. Hawai'i, of course, had a long and fatal history of Western plagues devastating the native population, and the ensuing panic drove people off the streets and into the presumed safety of their own homes. Churches suspended services out of fear of spreading the disease; movie theaters shut their doors indefinitely. Queen's Hospital was quickly overwhelmed with cases of influenza and emergency hospitals were established at Quarantine Island and, uncomfortably close to us, Pālama Settlement.

By this time I was also three months pregnant with our second child. Not wishing to expose Grace Eun or our unborn child to unnecessary risk, Jae-sun and I agreed that I would give up my job at the tailor shop, though I still took in some piecework I could do at home. We may not have made as much money, but neither did we want for anything of substance, and were even still able to donate our five dollars a month to the Korean Independence Fund.

So it came as something of a surprise when one morning my husband held up that day's edition of Dr. Rhee's Korean-language newspaper, the *Korean Pacific Weekly*, and said, "Here now, Grace Eun's mother, do you see this?" He tapped the front page with his finger. "This is opportunity. Go on, read it."

He handed me the paper, pointing out a story about the recent strike action taken by Japanese and Filipino laborers against O'ahu's sugar plantations. The workers were seeking an increase in wages— from a base pay of seventy-seven cents a day to a dollar and twenty-five cents—as well as changes to the inequitable "bonus" system. I remembered the back-breaking toil at Waialua and could scarcely blame the strikers.

"The plantation owners need new workers to replace them," Jae-sun said excitedly, "and are willing to pay up to three and a half dollars a day, plus bonuses!"

This seemed a huge sum and I was frankly skeptical. "Why would they pay someone three dollars a day when the strikers are only asking for a third of that?"

"As a wedge to use against the union. The planters would lose much more money in the long run if they give in to the demands. But in the short run, there is opportunity for much money to be made by someone like myself."

I was dismayed to hear this. "You wish to go back to the planta-tion?"

"Only for as long as the strike goes on. Even if it lasts only two more months, why, at three and a half dollars a day, I could earn nearly two hundred dollars in that time! Think of what we could do with such money! We could buy a home of our own. Or a boardinghouse! Perhaps even—open a restaurant."

This last he spoke casually, almost diffidently, but I did not underestimate its importance to him. Still . . . "It does not seem right," I said, "taking someone else's job. Even a Japanese."

"They have taken our country from us," Jae-sun replied coldly, predictably. "I won't shed any tears over taking one of their jobs! In fact, I will do it with pride, and as a spit in the face of the Japanese Empire."

Seeing my hesitation, he softened this a bit. "No one will lose their jobs permanently, *yobo*. The strike will last a month or two, the laborers will eventually return to the plantation, and you and I will have some extra money in our pocket—that's all."

Jae-sun earned barely two hundred dollars for an entire year's work at the cannery; to make such a sum in only two months' time did seem miraculous. "So," I said resignedly, "you have accepted a job, then?"

He looked surprised. "No, of course not. I merely wish to know what you think of the idea. Though I hope you will agree that this is an opportunity that does not come often in a man's life."

It wasn't the wistfulness in his eyes when he spoke of opening a restaurant that swayed me. Nor was it the money, though I did consider what it might mean for my children's future, as well as Blossom's. No, in the end what persuaded me was simply . . . that he had *asked* me. My father would have made such a decision on his own and only informed my mother after the fact. That Jae-sun sought my opinion—my consent—meant more to me than I could say. And because of that, I could not gainsay him this job.

"I see the wisdom in what you suggest. It *is* a great opportunity." I was not nearly as confident as I sounded, but the gladness in his face almost convinced me. "How soon would we leave?"

Startled, he said, "No, you misunderstand. *I* would go to the plantation, you and Grace would remain here, in Honolulu."

Had I heard him correctly? "You would go there—alone?"

"It will be better that way. You would not have to move, and I can always come into the city on Sundays to visit."

"But—my place is with you," I protested. "*Our* place—Grace's, too."

I had not expected the sudden panic I saw in his eyes. "No!" he blurted out. "You mustn't bring the children!"

His voice was raised not in anger but in alarm. Now I understood.

"Husband," I said, gently, "no harm will come to them. Or to me."

"You don't know that! A plantation is a dangerous place to raise a child."

I took his hand in mine and felt it tremble like a sparrow's wing.

"*Yobo*, no harm will come to us. I promise that I will not work in the fields if you do not wish me to. I will not bring Grace or our unborn child into the fields. And consider this: Given the spread of influenza here in Honolulu, it might even be safer for them there, away from the city."

He thought about that a long moment.

"You will go nowhere near the fields," he finally said—not a command but a restatement. I nodded.

"I lost a child on the plantation, too," I reminded him. "I promise you, I will not lose another."

Jae-sun had no trouble securing a job at the O'ahu Sugar Company in Waipahu, just outside Honolulu, and it took less than a week to pack up our belongings and arrange for transportation. Before we left, I stopped and said goodbye, for the moment, to the Kahahawais. The past year had seen Joseph Sr. remarry to a pretty eighteen-year-old Hawaiian woman named Hannah Pipi, with whom he soon had a young son named Arthur—

the first of four boys and two daughters. Esther, in order to make ends meet, had taken a job sewing burlap bags at the Hawaiian Fertilizer Company in Iwilei, where she met and began seeing a fellow employee, an easygoing Portuguese named Pascual Anito. With typical Hawaiian tolerance and *aloha*, all parties seemed to accept and embrace this extended *'ohana*. Joey—now, at the mature age of eleven, preferring to be called Joe, like his father—seemed happy to have a younger brother.

He even seemed to have gained something of an older brother in the form of a family friend named William Kama, who worked with Joe Sr. as a streetcar conductor, and who was visiting when I dropped by. Bill was a serious young man in his mid-twenties, of medium height and build, but he might have been ten feet tall for the way Joe Jr. looked up to him. A graduate of the prestigious Kamehameha School, Bill hoped to become a police officer.

"Joe's a good kid," he told me. "He just needs somebody to remind him of it." Bill promised me he'd do his best to keep him from playing hooky with Mack and Shorty, and "out of *pilikia*."

On Friday morning my family and I boarded a train bound for Waipahu, a few miles north of Pearl Harbor. Grace cried at first at the clamor of the locomotive as it clattered out of the station, but quieted when I held her up to the window to watch the landscape rolling past. It was a short trip to Waipahu—only nine stops, less than forty minutes—which helped reassure me that I was not leaving too far behind us the life we had begun building for ourselves in Honolulu.

We were not the only strikebreakers arriving that day, but were among a group of about thirty laborers—Chinese, Hawaiian, Korean, Portuguese—who disembarked at Waipahu. None of us, however, had expected to be escorted onto the plantation by a contingent of fifteen local police officers, who formed a buffer between us and a small number of Japanese gathered along Waipahu Depot Road. Some were local shopkeepers, but many were laborers who had been forcibly evicted from their plantation homes after the strike was called. They had taken refuge in nearby schools and temples and now looked upon us, their replacements, with understandable discontent. Once on the plantation grounds we even passed through what had been the Japanese camp—silent as a town full of *obake*, ghosts, the houses hauntingly empty, their doors and windows actually nailed shut.

In contrast to the white sands and crashing surf at Waialua, there was a lonely monotony about the landscape here. Waipahu was a flat, landlocked plain—acre upon acre of sugar cane and rice paddies—with only the stooped shoulders of low hills in the distance. When we reached the Korean camp we found that it stood within sight of the gracious homes of the plantation managers, but our own housing was so far removed from this it might have been on the other side of the world. We were to live in what amounted to a long barracks, four families to a building, each so-called "apartment" separated by freestanding walls that stopped well short of the roof. We had no privacy to speak of and were never free from the chatter of neighbors or the crying of their children. We also shared the housing with other, unwanted residents: cockroaches, centipedes, even scorpions, which stubbornly held their ground until repulsed by torches made of old newspaper.

The latrines were long sheds containing wooden benches with appropriate holes cut in them, situated above a trench of running water. There was also a copy of last year's Sears, Roebuck catalog, the pages of which were apparently used to cleanse oneself. It made the lavatories at Kauluwela look like a king's bath!

As I made my inaugural visit to these facilities—relieving myself of a stream of water into even fouler waters below—the last thing I expected was to hear a familiar voice:

"Did I not predict that this would be a great adventure?"

Glancing to my left I was startled to see—seated on the next bench, with her skirt hiked up to her waist—the diminutive figure of Wise Pearl.

We laughed and (taking time to adjust our skirts) embraced.

"It is good to see you again," she said warmly. "How is Mr. Noh?"

"It is good to see you as well. But I am no longer married to Mr. Noh. It is a long story, and as bad as much of it is, not one I wish to relate in an outhouse."

She laughed at this and we relocated outside, to more pleasant surroundings along the banks of Waikele Stream. I told her of my circumstances these past few years, the good and the bad, and asked for her discretion in regards to my divorce. I was a bit apprehensive about her reaction, but to my great relief it seemed not to trouble her at all.

"And have you and Mr. Kam been here at Waipahu all this time?" I asked.

"No, my husband was at 'Ewa Plantation when we married," she explained. "We spent three years there, where I gave birth to two healthy sons. But Mr. Kam speaks very good English as well as Japanese and Korean, and I encouraged him to apply for a job as a translator here at Waipahu . . . though at the moment, I'm afraid, there is precious little to translate."

I told her of our fellow picture brides, now both living in Honolulu. "It would be a fine thing to see them again," she said. "Perhaps we may take the train into town together sometime."

"I'm sure they would like that as well."

I was happy to find a friend here, much less an old friend; and pleased that it felt as if not a day had passed between us since our dockside weddings, almost six years before.

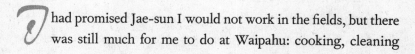 had promised Jae-sun I would not work in the fields, but there was still much for me to do at Waipahu: cooking, cleaning

house, and the inevitable laundering of work clothes caked in mud or blackened by soot from the sugar mill. It was familiar drudgery, made more challenging by the presence of a toddler who seemed unsettled by her new surroundings and clung anxiously to my skirt. My pregnancy often amplified my weariness, sapping me of strength and stamina when I needed them most. Thank Heaven for Wise Pearl, who was always there to lend a hand. She never seemed to lack for energy or good cheer, a useful corrective to my own moodiness—not just my hormones but the depressing return to plantation life, living by the shriek of the steam whistle sunup to sundown, and the unfortunate memories this evoked.

But the workers' community here was as welcoming as it was at Waialua, and I soon made many friends among the Spanish, Chinese, and Puerto Rican wives. Their children, and Wise Pearl's two sons, tried to befriend Grace, but she was painfully shy—as I had been at her age—and despite coaxing she usually retreated into the nearest corner to play with her doll.

My husband was not as young as when he last did field work; most days he came stumbling home bone-weary and sore, wolfing down dinner before collapsing into bed. I massaged his aching back and shoulders and rubbed ointment into sprained muscles. But he never complained or lost sight of why he was suffering this: Every payday he would proudly show me his wages and talk about the future this money would secure for us. Even after buying groceries I was able to deposit more than half of his salary in the bank; at his weariest, Jae-sun was buoyed by our little account book and what it represented.

I did most of our shopping at the plantation store, but there were certain items they did not carry, and though I shared Jae-sun's aversion to patronizing Japanese merchants, my family's needs came first. So without telling my husband I would sneak off to shop at the well-stocked Arakawa's Store on Depot Road. Mr. Arakawa was always cordial enough, but on the street I felt the eyes of the Japanese strikers on me and I shrank from the anger and contempt in their faces, lowering my eyes as I hurried back to the safety of the Korean camp.

When I next needed provisions I could not obtain at the plantation store, I decided to purchase them at Mr. Yi's general store in Honolulu, where I could also say hello to Beauty. With Wise Pearl minding Grace Eun, I boarded the 8:35 train, arriving in Iwilei at 9:15 A.M. But I scarcely expected the sight that greeted me as I left the train depot.

Refugee camps overflowing with hundreds of displaced workers from the plantations had sprung up like weeds all around the train station. I was stunned to see entire families living in canvas tents, cooking their meals over open fires, washing their clothes in metal buckets and drying them on lines strung between campsites. Instead of the scent of orchids or Chinese jasmine, the trade winds carried the rank smell of human waste from holes dug along the perimeter of the camp. In the midst of this squalor and desolation, *keiki* laughed and played as *keiki* did anywhere, but somehow that made the sight even harder for me to bear.

I hurried across King Street into Pālama, but if there was no refuge for these people, there was none for me from them. I saw dozens squeezed into a single shrine or temple, or camped in once-vacant lots between buildings. Some were Filipino, but most were Japanese—women in kimonos feeding their children meager rations of rice or *miso* soup as their frustrated and helpless husbands sat by, smoking cigarettes. Others lay blanketed on bedding inside their tents, even though it was mid-morning.

All at once our rude lodgings in Waipahu seemed positively palatial in comparison. And I wondered, with a queasy feeling, whether our current housing had perhaps been home to one of these families, who were now living in such squalid conditions.

I headed north on Liliha Street, where still more families squatted in abandoned stores and factories, each person staking out a cold sliver of concrete floor. Many lay on *tatami* mats, coughing or shivering as if feverish. With a sudden fright I realized how foolish I had been to come to Honolulu—these crowded, unsanitary encampments were obviously rife with influenza. Cursing myself for my stupidity, I quickened my pace, intending to briskly make my purchases at Yi's store, then board the very next train for Waipahu.

But a few blocks up the street, in another formerly empty lot, a baby was wailing—and that sound will always make a woman's head turn, if only for a moment. I looked and saw a Japanese woman sitting cross-legged on a mat, two drowsy toddlers leaning up against her with eyes closed as she cradled a baby, rocking it asleep with a Japanese lullaby I had heard in the sugar fields:

> *The guarded mountain,*
> *Mountain of the sacred grove—*
> *Along the foot*
> *Ashibi are flowering—*
> *What a lovely mountain is*
> *The mountain guarded like a crying child.*

But it was not the woman's song that had drawn my attention. I knew her.

It was the young Japanese woman from the *Nippon Maru*—the one who'd sat down beside me on the deck one chilly night, and whose friendly overtures I had just as coldly rebuffed. That young woman's face had been smiling, open, and cheerful, but this woman's was pale as chalk, her eyes beset with worry. She looked like a wraith cradling the spirit of a stolen child.

I knew I should not get any closer for fear of influenza, yet I still took a step toward her.

"Excuse me," I said, "but . . . did you travel here aboard the *Nippon Maru?*"

She looked at me and blinked, as if wondering why anyone would ask her this. Finally she replied, "A long time ago . . . yes."

Fool that I was, I took another step forward.

"I believe we met one night, on deck. I was . . . quite rude to you."

She looked more closely at me; a pale crescent of a smile appeared on her face. "Ah . . . yes," she said slowly. "So you were."

"Is—is your baby hungry?" I asked.

She shook her head. "No, just colicky. I have milk enough for her. But alas, these two"—she glanced at her two older boys—"are too old to suckle at their mother's breast."

"Does no one provide for you here?"

She made a little shrug at that.

"The union does what it can," she said, "but there are many mouths to feed—over six thousand of us, we are told, on Oʻahu. The men go fishing or catch crabs at the waterfront . . . that is where my husband is now. We get by."

"The plantation owners just . . . threw you out of your home?" I said in disbelief. "With your *keiki?*"

"Oh, yes. Even the sick and infirm. It made no difference to them."

I felt my face grow flush with shame and told her, "I will come back with food."

She smiled faintly. "It is kind of you to offer. But you weren't *that* rude."

"I will be back," I promised, and hurried to the nearest grocery store. There I purchased a five-pound bag of rice, a dozen eggs, a pound of dried bonito, two quarts of milk, soy sauce, miso, two pounds of *soba* noodles, a can of red *azuki* beans, and some crackseed— all of which cost about five dollars. We were making enough money at Waipahu that we could afford to be charitable, and since I managed our household budget, Jae-sun need never know of it. I carried the groceries back to the camp and humbly presented them to the woman.

"Please accept this paltry gift from an unworthy source," I said.

She hesitated to take them. "No, I could never repay this kindness."

"I am not asking you to repay it. Just take it—please." Wryly I added, "My husband hates *miso* and can't digest milk. What will I do with it all?"

She laughed at that, and finally accepted the gift.

"Thank you," she said, bowing, "for your *kampana.*" This was a Buddhist term that spoke of when "good people's hearts are moved" to do a compassionate act. "May I ask the name of our benefactor?"

"I am called Jin."

"Thank you, Jin-san. I am Tamiko. This is my firstborn son, Hiroshi, and my second-born, Jiro. The little one is Sugi."

"*Konichi wa,*" I said, then gave the boys the crackseed I had purchased. This was a sweet-salty confection popular in the islands; they snapped it up, thanked me, and happily began chewing the licorice-flavored candy.

I asked, "Which plantation did you come from?"—though I dreaded the answer.

"'Aiea." It was just a few train stops away from Waipahu. "At first we were housed in a church on King Street, but there were so many sick people there my husband thought it safer for us to be out in the open." With equal parts amazement and horror she added, "Have you heard? Even the *shichō*—oh, what is the word—the *mayor* of Honolulu, Mayor Fern, has died of the influenza!"

I had not heard. "*Aigo.*"

"Hawai'i is not what we imagined, back on the *Nippon Maru,* is it? Yet it's a lovely place, and so warm—the winters in Kumamoto were terrible, I could never go back to them. Do you live here in Honolulu?"

"No, I am just—visiting." It was nearly true. "And I must be getting home. But before I go . . ." I reached into my purse, took out several dollar bills, and started to hand them to her.

"No, no—you have done enough!"

"Call it a loan. You will repay me when you are rich, and I am poor." I bowed. "Good luck to you. Perhaps we will meet again."

"Yes, under kinder circumstances. Thank you, Jin-san."

I left and continued on to the Yi store, where I purchased the items I had come for and chatted briefly with Beauty. When I told her about Tamiko she said she would look in on the family next week and if there was anything they might need, she would supply it. Beauty truly had the good heart of which the Buddhist masters wrote; my *kampana* was compromised by shame and guilt. I thanked her and hurried back to the railroad depot. I remember thinking as I arrived that the encampment of tents and people looked like a war-weary army in a military campaign, stoically awaiting the next battle. And I feared I was on the wrong side.

*G*ently, I tried to suggest as much to Jae-sun, telling him what I had seen in Honolulu (though omitting any mention of my act of charity). But he simply said, "They chose to go out on strike. They can come back at any time of their choosing." Indeed, the Filipinos' labor union had already capitulated and called their members back to work.

I began to follow the progress of the strike more closely in the English-language papers and was shocked by their editorials, which claimed the strike was not economically motivated but a sinister attempt by Japan to wrest control of the sugar industry in Hawai'i—if not all of Hawai'i itself. They called it "the Japanese conspiracy." I read Jae-sun some of this virulently racist commentary and pointed out how the sugar industry sought to pit one racial group against another, as they did on the plantation by paying different salaries to different nationalities. "Next time it will be Japanese breaking a Korean strike, and who will benefit then?"

He grudgingly admitted that what I said made sense—and I believe I was beginning to sway his thinking when one afternoon he came limping home after a day in the fields, in a condition that made me cry out in shock and distress.

"Oh my Heaven! *Yobo,* what happened?"

His left eye was blackened; blood dripped from his nose; his right cheek was swollen purple-blue as a plum. I immediately ran and got ice from the plantation store, wrapped it in a towel, and placed it against his swollen eye. I swabbed his bruises and lacerations with iodine, which made him flinch. Finally I asked him, "Who did this to you?"

"I had an accident in the fields."

"Why did no one take you to the hospital?"

"It was on the way back from the fields," he amended.

"Husband," I asked again, "who *did* this?"

He sighed, knowing I would not let the matter rest.

"A few of us were on our way back from the north cane fields," he admitted, "when some of the strikers who had taken refuge in Hongwanji Temple approached us. They called us 'planter's dogs'— and a few other things I cannot quote. One word led to another, and here I am." He pointed to his discolored eye. "I believe the *haoles* call this 'a shiner,'" he said proudly.

"Oh, *yobo,* please. Let's go back to Honolulu."

"Never! I will be damned if I will run away with my tail between my legs, like the dog they say I am."

"Then report them to the manager, at least."

But to my surprise, he shook his head at this, too.

"They were angry, and thinking of their families' welfare," he said. "I will not report a man for that—not even a Japanese."

He stood, thanked me for my attentions, and staggered into

bed, bruised and exhausted. And the next morning went back to work in the fields.

We did not leave Waipahu.

Much of that year's sugar crop withered on the stalk for lack of sufficient manpower to harvest it, but by summer it was clear that the strike had taken a greater toll on the laborers than the planters. And by mid-year the influenza epidemic had claimed more than twelve hundred deaths in Hawai'i, a hundred and fifty of them displaced plantation workers.

Against all common sense I made occasional trips into Honolulu to aid Tamiko and her family, and thankfully I did not become sick, even though we often sat side by side and discussed our lives. Tamiko was also a picture bride, but in Japan such brides were actually married beforehand, in ceremonies in their home villages, to their absent grooms. She, too, had been disappointed at first by her husband's age and poverty, though she said she had come to care for him very much. I never dreamed that I would find I had so much in common with a Japanese person, even if my honesty with her could only go so far—a fact that weighed heavily on me as time went by.

In July the Japanese strikers' union sadly capitulated without receiving any concessions from the planters' association. The laborers went back to work, to all appearances defeated. But within four months the planters quietly raised the workers' basic wages from seventy-seven cents a day to a dollar fifteen, and revised the inequitable bonus system as well.

That system, however, had been good to our family: In four months at Waipahu we had managed to save over three hundred dollars—a small fortune by the standards of the time and the place. But I took no joy in it, only shame.

The day we returned to Honolulu was also the day Tamiko and her family left for 'Aiea. While Jae-sun haggled over new lodgings,

I took Grace Eun to Liliha Street, where the vacant lot was beginning to look vacant again—half of the squatting families having already left for their old homes at Kahuku, Waialua, Waimānalo, and other plantations. Tamiko and her two sons were gathering up their belongings as her husband was off buying tickets for the 4 P.M. train. She was happy to see me, but I was dreading this meeting.

"Tamiko-san," I said, "I've come to tell you something."

She didn't seem to be listening. "Oh, you," she scolded little Sugi, who had just soiled her diaper, "as though I didn't have *enough* to do."

"Tamiko-san, I must tell you—"

She turned and silenced me with a glance.

"There is nothing you need to tell me, Jin-san. I am not naive."

The knowing look in her eyes shamed me, as if she were staring through me, straight down to the bone.

Flustered, I said, "You don't understand." But somehow I knew she did. "I . . . I have not been honest with you."

"No, perhaps not," Tamiko said gently. "But you have been kind, and generous, and a good friend. It matters little to me what you did, or where you were, when you were not being my friend."

I was shocked and embarrassed—had she known all along?

"Not from the first," she admitted, "but things add up. Even in Japan, two plus two is still four." She smiled. "Honesty did not fill my children's stomachs, Jin-san—your *kampana* did. That is all that concerns me."

"But it was not true *kampana*," I protested. "It was tainted by guilt."

She laughed away my protestation.

"Not everyone who feels guilt does the kind or honorable thing. That is *kampana*. Now, that's enough said of the matter, but for this: Thank you."

And we spoke not another word about it, even to this day.

After they left for the train station, I visited the Yi store to purchase some household goods for our new rooms: laundry detergent, Borax cleanser, linoleum oil, among other items. I could not at first identify it, but it felt as though something was missing from the store. Beauty was there, folding a pile of work shirts, but she seemed distracted, even melancholy, and uncharacteristically disinterested in chatting. I went about my shopping, and Mr. Yi's son Jung-su had to go into the stockroom to get me a bolt of cloth for my sewing. When he returned, I realized what was missing and asked him where Frank Ahn, the stock clerk, was. "He didn't come down with influenza, did he?"

"No. He's gone," Jung-su said coldly. "His parents sent him to school in California. That will be five dollars and twenty-three cents."

I glanced over at Beauty, quietly folding shirts, and realized that she was doing her level best not to cry.

Twelve

In October I gave birth to a fine baby boy we named Harold Eun Choi—"Eun" now becoming a "generational" name, shared by brothers and sisters alike—and not long afterward, my husband and I birthed a different sort of joint enterprise. With our savings from Waipahu we were able to lease a small storefront on Buckle Lane in Liliha District, a neighborhood in which many Korean families and businesses were settling. It was a dusty little shop half a block from a stable—at quiet moments you could almost hear the flick of the horses' tails as they swatted away flies, and when the wind was right you could definitely sniff their neighborly presence. The crime rate here was high but the rent was low, and there was a large kitchen on the ground floor; and so we set about transforming this nondescript space into a restaurant. I scrubbed the grimy front windows and mopped the knotty pine floor. We purchased cookware, silverware, dishes, utensils, and a dozen sets of tables and chairs, as I fashioned tablecloths and napkins from inexpensive linen purchased at Yi's store. We spent more time debating what to christen this new offspring than we had choosing our children's names—finally deciding on Cafe Korea, which I carefully stenciled onto the front window, and below that: J. S. CHOI, PROPRIETOR. I have never seen my husband's face glow quite so brightly as when he first gazed upon that sign.

Like most businesses in the neighborhood, ours also served as a family home. The kitchen on the ground floor accommodated not only the restaurant but our own daily use as well. A stairway in the rear ascended to personal quarters above the cafe, a single large room with windows overlooking the busy street. Here was the bed Jae-sun and I shared, another for Grace, and a crib that used to be hers, now occupied by little Harry. In this one room we slept, dressed, played games, read newspapers, cut the children's hair, ironed sheets and clothes—in sum, lived our lives. There was a bathroom near the stairs and a long *lānai* off the main living area, where we often slept on hot summer nights. Sleeping was not easy even in cool weather, as throughout the night we could hear the rattle of streetcars and the blare of phonograph music from nearby saloons, though in time we grew used to the noise. Meals were taken downstairs at a little table in the kitchen alongside the chopping blocks and cutlery, the five-gallon stockpots and twelve-quart boilers of our new trade.

Here we would also celebrate the lunar new year, the Year of the Rooster, as we would other Korean holidays. Though our children were American by birth, we wanted them to have at least a foot in the land of their ancestors, and so they would learn to speak both Korean and English in our household.

Because there were no other Korean eateries in Honolulu at

the time, we set our cafe's prices comparable to similar items at Chinese restaurants: a large bowl of rice sold for a dime, a small bowl for a nickel; noodle dishes were twenty cents a plate; fire beef, pork, or chicken was available at upwards of forty cents per serving; and desserts like pastry, honey rice, and candied date balls sold for a quarter apiece. We thought it a reasonably priced menu.

But as restaurateurs we were babes in the woods. Uncertain how many customers we might expect at first, our first grocery order took home enough rice, noodles, red beans, soybean paste, eggs, and meat to feed a small army. When a small army failed to show up on our doorstep, we scaled back our expectations and our purchases—and though much of our initial order could keep till the following week, many other items were perishables that we were forced to hastily cook and consume ourselves.

Jae-sun was, of course, chef, and I served as hostess, waitress, and supplementary chef when required. Because my husband was not as fluent in English as I was—he once admitted to me that he understood at best half of any English conversation—I also handled most of our business dealings with non-Korean suppliers. That first week saw many of our friends from church come for dinner, as well as the newly married Esther and Pascual Anito (Esther had moved into Pascual's house on Kamakela Lane, not far from us). We averaged three or four customers each evening for dinner, most of them Korean, all fulsome in their praise for the food. A typical meal—a bowl of rice, a noodle or meat dish, dessert—averaged around fifty cents a person. A dollar and a half to two dollars a night barely covered our rent, let alone the cost of food and preparation. But many of our patrons returned on subsequent evenings, and so, confident in the quality of our product, we waited patiently for our business to burgeon in the coming weeks.

Alas, this burgeoning never came. After six weeks of operating at a loss we tried opening for lunch as well; this brought in perhaps another dollar a day, barely worth the extra time and expense, and we abandoned it soon after.

One morning I took Harold and Grace downtown to watch the show put on by Patrolman Pete Hose, the "Hula Cop," as he directed traffic at the corner of Merchant and Fort Streets. Pete was one of the few Negro officers on the Honolulu police force and had even performed his "traffic hula" for Charlie Chaplin when he visited the islands in 1917. My children seemed to enjoy it as much as the Little Tramp had, and afterward we took a stroll along the waterfront, where I noticed a food vendor with a pushcart, selling a curious bill of fare.

Onto a paper plate this vendor would ladle two scoops of rice, a slab of meat or fish, and another scoop of some sort of noodle dish called "macaroni salad." This culinary hodgepodge reminded me of *kaukau* time on the plantation and it was certainly popular with the stevedores, who lined up to purchase a plate for breakfast—and lunch and dinner, too—all for the price of a dime.

Intrigued, I asked the vendor, "What do you call this?"

He dug an ice-cream scoop into a vat of steamed rice, deposited two scoops onto a paper plate, and said with a shrug, "Kine mixed plate, I guess."

Later that day, the image of those customers queuing up for their "mixed plate" preoccupied me as I sat at a window table in our own becalmed cafe, with little to do other than watch the pedestrians pass by. I began to suspect that we had made a serious miscalculation. We had counted on the fact that Koreans were moving into this neighborhood, but the people I saw on the street were not just Korean—they were also Chinese, Japanese, Hawaiian, and Filipino. Koreans were still a small minority here, not yet present in sufficient numbers to support a restaurant that served only Korean cuisine. Nor was there one central Korean community in Honolulu; some lived in the upper Nu'uanu Valley, some in outlying Kaimukī, and many, increasingly, in Wahiawa, even farther away—too far to travel for the kind of meal that could as easily be cooked at home.

I told Jae-sun about the vendors at the docks and tactfully suggested that we consider expanding our menu to appeal to more than just Korean tastes. I expected him to be resistant to the idea, but he thought about it a moment and said glumly, "Perhaps you're right." I proposed adding a few recipes I had acquired on the plantation: Chinese eggplant in garlic, Hawaiian *haupia* pudding, Portuguese sweet bread. Jae-sun even grudgingly agreed to *saimin* noodles and *miso* soup.

We also sampled more American fare at other cafes around town, such as Harte's Good Eats, where Jae-sun stared in stupefaction at the salad of lettuce, tomatoes, and carrots the waiter placed before him. "Did they neglect to cook this?" he asked me in a low voice. "Should I send it back?"

"No, I believe it's customary to eat the vegetables raw."

He blanched. "Straight out of the ground?" I nodded. "God have mercy on their souls," he said, refusing to touch the salad.

I ordered a hamburger steak sandwich, something I knew was popular with *haoles,* and took a bite. I rather enjoyed it, as did my husband, though he found it lacking in sophistication: "This is all? Just a piece of meat between two slices of bread? Where is the poetry in that?"

"Not every dish need be poetic," I pointed out.

Even more disappointing to him was the "hot dog," which, alas, contained no dog meat and looked rather obscene in the bargain. We decided to add hamburgers to our menu but no frankfurters.

At an establishment calling itself the Palace of Sweets we tasted a dessert that was currently all the rage on the U.S. mainland— "apple pandowdy"—as well as various flavors of ice cream. "Much too sweet," Jae-sun said after a bite or two of vanilla. "There is enough sugar in this to stop one's heart."

"But might it not make a nice complement to *mochi?*"

He shrugged. "I suppose." He took a bite of the chocolate ice cream, then allowed, "This is not altogether detestable." He would later use it in preparing *pat bing su,* a traditional summertime treat.

It was on our way back from a diner on Hotel Street that I was startled to hear a woman's voice calling, "Jin-san! Hey! Jin-san!"

I half-expected to see Tamiko when I turned, but it was another young Japanese woman who stood smiling at me from the doorway of a barber shop. "It's me, Jin-san. Don't you remember Shizu? From Iwilei?"

By heaven, it *was* Shizu—but she looked considerably different than she had on that long-ago day when she'd helped me with my *kisaeng* hair styling. She was wearing a white barber's frock, with her hair pulled back in a conservative bun and with less makeup on her face, but still looking lovely.

"Of course I remember!" We met on the sidewalk in front of the shop and embraced. "But you are a barber now?"

It was not unusual—actually quite commonplace—to find a Japanese girl working as a men's barber in Honolulu. In fact, by the 1920s, it had come to be regarded as primarily a woman's profession. But I was surprised to find Shizu engaged as one, considering her last profession.

"Oh, well, after Mrs. Miyake get deported"—she lowered her voice discreetly—"I decide, eh, maybe time change career. I knew the owner here, Mrs. Origawa—she trained me as apprentice. Someday, who knows, maybe I open my own shop." Her eyes twinkled with mischief. "And what of you, Jin-san? Did you not become a *kisaeng?*"

I blushed and nervously glanced at my husband to see his reaction. It was only then I noticed how coldly he was staring at Shizu. When I introduced them he nodded politely at her, but the chill did not leave his eyes. Shizu asked whether I had heard from May, and I told her that she had returned to San Francisco; we parted with promises to stay in touch, and Shizu returned to the barbershop.

Once we had traveled out of earshot Jae-sun said bluntly, "I do not approve of your choice in friends."

Stung, I pointed out, "You like Beauty and Jade Moon and Wise Pearl well enough. And the Anitos."

"They are not part of a race who oppress our people."

"Shizu oppresses no one. She is a barber." I did not mention that she was also a former prostitute since this was unlikely to raise his estimation of her. "And if you are reluctant to have dealings with Japanese people, you are in the wrong city and the wrong line of work." I was too angry to hold my tongue and barely realized what I had said until after I had blurted it out.

Jae-sun considered this, then made a little grunt of acknowledgment.

"I will serve them and take their money," he said, "but I will not socialize with them. You are free to do whatever you wish on your own."

I was extremely glad I had not told him about Tamiko and her family.

The following week we introduced a number of new items, attractively priced we hoped, to our menu. In addition to my "plantation-style" dishes, we added a twenty-five-cent hamburger; a ham and egg sandwich for a nickel less than that; a sirloin steak for eighty cents; and various salads, which I prepared owing to my husband's distaste for the entire concept, at fifteen cents apiece.

And in an effort to make a fresh start, we rechristened ourselves the Liliha Cafe.

Slowly, business began to improve. Our Korean customers continued to patronize us, but now their ranks were joined by Chinese families ordering *gon lo mein,* Hawaiians sampling our *haupia,* and—though Jae-sun loathed cooking it—Japanese feasting on *saimin* and fried *tofu.* The hamburger sandwiches proved especially popular with *keiki* of all races. Within six months we were pleasantly surprised to find ourselves breaking even, and in less than a year we had even begun to turn a small profit.

This was provident, as that summer of 1921 I gave birth to our second son and third child, Charles Eun. Children born in the Year of the Dog are known for their good humor, and Charlie was a prankster from the start: he arrived a month early, the first of many surprises that he would present to us.

Grace, now three years old, seemed to find the appearance of this tiny infant in our home somewhat unsettling. "Why is he so small?" she wanted to know.

"He hasn't had time to grow, like you have," I told her.

She looked at him suspiciously and asked, "When will he be finished?"

I laughed. "Not for a while. You're a long way from finished yourself."

But Grace continued to regard him with uncertainty and anxiety, as indeed she did most things, despite all the love and attention I gave her.

It was not long after Charlie's birth—on a busy Saturday evening with the restaurant almost as full as my hands as I waited on tables—that I noticed someone standing outside on the street, peering through the window into the cafe. Thinking it might be a prospective customer I turned and looked—just in time to see a man turn and hurry away down the street. I caught only the briefest glimpse of his face, but the cut of his hair, the line of his jaw, the way he held himself, was enough to send a moment's shudder through me.

But then he was gone, and I told myself no, it could not be Mr. Noh, and did my best to banish the disturbing notion from my thoughts.

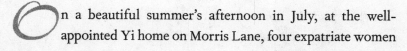

On a beautiful summer's afternoon in July, at the well-appointed Yi home on Morris Lane, four expatriate women from Kyŏngsang Province, far from home, gathered as a group for the first time in six years. Beauty had prepared hot rice water and Korean pastries for the occasion; I brought some homemade chestnut-cinnamon candies; and Wise Pearl came with a bouquet of fresh plumeria to commemorate our reunion, as our children played together in a living room that was larger than the entirety of my family's apartment above the cafe. Harold and Charlie played with Wise Pearl's two sons; Grace, for once, seemed relaxed, charmed by Beauty's daughter, Mary, who offered to share her dolls with her. Soon the house was filled with the laughter of *keiki* and the chiming musical tones of Kyŏngsang accents.

Jade Moon was the last to arrive, staggering through the front door under the weight of her third pregnancy, with toddlers Woodrow and Alma in tow. "Forgive this bloated apparition you see before you," she said, trying to catch her breath as she deposited her children alongside ours. "By God, how can something so small as a baby cause one to swell up to such grotesque proportions?"

"Nonsense, you look beautiful," I assured her.

She dropped into a chair and sighed in discomfort.

"I am a Zeppelin. A baby factory. No sooner has one rolled out than another is on its way." She took in the profusion of *keiki* running, tottering, or crawling around the room, then glanced at Beauty. "And how many of these heaven-sent darlings are yours?"

Beauty said, a little self-consciously, "Just this one." She gave Mary a gentle squeeze and smiled. "But a dozen more could not be more dear to me."

"Only one? And a lovely house like this, too? I hate you. I always have." Jade Moon popped a pastry into her mouth, which momentarily silenced her.

"It is good to see us all gathered in one place again," I said. "Who could have imagined, that night we first met in Yokohama, where we would find ourselves on this day, six years later?"

We caught each other up on our lives, and Wise Pearl proudly announced that she and her husband were leaving Waipahu Plantation. "We've purchased a carnation farm just outside Honolulu, in an area called Wilhelmina Rise."

"That's wonderful," Beauty said. "I love carnations."

"What are they good for?" Jade Moon asked skeptically.

"Oh, many things. They can be used in *leis*, and they are in great demand as a funeral flower."

Jade Moon nodded. "Death is always a good investment."

I told Wise Pearl that I had been under the impression that Asians were prohibited from owning property—as we were prohibited from becoming American citizens.

"Yes, but there are ways around that. The deed was entered into in the name of our eldest son who, having been born here, is a citizen. Even so, no bank would give us a loan; we had to save enough money to buy the land outright. It will be hard work, but no harder than working on the plantation, and at least now we will be laboring for ourselves."

Jade Moon's polite smile was more akin to a grimace. I could hardly blame her for being envious, spending her days as she did washing other people's laundry. I said, "Success will come to each of us, in turn, we sisters of Kyŏngsang." Then I added, "Though perhaps we might help one another to achieve this success."

My friends looked puzzled.

"We could form a *kye*," I suggested.

A *kye* is a kind of rotating credit cooperative, common in Korea. The members each contribute a fixed amount each month to a fund of cash that becomes available to each member in turn. In rural areas the money is often used to pay for things like road repairs, which are beyond the means of any one person, or to aid in marriage or funeral expenses. But many *kye* are formed purely for purposes of investment.

"Wise Pearl has noted the difficulty of obtaining bank loans without the necessary credit," I went on. "If we each contributed a certain sum at the outset, then more on a monthly basis, we could create enough capital to use in establishing a business, or expanding an existing business."

"That is an excellent idea," Wise Pearl agreed.

"How much would we have to contribute?" Jade Moon inquired warily.

"As much as we could afford, no more. Could you manage, say, ten dollars at the start, then five dollars a month thereafter?" I addressed Jade Moon specifically, for she was the one I hoped would benefit first from the fund.

"That sounds reasonable," she said after a moment's thought.

Wise Pearl thought so too, but said she would have to consult with her husband—as would I, though I did not imagine he would object. Beauty, however, said that ten dollars was well within her household budget and wrote a check for her share on the spot, which impressed us all.

"So the *kye* will have an initial balance of forty dollars," I said. "And after six months, if we are diligent, it will hold four times that much."

Jade Moon asked, "How would we determine in what order each of us would draw from it?"

"I believe it's usually done by bidding," Wise Pearl said. "Each bid represents a sum that will be paid to the other members as interest on the loan. The highest bidder takes home the money."

What she did not say was that those who need the money most will bid the highest. The only one among us who truly needed the money at the moment was Jade Moon, and thus I hoped that she would be the first beneficiary of the *kye*.

"Speak to Mr. Ha about it," I told Jade Moon, "and if he agrees, we will meet again and open a bank account."

Jade Moon laughed and opened her purse. "Mr. Ha," she said, taking out two wrinkled five-dollar bills, "thinks it is a splendid idea."

She added her cash to the fund, then looked around the table as if daring the rest of us to do the same.

Not to be outdone, Wise Pearl opened her own purse and deposited ten dollars in bills and coins onto the table.

I smiled and "anted up" my ten dollars, then raised my cup of rice water in a toast. "To success."

"Happiness, at least," Beauty added.

"Happiness be damned," Jade Moon said. "I will settle for success."

We agreed to meet for lunch on the first day of each month to administer the *kye,* though at first we chose not to bid on it since the fund was still amassing enough capital to be useful. At the end of six months' time our fund held a hundred and sixty dollars—a considerable amount by the standards of the day. Jade Moon and her husband began to consider the possibility of purchasing a small rooming house, against the day the *kye* would have enough money in it.

But this was much more than just a business connection: the four of us were bound together not merely by finances but by affection and kinship. Our common roots were in Kyŏngsang-do, but we had all been transplanted to the strange soil of Hawai'i, where we were growing in ways we could never have dreamed of in Korea.

Wise Pearl's carnation farm bloomed financially, and soon she and Mr. Kam were considering expanding it. "We have an opportunity to purchase another ten acres," she told us at a meeting, "but it would mean spending the modest profit we are now making, and then some."

"Do it!" Jade Moon advised her. "You will never be sorry to own land. How much is 'then some'?"

"We need another seventy-five dollars for the purchase."

"Is there enough in the *kye?*" Jade Moon asked me.

"Yes, more than double that," I confirmed.

"Let us bid, then."

In short order Wise Pearl had her money, and when the transaction was complete we all looked at each other with a kind of giggly wonderment. Four girls who a short time ago could not even leave home without an escort, now were starting businesses and buying property on an almost equal footing with men. It was exhilarating and, at times, a little frightening—nothing our mothers ever taught us could have prepared us for our lives here. We understood this, understood one another, as no one else could. Each meeting was an opportunity to exchange confidences as well as commerce; to seek counsel, to offer advice, or simply to trade gossip, swap recipes, or assist one another with babysitting.

Yes, Korea seemed very far away—but news from home, disseminated at church services, brought a few encouraging signs. In the wake of the March First Movement, the Japanese authorities had adopted a new approach to governing Korea, one of "cultural accommodation." They were allowing more freedom of education and expression, and undertaking many public works projects—such as the building of roads, bridges, and dams—designed to demonstrate that they were the friend of the Korean people and not their enemy.

A letter from my elder brother confirmed this, though he remained profoundly skeptical of the government's good intentions. He also delivered the dismaying news that Blossom—now fourteen years old, on the brink of marriageable age—had attempted to run away in an effort to find her birth family. Walking for miles on foot, she reached the next village before my father and brothers found her and brought her home. I winced to hear that Father beat her for her presumption. I remembered the frightened little girl who had climbed atop the inner wall, searching for some sign that her father was coming back for her, and I ached to think of her so unhappy. But I was helpless to do anything about it, until I could somehow convince my clan to allow her to emigrate to Hawai'i.

I now had to wonder: If Blossom was so intent on finding her own family, would she even desire to come to Hawai'i any longer? This was hardly a question I could ask my brother to put to her, however, and since Blossom could neither read nor write, she was mute to me, only a haunting silence between us. All I could do was try and put away—in addition to our monthly contributions to the *kye* and the Korean Independence Fund—an extra dollar or two for Blossom, and hope that when the time came, she would want to make the journey.

ortunately, the receipts of the Liliha Cafe continued to grow as word of mouth drew customers from surrounding neighborhoods like Kalihi, Chinatown, 'A'ala, and even Kaka'ako. We were also popular with local police officers walking their beat, whose meals were often given to them on the house in the interest of building goodwill. Chang Apana dropped by now and then, either with police colleagues or with his family, but would never let us pay for his meals. He seemed pleased that I had done well for myself, and I wondered how much of a hand he had taken in popularizing the cafe among his fellow officers.

We were soon able to hire a kitchen boy named Liho to assist Jae-sun with such things as peeling potatoes, deboning fish, and other odious tasks, and a part-time waitress, Rose, to help ease the burden on me.

On one particularly hot evening that summer, I had just taken a short break from my hostess duties to look in on our *keiki*, who were asleep in the apartment upstairs. I came down to find a man with his head bowed, standing by the door, who I assumed to be a customer waiting for a table. I had crossed half the length of the restaurant before I recognized him—and I came to an abrupt stop.

266

It was Mr. Noh.

I was shocked not just by his presence but by his appearance. He seemed much older than the five years that had passed since I had last seen him—not counting the glimpse I thought I'd gotten of him months before. He had dark bags under his eyes, he was unshaven, and he wore a rumpled *palaka* shirt and a pair of faded dungarees. He looked like a ghost of himself.

Even so, I felt a rush of fear. I glanced in the direction of the kitchen, comforted by the knowledge that Jae-sun was not far away—and slowly I found the nerve to walk up to my former husband, my heart racing the whole time. I stopped about three feet away from him and managed to ask, as calmly as I could, "What is it you want here?"

But there was none of his usual bravado in his reply. "I am hungry," he said in an equally low tone, "and I have no money for food. I know I do not merit your charity, but even so . . . could you grant me the favor of a meal?"

This was the last thing I had expected him to say, and I did not believe him.

"Get out of here. You're drunk."

He let out an unhappy laugh.

"No, this is a rare moment that I am not. You may smell my breath if you wish." He took a step toward me.

I shrank back. It was true, he did not reek of alcohol, but neither was his smell pleasant: I doubted that he had taken a bath in at least a week. "What has happened to you?" I asked, despite myself. "Are you not working at Waialua?"

"That was a long time ago," he said ruefully, "or so it seems."

A part of me, I admit, was not distraught to see my nemesis in this pathetic state, and relished the opportunity to scorn him and send him back, still hungry, onto the street. But then I felt ashamed for the thought, and I told myself that if I truly considered myself an individual capable of *kampana*, it should apply not just to those

I had wronged, like Tamiko, but to those who had wronged me as well.

He saw my hesitation and said, "But I understand—I ask too much of you," and turned to go.

I found myself saying, "Wait. All you want from me is something to eat?"

He nodded.

"And then you will go and not come back?"

"If that is what you wish."

I should have been terrified to have him here, just one floor below my home, where my children lay sleeping even now. But despite all he had done in the past, I did not feel—surrounded as I was by customers, and on seeing the spent shell he had become—as though I or my family were in any imminent danger.

"All right," I told him. "One meal. Come with me."

He bowed his head in gratitude.

I picked up a menu from the pile up front and, as if I were welcoming any random customer who had entered, took him to a small table in a corner of the cafe. I tried to hand him the menu, but he shook his head and told me, "I will take whatever you choose to offer me. Beggars cannot be choosers."

All at once I recalled the first time I had heard that phrase: also from Mr. Noh's mouth, on our wedding day, referring to his unlucky choice of bride.

And later: *She is lucky that anyone chose her at all.*

My anger roiled again inside me, but I did not show it. I merely nodded and told him I would be back with something for him to eat.

I went into the kitchen, where Jae-sun was contentedly juggling at least ten different dinner orders—completely in his element, whistling as he went from basting *bulgogi* to stirring a pot of Portuguese bean soup to filleting a three-pound tuna. I smiled as I watched him. I *was* lucky, though not in the way Mr. Noh had meant that day in court.

"What have you made too much of tonight?" I asked. It was inevitable that we would prepare a certain number of dishes in advance, in anticipation of a demand that did not materialize that evening. Usually we wound up eating these ourselves as a late-night supper.

"Um, probably the *bulgogi*," he said.

"Then give me an order of that, with rice and *kimchi*."

I decided not to tell Jae-sun of my former husband's presence unless I absolutely needed to. I took the food to Mr. Noh's table and placed it in front of him. He thanked me, picked up his chopsticks, and quickly took a big bite of *kimchi*, then an even bigger bite of fire beef. He barely chewed before he swallowed. Truly, he ate like a starving man, and I wondered what could have brought him so low.

"Ah," he said around a mouthful of beef, "your *bulgogi* is as delicious as ever."

"It is not mine. It is my husband's," I said pointedly.

If he was stung by that he did not show it.

"So you are . . . no longer employed at Waialua?" I asked him.

He shook his head as he ate. "I returned there after our—divorce. But then I began drinking too much—missing too much work—and they let me go. I went back to 'Ewa, but got into a fight with the head *luna* . . . broke his jaw." Each sentence was punctuated by a swallow of food. "After that, no plantation on O'ahu would hire me, so I went again to Maui, but . . . that did not end well, either.

"Finally I came to Honolulu, where I have been doing odd jobs here and there—enough to pay for a room, at least." He shrugged. "What did I tell you? I'm just *poho*."

"I think we make our own luck," I said impulsively.

He only nodded. "Perhaps so. You and your—husband—have certainly made your luck." His slight hesitation in saying "husband" did not escape my notice, and I admit I took some slight pleasure in it.

I excused myself to show some arriving customers to a table, and when I returned to Mr. Noh's table he had wolfed down almost all of his dinner. "You have shown me great kindness tonight," he said. "Certainly I do not warrant it. I behaved abominably to you. But when the drink is in me, it poisons everything. It's poisoned everything I might have been."

I could not let that pass without comment. "You were not drunk when you threatened me at the courthouse, or when you beat me for working in the fields."

His eyes clouded at this, but once again he merely nodded. "No, you are right, I was not," he allowed. "I was angry. Anger is its own poison, I suppose." He wiped his mouth with his napkin and said, *"Mianhamnida"*—the word that means both "Thank you" and "I am sorry for the trouble I have caused you."

I found myself unexpectedly moved by his use of this term.

"This was delicious; I shall not go to bed hungry tonight." He stood.

Softening, I asked, "Wouldn't you like some dessert?"

"No, you've been generous enough." He looked at me again, and this time he did not seem to be gazing into the past, but actually looking at me. "I did not mean what I said in court," he said. "I did it to hurt you and to keep you, if that makes any sense. You were a far better wife than I deserved."

He bowed, turned, and left with as proud a bearing as he could muster.

I never dreamed I would ever feel sorry for this man, but I did that night.

I could even, in my own way, understand the disappointment he felt from life. Though I was grateful beyond words for Jae-sun, our family, and our success, I still longed for one thing which I knew could never be mine: the dream of education that brought me to America, and which I had been forced to forfeit. But almost as satisfying to me was that September day in 1923 when I brought Grace Eun—now five years old—for her first day of kindergarten at Kauluwela Grammar School. She was terrified to enter the school, stubbornly holding on to my hand as we stood on the threshold. Plaintively she asked me why she had to go, why she couldn't stay at home with me. I stooped down beside her and said, "You know, when I was your age, I would have given anything to be able to go to school. I still would."

"Why can't you?"

"Because I'm too old. But you can go in my place, and learn all the things I cannot. And then you can tell me all about what you've learned, and that would be almost as good as if I went myself. Would you do that for me?"

She glanced uncertainly up at the imposing brick building— weighing the apprehension it caused her against her desire to help me—then turned back and, trying to be brave, said, "Okay, Mama, I will."

"Good girl," I said. "Who knows? You might even enjoy it." She gave me a look that suggested there was as much chance of this as there was of ice-cream pies falling from the sky, and then I led her up the front steps and into the school.

The corridors were filled with children of all ages, as well as parents like me searching for their children's classrooms. At the door to Grace's room I gave her a kiss on the cheek and handed her a lunch bag: "Learn something for me today, Grace." I watched her go in and nervously take a seat. The classroom smelled of chalk and ink and books; it smelled of learning. I never wanted to leave, but I did. My longing to trade places with Grace was equaled only by my joy and pride in knowing that my daughter—that all my children—would have the education I had been denied. That would have to be enough.

Thirteen

That September saw an academic achievement for someone else as well, and I was almost as proud of him as I was of Grace. Joe Kahahawai, now grown into a tall, strapping fourteen-year-old, had secured through his father's efforts an athletic scholarship to a very reputable parochial school called St. Louis College, which despite its name was really a secondary school. There he quickly excelled in sports, especially football, and my family and I were pleased to attend our first Sunday game in which Joe—now standing nearly six feet in a blue-and-red uniform emblazoned with the number 38—functioned as something called a "lineman," and a good one, too, judging by the cheers of the crowd. I gathered that the object of the game was to kick, throw, or carry the oddly shaped ball from one end of the playing field to the other, but the rules mystified me and I soon ceased to wonder why everyone would stop when whistles were blown, then wander about and reassemble like actors in a play who had forgotten their lines and decided to start all over again. I could appreciate how Joe seemed to literally explode out of his Kabuki-like stance—squatting with one hand ritualistically touching the ground—as if shot out of a cannon, but I was a bit taken aback the first time he tackled an opposing player to the ground.

"Was that absolutely necessary?" I asked Esther.

"Oh, but Jin, that's part of the game."

"To knock each other down?"

"Yes."

"But it seems so rude," I said.

After the St. Louis "Saints" won the game over McKinley High School's "Micks," we joined Joe and the Anitos in a celebration at Kamakela Lane that included Joseph Sr. and his wife Hannah, Joe's cousin Eddie Uli'i, and Bill Kama, who was now an officer with the Honolulu Police Department. "You're gettin' too big for me to box your ears," Bill kidded Joe, "so next time you get out of line—"

He grinned and playfully twirled a set of handcuffs. Joe laughed, turned around, and crossed his wrists behind his back. "Take me in, officer," he joked. "For my own protection." We all laughed.

More sadly, that same autumn Beauty's husband Mr. Yi fell ill, and at the age of seventy-nine any illness is a serious one. Pneumonia claimed him two weeks later, and he ended a long life in the comfort of his own bed, having overcome great obstacles to progress from plantation laborer to a wealthy and respected businessman. Our family attended his funeral service at the Korean Christian Church and then his burial at Puea Cemetery. Jade Moon and Wise Pearl also paid their respects, the latter bringing a lovely wreath of carnations. Beauty was saddened, of course, and even if she thought of Mr. Yi as more of a father than a husband, losing a kindly father is still a sorrowful event.

As we left the cemetery, Jade Moon took me aside and declared, with excitement unseemly to the occasion, "I've found a rooming house to buy!"

"Lower your voice," I said, "and at least pretend that you are bereaved."

"Oh, he was a thousand years old, we should all live as long. Would you come see the property with me tomorrow and tell me what you think?"

I sighed and said that I would.

The following day we took the streetcar to a neighborhood called Makiki, on the windward side of Punchbowl. It seemed a great distance away, though in truth it was closer than Wise Pearl's farm in Kaimukī. We entered a two-story clapboard rooming house in slightly better repair than the tenement I had lived in in Kauluwela. "The manager's rooms, where we would live, are on the ground floor," Jade Moon said as we entered the vestibule. "There are fifteen other rooms, most already occupied, each bringing in twelve dollars a month in rent. That is almost two hundred dollars a month in rental income!"

We ascended creaking stairs to the second story. "And what about expenses?" I asked. "Water, electricity, repairs?"

"Negligible, I'm told. Twenty or thirty dollars a month."

"Our water bill at the cafe is hardly negligible," I noted. "And these stairs could use some fixing."

"Mr. Ha is good with his hands. Whatever repairs need done, we will do them ourselves. It is a great opportunity."

The last time I heard that, I had found myself urinating into a trench at Waipahu. But I held my tongue.

Walking down the hallway, we passed open doors and windows through which trade winds passed sluggishly. Inside the tiny flats there were large families, mostly Hawaiian, Chinese, and a handful of Koreans. "The owner is moving to the mainland and wishes to divest himself of his properties here. He's asking only twelve hundred dollars for the building, and for a thirty percent down payment he will carry the rest of the loan himself! What do you think?"

"It seems like a good investment."

"We'll need three hundred and sixty dollars for the down payment. Is there enough in the *kye?*"

I nodded. "And a little more."

"I told the owner I could have the money for him on the first of next month, and he said that was acceptable to him." She beamed as she took in the faded walls around us, which to me seemed in dire need of replastering and a fresh coat of paint; but to her they obviously represented something else: "Just think . . . to *own land* again, as my parents did, and their parents before them!"

To Jade Moon, this aging and dilapidated boardinghouse meant more than just a comfortable income: it meant being a *yangban* again. Seeing the proud smile on her face, I could not help but be pleased for her, and gratified that we could help her realize her dream.

"It is perfect," she declared happily.

Given her name, she might have remembered the old Korean adage, "Even jade has flaws." Or, in other words: Nothing in life is ever perfect.

*T*he next day, as we were preparing to open the cafe for dinner, there commenced a pounding on our door so loud, so frantic, that I hurried to the front to see what the commotion could be. There was a pane of glass in the door, an interior shade rolled down over it; around the edges I caught glimpses of a woman's white dress and a child's braided hair. "Grace Eun's Mother! Grace Eun's Mother!" came a voice from outside, and as I hurriedly opened the door I was startled to see a tearful Beauty standing on our doorstep, her face flush, tightly gripping the hand of her daughter, Mary.

"Oh, my dear friend," she said plaintively as she entered, "forgive me! I didn't know where else to go, I don't know what to do!"

"What is it? What's wrong?"

She collapsed into a dining chair and began wailing:

"Oh God, what have I done? *What have I done?*"

I'd heard her utter these same words at the immigration station the day we first laid eyes on our husbands-to-be, but her tone now was even more desperate.

Whatever was wrong, the child should not have been seeing her mother in such a state. I took Mary by the hand and hurried her upstairs to play dolls with Grace. Before I left, Mary asked me, "Why is Mama so sad?"

"I don't know, little one," I told her, "but we'll make everything all right." I gave her a smile and went back downstairs to her still-weeping mother. "What on earth has happened?" I asked.

"I am lost—lost," she said. "And it is all my own fault."

"What is?"

"I have been an unworthy wife, and ungrateful. I admit it. But my child should not have to suffer for my mistakes!"

"For God's sake, what are you talking about?"

She made an effort to stop crying and in a shaky tone told me of how Mr. Yi's attorney had come to read his will earlier that day. It was only then that she learned that she had been completely disinherited from it.

"That cannot be right. You must have misunderstood."

"No, it was made quite clear to me," she said bitterly. "Mr. Yi left the entire estate to his sons. The store, his savings . . . even the house. Jung-su and Bae-su informed me they and their families would be moving into the house, and I need to be vacated by the end of the month."

I was dumbstruck at first, then managed to ask, "But *why?*"

She flinched from my gaze.

"Because I was weak, and foolish," she said, "and wished to laugh and talk with someone my own age. To feel a young man's skin against mine, and not the wrinkled touch of an old grandfather! Because I wanted to feel something for a man—what a woman is supposed to feel for a man. Oh, what a fool I was!"

"Are you talking about Frank Ahn?"

She looked even more mortified. "You knew?"

"I suspected as much." I sighed and took her hand in mine. "You are not the first woman to feel such things, or to be so foolish. But even if Mr. Yi was angry at you for your infidelity, surely he made provisions for his own daughter?"

"He did not believe her to be his daughter. Neither do his sons."

I confess, this thought had never crossed my mind. "Is she?"

"I . . . do not know," she admitted. "Jung-su said he and his wife were willing to adopt her, and raise her as their own. But"—her eyes flashed with anger—"she is *my* daughter! I may not know who her father is, but I know *I* am her mother! I can't give her up. I *won't*."

She collapsed again into sobs. "Gem, my dear friend, what am I to do? Tell me. What am I to do now?"

I wrapped my arms around her as I would an injured fawn. "You will not have to give up your daughter. As for the rest of it . . . we will find a way."

"I'm sorry. I know I've sinned. I know I don't deserve your friendship."

Before I could reply, someone did it for me:

"That is untrue."

I turned to see Jae-sun standing in the doorway to the kitchen.

"I am sorry. I could not help overhearing," he said, embarrassed.

Beauty smiled an unhappy smile. "It is I who should apologize. Please forgive my shameful display of emotion."

"You have understandable cause." There was neither accusation nor recrimination in his voice. "What you did outside your marriage was wrong . . . but what your husband has done is also wrong. He professed to be a good Christian; he should have forgiven you."

"I can understand him for not forgiving me," Beauty said. "But Mary . . ."

"Forgiveness can be difficult," Jae-sun told her. "I know this firsthand. But you and Mary have a place with us for as long as you need one. Don't trouble yourself over material losses. Make your peace with God. He will forgive you, even if Mr. Yi could not. You may be sure of that."

He discreetly returned to the kitchen, and I was never prouder to be his wife.

"I *did* care for him," Beauty said softly, "as a father." But the word was swallowed up in a sob, and I pulled her to me and held her as she wept.

*B*eauty and Mary moved in with us that day, and if it was a bit crowded in that one large room above the cafe, you could not tell it by the children. They played together in what we charitably referred to as the "backyard"—a rectangular courtyard between our building and the next, paved in concrete and filled with empty crates, which Harold, Charlie, Grace, and Mary overturned and imagined to be houses, boats, battlements, or warring airplanes. Above them flew flags of drying laundry from a cat's cradle of clotheslines strung between apartments.

Beauty was ashamed of the actions that had brought her to such reduced circumstances and asked that I not tell either Jade Moon or Wise Pearl what had happened. She was eager to help pay her way and offered to wait tables at the cafe—a well-intentioned gesture but a disastrous one. She spoke imperfect English and, never having worked on a plantation, little pidgin; taking meal orders for anything other than Korean dishes was a challenge for her, and trying to decipher what she had written down on the order ticket was equally challenging for me. I once stood for several minutes, puzzling over what "air pie" could possibly mean, until the Spanish couple at table three told me that they had ordered *paella*—phonetically, *pie ay-a*. Beauty assumed the second syllable was a modifier, hence "air pie." Another time I struggled to make sense of a dessert order that read, "horse, paid for," and only when I translated this back into Korean—*mal*, horse, and *sada*, to pay for—did I realize that the man at table five wanted *malassada*, a Portuguese sweet doughnut.

But Beauty was also quick to help out around the house—laundering, ironing, sweeping the rug, cutting the children's hair and even Jae-sun's. As my husband sat there in a straight-backed chair, a towel draped across his shoulders, with Beauty deftly wielding a pair of scissors, inspiration struck me and I asked her, "You seem to have a talent for this. Might you consider doing it for a living?"

"I suppose I could. But I have no experience, who would hire me?"

The next day I took her to Hotel Street and the shop where Shizu worked as a barber. Shizu was candid about the requirements of the job: "We work twelve, fifteen hours a day—afternoons, evenings, sometimes till nine, ten o'clock at night." Beauty had nothing against hard work and long hours, and so Shizu approached the shop owner, Mrs. Origawa, about taking on another apprentice.

Unfortunately, Mrs. Origawa was not interested in hiring another barber at that time. Shizu took us aside and told Beauty, "I'm sorry there is nothing for you here. But if ever I open my own shop . . ."

"Are you planning to open one?" Beauty asked hopefully.

"Someday, when I save enough money."

"How much do you need?"

Aigo, I thought, afraid of where this was leading.

"I have fifty dollars saved," Shizu told her, "but for rent, equipment, furniture—another hundred, at least."

Beauty looked at me excitedly. "There's that much in the *kye*, is there not?"

What could I say? "Yes, I believe so."

The entire situation had spun rather quickly out of my control. Soon, Shizu and Beauty were scouting commercial space in downtown Honolulu, where the majority of Japanese barber girls worked their trade, and pricing the cost of barber chairs, mirrors, lotions, razors, combs, scissors, and brushes. They decided the minimum expenditure they needed to set up shop was a hundred and eighty dollars. Shizu had fifty, so they would need at least another hundred and thirty.

There was four hundred and twenty dollars in our *kye*. But Jade Moon needed three hundred and sixty for her rooming house, and there was not sufficient funds for both her and Beauty. The thought of one of my friends having to lose out on the loan caused me great pain. But what could I do? I could not ask either one to give up their ambitions. I had to let things take their natural course.

At the next month's meeting—held in Wise Pearl's tiny farmhouse amid acres of red carnations spilling down the hillslope like lava flows—I settled Charlie and Harold in the living room to play with Mary and the other *keiki*. I continued to fret as we prepared to bid on the *kye*. Each member was to submit a written offer of how much they would pay in interest for the privilege of borrowing the cash in the fund—say, twenty dollars on a loan of two hundred. Whoever won would then distribute five dollars to each member of the *kye* as an interest payment, and they would be left with a hundred and eighty dollars of working capital.

For the hundred and thirty Beauty needed I had urged her to tender a bid of at least twenty dollars. But when the bids were all in and the numbers disclosed, it turned out Jade Moon had offered a bid of thirty, and therefore won the *kye*.

Beauty promptly burst into tears.

Jade Moon was understandably taken aback. "What? What's wrong?"

Beauty's resolve to keep silent about her situation blew away like an old dandelion puff. The truth spilled out, much to the dismay of her picture-bride sisters.

"Why didn't you tell us before?" Wise Pearl asked. "We could've helped."

"I was ashamed. I am still ashamed."

"Well, this changes everything," Jade Moon acknowledged. "I therefore wish to forfeit the *kye* to the next highest bidder"—which was, of course, Beauty.

"No, no! You won the money fairly—"

"*Take* it," Jade Moon said impatiently. "Are you a fool?"

I cleared my throat, and Jade Moon softened her advice: "I have a husband, a job, a home to live in. If Mr. Ha and I do not become landlords this year, we will not go hungry or homeless."

Beauty stubbornly held on to her pride. "I don't want to win out of pity."

"Then stop being so pitiful!" Jade Moon snapped, exasperated.

"You won fairly. I should have bid more. The money is yours."

Jade Moon gave her a smoldering look and I prepared for the bombast that would surely follow. But to my surprise she merely said, "Very well then. I win."

She reached into the strongbox, took out three hundred and sixty dollars in cash, then counted off thirty dollars—the price of her bid—and distributed ten dollars apiece to the rest of us. "Here is your interest on the loan. "Now"—she turned to Beauty—"how much did you need for that barbershop?"

Beauty was confused, but I began to see Jade Moon's reasoning and answered for her, "A hundred and thirty dollars."

Jade Moon counted off that precise sum and dropped it in front of Beauty.

"What's this?"

"A loan. To open your shop. We are now partners."

Beauty's eyes widened with disbelief and denial. "No, I can't accept—"

"It is not a gift, it is a *loan*. Give me back five dollars in interest. Go on, do it!"

Beauty meekly handed her a five-dollar bill.

"So now, on the first of each month you will pay me five percent of the shop's profits, until the whole amount of the loan is paid off."

"But there may not be any profits for a long while."

"I can wait. And in the meantime"—Jade Moon folded the remaining two hundred dollars and tucked it safely in her purse—"I will put this to work earning interest in the bank until I have enough to buy property. You see? We all profit from this."

"Thank you," Beauty said. There were tears in her eyes; she got up hurriedly and excused herself to go into the bathroom.

When she was gone Jade Moon sighed, "Good God! I thought we would *never* get her to take the damned money!"

"Woodrow's Mother, that was very kind of you," Wise Pearl said, in a tone reserved for miracles.

"She has been humbled," Jade Moon said with a shrug. "Who among us cannot understand that?"

After the meeting, Beauty headed straight to Shizu's shop with their newfound capital. Surprised and pleased at how the conflict had been so profitably resolved, I hoisted Charlie into my arms and shepherded him and Harold onto the streetcar at the top of Wai'alae Avenue. The car passed lot after lot of once-empty land here in Kaimukī on which the frames of new houses were sprouting like

bamboo shoots. "Someday," I promised Harry and Charlie, pointing to one of the wooden skeletons, "we will live in a house like
that."

Harold looked at it and asked, "Can't we have one with walls?"

I laughed. "Oh, and I suppose you'll want a roof, too."

Charlie shook his head, vigorously opposed to the idea, but
Harold just nodded meekly.

"If you insist," I said agreeably, "but it would be cheaper without the roof."

Harry's eyes didn't leave the shell of that half-finished house
until it was lost from view as the streetcar made its way down the
long hill toward Honolulu.

The trip to Kaimukī exhausted both *keiki* and they were
happy to take naps when we reached home. Jae-sun was not yet
back from his morning circuit of the fish and meat markets in
search of the choicest cuts for the evening's menu, and I decided
to go down and wash the breakfast dishes I hadn't gotten to this
morning.

But at the bottom of the steps, as I turned the corner of the staircase, I was jolted by the sight of a man rushing toward me with an
outstretched arm.

*B*efore I had time to scream he had grabbed me by the
throat and driven me back into the wall with bone-rattling
impact.

Only now, as I stood pinned like a butterfly to the wall, did I
fully recognize the man as Mr. Noh.

His face was not the chastened, humbled countenance he had
presented months before, but one transfigured by anger and alcohol.
I could barely breathe, but what air I could take in reeked of whisky.
There was a wild, familiar fury in his eyes, but something else,
too: something I would never have expected to see. Tears brimmed

in his eyes, even as his mouth was contorted in a sneer. Half his face was rage; the other half, grief.

"This should have been *mine*," he cried out, "rightfully mine!"

Oh Heaven, I thought; not him, not again! I gasped for breath and he loosened his grip a little—just enough to let me breathe, but not cry out.

"I could have led this life," he railed through tears. "This could have been my business! Those could have been *my* sons upstairs!"

At the mention of my children I felt a blind panic, like a bird trapped in a closet, banging helplessly from wall to wall.

Then, unexpectedly, his hand yanked me away from the wall. Without letting go his grip on my throat, he dragged me into the middle of the kitchen and began forcing me down onto my knees.

"If I cannot have this," he said coldly, "I will at least have *you*."

He kicked my legs out from under me, let go of my throat, and I fell to the floor, dazed. He dropped his full weight on top of me, knocking the breath from me, pinning my body to the floor. He squirmed out of his pants, then grabbed my arms in each of his calloused hands.

I felt another touch as hard, against my belly.

But instead of fueling my fear, this only fed my own anger, my rage at this man who refused to leave my life, who was now threatening not just me but my sons.

I shook off my pain and screamed at the top of my voice, forcing him to clap one hand against my mouth.

I brought my free arm down in a fist and pounded at his head, again and again. The blows distracted him from what he was trying to do to me and he had to let go of my mouth as he tried to seize my arm.

But rather than bring my arm down on his head again as he expected, I slipped it under him and grabbed the very thing he sought to shame me with—and with all the strength I could summon, I wrenched it first to one side, then the other.

He howled and let go of me, recoiling in an agony he richly deserved.

I scrambled to my feet, slipping once as I raced to the nearest counter, where I scooped up the first thing I saw: a fork. Mr. Noh came at me again; I threw the fork at him like a spear. He ducked to avoid it. I ran to the sink, where there were dishes soaking from breakfast. I threw a heavy plate at him, which missed its target, then another, which only clipped the side of his head. But this bought me the time I needed to get where I needed to go: the butcher's block.

I snapped up a carving knife, spun around, and as Mr. Noh lunged forward, enraged, I plunged the five-inch blade into his stomach.

I was surprised how easily it slipped through both cloth and flesh, as if I'd plunged the blade into soft butter. Mr. Noh let out a harrowing scream.

Then I pulled out the knife, and he screamed even louder.

He looked down in shock, his hand going to his side in an attempt to staunch the flow of blood leaking out between his fingers.

I brandished the knife at him and yelled, *"Get out!* Leave me alone! Or I swear to Heaven, I will kill you as you killed our daughter!"

He saw the hatred and the fury in my face, looked again at the blood gushing from the torn seam in his flesh, and realized that even this brutal act of vengeance would not be his, either.

Still holding his side, he turned and ran out the same back door he had come in by, trailing blood like a wounded animal.

I looked at the bloodstained knife in my hand—felt bile rising in my throat—and lurched over to the sink, where I vomited onto the breakfast dishes.

When I had finished, my legs gave out and I slid into a sitting position on the floor, and I either wept or laughed, I am not certain which.

ae-sun arrived home not long after to find me upstairs, sitting beside our still-sleeping sons, my dress spattered with what looked at first to him like a child's red water paint. I was no longer hysterical with fear, but I welcomed his strong and gentle arms around me as I related to him the horrors of the past hour. At the end of my story he was so furious that he wanted to go in search of Mr. Noh himself, and had he done so, I am sure that my former husband would not have survived the encounter. Instead we merely reported the incident to the police, who assured us that my attacker would have to seek medical help somewhere, and this would inevitably lead to his capture.

They were correct. My former husband was arrested at Queen's Hospital after receiving six stitches in his lower abdomen. The blade of my knife had not found any vital organs, for which I suppose I was grateful. In his second brush with the American legal system, Mr. Noh fared no better than in his first: though this time he was wisely represented by counsel, he was convicted on two counts of "assault and attempt to ravish." In lieu of jail time, his attorney petitioned the court to merely deport him to Korea, an idea which I, for one, could wholeheartedly endorse. A week and a half later, Jae-sun and I stood on Pier 12, watching as my former husband was escorted aboard the SS *Tenyo Maru*, bound for Yokohama, Japan. We lost sight of him amid the music and merriment accorded a departing vessel, but I did not take my eyes off the gangway until it was pulled back into the ship's bulwark, and I would not leave the dock until the great ocean liner was far enough away that it appeared to be just another whitecap cresting the peaks of distant waves. Then it vanished like so much foam melting back into the waters, and as it disappeared below the horizon I finally turned, took Jae-sun's hand in mine, and we walked away from the harbor.

Mr. Noh was out of my life—forever. I would neither see nor hear from him again. And now, for the first time since I had fled Waialua for Honolulu—indeed, since I had arrived in Hawai'i—I felt as though I could truly live without fear, and begin to enjoy the fruits of my new home.

Fourteen

oday the 1920s are often referred to as Hawai'i's "glamour days," though they were considerably less glamorous
for those who struggled under the crushing poverty of Kauluwela, Green Block, or Hell's Half Acre. But for our family, as for
many other Korean households in Hawai'i, the twenties were a
time of rising prosperity. There were now perhaps a hundred or
so Korean families living in Buckle Lane and adjacent Akepo
Lane—most of them having fled the plantations for the canneries,
even as others abandoned the canneries to become tailors, laun-
derers, shoemakers, or grocers. The twenties were also kind to
my Sisters of Kyŏngsang. As Wise Pearl's carnation farm flour-
ished, she and Mr. Kam invested more of its profits in additional

acres on which they raised barley, to be made into a kind of Korean taffy called *yot*. Shizu and Beauty's barbershop, on the corner of Merchant and Bishop Streets, was perhaps not quite as successful, but business was good enough so that Beauty was able to move out of our home and rent for herself and Mary a small one-room walk-up on River Street. Jade Moon collected some modest interest on her investment in the shop, and with that and the two hundred dollars from the *kye*, she and Mr. Ha were able to purchase another rooming house, smaller than the one in Makiki, this one in Pālama.

But even for the poorest of residents, there was still glamour to be had living in Honolulu—not the least of these being Boat Day.

Many "mainlanders" do not realize that Hawai'i is the most isolated group of islands on earth. In the days before air travel, the arrival and departure of ocean liners like our namesake, the SS *City of Honolulu,* was more than just a welcome novelty—it was a cause for celebration. As one of the great ships approached from around Diamond Head, it would announce itself with three piercing blasts of its whistle; by the time it steamed into the harbor hundreds of Honoluluans had flocked to the foot of Maunakea Street to greet it, whether or not they knew anyone aboard. There were so many men wearing pale linen suits and Panama hats, and women in white dresses and matching parasols, that the wharves looked whiter than the sands of Waikīkī. My children and I called it "Hawaiian snow." Scattered across these snowdrifts were summery eruptions of color: Japanese and Hawaiian women selling *leis* of red ginger, yellow orchids, green *maile,* pink plumeria, and golden *'ilima* blossoms. Each *lei* seller had dozens of stringed flowers draped like a hanging garden over her arm. *Hula* girls swayed to the music of the Royal Hawaiian Band, which serenaded the arriving passengers with "Hawai'i Pono'ī." It was always pleasing to see the smiles of the visitors as they took their first breaths of tropic air and bowed their heads to accept the fragrant, welcoming *leis.* "This is indeed a special place we live in," I would tell my *keiki,* "that people travel from so far to visit us."

Along with Boat Days, another source of free recreation for our family was the occasional Sunday spent at the beach.

For decades, the district of Waikīkī had been merely a patchwork of rice paddies and taro patches, foul-smelling duck ponds and mosquito-ridden marshes, prone to flooding during heavy rains. It might have stayed that way forever but for the dazzling jewel of a beach that graced its south shore, like a diamond necklace hung around the neck of a plow horse. But there was money to be made from that necklace, and in 1921, dredging began on a canal to divert the three ancient streams emptying into the floodplain. The result was a new, dry Waikīkī, where homes both large and small, garden apartments, hotels, and a variety of concessions—even an amusement park—now replaced the old farms and marshes.

Back then there were still only a handful of hotels on the sand, the largest being the Moana Hotel. At the height of the tourist season—winter and summer—Waikīkī Beach was crowded with visitors, but during the off-season there was more room for families like ours, from less affluent parts of the city, and my family and I would often enjoy the beach in the company of my Korean "sisters" and their families. In the fashion (and law) of the day, the men wore one-piece gray woolen swimsuits and the women were even more ensheathed, in knee-length bloomers and blouses with absurdly long sleeves. But we had no idea at the time how ridiculous we looked, and spent the day swimming and picnicking, listening to the soft, low beat of Korean hourglass drums played by Mr. Ha, or singing along to the sweet, melancholy melody of our nation's most beloved folk song:

> *Arirang, Arirang*
> *Walking over the peak at Arirang,*
> *The sorrows in my heart as many as the stars in the sky.*

Yet there was no real sorrow in us as we sang it, only a wistful nostalgia for a homeland that was slowly being supplanted by our new life in Hawai'i.

By this time Wise Pearl's *keiki* numbered four, while Jade Moon struggled to keep her brood of five out of trouble on the beach. The widowed Beauty still had only Mary, who was fast growing into a lovely girl with a heart-shaped face and sparkling brown eyes.

Harold, now three and a half years old, loved the water and couldn't spend enough time swimming in the surf, but Grace, almost six, was mortally afraid of the ocean and recoiled from the foaming waves lapping up the beach as if from the spittle of a rabid dog. Little Charlie was indifferent to the water, more interested in building sand castles, which he then would demolish with the zeal of a wrecking crew. "Boom! Boom! Boom!" he declared as his fist shattered a cylindrical tower the same shape as his sand pail. "No roof! No roof!"

Harry, meanwhile, had become captivated by the distant figures—out beyond the first shore break—who seemed to be standing atop the billowing waves, riding them in to shore: "Mama, how are those men *doing* that?"

"They call that 'surfing.' Look closely and you can see the men standing on long boards, like those over there." I pointed to the towering fifteen-foot surfboards propped up against the wall of the Moana Hotel, down the beach.

Mesmerized, Harry gazed out at the surfers and declared, "I want to do that."

"Perhaps when you are older," I said.

"I want to learn now!"

"You are too small. A wave like that would toss you so high into the air you'd never come down!"

Harry regarded me skeptically. "No, I wouldn't. Would I?"

"Well . . . maybe not *never*."

He looked smug. "Didn't think so."

"You might come down after six or seven days. But you know, there's nothing to eat or drink up there. You'd come back pretty hungry and thirsty."

That seemed to sober him and, chastened, he went back to playing in the placid waters closer to shore.

I tried to coax Grace into the water but she would venture no farther than ankle-deep. In truth, despite all the love Jae-sun and I had lavished on her, Grace seemed to suffer from many of the same insecurities I had been plagued with as a child. Even after a year in school, her teachers said she was anxious and "lacked confidence." Perhaps it was an inherited characteristic. But as I had succeeded in overcoming my fears, I was determined to help Grace do the same.

Charlie, meanwhile, was constructing a rather elaborate sand castle, in which I now recognized some disturbing shapes—not just the familiar pail-shaped towers, but a kind of cupola with suspiciously similar proportions to a rice bowl I had brought to the picnic. I now discovered that while my attentions had been focused on Grace, Charlie had ransacked the picnic basket and dumped the rice into a sandy grave, along with the *kimchi* I had packed in a tall jar that he used to make an admittedly impressive sand-tower.

I made my displeasure known, and only after I had finished scolding him did I suddenly realize that someone was missing. Where was Harold?

My annoyance with Charlie was quickly replaced by panic over Harry. He was a good swimmer, but even so I anxiously searched the rolling surface of the ocean for some trace of him. I looked up and down the beach, toward Diamond Head in one direction and the Moana in the other, but still no Harry. I told myself to remain calm, trying to think of where he might have gone; and then I noticed again the pile of surfboards stacked up beside the Moana.

After placing Charlie and Grace in my husband's care, I hurried down the beach.

The Moana Hotel was a large, modern white building with plantation-style verandahs facing the sea. On this autumn day the beach was populated mainly by local residents, surfers, and a handful of Moana guests: pale flabby *haoles* gleaming with coconut oil, looking and smelling like *haupia* pudding as they sunned themselves in beach chairs. I saw no sign of Harry on the grounds of the hotel. I looked seaward, where a handful of surfers wearing dark tank tops and trunks were serenely gliding atop cresting waves. When a surfer with skin as bronze as a new penny came ashore with his board, I went up to him and asked, "Excuse me, but—have you seen a little Korean boy? About four years old?"

The surfer looked over my shoulder and said, "Is that him?"

I turned to see another surfer riding a low swell in to shore, a small boy perched on the prow of the long board like a hood ornament on a Model T.

"Mama!" Harry called out, never happier. "Look! I'm surfing!"

I ran to him as the surfer beached the board and told him, "Uh-oh, jig's up. Everybody off." Harry obediently jumped off, into the shallows. I gathered up my son in my arms, so happy to see him that I barely chided him for going off alone. "Harry, you nearly scared Mama to death!"

The surfer on whose board Harry had been riding—a broad-faced Portuguese-Hawaiian with a few front teeth missing from his smile—looked at me, then at Harry and said, "Kid, you're a spitting chip off the old block."

In all the years I was to know this man, I was never sure whether his scrambled metaphors were accidental or intentional clowning.

"Sorry," he apologized, "my fault. Your boy came up, asked if I could teach him to surf, so I offered him a ride."

The other surfer grinned and said, "See, the *keiki* follow Panama around 'cause they know another *keiki* when they see one."

Panama expressed mock indignation. "If that ain't the Tarball calling the kettle black!"

"Hey, I may be short," the one called Tarball said, "but Panama's so short, other day he got beat up by some kid smaller than Harry here."

"She was not," Panama shot back, and they both exploded into laughter.

I soon learned that these amiable watermen with the colorful names were among a select group known as "beachboys," who served visitors to Waikīkī in a wide variety of capacities: surfing instructors, outrigger canoe pilots, island tour guides, drinking companions, and occasionally companions of a different sort for mainland *wahines* who could not help but be impressed by their charm, athleticism, and exotic good looks.

But this was, as I say, the off season, and the beachboys at Waikīkī today were here to surf, spearfish, or just enjoy a good time with their friends—among whom Harry and I were quickly counted. Soon two more came ashore: the genial "Steamboat Bill" and a tall, handsome figure of bronze who Tarball introduced as "my brother Paoa, the world traveler, finally home for a few minutes."

I gratefully invited Panama and the others to join our picnic, where we offered them cold noodles, rice, and fire beef, and in return Steamboat offered us *'ōkolehao*—distilled *tī*-root liquor. "Guaranteed," he promised, "to knock you on your *'ōkole*—and how!"

Jade Moon, fresh from chasing down two of her roving children, was quick to accept the challenge.

"We shall see about that," she said, quickly downing a shot of "Hawaiian moonshine," then requesting another.

"Whoa, I think I'm in love," Steamboat announced.

"I am a married woman," Jade Moon demurred. "But *this* one is single." And she mischievously pointed out Beauty, standing shyly nearby.

Beauty blushed in mortification and tried to hide behind me, but Panama's eyes lit up. "Now, now, don't go hiding your bushel under a tisket," which made even Beauty, who didn't fully grasp the absurdity of what he'd said, giggle.

The one named Paoa seemed quiet and unassuming, but now I noticed that although his brother called him Paoa, the other beachboys referred to him as "Duke." This was also not lost on Wise Pearl's ten-year-old son, John, who approached him and asked in a hushed tone, "Are you *the* Duke?"

"Well," Tarball's brother said, "my father was also named Duke. He'll always be 'the' Duke to me. That's why my brothers started calling me Paoa, to distinguish me from my dad."

"But you're the one who went to the Olympics, right?"

Duke nodded modestly. Jae-sun and I looked at each other with surprise. *That* Duke?

"Are your medals really made of gold?" John asked in awe.

"Sure thing. But let me show you something." The great Duke Kahanamoku—Olympic medalist, world champion swimmer, legendary surfer—took in the dazzling sweep of the ocean and told John, "*This* is worth your weight in gold. And it's all ours."

For the next few hours we all ate and joked and talked as if we were old friends. Steamboat strummed a ukulele and Panama showed Beauty's daughter, Mary, how to make a coconut hat. "Why do they call you Panama?" Mary asked.

He pointed to the big gap between his front teeth. "You heard of the Panama Canal? Looks kine like this." He took a big gulp of drinking water, then blew it out through the toothless gap in a gusher. Mary squealed in delight; Beauty laughed, too. Panama may not have been the handsomest of the beachboys, but I could tell Beauty was smitten.

Tarball, whose real name was Bill, took Harry out for another ride on his board and Duke offered to do the same for Grace—who backed away in horror at the idea. I explained Grace's fear of the water and Duke just nodded thoughtfully, then excused himself and headed back down the beach to the Moana Hotel.

When he returned a few minutes later, it was with one of the glass boxes that guests of the Moana used to view reef fish—the precursor to today's snorkeling masks. He asked Grace, "Have you ever seen how people throw coins off the big cruise ships when they come into the harbor?"

"They do?"

"Yeah, sure, all the time. Young boys go diving down looking for them, but they don't always find them all. I happen to know for a fact there's a quarter buried in the sand around here somewhere. You want to try looking?"

He started her searching on the dry sand and just when she was starting to get bored, I saw him slip a coin out of his pocket and bury it into the sand. When Grace found it a few minutes later, she cried out, "Look! A dime!"

"Well, that's swell," Duke said with feigned frustration, "but I *know* there's a quarter a little farther out."

He showed her how to use the glass box to view the sandy bottom of the shallows, pointing out frightened little puffer fish burying their heads in the sand and tiny sand crabs skittering sideways like tipsy spiders. Grace began to brave the deeper water without even realizing she was doing it. Duke turned her toward a school of silvery needlefish, slanting below the surface like a torrent of silver rain. When the water grew too deep for Grace to wade in, Duke picked her up in his big hands and gently floated her on the surface. She peered through her glass box at the schools of yellow tangs, blue-green unicorn fish, and black-and-white butterfly fish swarming around the pink coral heads. Grace was so entranced by this colorful undersea world that it didn't even occur to her to be afraid. And Duke didn't forget, as they came ashore again, to have her look again for that quarter in the sand—which, of course, she triumphantly discovered.

Grace was never afraid of the ocean again, and from that day on, Duke Kahanamoku was as much royalty to me as Lili'uokalani had been.

As the sun slid below the horizon our new friends invited us over to the gazebo at the end of the three-hundred-foot Moana Pier, where they were joined by Hiram Anahu, another beachboy as well as a talented painter and composer of popular songs. In the limelight of the newly risen moon the beachboys played ukulele and steel guitar, and sang both traditional Hawaiian standards like "Kalena Kai" and *hapa-haole* songs like "Honolulu Moon." Their voices were the sweetest I had ever heard, falsettos blending together in angelic harmony. This was a Sunday night tradition I would be lucky enough to experience again over the years—but I will never forget that first night out on the pier, listening to songs of moonlight and romance, and to the sigh of the tide as the moon tugged on it, its light scattering like daydreams on the waves breaking across the reef. I rested with my head on Jae-sun's shoulder; Beauty gazed adoringly at Panama, strumming his ukulele; Jade Moon cradled her youngest child in her lap as she looked up at the stars, sprinkled like sugar across the black bowl of the sky. These young men with their music and their magical voices were the very embodiment of *aloha*, of the spirit of the islands; but the true measure of their magic was that as we listened to them, we were not so much transported as transformed. Because for as long as we listened, reflected in the sweet light of their songs, we were all, every one of us, Hawaiian.

Sundays were always over too soon. The next morning Jae-sun would be up before dawn to make his daily pilgrimage to the O'ahu Fish Market, where limp stacks of bonito, skipjack, yellowtail, and *ono*, all fresh off the fishing boats, were piled high for inspection. Battalions of restaurant owners and chefs swarmed over the mounds of dead fish, checking for color and texture, hefting for weight and size. I went only once with Jae-sun. The place reeked of brine and seaweed, and the sight of so many deceased fish staring at me with open eyes reminded me unpleasantly of the butcher shop next door to Aunt Obedience's. Jae-sun was always frustrated that he could never find anything resembling mudfish—small minnows that live in the muddy mouths of rivers in Korea. These fish were but three or four inches in length, thin as pencils and usually dark with ingested sediment. Jae-sun knew an old recipe for a soup with stuffed *tubu*—soybean curd—that called for mudfish. First, he said, you placed the fish in brine, which made them—let's say "eject"—the mud, after which they shined like newly minted coins. They were then tossed live into a heated skillet filled with *tubu*—where, in an effort to escape the heat, the poor things would dive into the soybean curd, obligingly providing a stuffing for the *tubu* before expiring.

I never wished to see this in practice, much less partake of it, but Jae-sun had a yen to cook it and none of the local fish markets bothered to stock something as small and unprofitable as a minnow.

Then one day he came home triumphant from his morning pilgrimage, proudly showing me not only twenty pounds of fresh skipjack, but a large bottle filled with water and teeming with tiny live minnows. "Look!" he cried out. "They are not mudfish, but they will do."

"Did you find these at the fish market?"

"No, I finally used my head. I went down to the docks yesterday looking for a fisherman who would sell his catch to me directly, at a lower cost. I found a man with a small boat who said he'd be willing, if I committed to buy a certain amount each week." He opened the brown butcher paper covering a three-pound bonito. "This is of excellent quality, as you see."

"And you asked him to catch you some minnows?"

"He uses them for bait, so he gave me a jarful with his compliments. I can't wait to cook these up for a luncheon treat!" He took out a large skillet, which would shortly become the instrument of doom for the tiny wriggling fish.

"Ah," I said, "as it happens, I am having lunch with Beauty today." This was a lie, of course, but one I could make true easily enough.

"But this is a rare delicacy, and delicious!"

I slipped out of the kitchen before the butter greased the skillet.

While Jae-sun feasted on bait, Beauty was happy to share some fried rice with me at Sai Fu's Chop Sui House on Hotel Street. Panama Dave had swept her off her feet with his wit, romantic soul, and gentleness toward Mary, and she had fallen quickly and hopelessly in love with him. I was happy for her—Heaven knew she deserved some romance and laughter in her life—but when she began telling us at *kye* meetings about what "they" would do once they were married, Wise Pearl tactfully inquired whether Panama had actually asked for her hand.

"Not yet," Beauty admitted, "but I'm sure he will."

Now, months later, Beauty was fretting that the proposal still was not forthcoming. I suggested, as gently as I could, that perhaps Panama was simply not the "marrying kind."

"Oh no, you don't know him, he's so sweet," she protested.

"A man can be sweet and loving and still not be interested in marriage."

"He loves Mary. You see how good he is with her. He loves children."

"He has a childlike spirit, it's true," I said delicately, "and I'm sure he cares for Mary. But that does not necessarily mean he wants to be a father, or husband."

Beauty fell into a sullen pout and I elected to change the subject.

I returned to the cafe, where my husband was extolling the savory flavor of his *tubu* soup. He had saved me some, and I had to admit that it was tasty, as was the other fish he had purchased. We served it spiced and barbecued for *bulgogi* or grilled in a *miso* sauce. Thus began a long, fruitful business relationship, with our weekly order increasing steadily. After perhaps six weeks, Jae-sun came home with thirty pounds of bonito, yellowtail, and albacore, and with a certain diffidence he told me, "I've invited our supplier to the restaurant with his family. He only purchased this boat last year and I believe they struggle to make ends meet. I thought they might appreciate a taste of the fruit of his labors."

"We should prepare them something special, then."

"I was thinking perhaps *misoyaki*," he said with studied casualness. "They are Japanese."

I was more than mildly surprised, but said only, "Perhaps some *mochi* for dessert?"

"Yes, good."

"When will they be coming?"

"Tomorrow evening at six o'clock."

We spoke no more of it until the following evening at six, when a spindly Japanese man in a threadbare suit entered the restaurant with his wife and four children in tow. I was not looking at them but at him—there was an earnest grace to the way he bowed to me, smiled and said, "Hello. We have table. I am Taizo."

I bowed in return. "*Konicha wa*, Taizo-san. I am honored to meet you. My name is Jin—my husband has told me much about you."

"And he speaks of you with great fondness. This is my wife, Tamiko."

I looked at the woman standing behind him, holding an infant child, and surely betrayed my surprise at seeing my old friend from the *Nippon Maru*.

Tamiko smiled and bowed, then said, as if we were meeting for the first time: "I am pleased to meet you, Jin-san. This is my daughter Sugi, my sons Hiroshi and Jiro, and our newest child, who is also named Jin. Is that not a coincidence?" Her eyes glittered with amusement. "In Japanese it means 'tenderness.'"

Jae-sun appeared from the kitchen, greeting Taizo with evident warmth as he escorted the family to a table. As Tamiko and I followed behind our husbands we exchanged wordless smiles. But Jiro was regarding me uncertainly, perhaps with a faint memory of crackseed on his tongue. "I know you," he said at last.

"Of course you do," I said, pulling a chair out for him. "We are all going to be great friends."

As these ties were renewed, so were others. At the start of the Christian New Year of 1924, I had received a letter from my elder brother, informing me that Blossom, now sixteen years old, had made another attempt to flee the Pak home. The weariness in which he couched this news made me think that perhaps the time was finally right to again broach a sore subject. What's more, the following month would see the start of the Korean Year of the Rat. It had been the Year of the Rat twelve years ago, when Blossom first came to our home in Pojogae, and I took this as an auspicious omen. After consulting with Jae-sun, I wrote to Joyful Day:

> *It sounds as if little sister-in-law is becoming increasingly troublesome. Someone who so obviously hates where she is will hardly make for a pliant and dutiful wife. Would it not be better for all concerned if she were to come here to Hawai'i instead?*
>
> *My husband and I are prepared to offer you the sum of one hundred dollars—two hundred yen—to dissolve Blossom's obligation to the clan. We will also pay for her steamer fare to*

Hawai'i. You need do nothing but apply for the proper papers. If
Father will not consider sister-in-law's well-being, perhaps he
will consider what two hundred yen might do for his clan's.

The reply, which arrived a month later, was brief and to the point:

Little Sister:
    Father has given due consideration to your generous offer
and wishes me to tell you that he agrees to your terms.
    Please advise us on how you wish to proceed.

Your elder brother

I was ecstatic and wrote back to request they begin the process of applying for Blossom's passport and visa. Once they had obtained these, we would send them a steamship ticket and either mail or wire them the hundred dollars.

But in order for Blossom to enter the country, she had to be engaged to marry a man in the United States. I discreetly inquired of several young men of our acquaintance whether they would be willing to lend their names to the fiction of an arranged marriage. Ronald Yun, the twenty-year-old son of a neighbor, agreed to assist in this bit of subterfuge—even to marry Blossom if there was no other way to get her into the country, a marriage that would later be annulled.

To lend credibility to the sham, I had Mr. Yun send Blossom fifty dollars in "earnest money," which we provided.

My brother reported no trouble obtaining a passport for Blossom. I then had him apply for a visa on her behalf as the fiancée of an American-born man named Ronald Yun in Honolulu. Hundreds of women still entered the country this way, and I believed it would be only a question of how long we had to wait for the American embassy in Seoul to approve Blossom's visa.

But though my timing had been right in approaching Father, in another respect it could not have been worse.

*K*oreans were not alone, it seemed, in their antipathy toward the Japanese. Apparently many on the American mainland, including prominent members of Congress, were looking at the number of Japanese immigrants in Hawai'i—and other parts of the western United States—with mounting alarm about something they called "Oriental colonization." It was not a matter of race, they claimed, but of culture: Orientals, they said, were too alien in their values, and simply would not assimilate into American society. America's culture and values had to be preserved against this invasion from outside its borders.

The 1920 Japanese labor action against O'ahu plantations only fueled Americans' suspicions that the Japanese were out to undermine their economy and way of life. Immigration from China had been restricted before the turn of the century, and a so-called Gentleman's Agreement between the United States and Japan in 1907 stopped any further immigration from the Japanese Empire, including Korea. The only exceptions to this had been for students studying abroad and for "picture brides" like myself. But now, it appeared, we had committed an unpardonable crime: We were reproducing.

Birth rates among Japanese and Koreans in the United States had soared in recent years as laborers married, settled down, and raised families. We were apparently doing it too well relative to the birth rate of Americans in general, and white Americans in particular.

I was pathetically ignorant of all this as I began excitedly preparing for Blossom's arrival. We had purchased a two-tiered "bunk bed" for Harold and Charlie to sleep in, thus freeing up valuable floor space in our one-room apartment, in which we put the daybed that was to belong to my sister-in-law. Even though Blossom's arrival was still months away, I began excitedly cleaning house, making room in the closet, and clearing space for another family member.

But then, in December 1924, word came from my brother that Blossom's visa to the United States had been denied.

At first I thought it was some sort of mistake, but a visit to the passport office here in Honolulu revealed the appalling truth.

That summer, the United States Congress had passed—and President Coolidge signed into law—the Immigration Act of 1924, or as it was sometimes called, the Oriental Exclusion Act. Against the fear of a "Japanese conspiracy," it closed the door on any further Japanese immigration, including and especially the importation of picture brides.

It closed the door on Blossom.

The only exceptions now were temporary visas for students entering "an accredited school, college, academy, seminary, or university . . . and who shall voluntarily depart from the United States upon the completion of such course of study." Desperately I attempted to enroll Blossom in the Korean Girls' Seminary in Honolulu, but as she had never received a formal education of any kind in Korea, she was judged by the American Embassy not a "qualified" applicant and a student visa was also denied her.

It was our last hope, cruelly dashed.

I blamed not Congress but myself: If only I had thought to do this a year ago! I wept bitterly, feeling the greatest loss and grief since the death of my first child; and in a way, this was a kind of death, the death of a dream long held. Jae-sun tried to comfort me, but I would not be consoled. During the day, with Harold and Grace at school and Jae-sun at work, I would look at the daybed we had bought for my little sister and I would burst into tears— alarming Charlie, who hardly understood grief and would never know what he was missing by Blossom's absence in our home.

Just as I was beginning to reconcile myself to a life without her, I received another letter from Joyful Day—this one informing me that Blossom had once again run away. But this time she had done so bearing an Imperial Japanese passport. She could not travel to the United States with this document, but she might have been able to use it to escape to Japan or China. Despite their best attempts, my family was unable to locate her.

Blossom was gone, and my clan had only fifty dollars in "earnest money" to show for it. Father had reason anew to hate me.

With my husband's agreement I wired them the balance of the money owed them: they had, after all, lived up to their part of the bargain.

And now, in addition to my grief that my little sister-in-law would not be joining me in Hawai'i, I worried for her safety. The life of a runaway did not usually end well, and I fretted about where she was, whether she had money for food or a roof over her head. But all I could do was pray for her health and well-being.

My only consolation—a faint one—was the knowledge that Blossom would not, after all, become a Daughter-in-Law Flower growing in my family's bitter garden. At least I had helped, in some way, to assist in her escaping this fate; and wherever she was, wherever she came to rest, I prayed for her eventual happiness, and hoped she would not forget me . . . even as I would never, could never, forget the first real sister I had ever had.

Fifteen

In Korea the number three is considered a lucky number, and six—being twice three—is thought to be a profitable one. So on the sixth anniversary of the Liliha Cafe, we celebrated the luck and the profit that had come our way by inviting all the friends who had supported us to a private party at the restaurant. The buffet table was abundantly stocked with everything from *kimchi* and *mandu* dumplings to *kūlolo* pudding and—for the children present—hamburger sandwiches. Jae-sun was kept busy cooking much of the time as I greeted our guests, which included my Sisters of Kyŏngsang and their clans, the Anito and Kahahawai extended *'ohana,* our friends from church, and beachboys Tarball, Steamboat, Hiram—but notably not Panama Dave, the end of whose romance with Beauty had come as a shock to none save Beauty herself. It was pleasing to see so many faces dear to us gathered in this place that was both business and home to our family, and when I wasn't carrying in hot dishes, I drifted from one table to the next, visiting and chatting with one group of friends before moving on to another.

I stopped by the Kahahawais' table, where Joe, his family, and Bill Kama were raptly listening to Chang Apana casually relate how, over the course of his long police career, he had been pushed out of a second-story window, stabbed six times, run over by a horse and buggy, attacked with a sickle, and once even been shot at point-blank only to have the bullet stopped by his badge. Yet as celebrated as Chang had become for his true-life exploits, he had recently gained even greater notoriety for some that were purely fictional. An author of mystery stories, Earl Derr Biggers, had the previous year published a novel called *The House Without a Key*, which introduced a Honolulu police detective named Charlie Chan. Almost immediately upon publication of the story in *The Saturday Evening Post*, Honolulu was abuzz with speculation that Chan was based upon Chang Apana.

Now, it was true that Chang was also renowned for his powers of deduction: he once solved a crime by means of a silk thread found on a floor, and captured a murderer by identifying a certain kind of mud on the man's shoes. But that was all he and Charlie Chan had in common. Where Apana was wiry and two-fisted, Chan was fat and intellectual; where Chang was a man of a few choice words, his counterpart spouted aphorisms like "Alibi have habit of disappearing like hole in water" or "Death is the black camel that kneels unbid at every gate." Derr Biggers, who had vacationed in Honolulu in 1919, apparently ran across a news story about Chang smashing an opium ring and thought a Chinese police detective would be a refreshing change from the diabolical Oriental villains so common to mystery stories in those days. The character immediately caught the public's fancy and Chang Apana now found himself jokingly addressed as "Charlie" by his fellow officers, and his autograph was eagerly sought by tourists. He obligingly signed these *"Charlie Chan."*

"Detective," I asked him, "have you seen the chapter play yet?" Pathé had just released a ten-part motion picture serial based on *The House Without a Key*, starring the Japanese actor George Kuwa.

"Oh yeah, plenty times," he replied with a grin. "Eh, what do you know! Never knew I was Japanee!"

Everyone laughed, but the gleam in Chang's eye was not one of annoyance but amusement. I think he was flattered by the notion that his exploits had inspired a movie hero, if an unlikely one.

I moved over to where Joe Kahahawai was sitting next to his father. "And how are you, Joe?"

"Eh, good, how you—I mean, how are you, Aunt Jin?" Joe spoke pidgin among his friends, but was always careful to speak more conventional English around his elders, especially Esther.

"He's thinking about going back to school," Joe Sr. said proudly. Joe, having fared better on the football field than in the classroom, had dropped out of St. Louis College two years ago, when he was fifteen.

Joe wagged a thumb at his father: *"He's* thinking about me going back to school. Me, I'm not so sure."

I knew that since leaving school, Joe had drifted back into the company of his fellow Kauluwela Boys—or, as the police called them, the School Street Gang. This was not quite as sinister as it sounded: youth gangs in Hawai'i sometimes engaged in petty theft, but they were as likely to be found playing barefoot football on vacant lots as they were scuffling with rivals over "turf." Such conflicts generated their share of black eyes and broken bones, but never deaths as with mainland gangs. Far better, his father reasoned, for such clashes to take place not on the street but on the gridiron.

"I'd give anything to have that football scholarship you had, Joe," I told him. "If you don't use it, maybe I will."

Joe laughed. "I'd pay good money, Auntie, to see you make the starting kick against the Micks."

We all had a good laugh at the image of little me wearing Joe's enormous football jersey, and then I moved on to the children's table, making sure the *keiki* had adequate supplies of hamburgers and ice cream. Harry and Woodrow, each seven years old, were now the best of pals—they spent endless days together at the beach, swimming like fishes and bodysurfing under the tutelage of Panama and Tarball. I was happy to see Grace talking animatedly with Tamiko's son Jiro—my daughter was slowly outgrowing her painful shyness—even as I was unhappy to have to inform Charlie that ice cream was not to be used as a hair tonic, as he seemed to have convinced Wise Pearl's youngest son, Louis. After taking away Charlie's dessert and washing out Louis's hair in the kitchen, I was finally able to sit down and join my fellow picture brides at the next table.

Beauty was still moping over Panama: "I just don't understand it," she insisted. "He was always so happy to see me—right up till the day he didn't want to see me anymore." She burst into tears, not for the first time that day.

Wise Pearl patted her comfortingly on the shoulder. "None of this is your doing. He is just not the kind of a man to settle down, at least not yet."

"I thought that would change," Beauty said despondently.

Jade Moon took a swallow of the bootleg "Hawaiian moonshine" that Steamboat had brought, and spoke up.

"With all respect," she said, "why *should* it change?"

Beauty blinked in surprise. "What?"

"The man practically lives on the most beautiful beach in Hawai'i, is paid hundred-dollar tips for making rich men laugh, has love affairs with beautiful *wahines* from the mainland, and gets tipped for that, too! Why *should* he change? And where might *I* apply for such a position?"

Beauty said in a small voice, "I thought he would change for *me*."

Jade Moon emptied her drink and sighed. "Your problem," she said emphatically, "is that you are a romantic. You think love will solve everything, when in fact it rarely solves anything. My God—you are one of the most beautiful women I have ever met, you could have your pick of any man in Hawai'i. And who do you pick? The one least likely to become a husband! Why, if I looked like you, I would be married to a millionaire!"

Her voice was loud, as usual. I glanced over at the next table, where our husbands were chatting, unmindful of what was being discussed at the women's table. "Mr. Ha might fail to appreciate that remark," I said.

Jade Moon laughed shortly. "Mr. Ha induced me to Hawai'i with claims of being an affluent man, even as our friend's late husband purported to be young and virile, and not the withered old mummy that he was. We were all lied to, or have you forgotten? What was so romantic about *that*?"

"Our lives might have been even worse," Wise Pearl pointed out, "had we stayed in Korea."

"Of course—in Korea we would have been bartered like chattel to the best marriage prospects our parents could find for us. This is my whole point! Here, we have say over who we will marry. Here we have that power. Use it!" she urged Beauty. "Use it to better your lot in life, as our clans would have married us off to better themselves."

Beauty looked quietly thoughtful. As cold and calculating as Jade Moon's argument was, I could not rebut it on the facts.

"Do you not have wealthy men come into your barbershop?" she asked Beauty. "Do any of them ever ask you out?"

"Some do."

"Have you accepted any of these invitations?"

"A few." She shrugged. "I just haven't felt anything. No . . . tingle."

Jade Moon rolled her eyes. "*Tingle?* A bee sting tingles. Take my advice: Forget about romance! Find a wealthy man who will provide for you and your daughter, while you're still young and beautiful enough to attract one."

Beauty thought about that some more, then slowly nodded.

"Perhaps you are right," she said. "What has romance done for me? The first man I loved gave me a baby but no marriage, and the next one gave me even less than that."

"Now, wait . . ." I started to say.

With surprising vehemence Beauty said, "No! She *is* right. Men will not always look favorably upon me. I should use the blessings God has given me to my advantage, while I still can. Do they not say it is as easy to marry a rich man as a poor one?" She turned to Jade Moon. "Thank you for your advice. I will strive to be a new woman—the kind of woman you would be in my place."

I shuddered a little at the thought, but I confess that I did not take Beauty's pronouncement very seriously—not even as Jade Moon began earnestly counseling her on how best to ascertain a prospective husband's assets. I knew that Beauty often tacked into the wind like a swift but rudderless *sampan,* and when the wind shifted direction a few minutes later, so would she.

As proud as I was of the success of the Liliha Cafe, it was my husband's dream, not mine; and after six years of cooking, cleaning, and waiting tables, I was growing weary of the restaurant business. Jae-sun truly loved devising new recipes and new menu items, but for me creative expression came rarely these days, as when I would sew a new tablecloth, a new dress for Grace, or a pair of trousers for Harold. In truth, I missed my job at

Mr. Ku'uana's tailor shop: I missed working with needle and thread, the challenges that walked into the shop every day, the almost hypnotic tattoo of the sewing machine as it stitched.

I admitted as much to Jae-sun who, far from taking offense, pointed out that we now employed two kitchen staff and two full-time waitresses, and any of the latter could easily take on my hostess duties as well. "Why not open a little shop of your own," he suggested, "and take in some work as a seamstress?" This possibility had not even crossed my mind—I had been thinking merely of asking Mr. Ku'uana for my old job back, if only part-time. But Jae-sun noted, "This way you can set your own hours."

He suggested I open from eight in the morning to four in the afternoon, which would allow me more than enough time to cook supper for the children, assist them with their homework, and tuck them into bed, while Jae-sun and his staff readied the restaurant for opening. I found myself growing excited at the idea, more excitement than I had felt in some time.

I borrowed a little money from the *kye*, enough for a rental deposit on a small shop on King Street, with just enough room for a counter, a sewing machine, an ironing board, and a small cutting table. It was situated next door to a dry-goods store, C. K. Chow's, which specialized in imported fabrics from Japan and China. I reasoned that the nearness to such a store might send some business my way, and I turned out to be right.

Like so many girls in Korea, my shop was nameless: I merely stenciled the words TAILOR SHOP onto the front window and opened my doors for business. At first my customers consisted entirely of friends from church. However, my proximity to Chow's store soon yielded customers who came in with fine European broadcloth to be made into shirts, or colorful Japanese *yukata* fabric to be fashioned into a kimono. It would be a while before I earned enough to pay the full rent on the shop, but even so I was content to sit at my sewing machine for hours, keeping one eye on little Charlie playing with his toys behind the counter, interrupted only by the chime of the door as someone entered the shop.

I was surprised to find that many of the patrons of Chow's store were not just Japanese and Chinese, but well-to-do *haole* ladies from the Nu'uanu or Mānoa valleys who appreciated "Oriental fabrics." One who wandered into my shop early on was a Mrs. Quigley, a handsome woman in her fifties, impeccably attired in a white shirt-waisted dress and a *lauhala* sunbonnet. (Close-fitting cloche hats were all the rage on the mainland then, but in Hawai'i the bright tropical sun necessitated something more practical.)

"I usually go to Musa-Shiya," she told me, referring to the well-known tailor and clothier farther down King Street, "but I had a bit of a tiff with Mr. Miyamoto over some silk pajamas and Mr. Chow says you've done fine work for other customers of his."

"He is too kind."

Mrs. Quigley showed me some fine white China silk, which she desired to be made into a *holokū* for her daughter's evening wear. "She says she's bored to death of these old-fashioned Mother Hubbards, as she persists in calling them, and asked if there's any way I might—quote unquote—'jazz it up a little.'" She rolled her eyes. "God forbid anything these days isn't *jazzy* enough. I suppose I should be grateful she doesn't want one of those flapper dresses with their hemlines somewhere north of modesty yet south of complete disrepute."

I smiled. "Ah, but the two styles have much in common. Both are simple shifts—no cinching at the waist. Now, I have seen *holokūs* with short sleeves, or no sleeves, like the flapper dresses . . ." I drew a tubular shape on a sheet of writing paper, sketching in sleeves that ended just below the shoulder. "I have even seen them without the yoke. If we do away with that, and lower the neckline a bit . . ."

Mrs. Quigley nodded, intrigued.

"Hmm," she said judiciously, "why don't we make that . . . *two* 'bits'?"

I looked up at her, surprised.

"My daughter has a good bosom. And I *do* hope to see her married someday." She gave me a wink. I liked this amusing old *haole* woman.

"We could add some ruffles along the neckline," I suggested, "make them look like a *lei*, very Hawaiian . . ."

"Yes, that's quite nice. But I must ask you, dear: Have you worked with Chinese silk before?"

I wanted to say, "Yes indeed, I dressed some of the most fashionable ladies at Iwilei," but wisely left it at, "Yes indeed."

Mrs. Quigley "sized me up," smiled, and nodded.

"All right, then," she said. "I like the cut of your jib. Have at it!"

"Have at it" I did. I put more work into that *holokū* than anything I had ever sewn—hand-gathering the stitches, carefully fashioning a necklace of wide ruffles that looked something like a feather *lei*. I was quite proud of the finished product, and I had to admit: I was enjoying myself immensely.

Not long afterward, at our next *kye* meeting, held at my home, Beauty startled us all when she casually announced, "One of my customers, a man of considerable means, has asked me to marry him."

I looked at her in surprise. "I did not know you were seeing someone."

"I have only been out with him once."

"And he has already asked you to marry him?" Wise Pearl said.

"He has, and what's more, I have said yes."

"What!" I cried. "You're joking."

"I have never been more serious in my life," Beauty said.

"Now just a moment," Jade Moon said. "How can you be sure, after only one meeting—"

I was surprised but relieved that Jade Moon's would turn out to be a voice of reason.

"—that he truly *is* a man of means?"

Truly, would I never learn better?

"He has been a customer for some time, and owns a jewelry shop on Merchant Street," Beauty said excitedly. "He says I may pick out any ring in his store for my engagement!"

"Does he own a home?" Jade Moon asked.

"A beautiful one, near Punchbowl Hill."

"How old is he?" Wise Pearl inquired.

"He is forty-two, and widowed. One son."

"So you *have* known him a while," I said. "Is he handsome? Funny?"

"He is neither handsome nor homely," Beauty replied with seeming indifference. "And I cannot think of a single amusing thing he has said. In the past I put great stock in such things, and where has it gotten me?"

"He does not make you—'tingle'?" Jade Moon said mockingly.

"The rings in his store make me tingle," Beauty said with a sly smile, drawing a laugh from Jade Moon. Beauty giggled, and their shared laughter sent a chill through my bones.

Wise Pearl said dryly, "Would it be beside the point to ask his name?"

"He is from the Ko clan of Seoul. A prosperous clan."

I persisted in my foolish queries. "Is he at least a good father?"

This seemed to sober Beauty and she replied sharply, "I would not have accepted if I did not think he would make a good father to Mary. *She* is the reason I am doing this." She turned to Jade Moon. "Do *you* approve of my choice?"

Jade Moon bowed her head. "I could not have made a better one myself." Then she shocked us all by asking, "Have you shared a bed with this man?"

Beauty blushed fiercely. "No!"

"Good. Keep it so, until you are married. He is not the only one with baubles to bestow."

By Heaven, I should have thrown her over the side of the *Nippon Maru* when I had the chance!

"How old is this boy of his?" Jade Moon asked.

"Ten years—why?"

"Good, he's young. Ingratiate yourself with him. Do not let him turn against you as your first husband's sons did."

My face felt flush with anger.

Beauty said, "I had not considered that. You are wise."

I waited until Beauty had left before I confronted Jade Moon. "What kind of friend is it," I snapped, "who would teach a lovelorn girl to love only money?"

"What kind of friend," she retorted, "would have her waste her life on men who will never marry her or provide for her comfort? All I'm doing is turning her mind to more practical considerations."

"You are turning her into a conniving shrew!"

"She is simply recognizing her assets at long last, and exploiting them. Just because *you* married for love does not mean Beauty should, too. She can do much better than you"—she added quickly, "or I."

Her words inflamed my old insecurities like a poke to a forgotten wound.

Losing my temper, I yelled, "Leave my home!"

Jade Moon opened her mouth to say something, but before she could I repeated, "Get *out!*"

Realizing the depth of my anger, and perhaps too the line she had crossed, Jade Moon quickly left. I would not speak to her again until the next meeting of the *kye*, and even then, only barely.

*M*rs. Quigley so loved the *holokū* I made for her daughter that she gave me several other bits of piecework to do. When I completed these to her satisfaction, she asked if I might be able to come work for her at her home one day a week, doing everything from sewing together whole shirts to darning socks to mending ladies' unmentionables. This was a not uncommon arrangement for such affluent *haole* women—they called themselves *kamaʻāina,* Hawaiian for "native born," though the term had come to be regarded as synonymous with *haoles* descended from the first missionary families. For one day's work, she offered to pay me enough to cover my shop's rent for a week—so, of course, I agreed.

The following Thursday morning I took the streetcar to Mrs. Quigley's home in the Nuʻuanu Valley. I had seen houses like these from the outside, and just once—Liliʻuokalani's home, Washington Place—from the inside, but I was completely unprepared for the luxury I found within the gates of the Quigley estate.

Past a broad green lawn, a winding stone path wended like a mountain stream through a grove of tall coconut palms. As I walked up the path, gardens of helliconia and Chinese jasmine bloomed on one side of me; on the other, birds sang from the branches of a huge banyan tree, which also shaded a small fishpond. I followed the stone "stream" to its source, and no mountain could have been more impressive to me than the imposing Victorian mansion I now approached, two stories high, long settled on seven acres of lushly landscaped grounds.

I ascended the front steps onto a wide *lānai* decorated with white wicker chairs, tables, divans, and fragrant *lauaʻe* ferns spilling out of hanging wicker baskets. I rang the bell and the door was answered by a Chinese servant who asked my name, then politely ushered me inside.

We passed through a hallway decorated with fine Oriental rugs and calabashes of flowers adorning antique tables, into a spacious living area—it was far more than merely a *room*—the centerpiece of which was a marble pool and fountain, a stream of water spouting from the mouth of a marble fish. I had never seen such a thing inside a home before and, as impressive as it was, I could not for the life of me see the purpose of having it, other than the restful sound of bubbling water. My impolite gaping was fortunately cut short by the appearance of Mrs. Quigley, who greeted me warmly, offered me tea, then turned me over to a woman named Mililani, who managed the household staff.

I followed Mililani up a winding staircase to the second floor, and as we passed at least five enormous bedrooms I asked, "How many people live here?"

"In the main house? Mr. and Mrs. Quigley, their daughter, two sons, and Mrs. Quigley's mother. I live on the grounds out back. The gardener has his own quarters, too."

I reeled to think of how much money it must take to keep this house and all its employees running, but as I would see, it seemed to do so quite effortlessly.

Mililani showed me into a sewing room that was almost as big as our cafe's kitchen, and I spent the day doing a little bit of everything: mending lace doilies, letting out a few of Mrs. Quigley's older dresses, repairing a satin bedroom curtain. I was treated like one of the family—or at least like one of the family servants—and for lunch was served fresh papaya and little cucumber sandwiches.

Later, a young woman about twenty years old with bobbed black hair poked her head into my room and introduced herself as Mrs. Quigley's daughter, Eustace. "Oh, I just loved the *holokū* you made for me!" she said. "I hope you'll make all my party dresses from now on. I think your work is just the bee's knees!"

I assumed this was a compliment and told her I would be happy to do so.

Indeed, as I discovered, these *kama'āina* seemed to throw a party of some sort every other day: dinner parties, garden parties, dance parties, luncheons, afternoon teas on the *lānai,* picnics, horseback rides, and concerts. I never imagined anyone could enjoy so much free time as did these people. Mrs. Quigley asked me to assist with the decorations for one such garden party: I fashioned white tablecloths shaped like the blossoms of the *pua* tree, whose petals curved downward and so draped naturally over the lawn tables. These tables were then filled with a bountiful array of treats—coconut cakes, fruits, tea sandwiches, bowls of guava punch—the leftovers from which Mrs. Quigley insisted I and other employees take home. I watched from the window of my sewing room as men and women strolled the grounds, nibbling on little sandwiches and chatting as phonographs played Hawaiian ballads. I marveled to realize that there was a whole other Honolulu of whose existence I was only now aware: a Honolulu of elegant homes and gracious hostesses, where music was always playing and time passed as sweetly as a song. For the *kama'āina* who lived in this Honolulu, whose life was a long afternoon of amusement and painted sunsets, these truly were Hawai'i's "glamour days."

Or they were until September 18, 1928.

On that now barely remembered date, a ten-year-old *haole* boy, Gill Jamieson—a student at the prestigious Punahou School, as well as the son of the vice president of the Hawaiian Trust Company—was abducted from the school grounds and held for a ten-thousand-dollar ransom.

Nothing like this had ever happened before in Hawai'i— certainly not to a *haole* child. Everyone in Honolulu snapped up the newspapers' "extra" editions as fast as they were printed. In these pages we were to learn of the ransom note the kidnappers had sent the boy's father:

"We want you to have the utmost confidence in us," it read,

almost in the manner of an advertisement for gout remedy. "Have all fears swept aside. Do what we say and you will see your son again. Fight us and you will never see him again, nay, he will be but a shadow: lifeless."

It was signed, mysteriously, "The Three Kings."

The boy's father paid the ransom—in marked bills, it turned out.

It is no overstatement to say that the crime threw the island into turmoil. The police placed a cordon around O'ahu, National Guard troops were mobilized, hundreds of ordinary citizens deputized—even some twenty thousand Honolulu schoolchildren were recruited to engage in door-to-door searches. (Oddly, no one at the time questioned the wisdom of sending children to look for a kidnapper.) Jae-sun was one of the many volunteers who helped comb the city, even as I watched over our own *keiki* at home, prohibiting them from playing anywhere but in the safely enclosed alley between buildings.

But sadly, on Wednesday morning, police found the body of Gill Jamieson hidden in some brush behind the cottages of the Seaside Hotel, near the Ala Wai Canal. He had been killed by a particularly brutal combination of strangulation and a tempered steel chisel to his head.

No parent could hear this without feeling heartbreak, rage, and worry; but *haoles* in particular were shaken to discover that the bubble of privilege and security in which they had long lived no longer protected them from the sort of brutal crime the "other" Honolulu had always been prey to.

Because witnesses had identified the Punahou kidnapper as Asian, suspicion had quickly fallen on twenty-year-old Henry Kaisan, a former chauffeur for the Jamieson family. Kaisan was repeatedly interrogated, but just as repeatedly denied any connection with the crime. Chief of Detectives John McIntosh told the press he was "convinced that Kaisan has knowledge that will be of benefit to the police in the solution of the case."

But a number of prominent *haole* citizens, dissatisfied with the lack of progress their police department was making, allowed panic to override their good sense and organized a group calling itself the Vigilante Corps, to seek their own justice.

That weekend our friend Taizo told us how, close to midnight, he had been readying his boat to go out the next morning when he saw members of the Vigilante Corps gathering on Pier 2, calmly debating whether or not to storm the police station and administer their own justice to Henry Kaisan.

"Then they see me looking at them, and listening," he said, "and I think: If they can't get Kaisan, they settle for me. I said hell with the next day's catch, and hurried home."

We kept the cafe closed that night, just in case violence were to erupt. None did, but it was a long, tense night and we barely slept more than a few hours.

Then, on Saturday, a marked ransom bill led to the arrest of one Myles Fukunaga, a nineteen-year-old elevator operator at the Seaside Hotel. The young man promptly confessed to the police that he, acting alone, had kidnapped and slain the boy in a scheme to get money for his parents, who owed twenty dollars in back rent on their home to the Hawaiian Trust Company, and who, Myles felt, had been humiliated in the bank's attempt to collect the money.

"I killed the boy to bring happiness to my family, my mother and father," he told a newspaper reporter. "In their life they have always had many troubles.

"I expect and hope for the death penalty. It would be too awful to have to think about it for the rest of my life. I'd rather die.

"I know what is right and what is wrong—and I know I did wrong." He concluded, quite emphatically: "I am not insane. I am perfectly sane."

He asked for swift, merciless justice—and he received it. His trial began promptly on October 3; his court-appointed counsel didn't put on much of a defense, declining to call any witnesses. The state refused to allow a psychiatric examination of Fukunaga, despite the fact that he had tried to take his own life just six months before the kidnapping. After only two days of trial and deliberation, a jury unanimously convicted Myles Fukunaga of first-degree murder. Under territorial law this carried with it a probable sentence of death by hanging.

This was still more merciful than the death poor Gill Jamieson had suffered, and I shed no tears over Fukunaga's fate. But Tamiko pointed out to me that not long ago a *haole* man had poured gasoline over a Japanese plantation worker, then set him on fire, and was only charged with manslaughter. "And even then," she said, "the jury acquitted him." She thought the verdict in the Jamieson case was partly a product of anti-Japanese sentiment. There was truth in what she said, but at the time I believed that Myles Fukunaga had helped convict himself with his stubborn assertion that he knew right from wrong: *"I am not insane."* The jury merely took him at his word.

Or perhaps I simply did not wish to consider that prejudice against the Japanese could mean prejudice for all of us with different eyes and skin.

On that Thursday evening of Fukunaga's conviction, two plainclothes police officers—both native Hawaiian and searching for an escaped prisoner—intervened to break up an argument between a pair of drunken soldiers and a woman on the *lānai* of a tenement house off Liliha Street. The soldiers had apparently paid someone to take them to a brothel, and when they didn't find what they wanted, they became belligerent. When one of the policemen displayed his badge and told the soldiers to leave, Private Chester C. Nagle pulled out a pistol and shot both officers without a second thought, grievously wounding them.

Liliha Street was quite nearby our home, but the crime struck even closer than that: one of the policemen was Officer William Kama. He was shot in the forehead, and died hours later at Queen's Hospital, while his partner Sam Kunane, shot in the chest, remained critically injured but would live. Private Nagle ran away in an attempt to return to his ship, but was quickly found and arrested. He claimed that he shot the men "as self-protection."

All this greeted me from the front page of the next morning's paper, along with news of Myles Fukunaga's conviction.

I cannot say I knew Bill Kama well, but I knew how much he meant to Joe and his family, and so went to the Anitos' home to convey my sympathies. Joe was at the mortuary where Bill's funeral was to be held the next day, and I asked Esther to pass along my condolences and to let me know if there was anything I could do. She suggested making a donation to the memorial fund the *Star-Bulletin* had started for the benefit of Bill's widow and five children.

She also confided in me her worry over Joe now that Bill was gone. Last year, at age eighteen, Joe had agreed to return to St. Louis College, where he played another season of varsity football. But then a motorcycle accident caused him to miss too many classes. He was already several grades behind others his age, and finding himself even further behind—and the renewed butt of jokes for being a "dumb country boy"—he quit school for the last time in 1928 and took a seasonal job trucking pineapples at the California Packing Company cannery. When that season's work ended, he drifted back onto the streets in the company of his fellow Kauluwela Boys. When he wasn't tussling with other aimless young men, Esther said, he spent his time playing volleyball with his cousin Eddie.

At Bill's funeral Joe kept to himself, and I was able to give him only some brief words of condolence, as I did Bill's 'ohana.

A month later—late in the evening of November 15—I was

clearing tables in the cafe after closing, when I heard a tapping on the front window. I glanced up to see a tall, dark figure outside, his face partly obscured by our window stencil. For an instant I feared it was Mr. Noh, and dropped the plate I was holding. But even as the tableware shattered on the floor, the figure stepped to one side and I could see his sheepish smile as he peered in through the little triangle in the letter A. It was Joe.

Relieved, I opened the door. "Joe. What brings you here so late?"

He entered, a little wobbly on his feet. "'Lo, Aunt Jin."

But his breath preceded him inside. "Joe, have you been drinking?"

"Couple beers." Joe could never lie to me, though, and then admitted, "Eh, maybe more'n a couple. Aunt Jin, could I get some coffee before I go home?"

I knew what he meant was, *before Mama sees me like this.*

"Yes, of course. Come in back."

I hastily swept up the broken crockery, then took Joe into the kitchen, where Jae-sun and Liho had just finished washing the night's dishes. My husband saw at once the state Joe was in, greeted him warmly, and discreetly told Liho he could go home. I sat Joe down at our family table and poured him a cup of black coffee. Jae-sun left us alone and went upstairs to look in on the children.

"Thanks, Aunt Jin," Joe said, taking a hot swallow of coffee. He stared into the cup for a moment as if into a wishing well, then said, as if by explanation for his condition, "We were supposed to go out tonight, have a couple drinks."

"Who?"

"Bill. He'd have been thirty-two today."

I sat down beside him. "I'm sorry."

"Yeah," he said, his voice growing colder, "and that Army bastard's the one who gets the birthday present. You hear?"

"I heard he was being court-martialed for Bill's murder."

Joe shook his head. "Not murder. Yesterday they found him guilty of 'voluntary manslaughter'—that's all." He snorted contemptuously. "One shot to the head, *bam*—like you'd kill a dog."

I put a hand on his. "Oh, Joe."

"He says he didn't believe Bill and Sam were cops, 'cause he never heard of anything like a 'colored policeman.' Except somebody who saw the whole thing says what Nagle really said was, 'Hell, we don't care if you're policemen or not'—and . . ." Joe mimed a trigger being pulled. "Just like that. 'Cause they were only 'colored' Hawaiians. We don't get murdered—we just get manslaughtered."

I winced. "Has he been sentenced?"

Joe nodded. "Ten years."

"Well, that's something, I suppose."

There was a tension in Joe that I thought for a moment might bring tears to his eyes—but instead it erupted into a fist slamming on the table. I flinched.

"Something? It's *nothing*," he said bitterly. "After Nagle was arrested, you know what the Army provost marshal told him? 'If you confess, we'll have the case taken over by the Army. A soldier never hangs.'"

The words sent a chill through me. And now tears did spring to Joe's eyes, and he wept unashamedly, as for a lost brother. I went to him and held him, told him Bill was looking down on him now—that he knew Joe loved him and would see him again someday. After a few minutes Joe's sobs went dry and he just sat there, hunched over, breathing in the grief, breathing out more grief.

Joe was usually soft-spoken, but now his voice was almost like a rush of air beside me. "Ten years. He won't serve even that."

"You don't know that," I said.

"I don't seem to know much," he said disgustedly.

"That's not true. Bill believed in you. *I* believe in you."

Joe smiled faintly. "Yeah, he gave me hell when I quit school.

Told me, 'Look, if school isn't for you, figure out what *is*. Start doing something with your life.'"

"That's good advice, Joe. You can't do anything about Bill's murder, but you can try to live in a way that would make Bill proud."

"I guess. But how the hell do I do that?" he said.

"Well, what do you *like* to do?"

He shrugged.

"I like sports. I liked being part of a team." He hesitated in the manner of someone who'd been told too often he was "dumb," and was reluctant to share his thoughts. "I helped out with the National Guard when they were looking for Fukunaga. That felt pretty good. I've been thinking, maybe I could join up."

"That's a fine idea, Joe. And I think Bill would agree."

I freshened his coffee, and after another five minutes he had sobered up sufficiently to go home and face his mother. When he stood, he was steadier on his feet. "Thanks, Aunt Jin. Sorry to keep you up past closing."

"You know you can always come here, Joe. For anything."

He smiled, hugged me, and I saw him to the door. I watched him head up the street with less liquor in his step. Esther would no doubt smell the beer on his breath and wouldn't be happy. But I hoped she'd make allowances.

Shortly afterward, Joe did join the Hawai'i National Guard. It seemed to agree with him. He took well to military discipline and began competing on the Guard's boxing team, under the nickname given him by his teammates on the St. Louis College football squad: "Joe Kalani." I was hopeful this might be the first step in turning his life around.

Chester Nagle was sent to Alcatraz Island in San Francisco to begin his ten-year prison term, but observers at his trial seemed to think that the military board of review in Washington would reduce his sentence.

Joe was right. A soldier never hangs.

Myles Fukunaga, on the other hand, would die on the gallows a year later. I think all of us in Hawai'i hoped that his death would somehow cleanse us of what we had just been through—that his brutal actions were, in the words of one newspaper editorial, merely an "aberration" in the life of Honolulu—and that nothing so terrible could ever happen here again.

Sixteen

Jade Moon and I hardly spoke to each other anymore except at meetings of the *kye*, and then only on matters of business. These were painful occasions for me, as I was also forced to listen to Beauty's excited accounts of her wedding preparations and Jade Moon's inquiries about its profligate expense. Or at least it seemed profligate to me. Beauty appeared confused and distressed by the hostility between us, and in those moments she seemed the sweet young girl I had always known. Then in the next moment she would eagerly display the large diamond ring her fiancé had given her, or I would hear her eagerly confide in Jade Moon, "I bought Mr. Ko's son a new kite. I think he's starting to like me," and once again I would feel angry and heartsick.

Work was a welcome distraction from such matters, and around this time a new "wrinkle" in fashion appeared on the local scene. Some of my customers—students at secondary schools like Punahou—had begun bringing in bolts of *yukata* cloth they had purchased from C. K. Chow's next door. But rather than asking for it to be made into kimonos, they desired that shirts be fashioned from the fabrics. These were printed in bold Japanese motifs—birds, mountains, streams, pagodas—and often riotous in their colors. Men in America, even in Hawai'i, did not normally wear such bright garb, but I was happy to make whatever kind of shirt my customers requested. I cut my own shirt patterns out of old newspapers, creating front pieces, backs, yokes, sleeves, collars, and pockets. I knew I was not alone in receiving such requests: Musa-Shiya the Shirtmaker had produced shirts with equally striking designs, made from *tapa* cloth imported from Samoa, for students at a local dance studio. Clearly something new was in the air, and when my beachboy friends saw what I was working on, they quickly ordered similar shirts for themselves and even began recommending them to the tourists they served at Waikīkī.

Meanwhile, I had begun dreading *kye* meetings, and even considered not attending one to be held in the dining room of Wise Pearl's home in Kaimukī, but in the end I did. Beauty arrived late and seemed more subdued than usual. Jade Moon immediately saw that something was awry. "Where is your ring?" she asked, and only then did I notice that Beauty's hand was bare of jewelry.

She replied quietly, "The marriage has been called off."

"What!" Jade Moon was beside herself, even as I felt a surge of relief. "Why would he do such a thing!"

"He did not call it off," Beauty said. "I did."

"Are you insane?" Jade Moon cried. "Why would *you* do such a thing?"

"It is a personal matter. I don't wish to speak of it."

"Did you share a bed with him? I *told* you to wait until—"

Angrily, Beauty stood, strode over to where Jade Moon was sitting, and slapped her hard across the face.

Jade Moon jerked back, as much from surprise as from pain.

"I said it is a personal matter!" Beauty shouted, then stormed out.

After a moment I got up and followed her outside, where I found her leaning up against the clapboard walls of the plantation-style cottage, weeping. I went to her and she collapsed into my arms, once again the vulnerable little girl I had comforted after her disinheritance by Mr. Yi. Gently I asked what happened.

"I could not go through with it," she said.

"So I see, but why?"

She sniffed back tears and stood up a little straighter. "You know the custom here in America," she said, "of the wife taking the husband's name? Well, it may sound odd to you, but—when I first became engaged, I would try speaking my new name aloud: 'Mrs. Ko.' 'Hello, I am Mrs. Ko.' 'Mrs. Ko, you have a lovely home.' 'That is a lovely ring, Mrs. Ko.'

"Soon, this was how I began to think of myself—as Mrs. Ko. Mrs. Ko would not have to struggle to pay her bills. Mrs. Ko would live in a nice house and not a tiny one-room walk-up on River Street. Mrs. Ko's daughter would want for nothing. Mrs. Ko would not be taken advantage of as Mrs. Yi had been. And then . . . Do you remember the Hai Dong Hotel?"

"Of course. How could either of us forget it?"

"As Mr. Ko and I began planning our honeymoon, I could suddenly think of nothing else," she said. "I had been such a fool back then—a girl of sixteen who'd fallen in love with the photograph of a virile young man. Instead I met one old enough to be my grandfather and searched his face for some ghost of the man I had fallen in love with. I can never forget the feel of his body—like the wrinkled skin of a fig—as he lay atop me. Afterward, as he slept, I lay there and wept. I have never felt as lonely before or since.

"It was a terrible thing, a wedding night spent with a man I did not love. Yet here was Mrs. Ko, planning to do just that. In that moment I saw her as you might see someone whose face has been turned away from you, but now turns smiling to face you. I saw the cold appraisal in her eyes, the cunning in her smile, and decided I did not wish to be Mrs. Ko."

I clasped her hand and told her she had done the right thing.

I wish I could tell you that she never regretted this choice—but I cannot.

On October 29, 1929, the American stock market—inflated to unnatural proportions by years of speculation—burst like a tire pumped full of too much air, ultimately deflating in value by some twenty-six billion dollars. Figures like these were impossible to comprehend for a family that subsisted on perhaps thirty dollars a month, and at first we took as much notice of the event as we might of an airplane experiencing engine trouble high above our heads. This was only a problem for rich people, we thought, and so went about the business of our lives.

But six months after the crash, there were some twenty-seven hundred unemployed workers in the territory. Soon afterward the pineapple market collapsed, taking with it one of Hawai'i's largest industries. Tens of thousands of pineapples rotted in the fields; canneries closed their doors. Four thousand plantation laborers flocked to the city, looking for work that wasn't there. Many of them were Filipinos, who had been among the most recent wave of imported plantation labor; now there was talk not just of limiting Filipino immigration, but actually returning the workers already here to their homeland. We began to wonder when the government might decide that Koreans should be the next to go.

The sugar industry continued strong, but construction work plunged and even tourism began to decline. With dwindling numbers of visitors, hotel workers were laid off. Fewer tourists required fewer flower *leis*, and demand decreased for Wise Pearl's carnations. Shrinking jobs in hotel and other service industries meant reduced income for the customers of Beauty's barbershop, many of whom took to having their wives cut their hair. Meanwhile, every day on her way to work Beauty passed Mr. Ko's jewelry shop, which seemed to be weathering the depression quite nicely, and had cause to doubt the wisdom of her decision not to marry him.

Smaller incomes also forced families to cook meals at home rather than dine out. By the end of the year, business at our cafe had plummeted by forty percent. We lowered prices, reducing our profit margin, but things only worsened. My tailor shop fared a little better—the tourists who could still afford to come to Hawai'i were also able to afford colorful shirts as souvenirs—and I began funneling all my income from tailoring into keeping the restaurant afloat.

Of all my Sisters of Kyŏngsang, only Jade Moon and her husband could have been said to be doing well. People could cut their own hair and cook their own food, but they still needed a place to live; they could not make their own land or build houses out of air. Despite her frequent complaints about the costs of upkeep, Jade Moon had perhaps made the wisest investment of us all.

Financial problems in Esther's household were the cause of even worse troubles for her son. Joe had always had a temper—he once hit a man who refused to stop kicking a dog, though I could hardly fault him for this. Now, seeking to recover money owed him by an acquaintance named Hayako Fukinako, Joe got into a fistfight with the "four-flusher" and was arrested and charged with robbery and assault. Joe argued that he was just trying to collect on a debt; the jury agreed up to a point, acquitting him on the robbery charge but convicting him of assault. Joe received a thirty-day suspended sentence, and I hoped that this close brush with prison might shock him into thinking twice before using his fists.

But there was no reprieve from our own woes. By spring of 1931, I was forced to borrow money from the *kye* just to keep the cafe going for a few more months. When at the end of that time there was no improvement, one evening I gingerly broached the subject of closure to Jae-sun. He took in the suggestion with only a passive nod. We said nothing more about it and went to sleep. I woke around three in the morning to find myself alone in bed. I slipped on a robe and went downstairs, but Jae-sun was not in the kitchen. I entered the main dining room, then stopped at what I saw outside the front window.

In the glow of street lamps, I saw my husband in his pajamas, standing on the sidewalk, gazing up at the stenciled sign on the window that read LILIHA CAFE, J. S. CHOI, PROPRIETOR. His eyes, usually so bright and cheerful, reflected only disappointment and loss of face. My heart ached to see this, and I considered turning around and returning to bed before he noticed me. But no—I was his wife, and it was my duty to share his pain as I shared his success. I walked out the front door and joined him on the sidewalk, slipping my hand into his like a thread into a needle; and together we looked up at this sign, once the embodiment of a dream, now merely a remembrance of it.

*B*ecause our living quarters came with the lease on the restaurant, we now needed to find another place to live. Yet we barely had enough money left for the first month's rent on an apartment. One morning, as I packed up our belongings, I answered a knock on the back door to find Jade Moon standing in the alleyway. She looked awkward and uncomfortable—we had not spoken more than a dozen words to one another since Beauty had called off her wedding—but now she held out some sort of document to me and said, "This is yours if you want it."

"What is it?"

"A lease," she said. "There is a two-room flat available in our boardinghouse. On the second floor. It is a poor thing I offer you, I know, but if you need a place to live, it is yours."

I looked at the two-page lease, which called for a monthly rent of ten dollars. "That is . . . very kind of you," I said, quite taken aback, "but I am not certain we can afford even this."

"Then I will cut it in half. Here." She snatched the lease away, took out a pen and slashed a line through *Ten*, replacing it with a scribbled *Five*. "There. If necessary, I will cut it even further. It doesn't matter. You did not worry about money," she said, "the day the *luna* docked us half a day's pay. When you brought me in from the sun." For the first time since that long-ago day, I saw tears in her eyes. "But I understand if you cannot accept."

Touched, I told her I would discuss it with Jae-sun. In truth, we had no other choices. We moved into Jade Moon's rooming house within the week, and slowly she and I found that our friendship, though damaged, was like a fabric torn on the seam: not beyond repair.

Jae-sun went looking for work, and as there was little call for chefs he applied at canneries, loading docks, and rice mills. But he was competing with thousands of jobless men in the city of Honolulu. He would come home discouraged and dispirited, as did thousands of able-bodied men throughout the United States. His lack of proficiency in English did not help. He finally found occasional work—one day a week—at the docks as a stevedore. But the few dollars this brought home was scarcely enough to feed a family of five.

Thankfully, a good seamstress remained in some demand, and my shop now became our family's primary source of income. Mrs. Quigley continued to employ me one day a week, even when other *kama'āina* families were cutting back. I became the breadwinner, albeit often day-old bread, and we also ate much liver, tripe, and knucklebone soup. I patched and repatched Grace's dresses and Harry's trousers—everyone did during the Depression—and I ached when Charlie would ask me for a nickel's worth of crackseed and I had to tell him we couldn't afford it.

It was a struggle to earn enough to pay the rent on the shop and put food on the table, and I soon found myself working very long hours—twelve hours a day were not unusual. I came home exhausted, and it fell to Jae-sun to tend to the household while I worked. He was always happy to cook, of course, but I think he was less enamored of sweeping and cleaning the apartment. Each day he woke the children for school—"Easier to wake the dead, and the dead complain less"—and cooked rice gruel and *kimchi* for our daily breakfast.

On one such morning in September of 1931, the family had just settled in at the breakfast table when Harold—eleven years old next month—suddenly pushed his *kimchi* away, announcing with a scowl, "I don't want cabbage for breakfast anymore!"

"It is not cabbage, it is *kimchi*," his father said, puzzled.

"Whatever you call it, I don't want to eat it!"

"Why not?" I was baffled. "You've always liked it."

"The other kids say it makes me stink. They call me 'garlichead'!"

"What nonsense is this?" Jae-sun said. "Who tells you this?"

"Everybody," Harold told him.

"He's right," Grace agreed. "Nobody eats garlic for breakfast in America."

"Well, they do in a Korean house," Jae-sun declared, "and this *is* a Korean house, so you will eat your *kimchi*."

"*You* eat it," Harry said brashly, and ran from the breakfast table. He snapped up his schoolbooks and slammed out the door.

Jae-sun and I looked at each other, nonplussed, as Grace and Charlie meekly began picking at their *kimchi*.

"*I* like it," Charlie said with dubious sincerity.

"I will have a talk with the boy tonight," Jae-sun said as he opened his copy of the day's newspaper.

But another shock apparently awaited him in its pages, because after one look at the front page he quickly and quite uncharacteristically folded the paper closed and laid it on his lap.

He looked at Grace a moment, then asked, "Do the other children call you names, as well?"

She shrugged. "Only if they can smell my breath."

Jae-sun took that in soberly, as did I.

When breakfast was over and Grace and Charlie were on their way to school, Jae-sun again opened the newspaper. A headline shouted from the page:

GANG ASSAULTS YOUNG WIFE
Kidnapped in Automobile, Maltreated by Fiends!

After being kidnapped by a gang of young hoodlums as she was walking along one of the principal streets of the Waikiki district late Saturday evening, a young married woman of the highest character was dragged to a secluded spot on the Ala Moana and criminally assaulted six or seven times by her abductors, who fled in an open touring car and left her half-conscious on the road. She was picked up by occupants of a passing car as she staggered along the Ala Moana toward Waikiki in the early hours of Sunday morning and was taken home. She was later transferred to the Queen's Hospital.

Seven suspects, one arrested early Sunday morning by Detectives John Cluney and Thurman Black, and the other six Sunday afternoon by Detective Lucian Machado, are being grilled by Chief of Detectives John McIntosh. One of those held is said to be the owner of the car which the gang used to abduct the woman, and two of the others are said to have jail records, one having been previously arrested for rape and one for robbery.

I understood now why my husband had not wanted the children to see this. It was a terrible tale, and upon reading it I felt what any decent person would: sympathy for the poor woman, who was unnamed, and disgust and anger at her brutal attackers, "fiends" and "hoodlums" as the paper called them.

The story was on everyone's lips in Honolulu that day—it was all anyone who came into the tailor shop could talk about. In addition to what was revealed in the papers, word quickly spread via the "coconut wireless," or rumor mill, that the victim was a *haole* woman—the wife of a Navy officer stationed at Pearl Harbor— and that her attackers had been Hawaiian. This in itself was remarkable; though there had been many instances of *haole* men assaulting Hawaiian women, no one could recall an incident in which a Hawaiian man had sexually assaulted a white woman.

Soon the even more shocking news came that two of the men arrested on suspicion of being among these "fiends" and "hoodlums" were both local sports heroes, star players in "barefoot" football as well as boxers. One was Benny Ahakuelo, who had recently competed in the National Amateur Boxing Championship at Madison Square Garden; and the other, a member of the National Guard boxing team, was one "Joe Kalani"—aka Joseph Kahahawai Jr.

I felt physically ill the whole day, hoping it was all a horrible mistake. After work I stopped at the Anito house; Esther and Pascual had spent the greater part of the day at the police station. As Pascual put on a pot of coffee, Esther told me what Joe related to her: He and his friends Ben, Henry Chang, David "Mack" Takai, and Horace "Shorty" Ida—the latter just back from a stay in Los Angeles—had been out Saturday night joy-riding in a car Horace had borrowed from his sister Haruyo. Earlier in the evening Joe and Henry had run into Shorty while "crashing" a wedding *lū'au* at the home of their friend Sylvester Correa. After they left, they drifted over to the dance pavilion at Waikīkī Park, a gathering spot for local young people. Joe had had too many beers at the Correas' and was groggy as they drove back a while later to the Correa home. But the party was *pau,* over, and they were on their way home when at the intersection of King and Liliha Streets their car was nearly sideswiped by a Hudson sedan driven by a white man. As the cars came squealing to a halt, the man's Hawaiian wife called out, "Why don't you look where you're driving!" Joe shot back, "Get that goddamn *haole* out of the car and I'll give him what he's looking for!"

I winced. It was not hard to imagine Joe saying something like this.

"So this woman, Mrs. Peeples, gets out of her car, and"—a faint smile lightened her face—"all sides seem to agree she was quite an *imposing* lady."

"Joe said she would've made a good linebacker," Pascual added, chuckling.

"She gave Joe a shove; Joe shoved back. Then she grabbed him by the throat and started choking him. Joe slapped her on the side of the head and she fell back onto the running board of the car."

At this point all involved wisely decided not to pursue the matter any further. Joe got back into the car and they drove off—but not before Mrs. Agnes Peeples took down their license-plate number.

I asked, "But what does this have to do with the white woman who was assaulted?"

"The *haole* woman saw the license plate of her attackers' car," Pascual said. "It was only one number off from Haruyo Ida's car. And the police claim she has also identified Joe and the others as the boys who raped her."

I was stunned. It seemed impossible; absurd. *Our* Joe? "I don't believe it! Joe would never do such a thing."

"No," Esther agreed, "but I wonder about the other boys. There was that business with Henry and Ben and that girl at the schoolyard—"

When they were each eighteen, Henry and Ben had been arrested on a charge of rape against a seventeen-year-old Chinese-Filipino girl on a school playground. It came out at trial that the relations had been consensual, but though the two boys were acquitted on rape charges they were convicted on a trumped-up charge of sexual assault. They were sentenced to four months in prison, though Ben was released early by Governor Lawrence Judd so that he could represent Hawai'i in the amateur boxing championship in New York City.

"The girl consented," Pascual reminded Esther. "She said so at the trial."

"And what about Lillie Ching?"

"Who?" I asked.

"Ben's girl. She's six months pregnant with his child. Ben wants to marry her, but so far Mrs. Ching's refused to let him."

"Just because he got a girl in *pilikia*," Pascual said, "doesn't mean he would—"

Esther lost her usual poise in an anxious outburst: "How do you *know*? How do we know Ben, or one of the others, didn't do something terrible after dropping off Joe at home?"

I had never seen her look so tired and frightened.

Joseph Sr. arrived a few minutes later with what turned out to be the only good news of the day: "Benny's mother called Princess Abigail." Princess Abigail Kawānanakoa was one of the last of the

Hawaiian *ali'i*, and one of the most prominent citizens in Honolulu. "The princess called Senator Heen and said, 'Bill, somebody's got to represent these Hawaiian boys and see they get a fair trial.'"

This was the same William Heen who, as a judge, had granted me my divorce. He had gone on to become a state senator and was now in private legal practice. "He's a good man," I said. "He'll see to it the boys are treated fairly."

"You'll see," Joseph predicted, gently trying to calm the mother of his child. "This will all blow over in a few days."

*B*ut alas, it did not. The sudden tempest that had swept up Joe and his friends intensified into something resembling a typhoon. There was widespread outrage among the island's *haoles* over the treatment of this "white woman of refinement and culture," as the city's English-language newspapers called her, while the mildest description of Joe and his friends was as a "gang" of "local" boys—the latter an apparent euphemism for "nonwhite." It was the first time any of us had seen the word used in this way. And while these papers zealously maintained the anonymity of the victim, they did not hesitate to publish the names and home addresses of the "Ala Moana boys," as the papers had unfairly dubbed them—as if there was no question that they had committed the crime.

A few days later, a Japanese paper, the *Hawaii Hochi*, revealed the name of the victim: she was Thalia Massie, the wife of a United States naval officer, Thomas Massie, stationed at Pearl Harbor. The *Hochi* also disclosed that when first questioned by police, Mrs. Massie "could not remember the number of the automobile nor could she recognize the culprits because it had been too dark." But now, somehow, her memory had markedly improved, and she positively identified all but one of the suspects and even recalled their license number. Interestingly, a *haole* man was seen following

Mrs. Massie that night, and soon the town was buzzing with rumors that he was a Navy officer with whom she was having an affair—that it was he who had beaten and raped her, and she had accused the five boys to divert suspicion from her lover.

Meanwhile, the English-language newspapers laid the blame for this supposed crime on the most unlikely of doorsteps. They blamed the beachboys of Waikīkī and their "loose relations" with women tourists for encouraging miscegenation between whites and "half-castes." The beachboys wasted no time in condemning the crime, but it was an accusation that would be endlessly and absurdly repeated by the press here and on the mainland.

A more immediate problem for our family presented itself the next day, when the children came home from school and a confused Grace, now thirteen years old, asked me, "Did Joe do something bad to a lady?"

Jae-sun and I looked at each other, sighed, and sat down with the children to try and explain the situation as best we could.

"The police believe he did," I told her, "but that doesn't mean they're right."

"Then why do they think he did?" Charlie, now ten, wanted to know.

"People believe all sorts of things that aren't always true."

"This is what laws are for," Jae-sun told them soberly, "to determine what is true and what is not."

Grace thought a moment, then asked, "Mama, what does 'rape' mean?"

Jae-sun went pale, stood up, announced, "I have something I need to do," and quickly left the room.

I weighed my words carefully. "Rape . . . is something a man does to a woman without her permission."

"Doris says it happens between your legs."

Hearing these words from my young daughter chilled me in a way few things ever have.

"Yes," I told her. "That is so."

I explained the rest of it as best I could, telling her that if any boy tried to do the same thing to her she should scream, fight, kick, and run, if she could.

"Is that what they think Joe did to somebody?" she asked.

"Yes. But I do not believe Joe Kahahawai did this thing."

"Neither do I," Grace said.

There was silence for a moment, then Harold spoke up. "Mama? Can I ask you something?"

"Of course, Harry."

In the same sober tone Harry asked, "Do we *have* to eat stinky old garlic at every meal?"

Grace looked like she wanted to drop a plate on his head, but I just laughed.

"Well . . ." I said thoughtfully, "I believe I know what your father's answer to that will be. But I might be able to convince him to make his *kimchi* with less garlic, and to serve it only at lunch and supper, not breakfast. What do you say to that?"

"It's a deal," Harold said quickly.

I went downstairs and informed Jae-sun that henceforth we would be making our *kimchi* with half the usual amount of garlic.

"What! We'll barely be able to taste it!" he objected. "I'll do no such thing!"

"And we will not be serving it at breakfast, at least not to them."

"But a meal without *kimchi* is not a meal!"

"Would you rather the other children call them names?"

Jae-sun frowned. "No, but . . ."

"They are not Korean, *yobo*," I said gently, "they are Korean-American. They can be Korean at supper; let them be American at breakfast."

He sighed and muttered darkly to himself, his usual signal of acquiescence.

ven when I tried to banish the "Ala Moana case" from my thoughts, I found I had to confront it—as on Thursday, when I went to work at Mrs. Quigley's. She and her daughter were as overwrought over the case as most *haoles*, and it distressed me to hear them refer to Joe and the others, whom they did not even know, as "gangsters," "hoodlums," and "degenerates," parroting words they had read in the newspapers.

I put on my best Korean mask of dispassion and focused on my sewing. But toward the end of the day Mrs. Quigley came up to me and suggested, "Jin, dear, why don't you go home a little early? I'll pay you for the entire day, of course, but it worries me to think of you out after dark—now that we know how dangerous these streets really are."

"I have never encountered any trouble," I replied mildly.

"Well, let's keep it that way. Humor an old worrywart, would you?"

It was hard to be annoyed at someone who seemed so genuinely concerned for my welfare. I thanked her and left, but later, as I walked home from the streetcar stop, I had to ask myself: If Joe and his friends didn't do this thing, who did? And were the beasts who did it still out there? For the first time I understood how much better it must be for people like Mrs. Quigley to believe that the men responsible had been apprehended and were not still at large, threatening their daughters' safety. Had it been anyone but Joe who was charged with this crime, I might well have wanted to believe it myself.

The next day I received a visit from Esther, who had just come from a bail hearing at which a bond of thirty-five hundred dollars—an impossible sum—had been set for each defendant. Even though a bail bondsman required only a ten percent deposit, three hundred and fifty dollars was no small amount either, and at first only Horace Ida's family was able to come up with enough cash to secure his release. Eventually the bail was reduced to two thousand—but even two hundred dollars proved difficult for Esther to raise. She asked for help from her friends—not an easy thing for such a proud woman to do—and in addition to giving as much as our household could afford, I approached my own friends, as well as sympathetic customers of the tailor shop. Jade Moon donated five dollars, more than anyone else I knew. Wise Pearl's farm was barely eking out a living for her family, but she still managed to scrape up a dollar for the bail fund, as did Beauty and Shizu. Many of my customers could only contribute fifty, sixty, or seventy cents to the cause . . . but they did so out of a growing conviction on the part of many in Pālama that this case was looking, as one man put it, "like a goddamned *haole* frame-up."

In the seventeen years I had lived in Hawai'i, I had heard neighborhood boys occasionally taunt white boys with cries of *"Pilau haole!"*—"You stink, white boy!" But I had never seen this long-simmering resentment of *haoles* laid quite so bare, like a raw nerve suddenly exposed by a knife cut.

It took nearly a month for Esther to raise bail and Joe was the last of the five to be released. That night a quiet celebration was held at the Anitos' home, which our family attended. When Joe saw me, he immediately came over and hugged me, and the first words out of his mouth were, "I didn't do it, Aunt Jin."

"I believe you, Joe."

"I don't know why this lady says I did—why *we* did. We never went down Ala Moana that night." He shook his head. "After Shorty and Mack and the others got released, Captain McIntosh tells me, 'They're gonna leave you here to rot, Joe. What do you owe them? Tell me what really happened and things'll go easier for you.' I looked at him and said, 'We didn't do it. I had a rough-house with that Hawaiian lady, but we didn't do anything to any *haole* woman.'"

"McIntosh is a horse's ass," someone said behind me. I turned and Joe introduced me to Eddie Ross, a one-time Honolulu police officer, whose sympathies were clearly not with the department. "Joe, if you hadn't cuffed Agnes Peeples, McIntosh would've had to find some other poor saps to railroad," he told us. "Minute he heard about you boys, he decided, 'That's it, we got our men,' and to hell with anything that suggested otherwise. Just like the Fukunaga case. If those marked bills hadn't turned up, McIntosh would've had poor Henry Kaisan swinging from a gallows, and if the facts didn't fit, he'd have made 'em fit. The Navy wants someone caught, tried, and convicted—pretty much anybody'll do. You boys just came along and happened to fit the bill."

I nodded. "'Carve the peg by looking at the hole.'" Eddie looked at me blankly and I explained, "An old Korean saying. It means, Do things to fit the circumstances."

Joe looked more sad than angry. "You know the worst part, Aunt Jin?"

"What, Joe?"

"They kicked me out of the National Guard," he said softly. "I was prouder of being a guardsman than anything else in my life."

The hurt in his eyes was the hurt of the young boy I had met on the beach at Iwilei, taunted by his friends for being a *kua'āina*.

*T*he first day of the trial saw Honolulu oppressed by a spell of hot, windless Kona weather. Argument over the case in Honolulu was just as heated, with most *haoles* believing the prosecution's case, and most nonwhites, the defendants'. Hundreds of otherwise sane people stood in line for long, sweltering hours at the Territorial Courts Building for the chance to watch the first day of testimony in the First Circuit Court of Hawai'i. I admit, I was one of them.

Esther, Pascual, and Joseph Sr. were shown to seats up front, and

I was lucky to get a seat in the back of the courtroom along with a handful of other "locals." The largest portion of spectator seats was occupied by what appeared to be every starched, blue-nosed society lady in the city of Honolulu: the front of the courtroom was a field of wide-brimmed white hats bobbing like lilies on the water. Dressed in their Sunday finest, these women exuded a gaiety and excitement that seemed quite out of place in such grim circumstances.

I was startled and dismayed to see that one of them, sitting in the third row, was Mrs. Quigley.

The atmosphere in the courtroom was suffocating. Some women had the foresight to bring fans, while men fanned themselves with their hats, as District Attorney Griffith Wight made his opening statement. I was quickly infuriated by his characterization of Joe and the other defendants as little more than hoodlums.

Then Wight called his first witness: Thalia Massie, the victim of the alleged assault. She entered the courtroom supported by one of the prosecution attorneys and by a tall, slender, steely-eyed woman in her forties—her mother, Mrs. Grace Fortescue. This was my first glimpse of the woman around whom so much accusation and gossip had swirled these past two months. She was of average height, in her late twenties, with an oval face, dimpled chin, and a short bob of light brown hair. She was sedately dressed in a dark suit with a white collar.

After a few introductory questions, District Attorney Wight asked, "Mrs. Massie, where were you shortly after eleven-thirty P.M. the evening of September twelfth?"

"I was at the dance at the Ala Wai Inn," she replied in something of a monotone, "and I left shortly after eleven-thirty."

She went on to tell of how she had walked down Kalākaua Avenue and turned on John Ena Road—at which point an automobile drove up beside her and two men jumped out of it. One of them punched her in the jaw; the other dragged her into the backseat of the automobile.

"Would you be able to identify these two men?" Wight asked. She pointed without hesitation to Joe and Henry.

"I tried to talk with them, but every time I did Kahahawai hit me. I offered them money if they would let me go." In a soft but steady voice she told how she was taken someplace off Ala Moana Boulevard, to a clearing between trees where she was dragged out of the car by Chang and Kahahawai. Chang then proceeded to violate her, though "I struggled as hard as I could."

"After that, Kahahawai assaulted me," she continued, her voice trembling slightly. "He knocked me in the jaw. I started to pray and that made him angry and he hit me very hard. I cried out, 'You've knocked my teeth out,' and he told me to shut up. I asked him please not to hit me anymore."

As riveting as her story was, I knew for certain now that Mrs. Massie was either lying or terribly, horribly mistaken. Joe, like his parents, was a devout Catholic—he would no sooner hit a woman for praying than he would rape her.

She went on to describe her further violations—"from four to six times"—by Chang, Kahahawai, Ahakuelo, and Horace Ida. Eventually, she said, one of her attackers "helped me to sit up. He pointed to something and said, 'The road's over there,' then they all ran off and got away, and I turned around and saw the car"—the license-plate number of which she claimed to partially memorize.

She then stumbled up to Ala Moana Boulevard, where she flagged down a passing car and begged them to take her home.

The courtroom was silent as she related all this; everyone in it appeared transfixed by her tragic and seemingly heartfelt story. As the prosecutor finished his questioning, I sat wondering: Had Mrs. Massie been assaulted by an illicit lover, as was rumored? Perhaps by Lieutenant Massie himself, when he learned of the affair? Or had she truly been attacked by a gang of local youths, and somehow convinced herself that these five boys were they?

After a lunch recess, Mrs. Massie returned to the stand for

cross-examination by defense attorney Bill Heen, as impressive a lawyer as he had been a judge. He showed tact and respect as he began questioning Mrs. Massie, then cut to the heart of the matter: "Do you remember saying to the police officers on this night when you returned to your home that you thought these boys who assaulted you were Hawaiian?"

"I remember telling the people who brought me home that," she replied evenly. "I don't remember what I said to the police."

"Do you remember making a statement to the effect that you were unable to identify any of these boys because it was too dark?"

"No, I don't remember making any such statement."

"Do you remember stating, upon being questioned, that you couldn't identify the car—that you weren't sure what kind of car it was?"

"I didn't think about the car. Mr. McIntosh asked about it."

"Do you recall being asked whether you knew the number of the car and you said no?"

"Nobody asked me until Mr. McIntosh did. I didn't think of the number until Mr. McIntosh asked me," she finished lamely.

By the end of the day it was apparent that there was much that Mrs. Massie did not remember, and yet much that she remembered in conveniently full detail.

I tried to return for the next day's session, but thanks to the *kama'āina* ladies and Navy wives who had come to show their support for Mrs. Massie, there was not a seat to be had and I was turned away at the door. Many of these women had servants stand in queue for them in the miserable heat; then minutes before the courtroom doors opened at eight-thirty, the society ladies stepped into line, fresh as the morning dew, and took all the best seats. It was frustrating, but from this point on I was not able to witness another day of the trial. All I could do was read about the events in the papers—though their accounts were notably pro-prosecution—and occasionally visit Esther for a more accurate account of the day's testimony.

I also did my best to raise her spirits. She was afraid for Joe, of course—afraid that the jury would be carried away by the kind of mass hysteria that had sent Myles Fukunaga to the gallows. But she was also mortified to walk into that courtroom every day, feeling so many eyes upon her, seeing the spectators ogling her son with fear and repulsion. She had raised this boy to the best of her ability, under difficult circumstances, instilling in him a love of God while trying to shield him from the corrupting influence of a city she now wished she had never come to. And now to think that all these people believed she had raised a brutal rapist, a monster . . . She cried nearly every day of the trial, and all I could do was to assure her that those of us who knew Joe knew the truth, and soon everyone else would.

Indeed, it sounded as if Bill Heen and his co-counsels were doing an excellent job of undercutting, if not obliterating, the prosecution's case. They called on a series of police officers who testified as to how Chief McIntosh had not only failed to have the crime scene sealed off, a car he was riding in actually *erased* what were supposed to be the assailants' incriminating tire tracks. One officer testified that he had seen McIntosh coach Mrs. Massie into identifying Benny. And most damning, it came out that the license number of Horace Ida's car had been broadcast over police radio, and that Mrs. Massie had in all likelihood overheard it while at the emergency hospital—after which she suddenly, miraculously, "remembered" it.

All in all, the chief of detectives and the men he had entrusted with investigating this crime—most of them *haoles*—now appeared to be either fabricators of evidence or, at best, bungling Keystone Cops. And their credibility had been undermined by their fellow police officers—the majority of them "local" boys who clearly felt the defendants were being railroaded.

The case went to the jury on December 2. After four days of what was rumored to be rancorous debate, the jury informed Judge Steadman that they could not reach a verdict, and the judge reluctantly declared a mistrial on December 6.

*T*he boys were certain to be tried again, but barring some new evidence, there was little reason to believe a new jury would fare any better. Joe, his family, and the other defendants were relieved over the results, of course. But the mistrial sent shock waves of rage and indignation throughout the *haole* community—especially in the ranks of the Navy. On Wednesday, a scrawled note was found at the Submarine Base at Pearl Harbor: *"We have raped your women and will get some more."* It was signed *"Kalihi Gang."* Even Navy officials believed this to be a hoax, but word of it spread like a virus, infecting public thought. Tensions between locals and Navy men increased, as did shore patrols, though few residents trusted the MPs to intervene fairly. There were rumors that some Navy men were planning to burn down the city, starting here in Pālama, where the defendants lived. Few of us in the area slept soundly the night we heard of this.

Saturday evening, on my way home from work, I stumbled into the middle of a quarrel between Navy sailors and a group of Filipino men on Liliha Street. Shouts and curses quickly escalated as the two sides began throwing punches—and anything else at hand. I ran back the way I came and managed to get home, but rioting between sailors and locals had erupted all across town.

At our rooming house I found the indefatigable Jade Moon preparing to stand guard over her property, wielding a hastily purchased shotgun. "My grandfather stared down the Japanese Army with a deer rifle," she declared, "and I will do no less to the American Navy, if it comes to that."

"And what happened to your grandfather?"

"What do you think? He was shot deader than a wedding goose, a glorious idiot." She shrugged as she loaded the gun. "But what else is there to do?"

Jae-sun and I decided to keep the children barricaded inside our two-room flat, moving what little furniture we owned up against the front door, and settled in for what promised to be a long and frightening night.

For us, the night passed without incident. A detachment of Marines were ordered into the city to provide an armed escort of all naval personnel back to Pearl Harbor, and what could have been even more widespread violence was averted. But the next morning we learned what had forced the Navy to take these steps. I picked up the daily paper from our doorstep and was horrified to see, on its front page, photographs of Horace Ida—his face bruised and battered at the hands of a group of vigilantes the night before.

I hurried to the Ida home, where I was relieved to find him looking no better than his photograph but in surprisingly good spirits, surrounded by family and friends. "Are you all right, Horace?" I asked.

"Well, I've had better Saturday nights, that's for sure."

He told me how he had been standing outside a "bootleg joint" on Kukui Street, talking story with a friend, when four cars—bristling with sailors sitting in rumble seats and perched on running boards—pulled up to the curb. One of the Navy men leaned out a window, pointed him out and announced, "That's the guy!"

They shoved him into the front seat of a Chrysler roadster and took off up Kukui Street to Nu'uanu Avenue and then up Nu'uanu.

"You're gonna give us a full confession," the man told Horace, "or I'm going to blow your brains out and toss what's left over the Pali."

Near the top of the Pali the cars pulled off the road, where they had Horace take off his shirt and whipped him with their belts. The heavy buckles knocked the breath out of him and the leather straps stung like a jellyfish. They kicked and whipped him for fifteen minutes, as Horace insisted he was innocent. Finally one of the sailors hit him on the head with the butt of his gun, and Horace feigned unconsciousness, hoping they would go away, or at least stop beating him. He heard the men talking among themselves, debating what to do; but whatever else they were, apparently they were not murderers, and finally they picked him up and threw him into a cane field. He lay there until he heard engines roaring away, then limped back to the Pali Road, where he flagged down a passing motorist, much as Thalia Massie had two months before.

"You know," Horace said wryly, "I'm beginning to think I should've stayed in L.A.!"

The police offered to take the defendants into protective custody, but the boys declined, feeling they could defend themselves. The next night, a group of belligerent sailors pounded on the door of Benny Ahakuelo's home, demanding to see him, but police intervened in time—and when no further incidents occurred, we all prayed that the worst had passed.

The Navy, in the person of one Admiral Yates Stirling, made it sound as if Horace's abduction and assault was the fault not of the sailors who had perpetrated it, but of the people of Hawai'i for forcing his men to take such drastic actions. He began quoting—or misquoting—reports stating that forty "criminal assaults" had occurred in Honolulu in the past year. Stirling cabled Washington that forty "rapes" had occurred. These and other lies about our islands soon made their way to the mainland, spreading a kind of gleeful hysteria that was repeated, without any independent verification, by newspapers across America.

Honolulu enjoyed a brief respite from its troubles over the holidays, and on Christmas Day I attended a birthday party for Joe Kahahawai, who had turned twenty-two. He was hopeful that, once his name was cleared, the National Guard would readmit him. As the Christian New Year approached, the city remained relatively calm, and I held my breath against the hope that the goodwill of the season might last a little longer.

But on Friday, January 8, the late morning calm on King Street was broken by the shout of a newsboy touting an "extra" edition of the *Honolulu Advertiser*: "Ala Moana boy kidnapped! Read it here, five cents!" I rushed out of the tailor shop, one of a flock of people who quickly surrounded the boy, and handed over a nickel for the paper. My worst fears were realized in its blaring headline—KAHAHAWAI KIDNAPPED—and in the accompanying picture of Joe, staring out from the front page as if beseeching me personally.

Seventeen

A crowd was gathering like smoke around the police station, scores of people who had seen the newspaper story and were now roiling about the entrance waiting for some further word. According to the *Advertiser*, Joe had left his home that morning, accompanied by his cousin Eddie, to meet with his probation officer. But on the very steps of the judiciary building, Joe was "seized by two men and rushed into a waiting automobile. Eddie, jumping on the running board of the car, was shoved off . . . two white men and a white woman were in the machine."

"Has anyone heard anything else?" I asked a man in the crowd. He shook his head. "No mo' not'ing."

Someone next to him said, "I hear it was the same bunch of rotten apples what kidnapped the Japanese boy."

As more and more people converged on the corner of Merchant and Bethel Streets, uniformed officers made them form a single orderly line that soon stretched around the block and up Bethel, all the way to King Street.

Parked at the curb in front of the station was an old Chevrolet, not unlike the model owned by Esther and Pascual Anito. They were almost certainly inside the station, but these policemen were not likely to let me in to join them, unless . . .

I approached one of the officers and announced, as casually as I could, "Excuse me. I'm here to see Detective Apana."

He gave me a dubious look.

"He doesn't work cases anymore, lady. You want an autograph from Charlie Chan, we're a little busy right now—"

"Please," I said, trying to keep the growing panic from my voice. "Just tell him that Jin is here. He's expecting me."

This was a bold lie, but it gave the officer pause and he promised he would look into it as soon as the crowd was under control.

Five minutes later another officer came out, called my name, and escorted me inside. Standing in the lobby was the frail but straight-backed Chang Apana, chewing on a cigar as he barked at me: "Where you been? You very late!"

I had to stop myself from smiling. "I apologize, Detective, I was delayed."

To the officer who ushered me inside Chang said, "I take her from here, Kimo, t'anks." With a still-firm grip he took me by the arm and walked me through the lobby and into the officers' squad room. As soon as we were alone together, his face became less animated, more sober. He knew why I was here.

"*Mahalo,*" I told him. "I appreciate this."

"S'okay. You his auntie, eh? *'Ohana.* Only right."

"What about Horace and the others?"

"We got 'em," he assured me. "Protective custody."

"Thank God. Are Esther and Pascual here, too?"

He shook his head. "No—at morgue. Identifying body."

My heart felt as if someone had just squeezed it like a sponge.

I came to a sudden stop, my legs refusing direction from my mind. My heart was beating faster and harder than it had since the day I learned that Evening Rose had been taken away. *"No,"* I said, less a word than a moan.

Realizing his mistake, Apana gently guided me to his desk and sat me down. "Sorry. Paper's coming out with news, I thought you hear." He brought me a glass of water and I drank it, but my pulse was still sounding a drumbeat in my head. "You okay?" Chang asked, concerned.

I nodded, but I was far from all right. "How—how did it happen?"

"Eh, these bastards, they drive up, tell Joe sheriff wants see him, take off. Got caught Koko Head Road, Joe's body in back. On their way to blowhole."

The Hālona Blowhole, on the windward coast, is a popular tourist spot and one of the most dramatic sights on O'ahu. As crashing surf pounds the shoreline, water is funneled through a lava tube that forms a kind of chimney in the rock, spitting out geysers as high as fifty feet into the air. Then as the sea recedes the water is sucked back through the hole and out to sea—but not before anything unlucky enough to be in the water is pulverized against the walls of the lava tube.

The horrifying image of Joe's body, shattered and swept out to sea, brought angry tears to my eyes. "Was it the same men who attacked Horace?"

Chang shook his head, an itchy finger on his old blacksnake whip. "In car they find Navy man driving—also Mrs. Massie's husband and mother."

My astonishment briefly eclipsed my anger. "Mrs. Fortescue?"

He nodded. "They find her with Joe's body wrapped in sheet—like dirty laundry. Real cool cookie too."

"And these people dared to call Joe a beast," I said hotly.

Before he could say more a sobbing Esther, along with Pascual and Joseph Sr., appeared in the squad room. They had just returned from the morgue, and their faces all reflected the same horror and heartsickness. I embraced Esther and felt the grief that was wracking her body pass into mine. "They took my sweet *keiki*—my baby," she said, her words half-swallowed by her sobs. We stood there weeping and holding one another up.

"This is all they left me." Esther lifted her right hand, still clutching two pieces of jewelry she had been given in the morgue. One was Joe's wristwatch, its shattered face like crystallized ice, its hands frozen at 9:45—the moment, she was told, of Joe's death. The other was an engraved ring identifying Joe as an alumnus of the St. Louis College class of 1928. Its gold band encircled only empty air, like the hole that had opened up inside us all.

"They just killed him in cold blood?" I said.

"They were trying to force a confession from him," Pascual said, "and the gun went off. Least that's what they claim."

Esther appeared on the verge of collapse, and they still had to break the terrible news to Joe's sister, Lillian, before she heard it at school. We left together. Outside, the police's orderly line was beginning to crumble under the weight of hundreds more people pouring into the streets. The crowd would only grow larger upon news of Joe's death, as wild rumors flew around Honolulu about vengeful mutilations exacted upon him by his killers, all unfounded. By afternoon, thousands were mobbing the station, and officers had to fire tear-gas capsules to disperse the crowd, leaving the air as bitter as the feelings of many locals.

Jae-sun and I met our children at school and told them the news before they could hear it on the streets; then we all stumbled home together to cry. At nine P.M. we had just put them to bed when we heard the shriek of the siren atop the Aloha Tower, normally used to mobilize the National Guard in an emergency—five long shrill blasts that lasted a nerve-rattling seven and a half minutes. The children's calm dissolved after the second scream of the alarm.

"Did somebody else die?" Charlie asked, terrified. I'm not even sure he understood what death was, though he would soon learn.

"No, no, it's all right," I said as I held him, not knowing whether my words were even true.

"What if something's happened to Mack or Shorty?" Grace asked.

"What if the Navy's coming to burn us down?" Harold said anxiously.

"You are all safe," Jae-sun assured them. "We will let nothing happen to you, we promise you that."

We stayed with them for the next hour, until they finally drifted into an uneasy sleep. We learned the next day that the siren's sounding was only the result of a prank telephone call, but it sent people spilling into the streets again and briefly threw all of Honolulu into a panic. Joe's death had done more than just grieve those of us who loved him: it had set the entire city on edge, balanced on a precipice between anger and fear.

*T*he next day, Thomas Massie, Grace Fortescue, and their two accomplices, seamen Edward Lord and Deacon Jones, were arraigned and a grand jury was impaneled to formally indict them. But rather than being taken to O'ahu Prison, they were remanded to the custody of the United States Navy and given luxurious accommodations aboard the USS *Alton*, a decommissioned naval cruiser dry-docked at Pearl Harbor. Mrs. Fortescue was given a penthouse suite overlooking the harbor, with room service provided by the officers' mess. Horace, Mack, Henry, and Ben, held by the police in protective custody, were not even provided meals by the Territory of Hawai'i: their family and friends had to prepare food for them, as Jae-sun would do more than once during their stay.

This four-star treatment could not have spoken more loudly to the people of Hawai'i, demonstrating that rank—and race—had its privileges. Soon the deck of the *Alton* was deluged with flowers of sympathy and support from admirers all across the United States, aggrieved at the terrible injustice being done to them.

Meanwhile, Esther prepared to bury her only son.

His body was taken to Nu'uanu Funeral Parlor in Pālama, where it was on view in their chapel beginning the next evening, Saturday, at six P.M. My family and I were among the first to arrive and offer condolences to Esther, Pascual, Joseph Sr., and Lillian. As was common at Hawaiian funerals, ukulele music played softly in the background, and I was pleased to see that the deck of the *Alton* was not the only place overflowing with floral tributes. The chapel was brimming with wreaths, bouquets, and *leis* of every type and color: red roses, white lilies, pink aster, lavender orchids, red ginger. Joe's casket was banked high with flowers and *leis,* but I quailed to approach it. I wanted to cry, but even after all these years in Hawai'i, I was still Korean enough not to display such emotions in public. Quietly I steeled myself and looked inside the casket.

Clad in a dark suit, as if dressed for Sunday morning Mass, Joe rested like a shadow in a lavender casket. Around his neck was draped a *lei* of delicate orange *'ilima* blossoms—the kind favored by Hawaiian royalty—while a silver crucifix lay on his chest, nearby the spot where the bullet had pierced and drained away his life. I saw again the country boy gathering *kiawe* beans along the Iwilei shore; the hurt child blaming himself for his parents' separation; the young man who came to our cafe grieving the senseless loss of a cherished friend.

I leaned in to him and whispered, "Goodbye, my little Joey. Your Aunt Jin will always love you. No lie."

Grace, Harold, and Charlie followed, filled with a sobriety and grief no children their age should have had to bear. We took seats in the pews and watched as a steady procession of friends and *'ohana* filed past the funeral bier, including Joe's teammates from the St. Louis College football squad. Some looked upon Joe's face one last time with stoic sadness; others cried unashamedly, while many gave up a familiar wail of grief: *"Auwē! Auwē!"*—Alas, alas!

We would have liked to have remained all night, as family and friends traditionally did in Korea, but the children grew drowsy and fidgety and I convinced Jae-sun we should take them home and come back tomorrow. We made our goodbyes to Esther and her family, then left them to what surely would be the longest night of their lives as they maintained their vigil over the candlelit coffin, to the soft plaintive chords of the ukulele.

When we returned to the mortuary the next morning, I was startled to see that the flow of visitors had not ebbed, but actually swelled: there were hundreds of people patiently standing in line outside, not just Hawaiians but Chinese, Japanese, Koreans, Portuguese, even a few *haoles*. I recognized none of their faces. I asked one, a Filipino man, how he had known Joe. He told me that he had never met the boy in life, but felt he had to come and pay his respects to someone who could as easily have been his own son: "The *haoles* treat us all the same," he said. Others in line nodded their agreement, and an old Hawaiian said in disgust, *"Hilahila 'ole kēia po'e haole"*—translated for me as, "The *haoles* are shameless." It would not be the last time these words were spoken today.

The sentiments were echoed inside, where Bill Kama's older brother David stood at the foot of the casket and in a clear, impassioned voice declared: "Poor Kahahawai, these *haoles* murdered you in cold blood. They did the same thing to my poor brother. They shoot and kill us Hawaiians; we don't shoot any *haoles*, but they treat us like this. Poor boy, God will keep you; we will do the rest."

Around eleven A.M. the chapel fell into a hush as a contingent of police pushed their way inside. There was some agitation at first that this might be another act of violence against Joe, even in death—but the police were merely escorting in the remaining four "Kauluwela Boys," Horace, Mack, Ben, and Henry, released from protective custody to bid farewell to their childhood friend. Upon their entry a cheer went up from the crowd, but the boys kept grimly silent. Shorty Ida placed a bouquet of red gladioli at the foot of Joe's casket. One by one they approached it, and one by one they wept. After each had had a last moment with Joe, the police swept them out again, and the crowd gave up a final cheer.

The stream of mourners continued until three o'clock that afternoon, when Joe's casket was closed and taken by hearse to the Catholic church, accompanied by a squad of motorcycle policemen and an honor guard of twelve pallbearers walking beside the car. I was amazed at the size of the funeral cortege—over a hundred automobiles winding their way up Nu'uanu Avenue to Pauahi Street and thence to Fort Street—and like a ball of yarn gathering size as it rolled, the procession only grew larger along the way, as hundreds of onlookers joined the solemn march.

Our Lady of Peace Cathedral stood regal as a queen at the corner of Fort and Beretania, a coral-block building whose steepled bell tower and spire was crowned by a gilded cross and globe. Inside it was equally grand, with high vaulted ceilings of redwood and gold leaf. The nave was large enough to accommodate hundreds of worshippers, and my family and I watched with awe as every last seat was taken. Even the balconies were filled; the church was literally packed to the rafters with mourners. And there were hundreds more outside, crowding the palm-shaded sidewalks in front of the church, wending around the corner and up Beretania Street. Wouldn't Joe have been astonished to see this!

The casket was wheeled solemnly down the center aisle as the cathedral shook with the somber tolling of the bronze bells in the tower above. The candles on the casket and the altar flickered like stars in the wind. Then Father Patrick Logan began reading from the Latin liturgy:

"Réquiem ætérnam dona eis, Dómine: et lux perpétua lúceat eis. Te decet hymnus Deus, in Sion, et tibi reddétur votum in Jerúsalem . . ."

The words were strange and beautiful, the dead language come to stirring life—even as Joe's spirit, Jae-sun assured me, would be resurrected in eternal life.

"Kyrie eléison. Christe eléison. Kyrie eléison . . ."

After the Requiem Mass, Father Logan delivered a closing prayer in English, which ended with the words:

"And thou hast been delivered from the hands of thine enemies."

I felt an unexpected flush of anger at those enemies, and I struggled again to fight back tears. I had been prepared to quell my feelings of grief, but this suddenness of rage took me by surprise. I felt Jae-sun's hand on mine, and glanced over to see him trying to contain his own emotions. I closed my hand around his and took strength from my husband's compassionate presence.

The casket was taken back up the aisle to the waiting hearse and we filed slowly out of the church. We followed the cortege along streets lined on both sides with hundreds of people who solemnly stood and watched the procession pass by. Finally we arrived at Puea Cemetery on South School Street, not far from where Joe had spent most of his too-short lifetime. It was a small, ill-tended graveyard where the poorest of Honolulu's citizens found a last home no more gracious than the squalid tenements and shanties they had known in life. Already a crowd had gathered there to watch as Joe's body was returned to the *'āina*, the land. But once again we were unprepared for its size.

There were easily two thousand people squeezed onto this

small patch of hallowed ground. Many were dressed in their Sunday finest, while others had no such finery but came wearing their sorrow and respect. There were so many people that the cortege's police escort had to clear a path from the road to the burial plot, and then again at the grave to make room for the casket and family. I had not seen this many people gathered in mourning since Lili'uokalani's passing. Their faces were the faces of Hawai'i itself, reflecting every race, color, religion—and a shared grief. Only later would we realize that this was the first time in our islands' modern history that so many—from different cultures, each with its own traditions, prejudices, and strivings—would come together like this, moved by a single impulse.

"Mama," Grace asked me wonderingly, "do *all* these people miss Joe?"

I smiled for the first time that day . . . perhaps for many days.

"Yes. I believe they do."

The Reverend Robert Ahuna, a former state legislator as well as a Christian minister, officiated over the burial. First a hymn, "Angels Welcome," was sung in Hawaiian, and then Reverend Ahuna spoke, in a mix of Hawaiian and English, of Joe's accomplishments in sports and of how "this innocent man, obeying the law, had gone to report at the place where law is sacred, and it cost him his life." He reminded us that Cain had killed Abel in revenge and jealousy, and compared Cain's act to that which had befallen Joe: "And what was the cause of the bloodshed? Revenge. I call upon the Lord to pass judgment on those who committed this crime."

But gazing out at this vast crowd, his face softened and he said, "I am happy to see this demonstration of sympathy for the parents of him who lies here, who was the son not only of his parents, but of Hawai'i and the Hawaiians."

Joe's coffin was then lowered gently into the hillside beneath a thicket of trees, and those of us who were privileged to be Joe's friends each threw a single handful of red earth into the open grave. As I let the soil slip through my fingers, I finally gave up my tears, not caring who saw.

Two thousand voices now sang what had once been the Kingdom of Hawai'i's national anthem, "Hawai'i Pono'ī," followed by Queen Lili'uokalani's most famous composition, "Aloha 'Oe." Although both were sung in Hawaiian, I knew the latter's lyrics well from many evenings spent listening to the beachboys at the Moana Pier. I knew the words and knew their meaning, and through tears no longer denied, I sang along as best I could:

> *Aloha 'oe, farewell to thee,*
> *Thou charming one who dwells in shaded bowers*
> *One fond embrace, 'ere I depart*
> *Ā hui hou aku:*
> *Until we meet again.*

The next day's newspapers would declare that Joe's was the largest funeral in history for any Hawaiian not of royal birth. It was reported on respectfully, with no trace of hate-mongering or insinuation; but the same could not be said for the despicable Admiral William Pratt, chief of naval operations in Washington, who in a written statement asserted, "American men will not stand for violation of their women under any circumstances. For this crime they have taken the matter into their own hands repeatedly when they have felt that the law has failed to do justice."

Time magazine called this justification for murder merely "a friendly pat on the shoulder" to Lieutenant Massie—but the headline in the *Star-Bulletin* that day read, ADMIRAL PRATT CONDONES LYNCHING OF KAHAHAWAI. I did not know this word, "lynching," but when I asked Jade Moon about it she explained, "As I understand, it refers to a custom in the American South, where white men may punish the darker peoples with impunity by hanging them from trees."

I was speechless. How could such barbarity exist in a land of freedom like America? What country was this, in which I had been living all these years?

As fervently as the *Star-Bulletin* had helped to whip up public hysteria over the Ala Moana case, its editors now seemed to have peered into the abyss and decided to take a large step back from it, declaring, "We have before us a horrible example of what hysteria and lack of balance will do. That ought to be enough to arouse the sober judgment of every responsible citizen in support of orderly law."

Admirable words, though arriving far too late to do Joe any good.

That Thursday, at the Quigley estate, I was tasked with sewing floral slipcovers for the living room furniture, which required me to take measurements and do fittings. Nearby where I was working, Mrs. Quigley, her daughter, and a number of their *kama'āina* women friends who had come over for lunch chatted and twittered about the events that had captured the islands' attention:

"In the trunk of the *car*, can you imagine—"

"—actually *arrested*, like some common criminal—"

"—for simply doing what the jury didn't have the decency to do!"

Amid all this babble, Mililani and the rest of the Quigleys' household staff—all of them Hawaiian, Chinese, or Japanese— went about their business with faces stony and mouths shut. I followed their example, concentrating on finishing this work so I could retreat to the seclusion of my sewing room.

"The poor girl, first she's viciously attacked, now she has to see her husband and her own *mother* incarcerated—"

"Well, if you ask me, I think the brute got just what he deserved."

My stomach knotted upon hearing these words, not least for who had voiced them.

I suddenly heard myself addressing Mrs. Quigley:

"What did you say?"

She looked at me, surprised at my presumption in interrupting a private conversation; but her affection for me clearly outweighed the impropriety and she just smiled. "I only said, dear, that I think the brute got exactly what he deserved."

"Amen to that," another woman said, and they all chimed their agreement.

I put aside my work, stood, and walked over to my employer.

"You have been very kind to me, Mrs. Quigley," I told her, "but I cannot work here any longer."

"What?" She was clearly taken aback. "Why on earth not, Jin?"

"He was not a brute," I said, unwilling to mute the anger in my voice. "He was a boy who loved to ride his father's sugar train. Who took pride in being a National Guardsman. Who would never have done to anyone what was done to him. And he would never, *ever* have applauded such a thing, as I hear it applauded here today. He was better than that. He was better than you."

In the shocked silence that followed I strode out of the room; as I passed Mililani she gave me a small smile, quickly covered up.

At home I cried and apologized to Jae-sun for abandoning such a lucrative account in such difficult times, but he told me he would have done the same thing in my place. "We will not go hungry for the want of such blood money."

Mrs. Quigley's sentiments, it must be said, were mild compared to what was being said of Joe and his friends—of all of us—on the mainland. *Time* magazine continued to malign our islands as "a restless purgatory of murder and race hatred. The killing of Kahahawai climaxed a long chain of ugly events on the island of O'ahu growing out of the lust of mixed breeds for white women."

As absurd as this may sound, it was real enough for Bill "Tarball" Kahanamoku. He was dating a white switchboard operator at the Moana Hotel named Mary Davis—whom he would eventually marry—and out of cautious fear he made sure to walk on the other side of the street when taking her home.

MELTING POT PERIL! cried one mainland paper. Another declared smugly: HAWAIIANS MUST BE PUNISHED!

It was this last that surely must have alarmed the *haole* elite who ruled Hawai'i, and likely accounted for the sudden tilt of papers like the *Star-Bulletin* toward the rule of law. The U.S. Congress was also in an uproar, threatening to replace the territory's self-government with commission rule that would hand control of Hawai'i over to the military. This was not in the Big Five's interests, and so they now tried to scale back the racist hysteria they had helped foment.

Meanwhile, Mrs. Fortescue told the press, "I have slept better since Friday, the eighth—the day of the murder—than for a long time. . . . My mind is at peace."

She may have been the only person in Honolulu who slept so soundly.

Certainly not I, who was overwhelmed with anger and sorrow, and wanted nothing more than to escape from the tragedy and to take refuge in my sewing. But *everyone* who came into the shop seemed unable to talk about anything other than "the Massie case." They told me how the grand jury had indicted the accused on charges of second, not first, degree murder. (Soldiers never hang.) They spoke excitedly of how the defendants had hired the legendary attorney Clarence Darrow, who, I was told, had a reputation as a champion of the underdog, particularly black people. As these were the same black people who were often lynched, I wondered why he was representing people accused of doing the same to a dark-skinned Hawaiian boy. I was not among the hundreds who went to the harbor the day the SS *Malolo* sailed into port, eager for a glimpse of the "great man."

Unlike the first trial, I could not bear the thought of attending this one; of hearing the attorneys slander Joe's memory in defense of heartless murderers. But I could not avoid getting a summation of the day's events from my customers, few of whom actually got into the courtroom to see it. I heard of how Joe's cousin Eddie identified both Lieutenant Massie and Mrs. Fortescue as being in the Buick roadster, into which Joe was lured with a fake summons to appear before the sheriff. I heard of how Joe's clothing was found in Grace Fortescue's rented house in Mānoa, including a brown cap and a white shirt, thoroughly soaked with blood, with a bullethole in the front. And on a visit with Esther I heard from her how—as district attorney John Kelley had presented Joe's bloodied shirt to the jurors—she burst into tears, and this man Darrow jumped to his feet and insisted she be removed from the courtroom, which thankfully the judge denied.

She related to me how she had taken the stand to testify as to what Joe was wearing the day he was killed. "I had to sit there and say, 'Yes, he was wearing that cap. Yes, that was his watch, and ring. I know those clothes, I washed them all. They're Joe's.' And then Mr. Kelley brought me the shirt with the bullethole, and I couldn't help myself, I started to cry."

The district attorney was not trying to be unkind, but he was clearly determined that the jurors would see the full sum of the violent equation that had brought them to this place.

Darrow's defense invoked something he called "the unwritten law"—the right of a husband to avenge an attack on his wife. But just in case the jury did not believe that, Darrow also claimed that Lieutenant Massie had killed Joe in a fit of temporary insanity. The defendants freely admitted they abducted and bound Joe, and tried to force a confession from him. When Joe refused to do so, even with Massie holding a gun on him, Mrs. Fortescue said, "There's no use fooling around any longer. . . . Let's carry out our other plan." Massie told Joe, "You know what Ida got. That's nothing to what you will get." He then told Seaman Lord to "go out and get the boys"—promising, "Those men will beat you to ribbons."

Supposedly, under this trumped-up threat from unseen enemies, Joe—never one to be cowed by physical threats—blurted out a confession. In a fit of rage, Lieutenant Massie pulled the trigger, blacked out, and the next thing he knew, the police were arresting him and his confederates on Koko Head Road.

Small wonder that I continued to have difficulty sleeping, and would often get up at two in the morning to hand-sew in the calm darkness of our kitchen—as if by this act I could somehow stitch together the scraps of my old peace and contentment. But I was not the only one in our household whose slumber was disturbed. To my surprise, one night I found Harold—who had seemed the least affected by all these events—sitting in the kitchen, looking tense and troubled. I asked him what was wrong. He looked up at me, sheepishly, but there was more than embarrassment in his eyes; there was pain.

"I didn't tell you before," he admitted, "but I got into a fight today."

"Where? With who?"

"Woody and me were down Waikīkī, surfing, when some *haole* kid—tourist kid—gives us the stink-eye and says, 'Sure is a lotta garbage on this beach.' I ask him, 'Is there a problem?' He says, 'My pop says it's chinks like you coming here that's the problem.' So I say"—he managed a small smile—"'That's funny, 'cause my pop says your pop is full of shit.'"

"Harry!" My eyes widened in reproach, even as I was trying not to laugh.

He gave a little shrug. "That's when we started duking it out."

I sighed. "Well, you look none the worse for it."

"I did more duking than he did."

"You don't look too happy about it."

He hesitated. "They threw us off the beach."

"What? Who did?"

"The manager of the Moana Hotel. The *haole* kid complained about us, and even though he threw the first punch—and Steamboat and Panama took our side—they threw us off the beach." I now understood the hurt and anger in his eyes. "Can you beat that? These no-good *malihinis* come here, they do whatever they want, and they get away with it! They—"

He broke down, suddenly weeping, and I held him to me as he sobbed.

"No, they can't," I said, gently stroking his hair. "They won't. You'll see."

The following day I accepted a long-standing offer from Esther to secure me a seat in the courtroom—two seats, actually. On Wednesday, April 27, the last day of the trial, Harold and I found ourselves seated behind Esther and Pascual, two of only a handful of "locals" present on this final day. I wanted Harry to see the defendants as they were brought into the courtroom, no more privileged than he or I as they sat before a jury of their peers. I wanted him to see the American legal system at work, for better or worse—a system I could not help but believe in, as it had freed me from the tyranny of Mr. Noh. I did not know whether justice would prevail in this trial, but it seemed to me that Harry at least needed to see justice *trying* to prevail.

Unfortunately, this meant listening to Clarence Darrow's endless closing summation, which recapitulated in great detail the entire series of events from the alleged assault on Mrs. Massie through the Ala Moana trial, Joe's death, and the present circumstances—culminating in this question to the jury:

"Gentlemen," he said, "I wonder what fate has against this family, anyhow? I wonder when it will get through taking its toll and leave them in peace?"

He was not referring to Joe's family, of course, but to Mrs. Massie's.

He spoke of the pain of her "ravishment" and said, "I don't care whether it is a human mother, or the mother of beasts or birds in the air. They are all alike. To them there is one all-important thing and that is a child they carried in their womb, and without that feeling there would be no life preserved upon this earth."

He pointed to Mrs. Fortescue. "There she is—that mother—in this courtroom! She is waiting to go to the penitentiary. All right, gentlemen—go to it! . . . If this husband and this mother go to the penitentiary, it won't be the first time a penitentiary has been sanctified by its inmates!"

When the defense had rested its case, Harry turned to me and whispered, "What happens now?"

"Now," I said, "someone speaks up for Joe."

District attorney John Kelley paced before the jury and delivered a forceful summation, and a blistering portrayal of the defendants as cold-blooded killers who "let a man bleed to death in front of them, inch by inch." He excoriated Lieutenant Massie's so-called insanity defense and pointed out things he testified to that he should not have remembered had he truly "blacked out." Then he told the jurors, "Hawai'i is on trial. Is there to be one law for strangers and another for the rest of us?"

I could see Harry sit up a little straighter beside me.

And what will happen, Kelley asked, if the jury acquits Massie? "Why, they'll make him an admiral! They'll make him chief of staff! He and Admiral Pratt are of the same mind, they both believe in lynch law!"

But Kelley reserved his greatest scorn for the defense attorney's words:

"Mr. Darrow has spoken of mother love. He has spoken of 'the mother' in this courtroom. Well, there is another mother in this courtroom. Has Mrs. Fortescue lost her daughter? Has Massie lost his wife?"

He turned and pointed at Esther, who was now weeping.

"But where is Joseph Kahahawai?"

Darrow felt the sting of the courtroom's silence.

I leaned forward and placed a consoling hand on Esther's shoulder. Harold blinked back tears. I could not have asked for a better exemplar of the American legal system than John Kelley.

As Harry and I left the courtroom that day, I noticed Mrs. Quigley and one of her *kama'āina* friends leaving the courthouse as well. Perhaps she felt my eyes on her, because after a few moments she looked up and saw me. We briefly held each other's gazes—but I admit, I saw no anger or recrimination in her eyes, only sorrow, before she dropped her head and turned away.

After some fifty hours of deliberation, the jury of seven *haoles*, two Asians, two Hawaiians, and a Portuguese returned a verdict— finding all four defendants guilty of manslaughter in the death of Joseph Kahahawai Jr.

I was relieved and, I confess, a little surprised. After all that I had seen and heard, I thought there was a good chance the accused would escape the consequences of their actions. But the jurors had done a great service to Hawai'i and their country, affirming the rule of law over vigilante justice. Upper-crust Honolulu society may have been dismayed, but in Pālama there was celebration that Hawai'i had shown itself to be true not just to the American ideal of "equal justice under the law," but to the words of Kamehameha III that had become Hawai'i's motto: *Ua mau Ke Ea O Ka 'Āina I Ka Pono*—"The Life of the Land Is Preserved in Righteousness."

Unfortunately the rest of America did not live up to its founders' ideals, and the mainland exploded in a rage over the conviction of four people many considered to be heroes, not villains.

Only a few days later I was at work sewing together a shirt when I heard the door chime and looked up to see Esther Anito, shaken and pale, enter the shop.

"They've won," she said hoarsely.

"What? Who's won?"

She looked like a woman who had had everything taken from her and had nothing left to give up.

"I was at the courthouse," she said, "when the judge sentenced them each to ten years' hard labor at O'ahu Prison. But they were all *smiling*—like cats that had just swallowed big fat canaries. Then it was announced that the governor had commuted their sentences."

"'Commute'? What does that mean?"

"It means he reduced the ten years they would have had to serve in prison," she said, "to one hour 'in custody of the High Sheriff.' And then they all went off to the governor's office to pass the time and have their pictures taken for the press."

I was stunned. I could scarcely believe it. "Governor Judd did this?" He had always seemed like a good man to me.

"One hour," Esther said bitterly. "That's all my boy's life is worth: *one hour* of their time!"

She started to weep, as outside, newsboys began hawking extras announcing this latest, terrible turn in the case. I could not find any words of consolation for her, for there were none. Nor could I find any to console my children that night—especially Harold—when they asked me why the people who killed Joe were going free. The outcome had made a mockery of all my faith in the law, and I was helpless to shield them from this, their first taste of the world's injustice.

In the following days we would hear how the governor had been under intense pressure from Washington to grant the four defendants a full pardon, or else the territory would be placed under military rule. Judd had refused to consider a pardon, which would have wiped away their criminal convictions. "By their verdict the jury has built a monument upon which it is inscribed that lynch law will not be tolerated in Hawai'i," the governor declared, "and for the public good I propose to do nothing which would in any way tear down or destroy that monument." But it was a tarnished monument at best.

No matter his reasons, Governor Judd's actions were wrong and served only to demonstrate, as John Kelley had said, that there were two standards of justice in Hawai'i: one for *haoles*, and one for everyone else.

Four days after the commutations, amid the flash of news cameras, Thomas and Thalia Massie, Grace Fortescue, and Clarence Darrow left for San Francisco aboard the *Malolo*—leaving behind a Honolulu that would be forever changed by their brief and sorrowful transit through the islands. In that fall's elections, the Republican party—and the *haole* elite that controlled it—suffered their first major loss at the polls, thanks largely to the votes of young Asian-American citizens. It was the beginning of the end for the Big Five.

In an effort to close the books on the Ala Moana case—and to determine whether Horace Ida, Henry Chang, Ben Ahakuelo, and David Takai ought to be retried—John Kelley suggested to Governor Judd that he commission the Pinkerton Detective Agency in New York to conduct a thorough and impartial investigation surrounding the facts of the alleged attack upon Thalia Massie.

The report was not made public until a year later; even then, it was only quietly reported on in Hawai'i. The Pinkertons concluded that Mrs. Massie "did in some manner suffer numerous bruises about the head and body, but definite proof of actual rape has not in our opinion been found." It went on to confirm the boys' alibis: "The movements and whereabouts of the defendants on the night of the alleged assault remain precisely as they were accounted for"—and found no reason to doubt their "probable innocence."

Accordingly, the Territory of Hawai'i dropped all charges against the remaining defendants, clearing their names as well as that of Joe Kahahawai. It could not bring Joe back, but perhaps his spirit might sleep a little easier.

It was some, but scant, comfort for Esther, who would never quite recover from the loss of her son. Joseph Sr. also continued to mourn, and I wonder how his grief and the stress of the trials might have hastened his death, at the age of fifty, seven years later. But not long after the bitter pill of the commutations, he and his wife Hannah announced some joyful news, at least: They were going to have another child. Their fourth and final son was born to them on December 20—five days before the birthday of the half-brother he would never know—and his parents named him Joseph.

Eighteen

oe's murder and his killers' deliverance had a profound effect on me, plunging me into a melancholy the like of which I had not felt since the death of my first, unborn child. The injustice of it colored the way I now looked at life in America—or perhaps life here had already been colored by my naïveté, and I was viewing it clear-eyed for the first time. Hawai'i was ruled by a privileged elite who felt themselves above the law, and those of us with darker skin or a different cast to our eyes were merely second-class citizens. We had been brought here to do the hard manual labor that *haoles* would not stoop to perform, and that was what we always would be in their eyes: common laborers, who were simply not to be accorded the same rights as they.

Some people could drink from this bitter cup without it poisoning their lives, and I tried to tell myself that this was simply another kind of *han* to be borne bravely and silently; no worse, certainly, than what I had lived under in Korea. Had it only affected my own life, it might not have bothered me as much. But to think that my children could be struck down as capriciously as Joe had been, their lives not worth more than an hour of a *haole*'s life—that I could not bear.

Like a good Korean, I did not betray the extent of my desolation, certainly not to the children. My husband recognized what I was going through and tried to console me with a touch, a smile, a gentle word here and there. And Beauty understood as well, often spending mornings visiting with me in the tailor shop, since her business at the barbershop was largely confined to afternoons and evenings. We would talk about how our *keiki* were getting along in school, about our fellow picture brides, about everything and nothing; and in the calming drone of each other's chatter I found a welcome distraction from darker thoughts.

On one such morning Beauty and I were chatting when the door opened to admit two men in their early thirties: one a tourist and the other a beachboy of my acquaintance, Eugene "Poi Dog" Nahuli, a member of the Waikīkī Beach Patrol. This was a group founded in the wake of the Massie case to organize services and concessions at Waikīkī, and not incidentally to polish the tarnished public image of the beachboys. Poi Dog—the nickname came from a little terrier-mix he took to the beach with him every day—had the quiet good looks of a Duke Kahanamoku and an impish grin not unlike Panama Dave's. "Got a customer for you, Jin," he announced. He had brought in a guest staying at the Royal Hawaiian who wished to have a custom shirt made from a colorful cotton print—green Japanese pine trees against a dark blue background.

"Ah, this is very pretty," I said, starting to examine the fabric, when I felt a reproving kick to my ankle that could only have come

from the person sitting beside me. It was then I noted Beauty gazing hungrily at Poi Dog as if he were, well, not *poi,* but perhaps
kimchi.

I did not require a second kick and quickly made introductions.
Beauty was wearing her white barber's smock and Poi Dog looked
her over with a smile. "You a barber girl, eh?"

She nodded and smiled. "Yes, my shop is on Merchant Street."

"Just had a haircut last week," he said. "Guess it's 'bout time
for another."

She laughed, but he wasn't joking. He stopped by that afternoon for a shave, and they soon became inseparable.

That turned out to be an eventful week. Only a few days later I
was working on that Japanese print shirt when a dapper young
Chinese-American man in a business suit entered the shop, greeting me with a smile. "*Aloha.* I'm your neighbor, Ellery Chun—
from King-Smith Clothiers, next door?"

I met this with a blank stare at first. "Ah, you mean Chun Kam
Chow's?"

"Yes, he's my father. I changed the name a few weeks ago."

"I'm sorry. I'm afraid I hadn't noticed."

"Are you the owner of this shop?" he asked.

"Yes, my name is Jin. May I assist you with something?"

"I think you may," he said. "Are you also the seamstress who's
been turning some of the *yukata* fabric I sell into shirts?"

I conceded that I was.

"How long does it take you to put one together?"

I had never considered this before. "Well, cutting the initial
pattern consumes the most time, but once I have that, the actual
cutting of fabric and assembly of the pieces takes . . . oh, perhaps
two hours."

"That's impressive," he said. "Are you working on one now?"

"Yes, a friend of mine brought a customer in just the other day."

"May I see it?"

I brought out the two front pieces and the back of "the pine tree shirt," as I thought of it. "Yes, this is a lovely pattern," Mr. Chun said as he looked it over. "And you do impeccable work."

"You are too generous, I think."

"Don't give me that Confucian humility, I get enough of that from my father. You're very good. I've been watching the tourists come in here, placing custom orders, and I got to thinking, maybe they'd buy ready-to-wear shirts like these if someone were to offer them. How would you like to work for me?"

This was certainly the last thing I had expected to hear.

"You mean—make shirts for you to sell in your store?" I said.

"Right. Cut out the middleman."

"The middle of what man?"

He laughed. "Never mind, just an expression. How much do you usually charge per shirt?"

"Oh, about . . . thirty cents."

"I'll pay you fifty," he announced.

My eyes must have popped at this. "Fifty cents per shirt?"

"And to start I'll place an order for thirty—no, make that forty—shirts."

A bit of quick arithmetic yielded an impressive guarantee of wages.

"How long do you think it will take you to make that many?" he asked.

The largest number of shirts I had ever done before, in addition to my mending and fitting work, was four in one week's time. If I doubled that output, that would be four or five weeks—no, that was too long to make him wait. "Oh . . . perhaps . . . three weeks?" I said hopefully.

"Fine," Mr. Chun said. "Do we have a deal?"

He held out his hand, and after only a moment's hesitation I took it.

"It would seem so," I said with a smile.

*E*llery Chun may have been young—only twenty-two years old—but clearly he was already a shrewd businessman. An alumnus of the prestigious Punahou School, he had never imagined he would have anything to do with the garment trade. He graduated from Yale University in 1931 with a degree in economics and a desire to engage in foreign trade, but in the Caucasian business hierarchy of Honolulu at that time there was no place for a young, ambitious Chinese-American. When his father asked him to take over management of the family dry-goods store, its revenues declining as the Depression tightened its grip, he accepted out of filial duty—and not without a measure of frustration and resignation that this was the best he could do.

He promptly gave the store a more American name—after the closest streets, King and Smith—and was searching for something to stimulate new business when he took notice of what was coming out of my shop, as well as others around town like Musa-Shiya the Shirtmaker.

On my first day of work I gazed up at the hundreds of bolts of fabric stacked on the King-Smith shelves and began to wonder if I had been mad to promise so many shirts in so short a time. But all I could do was try, and not let Mr. Chun see how terrified and intimidated I truly was.

He showed me some shirt patterns he had designed and a bolt of Japanese silk called "*kabe* crepe," which had a crinkly, pebbled surface. The hand-screened print depicted slipper-shaped Japanese boats navigating a sea of blue surf and white foam, the waves looking rather like blue mountains capped with snow.

"This is lovely," I said, tracing the pebbled surface with my fingertip, "but delicate. I will have to hand-baste the seams—machine-basting is too likely to tear them."

"You're the tailor. Do as you see fit."

"Bamboo buttons would be lovely on this."

"Sounds swell. I'll look into getting some."

I examined another print, this one showing a flock of cranes in flight, and I thought of my mother's similar, elegant design for one of her wrapping cloths. I felt a pleasurable stirring inside me at this connection to a cherished part of my past—the first pleasure I think I had taken in anything since the commutations.

I smiled and said, "I will start on this one."

I spent an eight-hour day laying out and cutting the pattern pieces; fronts, facings, back, sleeves, collar, pockets, and for one design, a double yoke. Mr. Chun had purchased for me a fabric cutter with which I was now able to cut pieces for as many as five different shirts at one time, saving me considerable time. Once these were cut, I joined the pieces together and fashioned the buttonholes. My estimate of assembling one shirt in about two hours held true, and in not quite three workdays I was able to produce eleven finished shirts. Pressing and ironing took several more hours. I picked up a little speed with practice, producing thirteen shirts the second week and fifteen the next.

In addition to my work for Mr. Chun, of course, I had other customers to serve, and found myself working even later into the night than I was accustomed. Sometimes I would not get home until midnight, and all I saw of my *keiki* was their sleeping faces, which I would kiss before collapsing into my own bed. But at the end of three weeks' time I had, as promised, forty finished shirts to present to Mr. Chun—for which he paid me the generous sum of twenty dollars.

They were very attractive shirts, if I do say as much. I was especially fond of the cranes in flight—I had laid out the pattern so that the birds seemed to fly on a slight upward diagonal, providing a sense of lift and freedom. Mr. Chun was very complimentary of my efforts and put twenty of the shirts out for sale the following Monday on a table up front, with a sign in the window reading, HAWAIIAN SHIRTS—$1.00 EACH.

To our mutual surprise, by the end of the week they had all been sold—mostly to tourists, but a few to local *haole* boys. I had already begun work on the next batch, which I now rushed to complete before the remaining twenty shirts sold out. I soon found myself working a fifty-hour week for Mr. Chun alone, and producing between twenty to twenty-four shirts in that time.

These, too, sold as quickly as we could keep them in stock.

Eventually the demand would increase to the point that Mr. Chun had to contract out even more production to one of the few local clothing manufacturers, Wong's Products. But I could hardly complain about this: I was earning between ten and twelve dollars a week in wages at a time when many people in the United States could find no jobs at all. I now could afford the occasional treat for the children and meat for the stewing pot. For the first time since we had lost the restaurant, we could breathe a little easier. I was grateful to have such steady and lucrative work, which I also found rewarding, challenging, and—I hardly dared admit it to myself—fun.

The first time I brought home such large wages I showed it proudly to Jae-sun, expecting him to be as jubilant as I, but though he smiled and congratulated me, his reaction was muted. "I am lucky," he said graciously, "to have such a talented wife." Then he added, "Excuse me. I have some *chap chae* cooking on the stove," and he headed into the kitchen.

That night, as we lay in bed together, I said to him, "Someday you will have your own restaurant again."

He shrugged. "Perhaps. Perhaps not. But it matters little who feeds a hungry family. The important thing is, we are fed."

"Your job at the docks feeds us too. I know we were brought up to expect that the husband is the sole support of the household, but . . ."

"That doesn't matter to me," he said. "I have been in America long enough to know that the old Confucian ways do not apply here. It is just . . ." He paused. "It is a hard thing for a man to watch his wife working twelve-hour days, and not be able to contribute more. A hard thing to accept that his useful life is over."

"That's not true."

"It feels true," he said, and closed his eyes.

I placed a hand on his, but did not know what to say; so I said nothing.

That Christmas of 1932 was a happier one for our family than any since the loss of the restaurant, and seeing the looks of joy on the children's faces as they opened their (still modest) presents seemed to buoy my husband's spirits. Each year at this time we would also take photographs of the *keiki* to be sent back to my family in Pojogae in time for the Korean New Year. We borrowed Jade Moon's Brownie camera, dressed the children in their Sunday best, and took a roll of photos of them, singly or together. This was always a bit of an ordeal as we tried to get them to pose with polite Korean solemnity, but at the last minute they inevitably broke into giggles, laughter, and smiles—something my mother and brothers surely found shocking when they saw them. (I doubted my father even looked at them.) This year was no exception, but this time when I gazed at the developed photographs I found myself thinking: *They look so American.* My dismay at my own children's foreignness surprised and shamed me.

That spring Poi Dog helped Harold make his own surfboard— one of the shorter, lighter boards that were becoming popular— and Harry and Woodrow were soon spending even more of their time at the beach. After school, Grace—now fourteen years old— would lend a hand at the tailor shop, cutting out patterns, even doing some simple machine stitches on Mr. Chun's shirts. She had never expressed any real interest in sewing before, but she told me she liked being part of the business, and she had a good head for figures as well. We had always intended that she go to college, if we could afford it, and now she began to consider a major in business administration. It pleased me to hear her speak with enthusiasm about higher education, as much as it pleased me to have her in the shop with me; it felt like the thimble time I had shared with my own mother, and not for the first time I felt a pang of longing to see her face again.

It was during one of our late afternoons that Grace admitted to me shyly that there was a boy who had asked her to a dance that Friday at Waikīkī Park, and would it be all right for her to go?

After the many years of painful diffidence Grace had suffered through, I was pleased to know that she had grown into a lovely, confident girl who had begun attracting suitors. I smiled and asked her who this lucky boy might be.

"You already know him," she said. "It is Jiro."

My smile froze on my face. "Tamiko's boy?"

"Yes, he's always been sweet on me. When we were eight years old he asked me to marry him. I told him we were a little young and we should wait until we were at least twelve." She laughed. "So, may I go to the dance with him?"

I hesitated only a moment before replying, "Yes, of course. I would only ask you not to mention this to your father just yet. I confess, I'm not certain what his reaction might be."

"Oh, Mama, I know what they say about the Japanese in church, but Jiro is American, like me! Father's known him since he was a little boy."

"I know, but . . . humor me? If your father asks, tell him you are going to the dance with some of your friends. And Jiro *is* a friend, so it's not untrue, is it?"

"All right, Mother, if you say so."

We returned, to my relief, to our sewing talk. I told myself this was a harmless adolescent infatuation; it would probably run its course before Jae-sun even learned of it. And Grace was right: my husband *did* know Jiro, was good friends with his father. Jae-sun had learned, as I had, to distinguish between the Japanese Empire that oppressed our native land and the Japanese people we knew here in Hawai'i. But still, I was not certain how he might feel about our daughter becoming romantically involved with a Japanese boy—even Jiro.

And if I am to be honest, I was not certain how I felt about it myself.

Only a few weeks after this I was distressed to receive a telephone call at work from Wise Pearl: Her husband, Mr. Kam, had just suffered a heart attack, collapsing while at work with his two eldest sons in the barley fields. A doctor had been summoned, who examined him and had him taken to Queen's Hospital, from where Wise Pearl was calling. I closed the shop and went immediately to my friend's side. I found her sitting in the hospital's waiting room, hunched over like a small tree bent by the wind, with tears in her eyes. I realized I had never seen Wise Pearl cry before; she had always been too calm and self-possessed for that. But here she was, more distressed than I had ever seen her.

I went to her and clasped her hands in mine. "How is he?"

"Sleeping. 'Resting comfortably,' they tell me, though how they can tell he is comfortable if he is asleep I do not know."

"Where are the children?"

"Edwin and John are looking after the younger ones. I did not wish to bring them here when I was not certain of what the outcome might be."

Her words sent a shiver through me. "Is his condition that grave?"

"When John came running in to tell me," she said quietly, "I rushed out to the fields, and at first I thought he was dead. His face was as gray as the ash on one of his cigarettes. Then, as I sat down beside him, he opened his eyes and I saw he was alive. He reached out and took my hand in his. That told me how afraid he was: he had never held my hand before."

I was surprised to hear this. "Never?"

"Mr. Kam does not show his feelings readily, even to me. He was brought up to believe that self-control is the mark of a virtuous man. I have learned to take tenderness in an unguarded smile, rarely more than that.

"Now he held on to me like a baby holds on to its mother, afraid to be lost, and it was all I could do to hold back my tears for fear of frightening him more."

Those tears came to her now and I held her until she could find her voice again. "The doctors believe he will live, but his heart has suffered extensive damage. It could take many months for him to recover, and even then they say he should not go back to the hard physical work of farming."

"Thank Heaven. It could be worse."

"Can you believe, he actually protested when the doctors told him he should stop smoking because it was cutting his wind? Stubborn old man!"

"Yes," I said, "they're all getting old—aren't they?"

She nodded. "Mr. Kam will be fifty-nine next year, only one year away from his *hwan'gap.*" In Korea, one's sixtieth birthday is marked by a celebration of a full life-cycle as defined by the Zodiac. If one is born in the Year of the Pig, one's *hwan'gap* will also be in the Year of the Pig. Traditionally, it is often the time when a man retires from a life of work, as well.

"Jae-sun is fifty-six," I said. "Though he's still strong, I worry over him lifting freight at the docks. But I can't ask him to stop working and earning what little he is able to contribute to the household; I think that would kill him sooner."

"The boys and I can shoulder the load in the short term," Wise Pearl thought aloud, "but their father did so much of the work himself, I don't know how I'll keep the farm running without him."

"Can't you hire a man to help out?"

She shook her head. "It's difficult enough paying the mortgage as it is. No, this merely hastens the inevitable. I think I will soon have to start looking for a buyer for the farm."

"Will you be able to find one, during this Depression?"

"Eventually, perhaps. There is more home development than farming going on in Wilhelmina Rise these days. We may even be able to sell the land at a small profit—enough to set me up in a new business. A shop, perhaps, or a small hotel." She smiled sadly. "We are all reaching the same crossroads, dear friend—I've just arrived there a little sooner than you. Our husbands are growing old, and it is up to us now to fill the breach and provide for our families' futures."

It was with both pride and sadness that I realized I was filling that breach already. But I did not wish to think of the day my husband might be taken to a place like this.

As though we needed further proof of mortality, in December 1933, my old friend Chang Apana passed away at the age of sixty-nine—struck down not by a fall from a second-story window, or a stabbing, or a blow from an axe handle, but from injuries sustained in an automobile accident a year before. Even in his last years as a policeman Chang demonstrated he was still the best officer on the force, as when he solved the disappearance in Honolulu of mainland socialite Frances Ashe. The *Star-Bulletin* paid tribute to both the real-life detective and his fictional counterpart when they ran a photo of him on their front page with the headline, BLACK CAMEL KNEELS AT HOME OF CHANG APANA.

A happier event occurred a month later, when Beauty and "Poi Dog" Nahuli were wed. Eugene brought his little terrier, Keoni, who served as "best dog"; Mary was her mother's flower girl. I am happy to say that all of Beauty's Kyŏngsang sisters were in attendance. The modest ceremony was a far cry from the extravagant wedding she had once planned to Mr. Ko, but even Jade Moon had to admit that Poi Dog was sweet and seemed to genuinely adore Beauty.

Within a few months Mrs. Nahuli—or "Mrs. Poi Dog," as the other beachboys now called her—found herself pregnant for the first time in sixteen years. She was understandably nervous, since at that time thirty-seven was considered an advanced age to bear a child; but in July 1934, Mary received a healthy young baby brother named Franklin, so christened because he was born the same week that President Franklin D. Roosevelt arrived in Honolulu, the first U.S. president to visit Hawai'i while in office. Sixty thousand Honoluluans turned out to greet him, and many more lined the streets during his motorcade to catch a glimpse of this man who was laboring to get the country back to work.

King-Smith Clothiers was already hard at work with the success of its new garments, which were being advertised as "Hawaiian playsuits," "Waikīkī Beachwear," and most recently, "Aloha shirts." Other retailers like Musa-Shiya and Linn's Army-Navy Store had quickly followed us into the ready-to-wear market. Mr. Chun was pleased but not satisfied. As he said to me as we were examining a new *yukata* fabric, "You know, despite what the sign says, these prints aren't really very 'Hawaiian.'" In an effort to make something more "tropical" he began importing fabrics from Tahiti and Samoa—some with bordered floral designs suggested by Tahitian *pareus,* and others with tapa-cloth motifs. Javanese *batik* cloth also became popular in Honolulu around this time, and Mr. Chun began importing this as well.

Soon both Gump's Department Store and Watumull's East India Store were commissioning local artists like Elsie Das to create textiles using Hawaiian floral patterns, to be used in drapery and upholstery. Miss Das's were colorful, striking designs of native hibiscus, ginger, breadfruit, night-blooming cereus, even hula girls—beautifully hand-blocked in Japan onto raw silk. Mr. Chun, never one to be left behind a breaking wave, immediately saw the future of *aloha* wear and commissioned his younger sister Ethel—a graduate of the Chouinard Art School in California—to create uniquely Hawaiian tropical prints for King-Smith shirts.

Ethel Chun Lum was no stranger to the garment business—she had started out at the old C. K. Chow's, hand-painting pictures of Diamond Head onto the back of sweatshirts. She was a talented artist who produced many beautiful designs in such typically Hawaiian motifs as palm trees, pineapples, hula girls, and grass houses. Among the ones I remember best were her depictions of *mālolo,* or flying fish; a Hawaiian man fishing by the light of a torch; and a beautifully striped yellow, white, and black fish known locally as a "Moorish Idol." Ethel hand-painted these images, choosing colors in consultation with her brother, and then the color "croquis" would be sent to Japan to be roller-printed onto silk or cotton.

The shirts had not yet caught on with all of Hawai'i's residents—at a dollar or more apiece they were far too expensive for most locals—but tourists snapped them up to wear while they were in the islands and as gifts to friends and relatives back home. As a result, department stores on the mainland also began to purchase them, and suddenly there was an explosion of clothing manufacturers into the new market: familiar names like Watumull's as well as new ones like Branfleet, Kamehameha, Surfriders Sportswear, and Royal Hawaiian. Mr. Chun was soon laying plans to manufacture swimsuits, robes, and men's slacks.

But in fulfilling the growing demand for "Aloha wear"—a term which Mr. Chun had the prescience to trademark—we had completely outgrown my little shop. Mr. Chun phased out his contract with Wong's Products, deciding that King-Smith was a large enough concern that it needed its own factory, and he offered me the position of "head seamstress" and a generous weekly salary of fifteen dollars a week. This was a veritable fortune by the standards of the day, and though I was sad to give up the lease on my shop, where I spent many happy afternoons with Grace, I could hardly turn down Mr. Chun's offer.

And besides, Grace was now eighteen years old and, in the fall of 1936, would enter the University of Hawai'i as a business major. She would soon have little time to spend sewing with her mother. She had bloomed socially, and to my relief had had two or three other suitors besides Jiro in her last years of high school, including a very nice Korean boy named Albert. Jae-sun had eventually learned of her dates with Jiro, but chose to pin his hopes on Albert.

So it came as a surprise to both of us when Grace arrived home with Jiro one day near the end of her senior year and announced, "Mama . . . Papa . . . Jiro and I have decided that after graduation, we wish to be married."

Jae-sun looked suddenly like a man who had placed a month's earnings on the wrong race horse.

"Indeed?" he said, trying to cover his fluster, unsuccessfully, with a smile.

"I was thinking, maybe, of a July wedding," Grace said shyly, "like you and Mama had."

I could not help but be touched by this, but Jae-sun asked, somewhat nervously, "There is nothing that . . . requires . . . such an imminent ceremony, is there?"

"Oh, no, Papa," Grace assured him.

"No, no, not at all," Jiro agreed quickly.

Jae-sun's relief was palpable.

As for me, my first thought was, "But what about college?"

"Oh, I'll still go to school," Grace insisted.

Jae-sun cleared his throat. "Indeed? And how," he asked Jiro, "do you intend to support a wife attending college?"

"I've been offered a job at First Hawaiian Bank, Mr. Choi—as a teller. But I'm very good with numbers, and I hope it will lead to a better position in time."

"But can you afford a home of your own in the meantime?"

"I found the sweetest little apartment on Kewalo Lane," Grace said, "for only twelve dollars a month."

I looked at Jae-sun; he looked at me. We seemed to have exhausted all of our logical objections.

"Are you both very sure about this?" I asked.

"Oh, yes, Mama," Grace said. "I couldn't *be* more sure."

"I've loved Grace since I was eight years old," Jiro said, beaming. "I want to make her as happy as she makes me."

"Do your parents know of your plans?" I asked him.

"Yes, ma'am. They say they would be honored to have our two families joined in this way."

To my surprise, I saw my husband smile at this.

"Then we are honored as well," he said. He stood and extended a hand, in the American fashion, and Jiro took it with a big grin on his face. Grace looked thrilled. Jae-sun seemed genuinely pleased for them.

Why, then, was I forced to congratulate them with a less than honest smile?

Later, when we were alone together, Jae-sun said, bemused, "Well, I cannot say this is not a situation of my own making. I welcomed Taizo and his family into our home, though I scarcely expected this to happen."

"Are you upset, *yobo?*"

He shrugged. "How can I be upset about Jiro? He's a sweet boy, we've known him since he was a little *keiki*. I admit, I had hoped she would marry a Korean boy, but . . . if they are happy together, who are we to say otherwise?" He noted my hesitation. "You don't agree?"

"I agree that Jiro is a sweet boy, and I want Grace to be happy. I just . . . did not expect to feel this way."

"And what way is that?"

I hesitated, only now articulating this to myself.

"By American custom and law, she will lose our family name and take his. Our own children already feel little connection to Korea . . . hers will feel even less. I can't help but feel as though we are . . . losing something of what we are."

Jae-sun nodded. "Yes, I know. But this is inevitable, *yobo*. They have grown up in Honolulu. They speak Korean at home, English in school, and pidgin among their friends. They eat *saimin* and hamburgers as much as they do *kimchi*. As you once said, they are not just Korean, they are Korean-American. But they are something else, too: children of this place, of Hawai'i."

I nodded. " 'Local.' "

"Yes, local. I hear the word more and more, used with pride."

I shook my head in bewilderment. "I ran as fast and as far away from Korea as I could, when I was a young girl. Why should I feel the loss of it now?"

"You feel the loss of the world of your childhood," he said gently, "and of people left behind. Perhaps you need to look back before you can move ahead."

That summer Wise Pearl and her husband sold their carnation farm to a land developer, and for quite a bit more than they had paid for it. With this profit she was able to purchase a small house in upper Nu'uanu, which would now serve as both a family home and a small Korean-style inn. Mr. Kam's heart condition had improved, but he was still in no condition to work— perhaps never would be—and I was more grateful than I could possibly express when Wise Pearl offered Jae-sun a position as chef and general manager of the inn.

Wise Pearl brushed aside my thanks. "Mr. Choi has skills which we need," she said simply. "What could make more sense?"

Soon, Jae-sun was happily working full-time—cooking for guests, doing repairs, anything that was called for—and was more content than I had seen him since the closure of the Liliha Cafe.

Alas, this was matched only by my own discontent once I began work at the new King-Smith factory. Despite my title of head seamstress, in reality I became merely one of two dozen seamstresses, mostly Japanese and Chinese, sitting in a room filled with the stutter of sewing machines and the whir of electric fans. While I once made buttonholes with a series of careful zigzag stitches, there was now an entire machine to do that for me. While I once felt part of an exciting new enterprise, I was now little more than an extension of my sewing machine. I quickly found that I missed my shop; I missed the customers.

I told myself I was acting like a spoiled, well-fed kitten amid starving alley cats, and should be grateful to have any kind of job in these hungry years—though it did not make the job any less tedious.

When I mentioned this at our next *kye* meeting, Wise Pearl pointed out, "Once, in Korea, we would have been satisfied to merely put food on our families' tables. But here in America, we have had a taste of what is possible in life. Jae-sun aspired to be a chef; you aspire to be more than a seamstress. You should not be embarrassed by it. This is what America *is*: the opportunity to become something more."

Beauty suggested, "Why don't you start your own clothing line? You make such beautiful designs!"

"Yes," Jade Moon agreed, "you can produce these 'aloha' shirts as well as Mr. Chun! You could borrow money from the *kye*."

I shook my head. "No, there is too much competition. To do it right would require more capital than we have in the fund."

"I have some money left over from the sale of the farm," Wise Pearl offered without hesitation. "I would be honored to be your partner in such a venture."

I was greatly touched by this and thanked her. "But I'm not sure this is the right time for such an enterprise." Indeed, my thoughts, as Jae-sun had noted, were focused less on the future than the past.

*I*t was in the Year of the Ox that my life had changed upon meeting Evening Rose, and it was in this Year of the Ox—1937—that it changed again, with the receipt of a letter from my eldest brother:

> *Honorable Little Sister:*
>
> *It is with sadness that I must inform you of the passing of our father, Pak Dae Hyo, after a short illness. He died peacefully in his own bed surrounded by members of his clan. The cost of his medical care was paid in large measure by the money we received from you and your husband, for which Father was not ungrateful.*
>
> *Mother has taken the news hard but we are doing all we can for her. She asked me yesterday to read again from your last letter to us, and smiled to hear of your life in Hawai'i. She keeps the photographs of your children on her dresser. I think it would cheer her to hear from you.*
>
> *Your elder brother*

"Father was not ungrateful." I supposed that was the closest thing to an apology I could hope for in this life. There was still a little knot of bitterness in my soul over the way Father had treated me—but the anger, at least, was past. I wrote back expressing condolences I did not feel in my heart. Instead I felt a stab of guilt: I had always intended to return someday to Korea to visit Mother and my brothers, but now Father's death reminded me that time was not infinite. And then there was Blossom. Though I had no inkling of where she might be, I still harbored a faint hope that I might somehow locate her . . . or my old teacher, Evening Rose.

I found that I could think of nothing that day but Mother, Blossom, and Evening Rose, the three of them twined together in my mind like the stems of flowers in a vase. That night, as I lay in bed beside Jae-sun, I told him, "You were right, *yobo,* about the things I left behind in Korea. I think I would like to go back and see my mother . . . while I still can."

He nodded knowingly.

"I agree, this is something you must do. But I confess, I worry for your safety on such a trip. Not so much on the high seas as in the Sea of Japan."

I understood his concerns, of course. Several months ago, at the end of July, the long-simmering hostilities between Japan and China had come to a head when Japanese troops attacked and captured the city of Peking, capital of Chiang Kai-shek's government. Even as the Japanese offered peace settlements, they continued to battle their way across China toward the city of Nanking, capital of a rival "nationalist" government, smaller but increasingly the last bastion against Japanese domination.

"The Japanese have a formidable naval blockade of China in place," I noted. "Travel to Korea will not be a danger."

"Perhaps if you booked passage on a ship of American registry," he suggested. "America is still neutral. It would ease my mind a bit."

I agreed this would be a prudent move and the next day I went to the offices of the Dollar Line to purchase a ticket—second-class fare, this time, not steerage—from Honolulu to Yokohama, Japan, aboard the steamship *President Coolidge.* I then went to the Japanese Embassy to renew my passport, where it was eventually stamped and approved. I wrote Joyful Day to tell him I was coming, then informed our children that I was going to Korea to see their grandmother, whom they had never met. They accepted this with the same aplomb as if I had said I was going down to the corner drugstore. Only Charlie seemed excited. "Are you taking the China Clipper?"

"No, we can't afford an airplane. I'll be traveling by boat."

"Oh," he said, sorely disappointed.

"I will only be gone a few weeks," I assured them. "I will miss you all. I will bring your grandmother all your love."

And so, in early December, my husband and children accompanied me to Pier 12 and saw me off on my journey. The *President Coolidge* was a luxurious vessel, elegantly appointed in a style that would later be termed "Art Deco," but in these Depression days it was carrying little more than half its full capacity of nine hundred passengers. I watched from the stern, waving goodbye to my family as the ship slipped its moorings and was pushed by pug-nosed little tugboats into the channel. As the ship steamed away from Honolulu, I looked back at this city I had come to some twenty years before. Back then it had seemed a sleepy little port at the end of the world; today it was still a young city, slowly outgrowing the cradling green slopes of the Ko'olau Mountains. It did not take long before those mountains were only a small bump on the blue table of the horizon—a flash of green not unlike the kind seen for an instant as the sun sets—and then they were gone, and we were surrounded on all sides by wide ocean. All at once I thought of the kites which Blossom and I—perched like swallows atop the wall of the Inner Court—had watched fly free on that fifteenth day of the First Moon, perhaps to fly as far as America. And I smiled to think that one of them was coming home.

Nineteen

This ocean crossing passed far more pleasantly than my first: the second-class cabin was small, with narrow bunk beds and merely functional plumbing, but the accommodations were grandiose compared to steerage. I shared the cabin with a young Japanese woman returning to Tokyo from San Francisco, and found her a gracious roommate, even though, with my limited knowledge of Japanese and her equally modest command of English, we could rarely communicate more than a few words at a time. The *Coolidge* was so sparsely populated that at times it seemed like a ghost ship; every dinner table held empty seats and untouched place settings. When we reached Yokohama after nine uneventful days, there was distinct tension on the part of the customs officials, who took care to confirm our nationalities and intentions. "What is your destination, and the purpose of your visit?" one of them asked me sternly, to which I replied, innocently I hoped, "Pojogae, Kyŏngsang Province, Korea. A family visit." He looked me up and down, decided I posed no threat, and cleared me to board a rickety little ferry bound for Pusan, Korea.

The next day, I was surprised by the depth of the feelings that were stirred by my first glimpse of Mount Hwangnyeonsan and Mount Geumjeongsan, still straddling the city like the towers of some vast bridge. The chill in the morning air was bracing, colder than anything in Hawai'i. I headed down the ship's gangway and began the short walk to Pusan's railway station. I heard the music of my native tongue being spoken all around me; Korean faces greeted me with a well-bred lack of expression. Even the air seemed palpably Korean, fragrant with garlic and sesame and the mouth-watering smell of simmering red beans. The only notable differences I saw were that horse-drawn carriages, hand carts, and rickshaws, though still in evidence, were nearly outnumbered by trucks and automobiles; and there were more people wearing Western-style business suits or Japanese kimonos than there were a quarter of a century ago. Nor were women wearing the long hoods my mother and I had once been forced to wear outside our homes—and though the women I saw on the street were deferential to men, they interacted with them with a bit more familiarity than I remembered. Other than this, I felt as if I were cocooned in a memory of my youth, swaddled in the welcome sounds and smells I had grown up with.

Even the sight of the occasional brown-garbed Japanese military police posted on street corners did not distress me too much. A few of the policemen stood beside large washtubs, the purpose of which I couldn't fathom, but I gave it little thought, intent as I was on taking in the city's charms. One of these was an old man coming toward me wearing the traditional Korean white jacket and trousers: in Hawai'i, few Korean men wore these anymore, and I took pleasure in surveying the crisp white linen, the baggy trousers with their sensibly flexible waistline.

But as the pedestrian passed a Japanese policeman standing on the corner, the officer promptly dipped a bucket into one of the washtubs—scooped up a bucketful of dark, dirty water—and inexplicably hurled it at the man in white!

I stood, stunned, as the man came to a sputtering stop, his clothes now dripping with foul-smelling sewer water. A second policeman joined the first and threw another bucket onto him for good measure. The man's fine white suit was soaked—filthy. The police laughed and ridiculed his appearance, though they themselves were the cause of it. The old man said nothing, for fear of his life. He simply bowed to them, turned, and hurried away.

I did not dare ask the police why they had done this thing. When I saw one of them turn and look at me, I, too, hurried away, toward the railway station.

Shaken, I purchased a ticket for Taegu and within an hour boarded my train, the image of the old man's humiliation still livid as a wound in my memory. I wanted to ask one of the people sitting around me what it had meant, but I dared not since there was a Japanese police officer sitting a few rows behind me.

I distracted myself with the scenery passing by, intrigued not just by what was the same but by what was different. Many of the byways we passed were no longer dirt paths but rather modern, paved roads. There were newly built bridges and steel trestles; a man sitting beside me told me of a new dam the Japanese built that had put an end to the seasonal flooding that once plagued his village. Perhaps he mentioned this for the benefit of the policeman behind us, but it did seem as though Japan had brought much material progress to Korea. Gradually I began to wonder whether what I had seen in Pusan had merely been some sort of isolated prank.

I hired a taxi to take me to Pojogae, and the seven miles that had once required several hours to cover on foot were now traversed in only thirty minutes, even though the road was still a rough one; the trip was slow and bumpy, with several near blow-outs of our tires. Finally we reached the outskirts of town, where a group of women carrying their laundry in wicker baskets stared at us curiously, while other pedestrians fell away from us like flocks of startled poultry. Clearly, the sight of an automobile was still a novel one here. In fact, I marveled at how little Pojogae had changed. There was a new school made of concrete, and some of the old mud and stone houses had been replaced with wooden structures— but the village was still small, the dusty streets not yet paved over, and the white summits of the mountains around us might easily have been made of rice. If time was a river, Pojogae seemed to be a sandbar around which the currents of years swirled past, but never fully engulfed.

When I finally saw the fading sunlight sparkling off the blue tile roof of my ancestral home, my eyes filled with tears. This, too, had changed little. And playing in the street were two young girls with long braided hair, who could easily have been Sunny and myself. Perhaps they were. Perhaps I had floated downriver into my own past.

The girls gaped at the approaching automobile. One ran inside the house; the other boldly came up to the cab as it chewed its way up the gravel drive. The child's face was an oval of surprise, wide brown eyes taking in the car. She watched, fascinated, as I paid the driver and got out. Before I could greet her, she quickly bowed, assuming me to be of higher rank, then said breathlessly, "I am Bright Morning of the Pak clan of Pojogae, and I am honored to be meeting you."

I smiled at her careful formality and bowed in return. "I am Gem of the Pak clan of Pojogae, and I am honored to meet you as well."

She was startled. "We belong to the same clan?"

I nodded. "Today I live a long way from here, in a place called Hawai'i. But once upon a time, I grew up in this house."

The door to the house opened and a cloudburst of children—at least tenfold—rained down upon me, their parents not far behind. Three of these parents I recognized at once, even refracted through the lens of years that separated us: my brothers Goodness of the East, Glad Son, and Joyful Day. The latter was now forty-seven, while Goodness of the East was the youngest at thirty-three. They all looked hale and hearty, and the women I took to be their wives dutifully followed three steps behind. The children exhibited no such decorum, however, clustering excitedly around me. Joyful Day came up to me and said, "So, the frog comes back to the old well, does she?" He laughed and took my hands in his. "I have missed you, little sister," he said, more tenderly than I had expected.

"And I have missed my eldest brother," I said. Meanwhile, my nieces and nephews peppered me with questions:

"Are you really from How-why-hee?"

"Where *is* How-why-hee?"

"Is it true the roads there are made of gold?"

"Children," Joyful Day chided, "you will have time to talk with your aunt later. Let your *halmoni* pass through."

I looked up. Threading her way through the cloud of children—her hair white as cotton, her skin cobwebbed—was their grandmother, my mother. She seemed somehow to have shrunk; I remembered her being taller. But she looked up at me with the same joy in her face as I was feeling. "Daughter," she said softly, with tears in her eyes.

I embraced her and we wept for all the years apart. After a minute, she pulled back and gazed fondly into my face. "You are so beautiful!" she said.

"Oh, Mother, how I've missed you—and our thimble time together."

"We shall share some again, you can be sure of it," she said. "Come inside, and honor this old house with your presence."

The whole clan gathered in the men's rooms and my sisters-in-law put together a meal to celebrate my return. This house that had once been home to only three females—my mother, grandmother, and me—was now graced by considerably more. In addition to my brothers' wives, five of their eleven children were girls. All the cousins shared the generational name of Kyong—from a Chinese character meaning *bright, brightness,* or *shining*—so the girls were variously named Bright Morning, Bright Lotus, Shining Daughter, Obedient Brightness, and Shining Virtue. These were far more flattering names than I had been blessed with, and I gave my brothers credit for their forward thinking. The oldest girl, Bright Lotus, fifteen and very talkative, gave me another pleasurable surprise when she spoke of some lesson she had learned that day in school.

"You go to school?"

"Yes, we all do."

"Even girls?"

"Oh, yes. Our principal, Mr. Okura, says it's especially important for girls to go to school."

This made me very happy. "Does he?"

"Yes, he says we are learning the most important things a girl can know: how to be of good moral character and foster our womanly virtues."

My heart sank like a stone, but she went on excitedly, "And we are learning not just what it means to be a good wife and wise mother, but how to be a . . ." She lapsed into perfect, fluent Japanese: ". . . *nihon no teikoku no chuu na jitsu shiman.*"

Joyful Day, overhearing this, began to make his way toward us.

"Forgive your poor aunt her ignorance," I asked with trepidation, "but what does that mean?"

"It means, 'a loyal citizen of the Japanese Empire,'" she said proudly.

Before I could find a response, my elder brother came up and told his daughter, "Your aunt has had a long journey, I think she could use some air. Could you not, little sister?"

"Yes," I said. "I could, at that."

It was cold but not yet freezing outside; I bundled up in my winter coat and my brother and I were soon walking along the banks of Dragontail Stream, a stiff wind rippling its surface like a face wrinkled in surprise. "I should have prepared you for that, little sister," he told me. "I'm sorry."

"Does she truly believe all that?" I asked in dismay.

"For now she does. Whether she will continue to, I cannot say. And if I try to dissuade her from her views, she might bring it up at school, and then we will receive a visit from the High Police. Better to simply hope she grows out of it."

"I had thought, when she spoke of girls' education . . ."

He nodded. "Yes, I know. But the Japanese do not encourage girls to continue their studies after secondary school—the only colleges for women are private schools like Ewha."

"Is it still so bad, under the Japanese? I thought things were getting better."

"For a while they were," he said. "Then, in the Year of the Snake, a group of Japanese high school students insulted some Korean girls as they waited for a train in Kwangju. This led to violence, and eventually riots all across the country, and the government cracked down again.

"They make our children learn Japanese and would have us honor their Emperor as they do, as a god. Meanwhile, seventy percent of the rice we grow goes to Japan, and we still eat millet and beans."

I told him what I had seen in Pusan and asked him what it meant.

"The police have forbidden us to wear our traditional white garments," he explained, "but this is difficult if not impossible to enforce. So in the larger cities they set up those tubs full of foul, dirty water in order to embarrass and intimidate those who would continue to wear white."

I was speechless.

"So you see, Korea is still not free. And now China is lost as well."

"What do you mean, 'lost'?"

With the Japanese controlling all newspapers and radio, my brother explained, the only reliable news came from illegal short-wave radios and clandestine word-of-mouth. And the latest news smuggled from town to town was that Japanese troops had captured the city of Nanking—killing some forty thousand Chinese, soldiers and civilians alike.

"We'd best return to the party now," he suggested. "Before my Japanese daughter reports our suspicious behavior to the High Police."

He meant this as a joke, though neither of us laughed.

*B*ut the war still raged far from Pojogae, which for the moment rested peaceably in its little dimple of land. And these Inner Rooms, which had once seemed so oppressive and stifling, now seemed to cradle me gently within their walls. I slept that night on a mat in a room shared by two of my nieces, warmed by heat rising up from vents beneath the floorboards. After so long in tropical Hawai'i, it was good to feel a chill, and to be warmed by a Korean floor.

The next morning I gently sought to extract from my younger brother, Goodness of the East, any information he might have about Blossom. But even though it had been more than thirteen years since her flight from these rooms, my brother's bitterness was still fresh. "I do not know what happened to her and I do not care," he declared. "She is a vain woman, and dishonorable. Wherever she is, I hope she is rotting away like a bad tooth!"

Clearly he was of no mind to help me, and I changed the subject.

That afternoon Mother and I retreated, as in days long past, into the room where we had spent so many happy hours together, sewing. I'd brought a few of the shirts I made for Mr. Chun, and when Mother saw them she gasped: "Oh, so lovely!" She held one up, examining the design, the cut, the seams, even the coconut buttons. "You are a very fine seamstress," she said proudly.

"Oh, no," I told her, "I shall never be as good as my teacher."

She smiled and examined the other two shirts I had brought. Craftsmanship aside, she was fascinated by their startling images, so alien to her: *hula* girls, men riding surfboards, palm trees, pineapples, volcano craters, even the ocean waves. "Is this really what the sea looks like?" she asked.

"You've never seen it?"

"The farthest I have ever traveled was to Taegu, to see my sister." She looked at me with the hunger of one whose life has been tethered in one place like a balloon, as mine had once been. "Tell me about your life, your family—your home. Your brother has read me your letters, but I wish to hear it from you."

So we sat and I told her things I had never written of in my letters: the high hot sun on the plantation, the hard brutal hand of Mr. Noh, my desperate escape to Honolulu, and my eventual divorce, which shocked her, but not as much as I feared. I told her of my picture bride sisters, the divine gift of Jae-sun and my children, the beachboys' songs—but also of Joey's sad end and the cruel injustice that followed it.

I also spoke of the loss of my teacher and my little sister, my ignorance of their fates, and the nagging guilt that I might have altered these fates had I stayed. I even wondered aloud whether I should ever have left this house.

Mother just laughed good-naturedly.

"Nonsense," she told me. "It is a fine *chogak po* you have made. Far richer and more colorful than you would ever had stitched together here in Pojogae. And it is far from completed."

"I do not wish to add any more patches like the passing of Joe Kahahawai."

Mother considered that a moment, then got up, went to her wardrobe chest, and opened the bottom drawer. She rooted about inside, finally pulling out a carefully folded wrapping cloth. Sitting again, she unfolded it: it was a beautiful patchwork cloth with a green border enclosing a checkerboard of dozens of little rectangles and squares—red, yellow, gold, green, brown, blue, and black.

"You see these?" She pointed out a half dozen of the black rectangles, scattered randomly across the checkerboard. "I added these on the day my mother died, many years ago, because that was my mood that day. There is no pattern to where I placed them, as there is no sense to be made of death. One's eye may not go to them first, but next to them the blues look bluer, the reds richer, the golds more brilliant. Without them the cloth is pretty, but without character or contrast."

"Yes," I said quietly. "I see."

She placed a tender hand on mine. "Look around us, child. Listen to the sounds of war coming from the east. You could have made a *chogak po* here in Pojogae—but you might have had more patches like these than you could count."

*T*he next day I told Mother that I needed to go into Taegu "on business," looking for some Japanese fabric for Mr. Chun, and I made arrangements with a local farmer who owned a battered old truck to take me there. But the bumps and ruts I had felt riding in a new-model taxi cab now seemed more like mountains and gulches in a vintage Ford truck with questionable suspension. After half an hour of jolts and lurches, we finally reached Taegu, where I asked the farmer to drop me at the marketplace. Once he was gone I began a short walk to what I hoped would be a familiar sight.

I still remembered the way, and after five minutes I was rewarded by the sight of the little white house with the blue tile roof—looking much the same as it always had, but for the fact that the paulownia tree sheltering it had grown even more expansive over the years. The stone lantern still guarded the approach, and as I walked up the porch steps I told myself that there was little chance anyone I knew would be living there. But I knocked on the door anyway.

It was opened by a young woman in a gaily colored red-and-gold satin dress not dissimilar to the sort I had worked on at Iwilei. She seemed puzzled to find a woman standing on the doorstep: "Yes? Do you have some business here?"

I felt an odd surge of gladness that the house might have changed hands, but not its purpose.

"I am looking for an old friend who used to live here," I said. "She called herself Evening Rose."

"That name isn't familiar to me. How long ago was she here?"

"Longer than you have been alive, I suspect. Some twenty-five years ago."

"Oh!" she said with a laugh. "That *is* long. Perhaps our housemother might know. Please, come in."

She ushered me inside and had me wait in the vestibule while she went in search of the housemother. I looked around: Although the furnishings were new to me, the house was much the same, decorated with folding screens, rush mats, and lacquered tables. Most of the current generation of *kisaeng* were apparently in their rooms sleeping, but a few wandered up and down the staircase to the second floor, eyeing me curiously as they passed. Finally, the young woman who had answered the door came down the steps alongside a woman in her fifties, graying hair framing a still-lovely face. I confess, I did not recognize her at first, but she knew me at once. *"Aigo,"* she said on seeing me. "The student!"

The voice I could not mistake. It was Fragrant Iris.

I started to bow, but she came up and gave me a warm hug instead. "In this house we do not stand on ceremony! How are you, and where have you been these many years?"

When I told her I had been living in Hawai'i she expressed astonishment and delight. "I hear it is beautiful there."

"It is."

"Are you married?"

"Yes. Three children."

"I remember when you were little more than a child yourself." Her smile turned sad. "And I think I know what brings you here today."

I nodded. "Did you ever . . . hear from her again?"

The sorrow in her eyes presaged her words.

"Yes. We did." She motioned me to join her on a rush mat, and once we were seated she continued, "The police finally released her from prison, sometime in . . . the Year of the Dragon, I believe."

"The year after I left. But that's wonderful to know, she was freed!"

"She would not come back to work here," Iris said. "She didn't wish for us to suffer by association. Her patron paid to maintain a small apartment for her. The police watched her constantly, she said. But that did not prevent her from doing what she thought was right. It did not keep her from joining the demonstration in the streets on March First. She marched and cried *'Mansei!'* alongside thousands of others." Her voice grew soft. "And then the police attacked them as if they were an army—an army without weapons."

"I know," I said. "Even in Hawai'i we have heard of their brutality."

"By the end of it, thousands of lives ended at the point of Japanese sabers. I am sorry to tell you that Evening Rose was one of them. But know this: Your teacher died a patriot."

I had half expected to hear that she was dead, but the manner of her death caught me unawares. I felt numb, having found and lost my teacher all over again in the space of a few minutes. I thanked Iris, declined her offer to stay for tea, and stumbled out of the little pleasure house.

I thought I had cried all my tears for Evening Rose long ago, but as I leaned up against the trunk of a eucalyptus tree, I found that I still had some to give up.

I hailed a taxi and left Taegu.

That night a windstorm blew the few remaining leaves off the trees and rattled the paper windows of our ancestral home. The air grew more wintry and Elder Brother stoked the coals that warmed the floor of the house. I felt, if anything, even more despairing than I had in Hawai'i after Joe's death.

The next morning our household was visited, as it often was when I was a child, by our next-door neighbor, Mrs. Mun—Sunny's mother. Tiny and frail, but with alert brown eyes, she was ushered into the Inner Room, where my mother and I received her warmly. Oddly, though, Mrs. Mun turned to Mother and said, "I have come to tell your daughter something of a personal nature."

I could not imagine what this might be, but Mother respected it without saying a word, brought us a pot of hot rice water, then left us to sit and talk. I, of course, inquired after Sunny, and a veil fell over Mrs. Mun's eyes as she replied sadly, "My daughter passed from this life six years ago next month."

Even though it had been years since I had seen Sunny, it was still a shock to hear. "How? What happened to her?"

"She died birthing her third son, who is now five, so it cannot be said that her death was in vain," she told me.

"I—I am deeply grieved to hear it," I said softly. "I wrote her from Hawai'i, but never received a reply."

"No—she was too ashamed of how she had left you, and her intended husband. She could not bring herself to write you, but I know she wanted to."

Unashamed, I shed tears for my old friend. "I wish she had."

"We were shocked to see her return, and even more so to hear that she broke her engagement," Mrs. Mun said. "I was happy to have her back, but it did make her life, and ours, more difficult. Such matters may be taken in stride in Hawai'i, but here in Korea if a girl is engaged to be married, she *is* married. Everyone in Pojogae knew my daughter had been engaged to marry a man in America; no man here or in neighboring villages would consider marrying her. This presented quite a problem, as you can imagine.

"It took several years, but we were finally able to find a husband for her in Kyŏnggi-do—far enough away that no one knew of her engagement. She married a shopkeeper in Suwon, and I never looked upon her face-to-face again."

"Oh, I am so sorry," I apologized, swept away with guilt. "Had Sunny not come to Hawai'i with me—"

"No no," Mrs. Mun said, "you misunderstand. Every day I am grateful for what you did for her!"

Baffled, I asked, "What did I do?"

"You taught her *hangul* so she could pass some sort of test. She wrote me every week until the end of her life. My middle son would read her letters to me, and write down my reply." She patted me on the hand. "It was a source of great comfort to me then, and even more so now. Today my son will reread her letters to me, and"—she smiled—"I hear her voice again."

"I . . . I am glad."

"But that is only part of what brings me here. You see, after her return, my daughter became quite close to your little sister-in-law."

I was surprised but pleased. "Did she?"

"Oh yes. She and Sunny would do laundry together at the stream, and occasionally sew together. They both missed you, and I think they each saw a bit of you in the other. Until your sister-in-law ran away for once and all."

She leaned in to me and lowered her voice. "This is why I asked to speak with you privately. I know that Sunny taught your sister-in-law some *hangul* because I walked in on them once when they were supposed to be sewing. I never said anything. I don't know how much she learned—probably at least enough to read road signs." She smiled the faintest of smiles. "A day or two after Blossom ran away, I noticed that the money purse in which I kept our household funds was short about fourteen *yen*. I never asked Sunny if she'd taken it, or if she did, what she'd done with it. Any fool could plainly see how much your sister-in-law missed her clan, and wished to be gone from this house."

I was touched and grateful. "That was very kind of Sunny . . . and of you."

"It was the least we could do. You gave her the money, after all, that enabled her to come back to us."

"She said she would repay me, somehow," I remembered with a smile.

Mrs. Mun chuckled at that. "Which is what brings me here today. I have something for you, something important." She reached into a small purse she had brought with her. "Among my daughter's effects was—this."

She took out a small envelope, but did not hand it to me immediately.

"Her husband says it came a few days before she went into labor. If there was a letter in it, it has been lost. But he recalled that he later saw it on a table, with some folded currency inside it, and when he picked it up to examine it, he counted the sum of four-teen *yen*."

My heart began to race as I took the envelope Mrs. Mun now offered me. It was empty, and the return address read simply:

Nang Farm
Yudong Village, Kangwon-do

I stared incredulously at the address. "You believe this was—from Blossom?"

"I cannot tell you for certain that it is," Mrs. Mun said. "But I thought you should see it. Sunny would have wanted you to see it, I am sure."

"Thank you. Thank you very much," I said.

She smiled, stood, and gave me a shaky bow. I returned the bow, then saw her out of the house.

I sat back down and stared at the envelope in my hands, study-ing the address again. Was it possible? Could this be where Blos-som was living—on a farm up north—doubtless married by now? Living the bleak life of a peasant farmer's wife, working from sunup to sundown, forced to give up the best of their crops to the Japanese Empire? The possibilities were depressing to contem-plate.

Kangwon Province was many hundreds of miles away; it would take days to get there by train, I knew. And I had no real assurance that Blossom was even at this "Nang farm." I could write her there, but I was unlikely to get a reply before I left for Hawai'i. If ever there was a chance to see her again, I would have to travel to this "Yudong Village." If there was the slightest possibility that Blossom needed to be rescued from her situation, I had no choice: I would have to go to Kangwon-do. I could not leave her behind again.

*I*t had been twenty-three years since I had felt the bite of a Korean winter, and the farther north I traveled, the deeper into that winter I journeyed. The train compartment was well heated, but when I touched the window I could feel the chill on the other side, like the frigid breath of an ice spirit, pressing up against the glass with cold, implacable patience. In winter the arctic Siberian air rolls in across the Manchurian Plain and into Korea from the north, freezing rivers in their beds, gusting snow and wind from one side of the peninsula to the other. And yet the stark, bare trees we passed, their branches glittering with frost, looked oddly like the branching white coral I had seen in the warm waters of Hawaiian reefs.

All the while I sat in my seat and wondered whether this was a fool's errand—whether I would even find Blossom in Yudong Village, and if I did, in what circumstances.

It was a full day's trip to Seoul, and when I got there my journey had barely begun. A bus took me as far as the town of Ch'unch'ŏn, where I slept overnight in a small inn notable only for the high ratio of insects to paid guests; then the next morning I set off on the final leg of my trip. I hired a taxi to take me to Yudong, a sleepy little hamlet nestled at the base of Mount Palgyo, but when I inquired about the location of the "Nang farm," I was told it lay outside the village proper, and I was pointed helpfully in the general direction. This, as it turned out, was straight up Mount Palgyo, and the farther we drove into the foothills, the steeper the road. We passed a few farms and I inquired at them all, but none of the residents were named Nang and we continued on, passing an occasional church and a small schoolhouse. But once the rough gravel road turned into an even rougher unmarked trail, my driver informed me he had gone as far as he intended to. I paid him his fare, took my overnight bag in hand, and started up the trail on foot.

It grew steeper by the minute, threading through an endless

grove of bare oak and poplar trees that forested the hill. I passed a lovely stream, from whose clear waters I took a drink, then continued on and up. I had to stop several times to catch my breath, and as I took in the dense forest around me I wondered what kind of farm this could be that Blossom was living on, clinging like a billy goat to the side of mountain? The trail wound around the mountain like a watchspring, and just when I was becoming so cold and exhausted I didn't know whether I could go on, I came around a bend—and finally saw a house.

It was a small house, to be sure, made of rough-hewed stone, with a brown thatched roof like a mop of shaggy hair. It was built into the hillside, its rock foundation higher in front than in back; it looked snug and cozy amid the fallen snow. A wind-bell hung from the eaves, chiming a greeting to me as I started toward it.

I had drawn only a few yards closer when a woman came out of the house carrying a bucket, headed toward a well in back. She was a bit shorter than I, with long dark hair, an oval face, and delicate features. My heart found a rhythm it had long forgotten.

I stopped and called out excitedly, "Little sister!"

The woman turned, startled to hear my voice—any voice, perhaps, in this wild place—and gazed down the trail at me. I was almost afraid to move for fear of scaring her off, as if she were a deer, or some rare bird that might take flight.

She took a few steps closer, and I saw the dawning recognition in her eyes. When she was but a few yards away, she stopped and said in a hushed voice, "Sister-in-law?"

"Yes," I said softly.

We ran toward each other, meeting in an embrace long dreamed of. She squeezed me hard enough to take away what little breath I had left, but I held her just as tightly. *"Aigo, aigo,"* she said, and then the only sound I heard was her laughter and mine.

She pulled back and looked at me. Her black eyes shone like opals.

"I cannot believe it! I am so happy to see you," she said wonderingly. "I never dreamed I would again!"

"Nor I you." My words were swallowed up in a sob, and tears ran down my face, nearly freezing as they did. "I have missed you, little sister, so much."

"I've missed you, too," she said. "But how is this possible? What brings you from Hawai'i to our mountain?"

"I came back to visit Mother—and to look for you."

She looked amazed at this, and laughed.

"Well, you've found me! And look at you, you're half frozen for the effort. Come, come in, and have some hot rice water."

As we stumbled toward the little house together, I noticed that the hillslope behind it was covered with what looked like mats of straw—hundreds of them, blanketing acres and acres of uphill land. "Little sister," I asked, puzzled, "do you have so many animals that you need so much hay?"

She laughed again. "It's not for animals, it's for the crops. To protect them from the cold."

"What kind of crops grow on the side of a mountain?"

"Ginseng, of course. But I'll show you all that later. Come inside!"

She welcomed me into her home, to my surprise quite a lovely one. Its stone floor was plastered with mud and covered by straw mats, but a brass brazier kept it toasty warm. In the largest of the rooms there was a large rice chest made of burnished pagoda wood, colorful floor cushions tucked unobtrusively into a corner, and a rolled sedge mat that Blossom now unfurled for me to sit on. I warmed myself by the brazier as Blossom went to the kitchen to fetch a pot of rice water and two bowls.

"The children are still at school," Blossom said, "but here is a photograph we had taken last year." She handed me a portrait of herself standing beside a tall, handsome man in a traditional Korean jacket, vest, and trousers, as well as four children—two boys and two girls. They were posing solemnly for the camera, but there was a smile—a joy—in Blossom's eyes that I had not expected to find there.

"They are beautiful," I said. "What are their names?"

"This is Willow—she's seven. Plum Tree is five. The older boy is Brave One, he will be six next month; and the youngest boy we named Tiger, because he fought like one, at birth. I don't think he wanted to come out of there *at all*."

She beamed with obvious pride at these four fine children. "Your elder brother used to read me all your letters. As I recall, you have three children?"

"Yes. Grace, Harold, and Charles."

"Such strange names, if you don't mind my saying."

"They do not sound nearly so strange in America," I said with a smile.

"And your husband's name is—Jae-sun?"

I nodded. "He was as disappointed as I that we could not get you into the country. Then we heard that you'd run away."

"Yes. The passport was a great help to me, but so was Sunny."

"So I've heard."

"She taught me *hangul*, so that I might be able to read road signs and find work. The day I left, she invited me over to sew with her in her family's Inner Room, but instead I slipped out through a window. For two hours Sunny put on quite a show, talking and laughing as if I were still there—which allowed me to get a good head start on your father and brothers. By the time they even realized I was gone, I was halfway to Kimch'on!"

We shared a laugh at this, then she went on, "I wrote her asking for your address, so I could write you and tell you I was well, but I never heard from her."

I took a shallow breath. "Yes. Well, there is a reason for that. I am sorry to tell you, Sunny died six years ago, in childbirth."

"Oh, no! Our poor friend, how sad!"

"Yes. She was a good friend, to both of us." We talked of Sunny for a while more, then I asked her where she went after she reached Kimch'on. Now she looked even sadder than she had on learning the news about Sunny.

"I went looking for my clan," she said. "When I ran out of money, I would beg for food or do small jobs in exchange for meals. I finally reached our home village of Songso and asked anyone I knew if they'd heard from my family. One old neighbor of ours thought they'd gone to Chŏnjo, so I went to Chŏnjo."

"But that is so far!"

"Yes, it took me two months to get there—working here and there for a week or two, earning enough money to travel another ten or twenty miles, then finding another job. I cried when I discovered they were not in Chŏnjo.

"I didn't know where to look next. In desperation I even consulted a *mudang*. The woman shook her brass bells and tossed her coins into the air, and told me that I was troubled by ghosts."

I smiled, thinking of Jae-sun. "*Mudangs* say everyone is troubled by ghosts."

"She told me to exorcise the spirits by leaving some five-grain rice at a crossroads and to burn pine nuts on the fifteenth night of the First Moon."

"Did you?"

"No, it seemed a waste of rice. And then I remembered a cousin of my mother's who lived in Kwangju. I went to see him and it turned out he had received a letter from my mother—they were living in Chinju, not Chŏnjo. I took the address and worked in Kwangju until I had enough money for a train ticket to Chinju. I was so happy when I reached the station, and went directly to the address my mother's cousin had given me. But . . ."

Whatever happened next now brought tears to her eyes.

"Father was very angry to see me," she said softly. "He said he had brokered an honest sale to your father and that I had dishonored our clan by running away. He would not let me see Mother or my brothers and sisters. He told me to return to the house of my husband—it was the only honorable thing to do."

Her composure cracked and she began weeping. I wrapped my arms around her as I had when she was a small child, sitting on the wall of the Inner Court, pining for her family. But this was so much worse: to find your heart's dream and have it spurn you.

"Oh, my poor little sister," I said, "I am so sorry."

"It still hurts."

"Of course it does. I feel the sting of my father's hand to this day. We needn't speak of this any further."

"I left Chinju as quickly as I could . . . and on my way out of town, I left some five-grain rice at a crossroads, and burned a handful of pine nuts under a half-moon."

"Oh, sister . . ."

She started to say something more when the door to the little house opened and a tall, good-looking man entered, and Blossom's sorrow was quickly replaced by gladness.

"Husband! We have a visitor. This is my sister, come all the way from Hawai'i and America!"

Only a slight raise of his eyebrows betrayed his surprise. "I did not know you had a sister in America." He took a step toward me and bowed. "I am Always Well"—yes, that was his name: Sang-Ook—"of the Yu clan of Kaesong. My parents named me this, I think, so that I might save time answering people who ask, 'What is your name?' and 'How are you?'"

I laughed. "How thoughtful of them." I bowed and introduced myself in turn.

"He told me the same thing when I first met him," Blossom said. "I think he told it to all the girls."

"No, just the prettiest ones," her husband said, smiling.

"I was working in an apothecary's shop in Seoul," Blossom explained, "not long after the time I just spoke of to you. Mr. Yu came in to sell us what he said was the finest ginseng in the province, guaranteed to quiet one's spirits, drive out fears, and act as a general tonic for the heart, lungs, liver, and kidneys." She added with a shy smile, "The ginseng farmer, at least, proved a tonic for the heart."

He blushed at this. Flustered, he asked me, "Have you seen our ginseng fields?"

"No, not yet."

"Come then, let's show you."

They took me out to the straw-covered fields, arranged in vertical "beds" that reached high up the mountainside. "This land has belonged to my clan for generations," Mr. Yu said, "though it was long considered worthless. My older brothers inherited the rice fields in the valley, and I could have worked them, *for* them. But I desired something I could call my own, and agreed to take these four hundred acres on the slopes of Mount Palygo. My brothers thought me a fool, but I knew there was wild ginseng growing here, and that I could harvest it."

"But don't the trees make your job more difficult?" I asked.

"Actually, quite the opposite," Mr. Yu said enthusiastically. "Ginseng thrives amid trees. It's a temperamental plant, and too much direct sunlight will kill it. Here, beneath a canopy of oak and poplar leaves, the root thrives in the shade. We plant the seeds during the Ninth Moon, cover the seedlings with straw during the winter and remove it in spring. Did you know that it takes seven years to grow a mature ginseng root?"

Blossom rolled her eyes and whispered, "If you did not, you will now."

"You only get a crop every seven years?"

"Yes, but we stagger the plantings, so that every year brings at least one harvest. Then we plant goldenseal to refresh and replenish the soil. The joke is on my brothers now: I get paid more for one year's crop of ginseng than they do for their rice harvests. And they have to give some of theirs to the Japanese, who took one look at my land, decided it was worthless, and have not bothered us since."

"Isn't it remarkable," Blossom said, "how life clings to, and flourishes in, the oddest of places?"

"Yes," I agreed, "so it is."

"Right now it looks like the floor of a barn," she conceded, "but in spring it's like a green waterfall spilling down the mountain, with clusters of red berries everywhere. Oh, I wish you could see it! It's like a paradise, it truly is."

I smiled to hear her say this, but before I could reply there came shouts of "Mama! Papa!" and the fields were soon overrun by Blossom's four children, returning home from school. They were even more beautiful in the flesh than in the photograph. When Blossom told them I was their Aunt Jin from Hawai'i and America, the younger children expressed excitement, but the oldest girl, Willow, assessed me skeptically and said, "I don't believe it."

"But I am," I told her. "That's where I live now."

"Our teacher showed us this How-why-hee once on a globe, and it's way in the middle of an ocean," she pointed out. "How did you get here?"

"By boat."

"How long did it take?"

"Nine days," I said.

She shook her head. "I don't believe it."

"Willow!" her mother chided. "This *is* your aunt and she *is* from Hawai'i."

"Can you prove that's where you're from?" Willow asked.

Amused, I thought for a moment and said, "All right. I'll sing you a Hawaiian song." And I proceeded to sing the first verse of "Aloha 'Oe," partly in Hawaiian and partly in English.

Willow's eyes popped at these alien languages set to lovely

melody, and when I had finished she allowed as how I must be telling the truth, and we were best friends from that point on.

I spent the rest of the day and that evening with Blossom and her family, sharing a fine dinner with them, and took great pleasure in seeing the love and affection my little sister-in-law showered on her children. "They will never have to peer over a wall, as I did, to wonder where their father and mother are," she told me at the end of the evening, as the children dozed in their rooms and Mr. Yu left us to chat beside the smoldering embers of the brazier.

"I am happy to see what a wonderful family you have," I told her. "It is no less than you deserved."

"There was a time I could never have dreamed of it," she admitted. "After my clan rejected me, I was in despair. I wanted to die." In a low voice she added, "I considered dying."

I took her hand in mine and squeezed it, but she shook her head as if to dismiss my concern. "No, it's all right, you see. Because you stopped me."

"Me?" I said.

"Yes. In the still middle of the night, when I could easily have slit a vein and bled to death before morning, I reminded myself that someone had loved me, had *wanted* me, enough to bring me across the ocean, to be a part of her family." She smiled through the tears that now came to her. "And this was what saw me through that longest of nights."

The two of us cried, then, and held one another. "I *do* love you, little sister. And you are part of my family. You always will be."

We went on talking about our lives and our families well into the night; and then I dozed contentedly on a mat for a few hours, until it was time for the children to set off on their downhill trek to school the next day. I was to accompany them, as I was told I could use the telephone in their schoolhouse to call for a taxicab. But before we left, Blossom said, "There is something I would like you to have," and she handed me a copy of the photographic portrait of her and her family. I thanked her, tucked the photograph safely into my travel bag, and we embraced one last time. Neither of us knew whether we would ever meet in person again; but whenever I thought of her, I would always picture her amid the trees of this wooded hillside in spring, with green ginseng cascading down its face, and I would know that she was happy.

It was only when I pulled the picture from my bag on the train that I noticed what Blossom had written on the back of the photograph, in neat *hangul* lettering.

> *Dearest sister-in-law:*
> *A road need not be paved in gold to find treasure at its end.*
> *Love always—Blossom*

The tears I cried were joyful, cleansing. I could finally stop worrying for her—stop wondering. As I could for Evening Rose. I mourned for my teacher, and for Sunny, but rejoiced for Blossom: she was a bright patch of yellow on my *chogak po,* alongside two of blackest black.

*B*idding farewell to my mother was difficult, as both of us knew we were unlikely to see one another again. She wept much of the day before I was to leave, but when I left Pojogae she was calm and happy and presented me with a farewell gift. She handed me a bundled wrapping cloth, but there was nothing inside: the cloth itself was the present. It was the embroidered print I had always loved, the white cranes dipping their beaks into a river filled with gold-flecked fish. I thanked her, told her I loved her, hugged her, and never wanted to let her go. But eventually I did, and my elder brother took me by wagon to Taegu Station.

Ten days later, as the *President Coolidge* steamed into Honolulu

Harbor, I felt a rush of gladness at the sight of Diamond Head, sitting on its brown haunches like a faithful dog waiting at the door. I stood by the bow railing as a cool afternoon rain shower drifted across the city, sprinkling us with a light mist that smelled sweet and fresh. The mist gently bent the sunlight into a rainbow that had one foot in the city and another in the green foothills of the Ko'olaus.

Hawai'i is not truly the idyllic paradise of popular songs—islands of love and tranquility, where nothing bad ever happens. It was and is a place where people work and struggle, live and die, as they do the world over. Charlie Chan and Sadie Thompson are not real people; but Chang Apana and May Thompson were, and I treasure my memories of them as I love and treasure the real Hawai'i, which has offered me so many possibilities. I began to understand how my children—my *keiki*—must have felt about their island home. And when they and Jae-sun met me at the docks—Harry draping a pink plumeria *lei* around my neck, with its sweet perfume—I realized that I, too, was home.

A few weeks later, Mr. Chun did not hold it against me when I gave him my notice, telling him of my intentions to open a small dress shop of my own. By this time King-Smith was producing not just shirts but swimsuits, bathrobes, trousers, a whole line of Hawaiian sportswear. Mr. Chun hardly considered my shop serious competition and wished me well, thanking me for my years of hard work. I borrowed money from the *kye*, pooled resources with Wise Pearl, and found a small storefront to rent on Kalākaua Avenue, *'ewa* of the Ala Wai Canal. Above the shop was a workspace large enough to accommodate four sewing machines, two cutting tables, a press, and four seamstresses. I scrubbed and cleaned the floors and windows, and Jae-sun built yards of wooden shelving along the walls, suitable for holding a hundred or more bolts of fabric. I ordered as much *yukata* cloth from Japan as I could afford and drew up some simple patterns, which we now set about fashioning into ladies' dresses—as yet only a small part of the aloha wear market, but one I felt certain would expand in time. I called the shop "Gem's of Honolulu." Our first original design was of a flock of white cranes with long beaks, hand-blocked onto a blue silk skirt. In these humble circumstances the four of us—myself, Wise Pearl, my new in-law Tamiko, and after her classes, Grace Eun—shared our own thimble time, the hum of the sewing machines making a kind of music, as our laughing chatter became the rising notes of a song we would sing together for many years to come.

Hwan'gap: 1957

I was born in the Year of the Rooster—1897—and now, sixty years later, that old bird crows again. Today is my sixtieth birthday and the Zodiac has come full circle, signifying that one cycle of life has ended and another begun. On this, my *hwan'gap,* my children honored me and my husband with a fine celebration, renting a banquet room at the Royal Hawaiian Hotel that looked out onto the beach where our family spent so many festive Sundays. A band played a mix of traditional Korean music and favorite Hawaiian melodies, with invited guests like Steamboat and Tarball occasionally sitting in for a song. Sadly, some of the beachboys we knew—Dude Miller, Tough Bill Keaweamahi, Hiram Anahu— are now gone. I attended Hiram's funeral here on the beach eight years ago, watching as his ashes were taken out to sea in an outrigger canoe and scattered across the reef—into the surf he had loved and sung of all his life—by his fellow watermen. Happily, despite a crown of snow-white hair, Duke Kahanamoku—who now holds the mostly honorary title of Honolulu sheriff—is still among us, as are his brothers Sam, Louis, Sarge, David, and Bill (aka Tarball). Even Panama Dave was here, clowning as usual: at the age of forty-five Panama had married for the first time and Beauty finally forgave him for the end of their romance.

I was fortunate, too, that neither time nor space had separated me from my Sisters of Kyŏngsang, all of whom celebrated this day alongside me. Beauty, Poi Dog, and their two children, aged seventeen and nineteen, were there, as was Mary and her young daughter. Beauty still lives up to her name, though like all of us her hair is more gray than black. Her barbershop evolved over time into a hair salon for women, one of the city's most successful. Jade Moon—wearing an elegant blue silk dress of the sort she used to launder for others—managed to consume a glass of rice wine and a shot of vermouth even before she had finished wheeling her invalid husband to the banquet table. They have done very well in real estate and own some thirty properties across O'ahu. Wise Pearl's first husband, alas, succumbed to heart failure during the war. She remarried a few years ago to a big sentimental Hawaiian named Lono whose affections for her were never in doubt, and she sold her part-ownership in Gem's in order to convert her little Korean inn into a budget hotel catering to tourists, which she and Lono now run.

As for Gem's of Honolulu—it has grown from a four-woman shop to a manufacturer of both ladies' and men's wear that employs a staff of seventy-five and has an annual revenue in six figures.

Also among our guests this day was my old friend Ellery Chun, who had closed King-Smith Clothiers in 1945 to become vice president of American Security Bank. There was no question but that he had finally succeeded in becoming a respected member of Honolulu's business establishment. At the same table sat Pascual Anito, a widower since Esther's death five years ago, as well as Tamiko, Taizo, and their very large clan, including those grandchildren we shared.

Most important, Jae-sun—frail but in good health and spirits at the age of seventy-eight—sat with me at the head of a low table overflowing with food and lavish gifts ("too expensive," my frugal husband would later sigh). One by one our children and their children approached us. Each was obliged to perform an elaborate, stylized bow—a *se-bae*—before offering us a glass of wine from a bottle of homemade rice wine sent all the way from Korea by my sister, Blossom. With three children and ten grandchildren, that made for a great deal of wine, and by the end of this ritual I was aglow with more than just happiness and parental pride.

But I *was* proud, very proud, of what our children had so far accomplished in their young lives. Grace graduated from the University of Hawai'i with a degree in business administration, which she puts to good use managing the day-to-day operations of Gem's. Harry is an engineer with his own consulting firm—which he likes to say he operates to subsidize his surfing—and Charlie is a high school principal in windward Kailua, pursuing his master's degree in education. Had I only been fortunate enough to take vicarious satisfaction in their achievements, I would have been a happy woman. But just after the close of the Second World War, I was given an opportunity to realize a dream I had long since given up on.

In 1946 the Territory of Hawai'i introduced the first academic adult education program since 1827, when the Christian missionaries had schooled nearly the entire native population in reading and writing. I was already proficient in English and quickly earned a grammar school diploma. This was followed, in a year, by my high school diploma. It was a moment I had not dared to dream of in more than twenty years, and my children were as proud to attend my graduation ceremony as I had been at theirs.

But in addition to the courses I have since taken in English, history, and literature, I also take pride in another class I recently graduated. Five years ago the United States Congress passed the McCarran-Walter Immigration Act, which for the first time allowed men and women of Asian birth living in the United States to become American citizens. I enrolled at once in the Adult Education Citizenship course and, along with hundreds of others of Chinese, Japanese, and Korean heritage, took the oath of allegiance the following year.

I am proud to be able to finally call myself an American, as proud as I am of my Korean heritage—and of this special place I call home, Honolulu. The Big Five and the "*haole* elite" no longer rule Hawai'i; the faces of our mayors, our representatives, our business leaders, are no longer exclusively white but Hawaiian, Chinese, Japanese, Portuguese, Filipino, Korean, and more. Hawai'i has often been called a melting pot, but I think of it more as a "mixed plate"—a scoop of rice with gravy, a scoop of macaroni salad, a piece of mahi-mahi, and a side of *kimchi*. Many different tastes share the plate, but none of them loses its individual flavor, and together they make up a uniquely "local" cuisine. This is also, I believe, what America is at its best—a whole greater than the sum of its parts. I only wish Joe Kahahawai could have lived to see what Hawai'i has become—what he unknowingly helped it to become.

I stand here on the fifteenth floor of a high-rise apartment building on Ala Moana Boulevard, always in sight of the vast Pacific I first crossed more than four decades ago. The life I have led here in Honolulu is so much richer than I could ever have imagined for myself as a child. I married a man who encouraged me to be myself, who saw me as a partner in life and not a mere vassal toiling in Inner Rooms. I watched my three beautiful children grow and learn and accomplish much in their lives. And as I told our assembled guests at the celebration, I have been privileged to have had three sisters—none of us bound by blood, but no less sisters for that—who have shared this journey with me, each of them, like everyone in the room, a unique and beautiful patch on my *chogak po*.

At this, Jade Moon rose from her seat—a sight to give anyone pause.

"If so," she said, holding her glass aloft in a toast, "then you have been the seam that holds us all together." She drained her glass to loud applause, then added, "And will someone please tell these fool waiters that we are out of wine?"

I replenished her glass myself amid much laughter.

Not long ago a newspaper reporter—interviewing me about the aloha shirt industry and my own small part in it—asked whether there was anything in my life that I would have done differently, or not done at all, had I the chance to do it all over. I did not hesitate for a moment. As I told him then, I tell you now:

"I have no regrets."

Author's Note

If there is a common theme linking *Honolulu* with my previous novel, *Moloka'i,* it is not just the history of the Hawaiian
islands but the significance of the ordinary people whose lives—
many quite extraordinary—make up that history. Immigrants have
played an enormous role in the life and culture of Hawai'i, but
their individual stories have often gone undocumented. Fortunately, this is not the case with the "picture brides" of China, Korea, and Japan, who bravely left their homes for the promise of a new
land and a new life (though for some, admittedly, it was an empty
promise). The last of these women are gone now, but their voices
and stories have been preserved in a number of noteworthy books
and articles, which were instrumental in helping me to tell Jin's

story: *Korean Picture Brides* by Sonia Shinn Sunoo, *The Passage of a Picture Bride* by Won K. Yoon, *The Dreams of Two Yi-min* by Margaret K. Pai, *Passages to Paradise* by Daisy Chun Rhodes, "A Picture Bride from Korea: The Life History of a Korean American Woman in Hawai'i" by Alice Chai, "The Heritage of the First Korean Women Immigrants in the United States" by Harold Hak-won Sunoo and Sonia Shinn Sunoo, and "Contributions of Korean Immigrant Women" by Esther Kwon Arinaga. Also useful were *Winds of Change: Korean Women in America* by Diana Yu, "The Koreans in Hawaii" (Master's thesis) by Bernice Kim, *The Ilse: First-Generation Korean Immigrants in Hawai'i, 1903–1973* by Wayne Patterson, *The Koreans in Hawai'i: A Pictorial History 1903–2003* by Roberta Chang and Wayne Patterson, and *Beyond Ke'eaumoku: Koreans, Nationalism, and Local Culture in Hawaii* by Brenda L. Kwon.

Providing insight into Korean culture and the status of women were *Things Korean* by O. Young-Lee, *Women of Korea* edited by Yung-Chung Kim, *Women of the Yi Dynasty* edited by Park Young-hai, "Women and Education in Korea" by Lium Sun-Hee, *Korean Women: View from the Inner Room* edited by Laurel Kendall and Mark Peterson, *Village Life in Korea* by J. Robert Moose, "The Tradition: Women During the Yi Dynasty" by Martina Deuchler (in *Virtues in Conflict* edited by Sandra Mattielli), "Women in a Confucian Society" by Yunshik Chang, and *Rapt in Colour: Korean Textiles and Costumes of the Chosun Dynasty* edited by Claire Roberts and Huh Dong-hwa.

Joseph Kahahawai is another ordinary person whose death had a profound impact in shaping Hawai'i in the twentieth century, but whose life and character has until recently been largely ignored, even as it was demonized by the media of his time. It was sociologist Andrew Lind—as quoted in Jonathan Y. Okamura's article *"Aloha Kanaka Me Ke Aloha 'Āina"*—who noted that the word "local" was first used during the Massie case to describe non-whites living in Hawai'i. The idea of the Kahahawai murder as the precipitating event for the birth of "local" culture was then posited by John Patrick Rosa in his dissertation *Local Story: The Massie Case and the Politics of Local Identity in Hawai'i*. As Rosa writes, "[T]he killing of Joseph Kahahawai came to be seen as more than just an injury against the Native Hawaiian community. Kahahawai's murder was cast as a story of local oppression, telling Native Hawaiians that they had more in common with working-class peoples of color and that they were part of an emerging local culture."

This theme was brilliantly expanded upon by David R. Stannard in his book *Honor Killing: How the Infamous "Massie Affair" Transformed Hawai'i* and by PBS's *American Experience* documentary, *The Massie Affair*. Equally fine, and complementary to the above works, is Cobey Black's *Hawaii Scandal*, which vividly captures the social milieu in which young Joe Kahahawai grew up. (My thanks to Ms. Black for her *aloha* and her willingness to answer a fiction writer's questions.) I owe a considerable debt to all these authors' seminal research, and have supplemented their accounts of Joe's life with details derived from my own research. Sometimes these details were as small as the information, gleaned from Honolulu city directories, that Joseph Sr. had been a locomotive driver for the Pioneer Sugar Mill on Maui—an interesting bit of color I encountered nowhere else—or that William Kama worked for Honolulu Rapid Transit & Land Company before becoming a policeman, which accounted for how he came to know the Kahahawai family.

I have also drawn to some extent upon other accounts of the Massie and Fukunaga cases: *Something Terrible Has Happened* by Peter Van Slingerland, *The Navy and the Massie-Kahahawai Case* by John Reinecke (writing anonymously), the "Reaping the Whirlwind" chapter of Dennis M. Ogawa's *Jan Ken Po: The World of Hawaii's Japanese-Americans*, *Rape in Paradise* by Theon Wright, and *The Massie Case* by Peter Packer and Bob Thomas.

Joseph Kahahawai Jr. was a complex and sometimes contradictory individual: soft-spoken but short-tempered, intelligent and yet academically indifferent, competitive but not ambitious. In real life, of course, we meet people who embody such contradictions, but since we can't see inside their heads we don't expect to understand how all the pieces connect. In fiction there is a different expectation, and an author of historical novels, writing about a real person, must try to reconcile some of these contradictions. While I don't presume to suggest that the dramatic and psychological choices I've made necessarily reflect Joe Kahahawai's true inner self, I do hope my portrayal of him does justice to a young man who saw precious little justice in his short life.

What little we know of May Thompson we owe not merely to Somerset Maugham, who immortalized her as "Sadie" Thompson, but to the diligence of his biographer Wilmon Menard, author of *The Two Worlds of Somerset Maugham*. In researching his book, Menard did more than just uncover the fact that Maugham's Sadie had been inspired by a real-life prostitute with the same surname, with whom Maugham shared passage to Pago Pago. Menard actually traveled to Samoa and spoke to people who had met "Sadie" there. (Among these were the parents of future playwright John Kneubuhl, who was also the person, in real life, who brought to Hawai'i the Samoan *tapa* cloth mentioned in Chapter Sixteen, which Musa-Shiya made into a proto-*aloha* shirt.) Most significant, Menard interviewed Iosef, the Samoan man with whom May had pursued her doomed romance. Menard's interest in documenting "the real Sadie Thompson" persisted even after publication of his book; in 1992 he published an article in *Honolulu* magazine, "The Iwilei Floozy," in which he revealed May's given name for the first time.

Maugham's *A Writer's Notebook* furnishes details, not found in his short story, of his visit to Iwilei, much of it quite helpful to me in envisioning and describing the stockade. Also helpful was a remarkable, though much more obscure, document: *My Life as a*

Honolulu Prostitute by "Jean O'Hara." A self-published autobiographical booklet—hand-mimeographed "BECAUSE NOBODY DARED PRINT IT!!!"—it is an earnest and entertaining exposé of "vice conditions" in the Honolulu of the 1940s, and offers a wealth of information about prostitution in Hawai'i. Sixty years later, what appears to be the last surviving copy is preserved in the library of the University of Hawai'i at Mānoa.

In the end, of course, my portrayal of May is as fictional as Maugham's: I've embellished her life and her personality, as is a novelist's right and obligation to his story. But I take some satisfaction in hewing a bit closer to the essential truth and tragedy behind May's trip to Samoa.

(There is a legend, by the way, that "Sadie" stayed on in Pago Pago and eventually opened her own brothel, calling it the Sadie Thompson Inn in a bid to reap some profit from Maugham's fictionalization of her. It's a nice story, but one not supported by the facts. According to a ship's manifest in *Passenger Lists of Vessels Arriving at Honolulu,* May Thompson returned to Honolulu aboard the SS *Sonoma* on January 10, 1917, and the *List of Vessels Arriving at San Francisco from Honolulu* confirms that she left Hawai'i aboard the SS *Maui* on June 15, 1917. There is some circumstantial evidence—from census records—that she may have returned to her hometown in Nebraska, where she lived for at least the next twenty years; but since I couldn't prove this to my own satisfaction, I left May's final destination vague. Perhaps someday, like Wilmon Menard, I'll follow up on this with more conclusive research and publish it as a nonfiction piece.)

Chang Apana, on the other hand, required little or no embellishment on my part. This guy really did arrest forty men at one time, fall out of a second-story window, get sideswiped by an axe, and solve innumerable crimes through a combination of shrewd deduction and two-fisted action in his long and storied career. Interested readers can learn more at the Web site of The Charlie Chan Family (including an informative article by Earl Derr Biggers on Apana) or at the Chang Apana exhibit in the Honolulu Police Department Museum. Two other valuable sources of information on the detective are "Will the Real Charlie Chan Please Stand Up?" in Jim Doherty's book *Just the Facts: True Tales of Cops & Criminals,* and the documentary "The Real Charlie Chan" on the *Charlie Chan in Egypt* DVD, available as part of the *Charlie Chan Collection, Vol. 1,* from Fox Video. I'm amazed that no enterprising historian has yet written a dual biography of Chang Apana and Charlie Chan.

Other books that contributed to my understanding and depiction of Hawai'i in its territorial days include *Hawai'i's Forgotten History* by Rich Budnick, *Growing Up Barefoot in Hawai'i* by Peggy Hickok Hodge, *Hawai'i's Glamour Days* by Maili Yardley, *I Knew Queen Liliuokalani* by Bernice Piilani Irwin, *Hawai'i in Love* by Toni Polancy, *Waikiki Beachboy* by Grady Timmons, *Memories of Duke* by Sandra Kimberley Hall and Greg Ambrose, *Pau Hana: Plantation Life and Labor in Hawaii* by Ronald Takaki, "Assimilation in a Slum Area of Honolulu" by Kiyoshi Kaneshiro, *The Garment Manufacturing Industry of Hawaii* by Emma Fundaburke, *Aloha Attire* by Linda B. Arthur, *The Aloha Shirt* by Dale Hope and Gregory Tozian, *The Art of the Aloha Shirt* by DeSoto Brown and Linda Arthur, and *Hawaiian Shirt Designs* by Nancy N. Schiffer.

I am greatly indebted to my friend Sally-Jo Keala-o-Ānuenue Bowman, who graciously agreed to read my manuscript and then gave me careful and considered comments on everything from character motivation to street names to horticulture and sewing. Her assistance was truly invaluable and deeply appreciated. (For anyone interested in what it really means to be Hawaiian, I commend to your attention Sally-Jo's book *The Heart of Being Hawaiian.*) Hope Dellon has the sharpest eye and best story sense of any editor I've ever worked with; once again she has made me look the better for it. Amy Adelson also assisted me in thrashing out more than one troublesome plot point. My thanks go as well to Robert

Eric Barde, author of *Immigration at the Golden Gate: Passenger Ships, Exclusion, and Angel Island,* who generously provided me with a translation of the chapters on "Asiatic steerage" from Michio Yamada's book *Japanese Emigration History As Seen Through Ships.* Tamara Leiokanoe Moan provided expert research assistance on those occasions when I could not get to Honolulu myself. B. J. Short and Charley Myers of the Bishop Museum Library and Archives were an indispensable source of articles and photographs; William F. Wu shared his knowledge of Asian immigration and culture; Jan Morgan at Kohala Books recommended reference books. I am grateful, too, for the assistance of the staffs of the Hawai'i State Archives, the Center for Korean Studies at the University of Hawai'i at Mānoa, and the Hawai'i State Library, as well as Susan Fukushima of the Japanese National Museum. For miscellaneous advice, encouragement, and research assists, *mahalo* to David Wells, Angela Claus, Rebecca Claus, Nora Steinbergs, and Priscilla Claus, and, of course, my agent Molly Friedrich. As ever, my wife, Paulette, was my "in-house editor."

Finally, there is one other character in this story drawn from real life. May Thompson's cat, "Little Bastard," shares a few antisocial tendencies with our cat Casper, who eventually outgrew his bad habits (mostly) to become the sweetest cat anyone could want. Casper is a whole book unto himself, but since he died just as I was completing the first draft of *Honolulu,* for me he will forever be a part of this one. Goodbye, little pal. *Ā hui hou aku.*

Reading
Group
Gold

HONOLULU
by Alan Brennert

About the Author
- A Conversation with Alan Brennert

Behind the Novel
- Snapshots from Honolulu's Past

Keep on Reading
- Recommended Reading
- Reading Group Questions

A
Reading
Group Gold
Selection

For more reading group suggestions,
visit www.readinggroupgold.com.

ST. MARTIN'S GRIFFIN

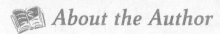

About the Author

A Conversation with Alan Brennert

Did the idea for *Honolulu* come out of your research for your previous book, *Moloka'i*?

In a way. One of the most colorful periods of modern Hawaiian history was the so-called "glamour days" of the 1920s and '30s. Though I read about it in my research for *Moloka'i,* it was a time period I couldn't really explore in depth in that book since my main characters were held in isolation at Kalaupapa. These were the years when Hawai'i made its deepest impression on the American consciousness, the years of Matson liners, the China Clipper, Hollywood celebrities vacationing in Honolulu, and the *Hawai'i Calls* radio show that broadcasted popular *hapa-haole* music to the mainland. I found myself wanting to tell a story against that romantic backdrop.

But *Honolulu* also presents a very different picture of Hawai'i in those "glamour days."

Yes, there were almost two Honolulus existing alongside one another—or, more accurately, interwoven, like the Korean patchwork quilts I write about in the book. Because at the same time this romantic, glamorous image of paradise was being exported to the American public, many Native Hawaiians and immigrants to Hawai'i labored on plantations for low wages or lived in poverty in Honolulu tenements. So *Honolulu,* the novel, is partly about this collision of image and reality . . . and how, in fact, the reality was far richer and more captivating.

*About the
Author*

What led you to choose as your protagonist a Korean picture bride? What was compelling for you about Korea and the Korean experience in Hawai'i?

When I first read about the Hotel of Sorrows, it struck me that the story of a picture bride neatly dovetailed with that of the two Honolulus. I chose a Korean bride because there had already been novels and even a movie about Japanese picture brides. But the more I researched it, the more fascinated I became by the role of women in Korean society. It wasn't hard to see why so many women jumped at the chance to become picture brides: to gain a degree of freedom and adventure in their lives that they might never have experienced had they stayed in Korea. It seemed an ideal motivation for my protagonist—and then of course as soon as she arrived in Honolulu, all those expectations would be rudely dashed when she met her husband-to-be. When I had these two elements joined in my mind—Jin's personal journey and the rich background of the city she comes to—I knew I had the alloy of a story, a novel.

The protagonists in both *Moloka'i* and *Honolulu* are women. You do an excellent job portraying their perspectives—their voices feel authentic. How do you go about writing a book from the viewpoint of a woman of another time, place, and culture?

To me, the two most important tools for a writer of historical fiction are empathy and research. Jin's childhood issues—of feeling homely and out of place—are certainly ones I could identify with myself (boys can feel that way too, growing up) and which are fairly universal. People feel the same emotions the world over, and that's essential to making a reader connect with a character; but just as interesting, I find, are the differences, the particulars of a character's time and place and culture. I try to make those as specific and accurate as possible. But unless a writer has grown up in that culture, you simply have to immerse yourself in everything you can read on the subject in search of specificities that add flavor, texture, and dimension to the character and the story. A young girl growing up in America in the 1900s might share Regret's desire to read and be educated, but it's the particular impediments to this in Korea—and the solution, in the form of Evening Rose's tutelage, the irony that a woman of the lowest status is allowed the most education—that I think enrich the narrative.

In both of your books, there is a distinct leaning
toward representing the experiences of native
Hawaiians, and it's fascinating and refreshing. In
your visits to Hawai'i have you developed rela-
tionships with native Hawaiians?

I do have some friends of Native Hawaiian heritage. I felt it was important to acknowledge that
Hawai'i's multicultural society, as unique and wonderful as it is, was achieved at a cost. That cost was
to Native Hawaiians—whose country, after all, it
was originally. That's why Queen Lili'uokalani is in
the book: She's one of only two characters who
also appeared in *Moloka'i*—the other is Governor
Lawrence Judd—and I included her in *Honolulu*
both to complete the narrative "arc" begun with
her overthrow in *Moloka'i*, as well as a kind of
grace note, displaying her dignity and pride even
in face of the loss of her kingdom, something
Hawaiians have lived with for the past hundred
years.

But at the same time, it must be noted that
Hawai'i's remarkable polyglot culture increasingly
mirrors the kind of multiethnic society America
is becoming—and that in many ways the story
of *Honolulu* is really the story of America itself.

Interview conducted by Stephanie Deignan, events coordinator
for Copperfield's Books.

Excerpted from www.copperfieldsbooks.com.

Reprinted with permission.

ALAN BRENNERT was born in Englewood, New Jersey, to Herbert E. Brennert, an aviation writer, and Almyra E. Brennert. Since 1973 he has lived in Southern California, where he received a B.A. in English from California State University at Long Beach and did graduate work in screenwriting at UCLA.

In addition to novels, he has written short stories, teleplays, screenplays, and the libretto of a stage musical, *Weird Romance,* with music by Alan Menken and lyrics by David Spencer. He has developed screenplays for major studios, as well as miniseries, pilots, and television movies, and earned an Emmy Award for his work as a writer-producer on the television series *L.A. Law.* His short story "Ma Qui" was honored with a Nebula Award in 1992.

His novel *Moloka'i,* about the forced segregation of leprosy patients to the settlement of Kalaupapa in Hawai'i, won praise from *The Washington Post, Chicago Tribune,* and *Publishers Weekly,* and became a national bestseller in paperback as well as a favorite selection of reading groups across the country. It received the "Bookies" award for Book Club Book of the Year, sponsored by the Contra Costa Library.

He is currently at work on a new novel. For more information about Alan and his work, or to contact him about speaking to your reading group, visit his Web site at www.alanbrennert.com.

Snapshots from Honolulu's Past

Queen Lili'uokalani, the last reigning monarch of Hawai'i, seated outside her home, Washington Place, ca. 1917, the last year of her life. (Library of Congress)

Joseph Kahahawai, boxer, football player, and National Guardsman, murdered by Thomas Massie, Grace Hubbard Fortescue, Deacon Jones, and Edward Lord. (Library of Congress)

Behind the Novel

Detective Chang Apana, one of the most honored and colorful law enforcement officers in Hawai'i's history. (Honolulu Police Department)

Duke Kahanamoku, five-time Olympic champion, legendary surfer, and later the honorary mayor of Honolulu. (Library of Congress)

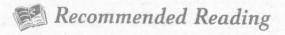 *Recommended Reading*

Sunset in a Spider Web, adapted by Virginia Olsen Baron and translated by Minja Park Kim, contains many lovely *sijo* poems of old Korea by the *kisaeng* Hwang Chini and others.

The Trembling of a Leaf by W. Somerset Maugham collects eight of his short stories set in the South Seas, including "Rain." It's worth noting that although Maugham later spoke unflatteringly of his bawdy rooming-house neighbor, May Thompson's fictional counterpart Sadie is the most winning character in the story and the author clearly intended for her to win the reader's sympathies as well. Maugham was too fine a writer to let his personal animosity get in the way of a great character.

Think of a Garden and Other Plays by John Kneubuhl showcases three stage plays set in Hawai'i and the author's native Samoa (where his parents, who owned a trading post on Pago Pago, met Maugham and May on their rainy stopover). Kneubuhl was a preeminent playwright on Polynesian/Pacific themes, as well as a prolific writer for television in the 1950s and '60s.

And for anyone curious about modern Honolulu in the years after Jin's story ends, I highly recommend **My Time in Hawaii** by Victoria Nelson, a beautifully wrought memoir of "her time" in Honolulu, spanning the years from 1969 to 1981.

Keep on Reading

 *Reading Group Questions*

1. How do you feel about Jin's decision to leave Korea? What might you have done in her place? How do you regard the various decisions she made after learning the truth about her fiancé in Hawai'i?

2. How would you interpret the poem by Hwang Chini on page 32 within the context of the novel?

3. Korea and Hawai'i were both small countries in strategic locations that came to be dominated by more powerful nations. In what other ways were the Korean and Hawaiian societies of the time both similar and different?

4. Compare and contrast the lives of a Korean *kisaeng* and an Iwilei prostitute.

5. How does the author weave real people and events into the lives of his fictional characters, and how do they contribute to your understanding of Jin's circumstances? If you were already familiar with any of the historical figures, how do you view them after reading the novel? For example, the author is uncertain of May Thompson's fate in real life—what do you think she might have done after leaving Honolulu? What do you think about the governor's decision to commute the sentences of Lieutenant Massie and the others convicted in Joe Kahahawai's death?

6. How have Americans' attitudes toward immigrants changed—or not changed—since the 1900s?

7. The biography *Passage of a Picture Bride* describes its real-life subject as having a "positive outlook and broad-mindedness, unusual traits among Korean women" of that time. How does this statement apply to Jin and her fellow picture brides?

8. What binds Jin and her "Sisters of Kyŏngsang" together, other than the *kye*? What purpose do they serve in each other's lives?

9. What is the significance of the patchwork quilts not just to Jin's life, but to the life of Hawai'i itself?

10. At the end of the novel, Jin says, "Hawai'i has often been called a melting pot, but I think of it more as a 'mixed plate'—a scoop of rice with gravy, a scoop of macaroni salad, a piece of mahi-mahi, and a side of *kimchi*. Many different tastes share the plate, but none of them loses its individual flavor, and together they make up a uniquely 'local' cuisine. This is also, I believe, what America is at its best—a whole greater than the sum of its parts." What do *you* believe? What is gained and what is lost—both in Hawai'i and in the United States as a whole—in becoming a multicultural society? How might this be particularly relevant to Native Hawaiians?

FROM THE BESTSELLING
AUTHOR OF *MOLOKA'I*
AND *HONOLULU*

comes the spellbinding story of a family
of dreamers and their lives within the
legendary Palisades Amusement Park

PALISADES PARK

by Alan Brennert

Available April 2013

FIND US ON FACEBOOK:

 Facebook.com/PalisadesParkBook